STAND NEXT TO ME

CALLE J. BROOKES

LOST RIVER LIT PUBLISHING, LLC

I had withdrawn in forest, and my song
Was swallowed up in leaves that blew alway;
And to the forest edge you came one day
(This was my dream) and looked and pondered long,
But did not enter, though the wish was strong:
You shook your pensive head as who should say,
'I dare not—too far in his footsteps stray—
He must seek me would he undo the wrong.'
Not far, but near, I stood and saw it all
Behind low boughs the trees let down outside;
And the sweet pang it cost me not to call
And tell you that I saw does still abide.
But 'tis not true that thus I dwelt aloof,
For the wood wakes, and you are here for proof.

A DREAM PANG
-ROBERT FROST

1

HER DRESS COST MORE THAN SOME USED CARS. HER hair had taken hours to style at a private salon. Shelby Jacobson looked good. Looked expensive. Looked confident, wealthy, and well-bred. Like the world was *hers*.

Exactly as she had wanted to look.

It was all a sham.

Shelby would never let the people around her know that.

Her brother held her elbow in his. Protectively. His wife of seven months, Izzie, walked just ahead of them, looking stunning in deep red.

Shelby knew what they were doing. Paving the way. Protecting.

Izzie walked next *to him*.

Jake MacNamara.

Why did it have to be *him* tonight?

Shelby shivered. She wished anyone other than Jake was with them. He saw right through Shelby to the quivering mass of pitiful she was inside.

Jake despised her. Usually, it didn't matter what the man thought—Shelby had no real love for him, either. But tonight...

Technically, he was the man escorting her to this little shindig. Her brother knew that that was the last thing Shelby wanted.

She'd rather be staked out naked to an ant hill in the dry Texas heat—fire ant hill, at that—than spend two minutes with "Don't ever call me Giacomo" Jake MacNamara, wonder boy of the Texas State Police.

As if he knew she was staring at his back, the man in question turned. Looked right at her. Shelby fought the instinct to avert her eyes, like one would with a stray dog. He—more than any man she had met in a long, long time—disconcerted her.

That was the last thing she needed tonight. People would be looking at her, staring. Wondering about her. Judging her. Thinking she had no business being where she was, having what she had now.

Including people from the TSP.

The last people she ever wanted to see.

She pulled in a deep breath. She could do this. Could get through the next five hours of interacting with the Texas State Police for her brother and his wife. They were all the family she had. She would do anything for Allen and Izzie. Anything.

Even spend an evening with Jake. It ended at midnight. She just had to make it to midnight, and then Allen would take her home, and she'd be free.

"You all good back there?" Jake asked, his eyes on her and not Allen. He was always watching her.

Shelby nodded. "Of...of...of course."

"Neither one of us are too fond of crowds," Allen said smoothly. He covered her hand with his. Squeezed. Looked at her with gray eyes identical to her own.

Allen was her great protector, and he always had been. Ten years her senior, he had been there for her from her first steps to the day they had buried their parents. Until this very moment. Protecting always.

She was his greatest burden—and she was well aware of it.

Shelby would do anything to make life easier for her brother.

"Really? I would have thought this was just your cup of tea, this crowd." Jake smirked at her for just a small moment. Challenging. Trying to disconcert her. He so loved to throw her off her game whenever he could. Sometimes, he would say things just to get a rise out of her. Shelby had figured that out rather fast. She just hadn't ever figured out why *her*. "All fancy and glittery with green—and men who will fawn all over you."

"Jake, you're an ass. Behave yourself," Izzie said with a firm warning in her tone. "Shelby, just ignore our pet idiot. You are gorgeous, and there are beautiful men inside waiting for you to dazzle them. I heard most of the Barratt cousins will be here tonight. Mac was asking about you, Mel said. Or was it Alex again? It's hard to tell those two apart. I'm sorry Jake thinks it's ok to be a butt already."

She'd apologized to Shelby a thousand times—for her uncle. Jake had a thing against people who came from a moneyed background as Shelby and Allen had. Everyone who had ever met him probably knew that.

Shelby checked discreetly—at least he hadn't worn the work boots he favored tonight. She wouldn't have put it past him. As a statement for all that he despised.

Jake felt free to snip at Shelby whenever he wanted. She annoyed him on every level. He'd let her know that, too.

It had just gotten worse in the past six months when the rest of Logan's estate had been released to Shelby. All tens of millions that no one had even known existed.

Jake's attitude made Izzie and Allen angry. It made Shelby feel like a great big wimp.

Shelby agreed with Izzie. The uncle who'd raised Izzie from the age of fourteen was a total braying asshole. Shelby was stuck with him. At least for tonight.

"I was just commenting." His black eyes looked at her with

challenge. Jake was part Italian, on his mother's side. It showed in the dark hair and dark eyes and slightly darker olive skin. In the Italian he sometimes spoke when he was feeling strongly about something.

It wasn't fair that he looked so good.

Jake was walking sex appeal.

He looked like a male model, especially tonight. The man was made for tuxes.

The gorgeous exterior hid the heart of a troll, though.

At least, where she was concerned.

"Sure...sure...sure you were." She forced herself to take a breath. To slow down when she spoke, to control the stutter that came out a bit more when she was anxious.

She was always nervous with him.

Shelby hated this.

She'd far rather be home in her living room, behind the walls that kept the world out than *here* at the Barratt-Finley Creek hotel at an honors ceremony for heroes of the storm. She was one of the guests of honor.

Shelby didn't feel like a hero at all.

Far from it.

She wanted to forget the things she'd seen a year ago when the F4 tornado had struck Finley Creek. She'd just been there, did what she'd had to.

She'd been in the TSP parking lot, waiting on her friend Daryn to end her shift as the assistant ME before they headed to Garrity three hours away. To where their friend Zoey had been waiting.

That hadn't happened.

Shelby had seen the storm coming, and she had been so exposed. She'd stepped out of her car, ready to run toward the TSP. To any kind of shelter at all. Daryn's brother had been there in the parking lot, too—he had been commander of the small Finley Creek: Missing Persons unit for years.

He'd yelled for her to get to him, instead of the building so far away.

Darrell had grabbed her, and they'd run. Away from the storm. Darrell had wrapped himself around her at the last moment—and pulled her toward the drainage ditch that had run in front of the building.

The world had exploded around them. Just like in the movies about tornadoes. She had been terrified they'd just be sucked away.

When it had ended, she and Darrell had been the only ones outside who'd gotten lucky.

Four other people in the TSP parking lot hadn't been lucky at all. Shelby and Darrell had dug the first one out themselves. And then the second.

Darrell's truck had been spared major damage. He had had search-and-rescue equipment in the back. Equipment he had taught Shelby how to use years earlier.

When she and Daryn had been so afraid of the world, the only place they'd felt safe was outside of the city.

Darrell and the outside world had saved her back then.

She, Zoey, and Daryn had learned the basics of rock climbing and hiking and camping first—there were tons of cliffs in nearby Value at the reservoir—and Shelby had learned to breathe again. Outside, she'd been able to heal.

Darrell had started teaching them the basics of search and rescue. Shelby had taken it further than the other two women; she'd let him teach her more. And more.

Until she felt confident in something again.

It was coincidence, circumstance, that had had her and Darrell teaming up to start search and rescue of the destroyed TSP building. She hadn't felt adequate, even for one minute. She had just kept going.

He was the true hero. Not her.

She hadn't been *thinking*, she'd just been…helping.

No one would listen when she'd said that. No one understood that Shelby just wanted to forget the nightmares. All of
them.

That was all she had ever wanted.

He was worse than the lowest kind of dog, and
Jake knew it. He shouldn't keep poking at her. He knew himself
well enough to know it was his only defense against her.

Shelby Jacobson twisted him up in the gut every time she got
within six feet of him.

It took everything he had to keep from drooling every time
he looked at her. Shelby should always wear low-cut dresses in
the deepest burgundy, with her hair swept up in those curls and
pinned with what he suspected were diamond combs. It left her
shoulders bare, and tempting.

Taunting a man, teasing him to touch. Jake's fingers flexed,
wishing he could do just that.

Except for that one scar. Right there. He could see the edge
of it where it marred her skin. A bullet and shards of glass had
struck her—when a killer had been aiming at Izzie. "Sorry, Iz. I
don't mean to be a jerk."

His niece's dark eyes—identical to his own—showed him
exactly what she thought about that. She'd lectured him a good
three dozen times on how he interacted with her sister-in-law—
just this month.

He couldn't seem to help himself. The Jacobsons got under
his skin. Always would.

He'd *given* Izzie to Allen in marriage—he snorted at that—
just after Christmas. She was wildly happy. That didn't mean he
trusted the guy.

Allen was too old for Izzie, for one thing. He and Jake were
close to the same age. The guy was too polished for Izzie, too.

Sophisticated and comfortable in the world of the wealthy. Jake had to admit, Allen Jacobson seemed to adore Izzie.

So far.

Everything he'd dug up on Allen showed that the man was exactly as he appeared to be—no matter what Jake's gut was telling him. A wealthy trauma surgeon who had been born into the upper-crust lifestyle. Same for the sister.

There was more to *her* than that.

Shelby Jacobson had secrets. They were right there in the storm-colored eyes too perfect to be real.

Her eyes called to him in his dreams. Tormented him.

Jake wanted to know what it was that scared this woman who had everything in the world she could want.

It had just been handed to her—she hadn't worked for it, not even for one moment. Almost twenty million dollars had been deposited into accounts in her name once the estate of Dr. Logan Lanning had been settled more than a year ago. Six months later, another part of his estate had been magically "discovered" in offshore accounts.

Almost forty-nine million dollars' worth. Most of that money had gone straight to Uncle Sam—and the woman in the burgundy dress.

Jake wanted to know why. Why *her?*

Why would Logan Lanning leave tens of millions of dollars to his friend's younger sister and no one else? He'd left only nine additional million to Allen—a man who'd been his closest friend since high school.

Yet seven times that much had been left to Shelby.

Jake had to admit that ate at him. Other than the deaths of her parents when she'd been a teenager—and he knew how traumatic that had to have been for her—everything had been easy for her. Best schools, everything she'd ever wanted, and one of the most beautiful women he had ever seen—she hadn't had to work for anything.

She didn't have to work at all. Would never have to again.

A year ago, Shelby had graduated with a master's degree. In social work. Within six months of that, she had inherited millions. Do-gooder with a never-ending bank account. She was a walking contradiction.

He wanted to figure her out and move on.

He was a hunter. Of men. It was in his blood. He had answers he needed to find. Including answers about her.

Logan Lanning topped his list of questions, even now, almost two years after the bastard had nearly killed three women. Three years after Lanning had focused on Jake's niece as a target, too.

Lanning was dead, but the questions remained.

"It's Shelby you need to be nicer to," Izzie continued, as they entered the ballroom at the Barratt-Finley Creek. The conversation buzzing was already a steady hum that grated on his nerves.

Jake hated crowds. Hobnobbing with the rich and famous of Finley Creek was *not* something he would ever enjoy. He was a working-class man from a working-class family, and he knew where he belonged. Where he *wanted* to belong.

This Cinderella's ball wasn't it.

He was more the mouse turned into coachman than Prince Charming, after all.

"Shelby knows I'm nowhere near nice. It's one reason why she doesn't like me." That was the truth. The moment he entered the room, she couldn't get out fast enough. Each and every time.

That was probably his fault. He didn't always have a filter where she was concerned.

He had said some truly jackass things to her, too. Usually when it was just the two of them, or when Izzie and Allen were distracted. "She finds me fascinating against her will, though."

Her storm-blue eyes met his for just one long moment. Her eyes...the secrets they held...

Damn it. He wanted to know everything about her.

"*Fascinating* isn't the word for it. *Irritating* is more like it. Like a cold sore that won't heal. Or a blister."

Her calm delivery drove him mad. She always used that tone. Always hesitated before she spoke in a way designed to make a man anticipate what she was going to say. Jake was almost certain she was lying every time she opened her gorgeous mouth.

Storm-blue eyes were watching every move he made. The way one would watch a particularly disobedient dog taking a dump on the sidewalk.

She always looked at him that way—like he wasn't fit to be within ten feet of her. It drove him crazy.

He'd known women like her before.

Jake wasn't interested in repeating that experience.

Even if he did dream about her all the damned time.

It was just because he hadn't figured her out yet. Once he did—he'd forget her and move on.

2

Melody Beck Barratt, a former TSP detective who'd been shot and partially paralyzed several years ago and was now married to what seemed like the richest man in the world, was their hostess for the evening.

Everyone who was anyone in the high society set in Finley Creek or Barrattville *knew* and at least pretended to adore Mel.

Mel found her way to their table about an hour into the event.

She placed one hand on Shelby's shoulder. Shelby knew Mel well—and liked her. Shelby's brother had been good friends with Mel's family for a long while now. Mel was nice—but a bit pushy when she felt she knew what was best for someone. She and Izzie were trying to make Shelby their pet project lately—and it was interfering with Shelby's own plans.

Shelby had some very definite plans. She just hadn't shared them with her brother yet.

Izzie was almost as fiercely overprotective of Shelby as Allen was. Not what Shelby wanted, but Izzie was taking her cues from Allen. Shelby didn't know how to tell them to back off without hurting their feelings—and that was the one thing she would never do.

Hurt her brother again.

Allen was looking at Shelby with that particularly worried look in his gray eyes that told her he was sure to say something to her later. She bit back a sigh.

She loved him, but...it was time he stopped hovering over her all the time.

He had his own life to think about now.

Her big brother had taken his stand-in parent duties seriously. It had been twelve years since they'd lost their parents. Shelby was almost twenty-seven now. It was time he just accepted that he couldn't make everything perfect for her.

Let her do what she had to do to get through. To live the life she was trying to build for herself. That was all she wanted.

To move on. To find the *answers,* and then move on.

Into the life that was *far* different than she had ever imagined it would be. Her parents had been reasonably well off, but they'd had still had to work for a living. They'd made wise financial decisions—her mother had particularly enjoyed investing—and Shelby and Allen had both had small inheritances. Allen had turned them into a decent portfolio for both of them.

Logan had changed everything. For both her and Allen.

Every penny had been money Logan had earned through his hard work and dedication. *Every* penny—no matter what people said about him. People said a lot about him—most of it not good. Shelby hated that. He had hurt people—but he had loved her and Allen a great deal.

She was still trying to reconcile that.

Allen looked beautiful in his tuxedo. Happy. Shelby hadn't seen her brother that happy in a seriously long time. Izzie was all Shelby could have wanted in a sister-in-law.

Too bad Izzie had a *Jake* attached.

She shot another look at Jake, where he sat trying to charm some woman who had mysteriously found her way to their table. It took Shelby a moment to place the woman underneath the garish, ash-blond hair and thick makeup. When she did, Shelby bit back a smirk of her own.

Perfect.

It took everything she had not to tell Brianna Claireson that Jake's annual salary wouldn't be enough to keep her in the diamonds and champagne she was accustomed to. Brianna built her friends list based on how much they had in their pocket-book. If she wanted more from Jake, that woman would literally call it slumming. And it would involve one thing.

Of course, Jake probably wouldn't mind. He was such a dog at times. Women came at him like he was Hunter Louis Clark, hottest guy in Hollywood, or something.

Brianna liked hunting blue-collar men and bending them to her will.

Shelby and Brianna had tangled before. Viciously.

Brianna had despised Shelby from the moment they had met, even though the woman was a good six or seven years older than Shelby, and far more experienced.

It had gotten worse, especially five years ago.

Over Logan.

Brianna had wanted him, desperately.

She'd seen Shelby as the primary rival to all her future plans.

For a while there, Shelby *had* been.

Even if only Shelby and Logan had known that. She missed him so much. She'd far rather have had Logan tonight than...Jake.

Jake shot her a look. One that told her what he was thinking.

He was measuring Shelby against Brianna—and finding Shelby lacking.

Well. Jake deserved what he got. It wasn't Shelby's job to

protect him. Far, far from it. She sent him a smirk and turned away.

Jake got what Jake deserved.

Someone touched her shoulder, and Shelby fought the instinctive urge to jerk away. Strangers coming up behind her would always throw her off. Always.

She looked up into the gorgeous face of Daniel McKellen. Head of the Major Crimes unit at the TSP.

Jake's boss.

One of the very few TSP men that Shelby even halfway trusted. She released the breath she'd been holding and smiled up at him. "Jake, Izzie. Allen...Shelby. It's nice to see you." He touched her shoulder again lightly. Looked right at her. Gave her the shivers—the man had dark hair and beautiful eyes, too. There was appreciation in Daniel's brown eyes when he looked at her. "You and Izzie both look gorgeous. Far too gorgeous for these two. Shelby, why don't you leave Jake to his...new friend...and join me for the next dance? My date has abandoned me already."

Daniel held out a hand to her. Shelby couldn't resist. He was offering her a few minutes of distance between her and Jake—and Brianna Claireson.

That was worth far more than Daniel's weight in gold.

She took his hand and stood.

3

Jake barely listened to the woman sitting next to him. Brianna Claireson wasn't a woman he was interested in knowing, not even for a moment. Brianna had been shooting looks at Shelby since she'd stopped by their table to introduce herself to him all breathlessly and flirty.

For the third time.

Brianna didn't remember him when he was flashing a badge instead of wearing a tux. He'd purchased the tux on Shelby's orders, for Izzie's wedding almost eight months ago. Shelby had demanded to know his sizes and had told him where to be for fittings—as if he wasn't capable himself. She'd printed him up a fitting schedule. Circled the address of the shop in red. Then called to confirm he was where he was supposed to be. Each time. As if he wasn't capable at all.

The woman just irked him to his toes.

Brianna was jealous. That was painfully clear. Either that, or she felt intimidated by Shelby.

He could see why. Brianna was nothing like Shelby. Not by a long shot.

Shelby was the most gorgeous woman in the room. He might

not like her much personally, but he would never deny that she was beyond hot—especially in that dress that made her look too damned expensive for a mere mortal man to even look at.

She was way out of Jake's league.

Shelby Grace Jacobson was hot enough to have him waking in a sweat some nights, after some of the steamiest dreams he'd had in a long, long time. He'd just about gotten used to it—every time he saw her, he had fantasies for a week after.

Allen said something, flirting with Izzie again. Jake got that they were still in the newlywed stage, but did they have to shove their relationship in his face like they did? Allen pawed at her all the time. Izzie was pawing right back.

Izzie was doing it on purpose—because she knew how Jake felt about Allen. She was rubbing it in Jake's face on purpose just to goad him. His niece was rather wicked like that.

Jake turned back to see Daniel McKellen, his damned *friend*, staring down at Shelby like she was the star of his own hot dreams. To his shock, Shelby accepted Daniel's request and took off across the dance floor with a man Jake had until that very moment considered a good friend.

One of his closest friends, actually.

That traitor.

"Shelby and Daniel look so gorgeous together," someone said from behind Jake, as the Claireson woman took off, finally. Jake turned. There was his second-favorite girl, dressed in jade green—with the lovesick mayor trailing after her like a total goon, like Turner Barratt always did. "I can see that she likes him, too."

Jake turned back to the pair in question. Daniel was just as tall as Jake's own six three. Shelby was around five eight or so, but with the three-inch heels, was only a few inches shorter.

Shelby's hair, warm chestnut brown, had been twisted into one of those fancy twists he despised. He loved it when it was down and wild around her shoulders. Made a man's fingers curl to touch. To bury in that hair and hold her still while he kissed the hell out of her. Daniel turned her on the dance floor. Jake's tongue almost hung out of his mouth as the drool doubled.

The back of the damned dress was missing. Nothing was there, not even a bra strap. How was that even possible? Shelby was curved in all the right ways—things were defying gravity in ways he was so stupidly curious about.

He wanted to know what was under that dress.

All that creamy skin was right there under Daniel's hand. Someone needed to punch Daniel's lights out. Daniel's hand rode *low*. Far lower than it should. Surely Daniel wasn't about to cop a feel right there for everyone to see?

If the man even tried it, Jake would rip his face off. As a friendly warning.

Anger tightened his gut. Daniel wouldn't be that stupid.

"Jake, Allen, you both look great. Izzie, red so suits you," Annie said. "Love how you've tamed the troll hair."

His niece didn't have troll hair. She had natural curls just like Jake's mother had had. Beautiful, even if Izzie hated them and had forever.

"Thanks. How are you feeling?" Jake barely looked at the mayor's pretty little wife.

He'd had a hand in raising her and her sister, too. If he could call riding herd on her, Josie, and Izzie *raising* them.

Wrangling them had been more accurate.

That, and transporting them wherever they'd needed to go. He'd spent several years just playing taxi to three young girls.

He hadn't done half bad a job raising them, he didn't think.

Jake barely heard what they were saying, all his attention on Shelby and Daniel. Shelby was laughing at something Daniel and Daniel's date, Haldyn, were saying. Laughing. A genuine laugh.

He hadn't known she could laugh like that.

Damn, she was the hottest woman in the damned county. He'd bet a million on it—if he had that kind of money.

Maybe he could borrow a million from her brother and make that bet. Bound to be a substantial return.

No other woman in the room held a candle to that one.

"So what's Jake scowling at now?" Annie asked. She nudged his shoulder, and then followed his gaze. "Seriously? You and Shelby into it again?"

"He'd better not be into it with her at all," Allen said, a clear warning in his tone. "Shelby's already nervous enough as it is. This...kind of event is not easy for her, whatsoever."

"She'll be ok. She has us to help her get through," Annie added, real compassion in her tone as she patted Allen's hand. It had Jake's attention sharpening. Had the questions building. "Daniel is a great place to start. He won't do anything to over-whelm her too badly. He knows how tough this is for her. And she'll have her family on stage with her."

Jake had the feeling they were speaking over his head.

He had yet to figure out just what about the TSP freaked Shelby out so completely that even the mention of it would be enough to have her paling before a man's eyes. Jake hadn't been able to find her name in the database anywhere— except for one speeding ticket when she'd been twenty-two years old.

Nothing. He'd searched more than once.

Yet something had happened. He would almost guarantee it. No one would tell him just what it was. And that wasn't good enough.

4

RESCUE CAME IN AT THE STRANGEST PLACE. BEFORE
the worst part of the evening, when she was to be paraded on
the stage for the world to see, a small woman in a black dress
marched right up to their table, shot a cranky look at Daniel and
Jake's friend Dom—who had somehow shown up at their table
—and grabbed Shelby's hand. Charlotte looked at Daniel's date
and sniffed once. "Haldyn, come on. You and Shelby need to
keep much better company than these lunatics. Let's salvage the
rest of your night."

Charlotte tugged on Shelby's hand. Shelby and Haldyn went
quietly. Just like that, Shelby found herself at a table with a
handful of women she called her friends. She gave a real,
genuine smile as Charlotte hassled Haldyn about her choice in
dates.

"What...what...what are you all doing here?" They hadn't
been invited, but she was seriously glad to see them all.

"Powell said you needed some emotional support from
rational women like us. We're the rescue squad. She black-
mailed her brothers into being our tickets in. Oddly enough,
they didn't protest too much. I do think Madison has to kiss

one of Powell's brothers later. Something to do with a bet between the brothers? I'm not clear on the details," Charlotte Fields said. Shelby had known her for about a year and a half now, through the children's choir Charlotte had organized. Daryn had put Shelby in contact with Charlotte—who worked in the same department as Daryn at the TSP—when Charlotte was having trouble funding the project. Shelby had been glad to help.

Even if it had just been with Logan's money at first.

She'd ignored the TSP part of things. Deliberately.

Through Charlotte, she'd met Madison. To her surprise, her closest two friends in the world were right there at the table next to Madison, too. She'd known Daryn would be there with her husband Mike, but...Zoey had been scheduled to work. "Zoey?"

"Powell rounded up some brothers. Char and Madison are their plus-ones tonight. I already had an invite, but I came with one of her brothers as well. I traded shifts with the Incredible Blond Hulk to get tonight off." Zoey hugged her quickly. "You look gorgeous."

"I don't feel it. I-I-I hate these kinds of things."

"I grabbed us a table," Powell said, looking like a little fairy in her silk dress. "Had my brothers run interference. *Now* we can sit down and enjoy ourselves."

"As if anyone would mess with Powell," Haldyn said, quietly. She rarely spoke, something she and Shelby had in common.

They were an odd group, Shelby thought.

They had made room for her and Zoey.

Zoey's sister, Pen, was a part of the choir, too. When the choir had needed a pianist, Pen had volunteered Shelby, and then convinced Shelby to do it. Badgered her, actually.

Pen was a bit of a steamroller when she wanted to be.

"Where's Pen?" Zoey and Pen were related to many of the people here tonight. That did explain Zoey's presence. She had

had an invitation. Trading shifts with her co-sheriff—that was a tough one for Zoey. The two didn't exactly get along.

They made Shelby and Jake look like best buddies.

"She's around with her friends. They are having a good time. Mel has a security guard around to make sure they aren't...bothered."

"Bothered by what?" Charlotte asked.

"Some of the men in this crowd," Powell said with a frown. "Don't always handle not getting their own way well. And they like the younger girls."

"Mel is aware," Zoey said. "And I'm watching them, myself."

"Probably a good idea for none of you to go anywhere alone, just to be on the safe side." Powell usually was the most serious, cautious one of the group. "And I think Victor Scott may be drunk. He's asking a lot of strange questions. Just be prepared."

"I'm glad you are all here," Shelby said impulsively as she ordered another water from the server. She settled in the chair between Zoey and Daryn and slipped her shoes off beneath the table. "I-I-I do not like the idea of being the entertainment."

"I'll be up there with you," Daryn said. "Darrell and Mike, too."

"And Jake and Dom," Madison said, leaning forward with a wicked expression on her face. "Just stand behind those two. No one will be able to see you behind their massively broad...egos."

"Ignore her," Charlotte said. "But she's right. Those two cavemen will get all the attention up there, as gorgeous as they both are. You just stand there to one side, and no one will notice you."

"They'll notice her," Powell said wryly. "Shelby's flat out stunning. And she is in so many of the photographs from after the storm. People were intrigued by her. Rich Lady Rescuer. We all know that." Powell sent her a significant look. "Probably would be a good idea for you to stay between those two, though. Limit exposure, if you can."

Shelby's breath caught a little. Powell was her attorney. She knew exactly why Shelby didn't want to be the center of attention right now.

Shelby got to spend a good hour with her friends, laughing and actually enjoying herself. She had always had Daryn—they'd been friends since they were in high school. Zoey had joined them in their first semester at FCU, though she'd only been a part-time student and older than them by a few years.

They'd stuck together since then.

Now, they were adding friends to their circle. Growing.

Shelby liked to think she had finally grown up and was ready to let more people into her safe little world. Even if they were with the TSP.

Only Zoey was an actual cop. Haldyn, Charlotte, Madison, and Daryn were all forensic scientists. Shelby had friends who she cared about. And who cared about her in return.

Shelby was starting to get herself back now. Finally.

It had only taken five years to do it.

Shelby looked up to where her brother had just taken his seat after helping Izzie into hers.

It drove Izzie crazy when he did that. The old-fashioned manners their mother had insisted on. Shelby had seen Izzie's cheeks turn bright red when Allen's hands would stray just a little.

A small smile hit her lips. Her brother was finally happy with a woman who adored him. Daryn was happy with the detective she'd snagged after the storm, as she put it. Zoey and Pen were doing ok, happy now that Zoey was doing better financially with her promotion to sheriff and they had found a wonderful family that they had been separated from years ago.

And Shelby…Shelby was becoming happy.

Nothing could take that away from her again.

She wasn't going to let it.

Her eyes met devil-dark ones across the empty tables.

Jake was watching her.

Shelby wouldn't let herself look away first.

"You keep challenging him like that, and that junkyard dog is going to turn on you," Powell whispered in her ear.

"That's Jake. Izzie's uncle. His bark is worse than...than... than his bite."

"I see. I thought was him. He cleans up very, very nice. Doesn't like rich ladies though."

"I know. He's made that clear."

"I've met him a few times. Got the feeling he didn't respect my bank account. Some guys are like that."

"Jake is." And it was best to stay far, far away from him. "He...he has issues with money. Rather, women with money."

"Sometimes women with money intimidate the old-school "me provider" types. I've learned to just go on by that kind of man, personally. I have money. I like making more money. I love the challenge of it. Nothing wrong with that. Is he going to cause problems now?" Powell asked as four tall men who Shelby recognized as Barratts showed up at the table—followed by a fifth that she knew was Powell's twin brother.

He held out a hand to her. "I have been waiting all evening to ask this of the most beautiful woman in the room. Would you do me the honor?"

Shelby almost hesitated. She was having an actual good time with her friends. But there was a kind look in his eyes. Powell had brought her friends here for her—that mattered. She wasn't going to be rude to Powell's beloved twin now—and Powell adored him. She spoke of him so often. "Of...of...of course."

"Excellent. I am Brandt Barratt, by the way. The best of the Barratts." He gave a confident smile that made him even more gorgeous. Wow. Barratts were very good-looking men. That this one was five-foot-nothing Powell's twin was just crazy. He had to be six and a half feet tall.

His name caught Charlotte's attention. "You were in Masterson. With Marin and Maggie, that day."

He turned toward Charlotte. Studied her for a moment. "And you would be the infamous Chuckie Talley? I think we've met before."

Charlotte laughed. "Only the TSP idiots call me that. I go by Charlotte. Plan to return to Masterson soon?"

He spoke with Charlotte for another moment, and then he led Shelby to the dance floor. He was a beautiful dancer. He didn't hold her too tightly. She liked him—Brandt had the same eyes as his twin sister.

"What do you have planned in Masterson, Mr. Barratt?"

"Please, it's Brandt." He shot her a gorgeous smile. "There is a woman there. And just between us, she is Charlotte's younger cousin. They have the same green eyes. I have been too shy to tell her how I feel. Powell freaks every time I mention returning to Masterson, considering that I was almost killed there recently. I'd be out of her control there, you see. She so loves to boss me around. And she's afraid, after what happened up there before."

"I remember the news. Are you better now?"

"Fully recovered. With a new lease on life and a bullet fragment sitting in my collarbone forever. And plans. I have great plans for my future. That woman in Masterson? She terrifies me. Some women are just like that."

Shelby enjoyed the rest of the dance with him. He told her all about the woman he had a thing for.

Love.

It was beautiful to even think about.

5

Victor Scott had everything. Correction, Victor Scott had *once* had everything.

Now...now, he had nothing. Not since the moment when he had buried his thirty-two-year-old son and realized that he had nothing left.

He was sixty-five years old now, and he had nothing.

No children, no loving wife, no grandchildren.

But he did have an expiration date.

He'd learned of that very thing two weeks ago. Now, now he had to face what his life had become. And what was left of it.

Victor had no one to leave his legacy. The only relative he had left in the world was his younger half sister's daughter somewhere along the northeast coast. Victor didn't even know that young woman's name.

He had his attorney tracking her down, just in case his final plan didn't come to fruition on time. Her mother had walked away from the Scott fortune more than twenty years ago.

He essentially had no one.

No one to train in how to manage the millions he had

amassed since his father had sat him down as a ten-year-old and explained the basics of economics to him.

He was a *Scott*.

Scotts were made to make money.

He had done that, many, many times over.

He would have been proud the day he turned it over to Kyle.

Kyle was in the ground. Gone forever. It was time for Victor to stop looking toward regrets, toward the past, and plan for the future.

His very line depended on it. He had much he had to do now.

That saucy little upstart wife of Houghton Barratt had some of the best events in Finley Creek. Her benefits and galas were often filled with attractive, intelligent young women moving around.

From all socioeconomic levels in Finley Creek.

They were perfect, and thanks to his fortune, he would find one to do exactly what he needed.

Victor studied his options now. *One* of them had to fit his needs. He just needed one—the perfect fit.

There were many who weren't of his socioeconomic background, but they were well connected. Some were even connected to the governor of Texas, the heads of two local hospitals, Carrington Medical Group, plus the mayor of Finley Creek.

That was an important distinction.

Finley Creek was a small city of fifty thousand or so. There weren't a great deal of women who would meet his needs.

Not as quickly as he needed.

He could overlook a less than stellar pedigree if the woman he chose fit all his other requirements. He was willing to see the woman he finally chose was well compensated. For life. That could be an important factor in his plan.

Victor would start his hunting tonight—then, tomorrow, he had other business that would demand his attention.

It was time he cleaned house.

The legacy his next son or daughter—he could not be choosy at this point—inherited would be as perfect as Victor could make it.

He would leave no room for mistakes.

He had some mistakes of his own to clean up—and some of his late son's. Then...then, everything would be perfect for the next Scotts to come.

His child's mother would have to have intense training to ensure she could preserve his child's legacy until he was old enough to take it on for himself.

There was no room for mistakes now.

Victor would make his list tonight. Victor's gaze roamed the room as he made note. He would start with the beautiful young women at the tables near the rear. He would start there.

He studied them for a long moment, impressed by what he saw. They were the type to grab a man's attention, certainly.

He would learn of all of them that which he could, and then he would decide.

If the shoe fit, the woman would be blessed beyond measure. He had to choose tonight.

Victor's time was running out.

6

ALLEN HAD GOTTEN CALLED IN FOR A PARTIAL amputation less than an hour after the benefit had started. He had taken off, leaving Jake with both Izzie and Jake's "date" for the evening.

And a warning to behave himself with Allen's sister. Or else.

Jake didn't mind seeing the back of Allen. Izzie was disappointed, but she covered it. There was no accounting for the girl's tastes. She always had been a perverse little creature. Izzie and Annie both.

Shelby returned to their table, but it was obvious she didn't want to.

Not that she stayed long.

Izzie and Shelby were led away from the table by two of the mayor's cousins. Both women went willingly, Izzie laughing at the Barratt's crestfallen face when she told him she was perfectly happy with her husband and not about to run off with him. Barratt kept making jokes.

Jake had to say that most of the Barratts he'd met weren't that bad for a bunch of rich guys. Not as bad as Allen. The

Barratts seemed genuine as a family. A little cocky, but most rich guys were.

So were a lot of cops, in his experience.

He could tolerate the Barratts, but that attorney Mac Barratt had his hands too low on all that silky skin of Shelby's.

The man should know better.

If he didn't move his hands soon, Jake was going to go break his fingers.

She was his date tonight, after all. Even if she seemed to have forgotten that fact.

Jake sat there alone and glowered at the pair. Shelby just ignored him. Like always.

Someone said his name and people settled in the chairs next to him.

He looked up and there they were—men he could actually stand to spend time with. Finally. They had an actual purpose for being there tonight, after all. And it wasn't just for photo ops.

They were hunting. Like always.

Jarrod Foster pulled a chair from the next table over. "Girls tell you to shove it, yet?"

"Allen got called in, thankfully. Was ready to punch the guy." Allen really needed to keep his hands off Izzie in front of Jake. "I'm in charge of babysitting his sister tonight."

"I can think of far, far worse things. In fact, you take Izzie on home and read her a bedtime story and tuck her in, Daddy. *I'll* see to it that Shelby makes it home just fine," Jarrod said, smirking. "She half likes me, and I'd love to get close to her. Real close."

"So who did you bring tonight then? All alone? At least we all *have* dates." Jake would not knock Jarrod's teeth out. That just wasn't done around this place.

"Haldyn did me the honor, so when you see her, Jarrod, don't be an ass," Daniel said, settling into the chair next to Jake.

Daniel had been known to throw a punch where his date was concerned.

The most recent blow had been directed at Jarrod after a particularly vicious *discussion* between Jarrod and Haldyn on a crime scene one day. Jake had threatened to arrest both Daniel and Jarrod on assault charges if they didn't behave themselves.

He'd only been half joking. Jarrod and Haldyn would never get along. That was rather a given around the TSP.

"Haldyn is here?" Jarrod asked, looking around. "I must have missed her. Pity."

"Or she was avoiding your ass," Jake liked Haldyn just fine—she was quiet and reserved and damned good at her job. Hot as hell, too. "Leave Hal alone. I did see her already, and wow. She should always wear tight, short, little green things like that. Make's a man's heart pound, right, Dan?" Jake asked.

Jarrod coughed. "I'll make a point of saying hello to her, then. Since we're on the same team and all."

Daniel almost growled.

Haldyn, Charlotte, and Madison made up a portion of the forensics lab at the TSP. They all looked damned good tonight, too. He bet that ate at Dom—who'd had a thing for Madison a hell of a lot longer than his father had for Madison's mother. It was getting complicated around here.

Dom took the empty chair across from Jake. Sean Callum showed up out of nowhere, surprising Jake, with Mike Evers in tow.

Hell, Callum shouldn't even be there—his wife had just had the baby three weeks ago.

He questioned the other man. Callum shuddered. "I'm here *representing* the wife and me. We were the most special rescue, after all. And I'm here for Shelby. Photo op and moral support. So what do we know now? Anything new? I think most of the task force is here, tonight. Even saw the Addys near the rear of the ballroom wrapped up in each other like a pair of squid."

Jake studied all the high-class assholes around him. Making mental notes and trying to ignore burgundy silk and creamy satin shoulders as she was twirled around and around again.

All the men wanted to dance with her. All of them—damn them all.

"Well. Look at us now. We've moved up in the world," Gunnar Erickson said, shooting a glance at the now empty tables around them, as he was the last to join them. "Anybody got a list of names to add to the suspect pool?"

Jake hadn't been looking at the people around him as potential leads. He'd spent most of the evening trying not to stare at Shelby.

He kept that to himself.

"Been busy. I'm on guard duty tonight," Jake said. "Keeping an eye on Izzie is a full-time job—and I got her sister-in-law to babysit, too."

"You weren't paying the least bit of attention to your niece. Not that I blame you," Callum said. "Shelby...Wow. If it wasn't for my wife..."

"If she'd ever look in my direction, I'd already have asked her out myself," Daniel said. Jake half thought Daniel was serious, even with Haldyn right there and available. Hell, what was Daniel thinking? He didn't think his friend was that much of a dog. "She's too afraid of any man with the word TSP associated with him for that to ever happen."

"Someday, I'm going to find the bastards responsible," Mike said, tightly. "For what happened to her and Daryn that day. And I'm going to make them pay. With my fists."

"When you do," Callum added. "I'll hold your coat while you kick their asses."

"Agreed," Daniel turned back to the reason Jake's buddies had all crowded Jake's table. "I heard back from my contact in Mexico City."

Just like that, talk turned to the case none of them would ever admit they were working on.

Jake tried to concentrate on what they were saying. He could see Shelby, wrapped up in the arms of some older rich guy who was looking down at her like Shelby was the answer to all his prayers.

Shelby had a slightly panicked look on her face. He wanted to storm across the ballroom and rescue her. A totally stupid, dickhead idea.

It wasn't his place to coddle Shelby because she hated crowds. Hell, most sane people hated crowds. Why should she be so special?

Because it was her?

The other men knew something about her that Jake didn't. Something had put that expression on Mike's face when he'd spoken about his wife, Daryn.

Like Mike knew exactly what had happened to Shelby.

So did Callum. And Daniel.

Hell, Jake was starting to think that he was one of the few that didn't.

Damned if he didn't recognize the rich guy holding her now. He was at the top of Jake's suspect list, after all.

The man had his hands all over Shelby. Jake barely kept himself from growling and storming over there, just in time.

7

JAKE GRABBED HIS FAVORITE FEMALE OF ALL TIME BY the hand, five minutes after she and Annie and Turner returned to the table, ending the case discussion instantly. "Come on and dance with me, kid. Make me look less like a fool. I can't have McKellen looking better tonight than I do."

He wanted to get closer to Victor Scott, too. The old goat was looking down at Shelby like she was his own personal Cinderella. Like he was ready to carry her right out of the ball-room to his...pumpkin.

Izzie just snickered. "As if that were possible."

Izzie had always been into dance and gymnastics as a kid. She'd made him learn ballroom dancing when she was all of twelve years old. He wouldn't look like a fool out there. And it would be one way for him to ask his niece about Shelby once again.

Jake waited until they were clear across the dance floor from their table—and from that disloyal ass, Daniel—before he asked. "What's going on with Shelby and the damned TSP that has everyone at that table knowing more than I do? Just what happened to her that was so bad? She get arrested and big brother have to buy her way out of it?"

Pain went through Izzie's eyes in an instant. Jake tensed.

"It wasn't like that at all, Jake. Not at all."

"Then just what exactly was it?"

Her attention shifted. He followed with his own. Daniel was dancing with her again. Victor Scott was stalking off the dance floor, looking disgruntled.

Jake hadn't forgotten what Daniel had said. Daniel wanted Shelby?

Hell, of course he did. Jake did—and he didn't even like the woman.

"It's not my story to tell, Jake. But...she was hurt. Badly. When she was twenty-one or so. Her attackers were off-duty TSP. She barely escaped being assaulted. Logan Lanning rescued her just in time. Shelby and Daryn Evers. They were just kids, really. Sheltered, especially Shelby. From what I've been told the four men responsible stalked her for a few months after. They nearly ran her off the road one time; they almost killed her that day. They ticketed Allen twice, too. Harassed him. Allen called in some favors with someone—I think it was Turner's uncle, or something—and the men were transferred to Houston. That she's here, in a room full of cops...Her friends are here to help her get through it. That's Powell and Zoey's doing, I think. Just give her a break; Shelby is extremely shy, and she's terrified of the TSP. Tonight, a benefit *for* the TSP, it's a literal nightmare for her. So just...be kind. For me?"

There wasn't anything he wouldn't do for Izzie. She knew that.

Jake felt lower than a slug. Izzie wouldn't lie to him, and she believed what she said. Completely.

"I didn't know. Did anything...happen to those SOBs?"

"Not a thing. For all we know, they're back in Finley Creek or Wichita Falls by now. That's her biggest fear, I think. That they'll come back. Find her again. Shelby doesn't trust the TSP to protect her if they do. How can she?" Izzie's eyes were filled with worry. She cared about her husband's sister a great deal. He knew that, too. Now, he felt like that stupid dog shitting on the sidewalk. "Who could she call for help?"

As he imagined Shelby's experience, Jake fought the nausea Izzie's whispered words brought. "Why didn't you ever tell me?"

"Frankly, it's none of your business. If you would just quit snipping at her so much, I wouldn't have told you at all. She could lock herself away forever. She just hasn't yet."

The dance ended. He had a lot of questions—but now wasn't the time to go digging. He would. He wouldn't stop until he had proof—and names. "I'll stop being an ass to her, Iz. I swear."

"Good. Because...I think you're getting in the way of her healing now. Making it worse for her. She doesn't need to be fighting with Mr. TSP every time your paths cross. It isn't fair to her at all."

Hell, that was the last thing he wanted. He looked for Shelby again. He found her, with Daniel practically wrapped around her, in the center of the dance floor.

Looking cool and calm as always. Like nothing rattled her. Who was the real her? The woman in front of him or the one Izzie described? "Who were they, Iz? Get me their names, and I'll find out exactly where they are right now."

"Allen's never told me. They were never charged, never prosecuted. Only Shelby and Daryn know who they are now. Maybe. I don't know. They might not have even known the attackers' last names. Or first names, for that matter."

"And Allen won't give me that information?"

"Not in a heartbeat. He would never betray her trust like that."

Well, hell. He should have expected that. He hadn't exactly

played nice with the Jacobsons, after all. He'd have to find his answers somewhere else.

If there was truth to what his niece said, he'd find the sonsofbitches and make them pay. As soon as he possibly could. No one should betray the badge like that.

It damned near destroyed him just thinking about Shelby being hurt.

He'd kill for that woman, if he ever had to.

Without hesitating.

That was just the way it was. Of course, that was not something he would ever tell her. A man had his pride, after all.

8

SHE WAS A BEAUTIFUL WOMAN, WITH BROWN HAIR just hinting at fire. The eyes were big and beautiful. Soft.

Intriguing.

But if she was dating that fish-shit from Major Crimes that could be a major problem.

She had come as Jake MacNamara's date for the evening. That was definitely a concern.

One he did not need to face now.

He paused near a column for privacy. Studied his prey.

There was young redhead, around the age of twenty. She looked very much like his hostess for the evening.

One of Melody Beck's sisters, he believed.

He considered it for a moment. A connection for his future heir to Houghton Barratt would be fortuitous. And after he was gone, Barratt would protect that child. That could not be discounted.

But the girl was at least forty years younger than Victor.

He wanted a woman with a bit more maturity, so that he could be guaranteed she was experienced enough to manage the responsibilities his wealth would bring with it.

If she was a Beck, the youngest perhaps, then she was not accustomed to this type of life, nor mature enough.

No. That girl would have to be marked off the list.

But he watched her as she joined three other beautiful women near the back of the tables. They were incredibly young.

They were quite beautiful. Would be stunning and intriguing when they matured.

He would not be around to see it. Nor did he have time to nurture such growth. He needed a woman already established in this world.

He would be best served by turning his attention elsewhere.

The first table he had focused on had his best potential. He would have to try harder.

Open himself up a bit more. Delve deeper into the women on his chosen list.

Victor was naturally more reserved. It was easier to keep secrets that way.

9

SHE'D MADE IT HALFWAY THROUGH THE EVENING without running out, screaming into the night. Shelby considered that a win. After she'd danced with Daniel again, he'd joined their table completely. Putting himself and Haldyn right between her and Jake, thankfully. Protectively.

That was her—the woman random men decided to protect.

Yay.

Apparently, they thought she needed it.

Jake was better behaved after that. Probably because Haldyn would call him a stupid frog again if he didn't.

The latter half of the evening was going to be the worst. That's when the honors ceremony and the personal stories would be presented. Accounts of so-called heroism. And, to her dismay, photos. Thanks to cell phones, there was documentation of the horror of that day.

She would be in some of those photos. It made her want to vomit just thinking about them. The last thing she ever wanted was the attention of the TSP coming in her direction.

Ever. Especially now.

Annie—plus her shadow, the mayor—and Izzie were off

visiting with friends of theirs at other tables. They were good friends with the Barratts and the Becks, Mel's and Turner's family.

She had no idea where Jake had slithered off to. Probably flirting with Brianna or someone of her ilk.

Shelby was glad; she needed a moment or two to decompress before the hard part of the evening began.

She settled back at the table and sipped her water slowly, watching an obviously annoyed Zoey fend off the advances of an older businessman on the prowl and watching Madison and Charlotte enjoying themselves with Powell's older brothers, Alex and Mac. Right before her eyes, Alex scooped a laughing Madison off her feet and kissed her in front of dozens of people.

Madison turned beet red, but everyone was laughing.

Powell was in a serious discussion with her twin, Brandt, in one corner. Shelby laughed aloud when he reached out and patted Powell on the head obnoxiously before walking away.

There was one more person she looked for—Zoey's younger sister, Pen. This crowd would be more than Pen was ready for, too. Pen and her three friends were easy to spot—next to Pen's brothers and other sister over at their table. Protected.

The sight of her friends and family helped Shelby relax a little. She wasn't alone. She was safe.

Shelby slipped her heels off under the table. Shelby forced herself to breathe slowly. To calm herself. She had strategies in place. She could deal with this. She could. It was just a few hours longer.

She had friends here tonight.

Even among the TSP. Daryn was still here somewhere, along with her husband Detective Mike Evers.

They'd stopped fighting each other—and the attraction they'd felt for one another—right after the storm. Mike had basically never left Daryn's side after that.

Poor Mike had been searching the rubble for his friends—

and his younger sister, A.J., who'd worked in forensics the day of the storm. Shelby had pulled Sean and A.J. free herself. They had been the last to be found in the rubble.

Alive, anyway.

There were photos of that rescue on prominent display right now. One focused on Shelby's face as she wore a blue helmet and protective gear and crawled through debris, Sean Callum right behind her. Her eyes and mud-streaked face were the focus of the photo.

It had become iconic for the Finley Creek tornado. It had been blasted on news sites clear around the world. For weeks.

Her face.

She hated it. Wished it had never been taken.

She just couldn't escape. Someone she didn't want to see it could. Could make the nightmares come back all over again.

Shelby had to find out who *they* were first.

10

She was alone for the first time all night. Shelby was sitting in the corner, half hidden. Jake checked the clock to make certain it wasn't anywhere near midnight.

He'd hate for Shelby-rella to disappear at 12:01 or something.

He couldn't help himself. He redirected.

Izzie's words rang in his head—they hadn't stopped since she'd told him.

Those who carried the badge were to protect, not hurt.

Most of the cops he knew felt the same. *Most* of the cops Jake had known through the years were good people, dedicated to making their streets a much better place. Willing to die if that was what it took.

To *help*. Not to hurt. Like he'd always told Izzie, Annie, and Josie—ninety percent of any group were good people. But there was always that ten percent that gave everyone else a bad name.

It was his job to flush those bastards out. It was why he liked Major Crimes. And it was what he'd been working on since Elliot Marshall had taken over as police chief more than three years ago.

Cleaning the devil from the TSP.

He was finally getting close to finding out the worst devil of the lot.

"Hiding again?" he asked softly, coming up behind her. He reached out a hand to touch her shoulder.

She jerked, spilling her drink over the table.

There was fear, panic in her eyes when she turned. Jake held up his hands and stepped back. "Sorry, didn't mean to scare you."

He had terrified her.

For the first time since he'd first seen her walking into W4HAV, he realized bone-deep fear was in those storm-blue eyes of hers. It took a moment for it to go away.

Damn.

Shelby was truly afraid of him. Even with the way she snipped at him at times. He hadn't seen it before.

Trauma was a real bitch. He had seen what trauma had done to Izzie and Annie firsthand. His niece was still healing from what that bastard Henedy had done to her. It would take her a lifetime to heal.

That was the way trauma worked.

That the TSP had caused Shelby's just pissed him off. He grabbed a cloth napkin and batted at the spill on the table. He needed to do something before he pulled her close and made promises he couldn't keep.

"What do you want, Jake?" she asked after a moment. She eyed him like he was the snake about to strike her delicate ankles.

"Just needed a break from the crowd, myself. Before we get paraded up there like good little boys and girls. What are you doing back here? Finally pry Daniel off of you? Was he getting a little slobbery? Did Haldyn get jealous? Challenge you to a wrestling contest? I would love to watch that. You and Haldyn... yeah, I'd watch. I'd give a year's salary to watch, actually."

"Daniel is just a friend, as is Haldyn. She says *they* are just... just...just friends. Not that it's your business. Where's your girlfriend Brianna? She finally find out you can't afford her?"

"She isn't my type." Well, so she was feeling a little snippy with him. Jake bit back a smile. He preferred that over his imagining her sitting here quaking in terror. She shot him a cool look out of storm-blue eyes.

"Why not? She not into Jell-O wrestling in the backyard?"

Sometimes, her eyes looked blue, and, sometimes, they were storm-gray. He had yet to figure out what color to call them. He would never admit it, but he had spent far too much time than he wanted to admit just thinking about her eyes.

And other parts of her. What they would feel like, look like, taste like. Especially her lips. What he would do to her if she'd ever lower herself to his level. Just for a weekend or so.

There were so many things he'd imagined doing to her. Things they would hopefully both enjoy.

Now, he felt like a dog. Shelby was a year older than his niece. Ten years younger than he was. He suddenly felt like a pervert. "Are you into Jell-O wrestling? Because if you are, I'm ready to hit the market near my place and buy every box they have."

He shot her his best smile.

Her eyes narrowed. Mistrust was there for him to see. "Wh-why don't... don't... don't you go away?"

She stuttered more when she was talking to him. He'd noticed that before. Nerves—Izzie had said it was nerves. He hadn't believed her then. Now, he wondered. "I don't want to. The last place I want to be is in the middle of the fancy-schmancy crowd around here tonight."

"Me... eith ... me ...too."

"Look at that. We've finally agreed on something."

"Wonders do happen."

He wasn't going anywhere.

He'd seen several men he recognized in this crowd—men he knew were real dogs when it came to women. Beautiful women, especially.

A beautiful, wealthy, vulnerable woman like her?

They'd been eyeing Shelby all night.

Especially that little weasel Jody Callahan. He'd been going on and on about Allen Jacobson's sister ever since all that bull had happened with Izzie and Allen and the Henedys last October. Saying how hot she was, and how he wished he'd get some time alone with her.

Jake had punched him once, just to shut him up. Told the little prick that Shelby was a part of his *family*. To watch his damned mouth or Jake would shut it for him.

Callahan brought up her name to Jake at least once a month. Panted over the woman he would never get.

The prick thought he'd have a shot with Shelby if he could just get close to her. He'd wanted Jake to help him get close to her. That conversation hadn't gone well for Callahan after that. Not by a long shot.

Callahan was circling closer to her now.

No, not going to happen.

Jake wasn't about to let her get caught alone with the wolves of the TSP. Not after what Izzie had told him.

He'd stand between her and the masses that were the TSP tonight—hell, most of his colleagues at the post were afraid of him, anyway.

He might as well take advantage of that.

"You really want me to leave you alone? The boys are starting to realize we didn't come together. They're going to start hunting. Especially with you in that dress, looking like you do."

A look of anger went across the stormy eyes—they were blue tonight, he thought—and she straightened. Jake bit back the slobber as the pose accented every curve she had. Shelby had perfect curves. Beautiful curves. Curves Jake wanted to touch.

"That's what it's all about for men like you, isn't it? How I *look*? Not how I think or f-f-feel? What I do? I didn't always look like this. I was awkward, too tall, too pudgy, with braces and acne and a stutter. When I was twenty. But now...now that I lost a few pounds, and the braces, and my skin cleared up, *now* people want to give me attention? I don't want it. At all. I just want to be left alone."

There was so much damned *pain* in her words that he almost backed up. So much longing to get just that. To be left alone. "That's not what I meant."

"I know what you think when you look at me."

"I don't think you do."

She leaned forward, just enough to have that dress gapping a bit in the front. Jake forced himself to keep his gaze in gentleman territory. His mother had raised him right. He wasn't an animal. Or a creep. He wasn't about to sneak a peek. "Really?"

"So tell me, what do I think when I look at you?" Jake sincerely hoped he'd hidden how he felt about her in certain ways well enough.

"You see the outer package and the money that surrounds me. You hate it. I know you hated Logan. Izzie told me what he did to her. You hate me because you hated him, and you don't like my brother at all, probably for the same reasons—Logan and money. Money, money, money—that is all you see. Even though Allen is the best man I have ever known. All you see when you look at me is the spoiled rich girl you despise. And I am not good enough to be anywhere near your sphere. Even though I have never done any...any ...anything to you."

"That's not all I see." Hell, he *had* hurt her, deeply. Over and over. Why hadn't he ever realized that before? He was a cranky, cantankerous asshole at times, but the last thing he had ever wanted to do was hurt her.

He owed her one hell of an apology. Now was as good a time as any.

"Then what? Tell me. Because...I am tired, Jake. Very, very tired of fighting all the time. Of fighting everything. Including you."

There was a world of hurt in those words. Hurt that he had caused. "I look at you...and see the woman who haunts me at night."

Surprise now. For the both of them. He hadn't meant to say those words, not at all. Her eyes immediately turned wary. "What?"

"I mean I can't figure you out, and that bothers me." There was no way in hell that he was going to let her know for even an instant that he'd been attracted to her from the moment he'd met her. There was no point in that. He could list all the differences between them instantly—he was too old for her, she was too damned rich for him, he didn't like where that money had come from, he couldn't stand her brother, he didn't trust her, they were of two different worlds...

Were they? She was right in front of him, in his world. Connected to his world in one very clear way: Izzie. Izzie was treating Shelby like the sister Izzie had never had. She and Annie and their pal Nikkie Jean all three were.

Shelby was everywhere Jake turned lately. Tempting him.

"Why do you even care? Because you don't like my brother?"

"It's not that I don't like him. I just don't understand him." That was the truth. Jake had been digging into problems associated with Finley Creek General Hospital for more than two years now. Trying to find the connections between the hospitals, the local government, the construction industry, and a million other things that just weren't adding up in this little city of fifty thousand or so.

The Henedys' names had come up repeatedly. So had Victor Scott's.

"Allen is the best man I have ever known. You...you can't even compare."

"That. That look right there. That's the look that drives me crazy, woman."

"Don't call me *woman*. What look?"

"The one that says I'm no better than a rodent in your kitchen. Not that you'd ever see it, considering the servants you probably have..."

"I don't have a single servant. I have a cleaning crew come in once a week. That's it. Why do you constantly bring up Logan's money? I didn't ask for it. I'd rather he be alive and getting help for his addiction than have all his money. He was... my... my... my...friend. When I needed him most. And I loved him. More than you can ever know."

A wild look of grief turned the eyes from blue to gray in an instant.

"We'd probably best not talk about Logan Lanning right now."

"We'd probably best not talk about *anything* right now."

Jake leaned closer, wanting to make certain she didn't miss his words as the band struck up again. "Maybe that's our problem, Shelby Grace. Maybe you and I haven't spent enough time talking about anything to know each other. Maybe I'm ready to fix that."

11

SHELBY SHIVERED. THERE WAS A LOOK IN HIS DARK eyes she had never seen directed at her before. He looked almost hungry.

Predatory.

That scared her. One of the few things she'd been able to say positively about Jake MacNamara was that he had never thought about her *that* way.

When she'd been injured before, he'd carried her into the hospital. She'd known he'd keep her safe—because Izzie had been right there, they'd been somewhat friendly, and Shelby had known about Izzie's relationship with Allen. She hadn't been able to say the same about the other TSP deputies there that day.

She just didn't trust Jake for one other reason: he'd made it clear from day one that he despised her. Even when she'd been all bloody and terrified, he'd been less than friendly. Now, here he was, right in front of her. Trying to tell her that he *didn't* despise her?

He must be drunk. That was the only explanation she had.

"I don't think that's a good idea. I think we should just keep to our corners and stay away from each other. I don't like you, Jake—and I never will. It's just because of Izzie that I tolerate you at all. Surprised you haven't *detected* that."

She was so sick and tired of people, men mostly, intimidating her. This was not the person Shelby wanted to be. At all. She wanted to be as fierce and take charge as Zoey or Charlotte…she wanted to not *hurt* so much all the time.

Before she'd been attacked, she hadn't been this afraid. She'd been quiet, studious, focused on getting her degree, but she'd not been afraid of the entire world then.

She hadn't even wanted to go to that party, but a so-called friend had driven her and Daryn there. They hadn't even known where they were going.

It was just supposed to have been a simple party. They'd stay a few minutes while Joanne had found the guy she had been interested in, and that was it. But that hadn't been it at all.

Joanne had brought them there where they could be hit on. On purpose. As a *joke*. She'd thought Shelby was too naive and needed a lesson in the *real* world. To Joanne, that had meant men.

Shelby had never forgotten that betrayal.

It had escalated.

Daryn and Shelby had been separated that night on purpose. Because they had been the prey. It had been a game to the men involved. They'd toyed and taunted—even more so after she'd stuttered when she'd said *no*.

She'd said no. Said she'd wanted to go home.

It had been a game to them. Yet it had almost destroyed her. She was still finding her way back to *Shelby*, five years later.

"I'm sorry for making you feel that way."

"What are you really after?" It was time she stopped just passively letting life happen. She'd made that decision the instant Daniel and Callum had turned over the keys to Logan's house to her after the TSP had kept Logan's house as evidence after his death.

Jake was a good place to start.

It felt like confronting the demon in front of her was Shelby finally taking control.

"I'm after...calling a cease fire. That's all. I've been a jerk. Maybe I am sensitive over the money thing. And I did so despise Lanning."

Logan was dead. It was time Jake moved on.

Time they both did.

Shelby was trying. She honestly was. She had one more thing she'd promised Logan that she would do *first*. Then, she was going to fight to build that life for herself. No matter what it cost.

But...Logan's promise first. She owed him that much.

"The Logan I knew when I was younger...he wouldn't have done that then. And I'm so sorry for what he did to Izzie. To all of them. He was broken and hurting." A part of that was her fault. Shelby would never forget that.

"It wasn't your fault. I've never blamed you for it. Maybe I did take my anger out at you. And for that...I am beyond sorry. So...peace? For our family's sake?"

"Like it or not, we're stuck with each other." Shelby shot him a direct look. They were; the baby Izzie carried now just cemented that. "Maybe we should just agree that we don't like one another, and we're going to just be civil around Izzie and Allen? That might be the best we're going to get."

"Deal." He held out a hand to her.

Shelby stared at it for the longest time. She finally reached out. "Deal."

His warm fingers wrapped around hers. Instead of sealing the deal, he tugged lightly. "Then dance with me. Because that ass Callahan is on his way over here. And he's got it bad for you. The last thing you want is him getting his hands on you the way he's wanting. Come on, just one dance. We'll call it an act of peace."

She wouldn't have. Except he was right. She saw Detective Callahan, and he was definitely intent. Hunting.

She was the only woman on this side of the room now.

Shelby didn't hesitate.

She stood.

And kept her hand in Jake's.

12

Jake might get on her nerves, but at least Shelby could say what she wanted to him. After about a month of knowing him, Shelby had let her filters go where he was concerned.

If Jake's hands went where she didn't want them, she'd tell him. He'd say something completely crass, but he'd move his hands. She did trust that. "You are a bit demanding."

"Ah, but I can dance really well." He shot her a beautiful grin.

He was taller than Mr. Scott—the last man she'd danced with before taking a break—by a good four inches or so. Even in her two-inch heels, he was still quite a bit taller than Shelby. His shoulders did a good job of blocking the sight of the crowd for her. She pulled in a deep breath and exhaled as the orchestra picked up again.

Jake did dance well. Jake didn't smell like rotten onions, or unwashed musty sweat. Some men didn't understand that tuxedos needed cleaned occasionally.

No. Jake smelled like peppermint and some type of woodsy scent that wasn't off-putting in the least. He pulled her closer, probably a bit closer than he should. Like an idiot, she found herself almost breathing him in.

Shelby found she didn't mind. His arms kept the rest of the room at bay. It was hard to focus on anyone *but* Jake, after all. "Enjoying yourself tonight, Uncle Jake?"

Jake growled a bit, just like she knew he would. Shelby bit back a grin as he spun her into the music and pulled her far too close this time. He hated it when she called him Uncle Jake. It was the number one reason she did it whenever he least expected it. Sometimes, she wanted to rattle him.

Feeling Jake pressed against her like this had her more than just a little rattled, too.

"I don't feel familial toward you at all, especially tonight. Don't call me Uncle Jake."

"Oh, but...Izzie said I could call you that. Since we're family now." She gave a deliberately coy look and batted her eyelashes as he spun her and then pulled her closer. "And you are so much older than me."

She was needling him. Shelby was enjoying it.

It was best to get the upper hand with him. Sometimes, she said things to Jake she would never dare say to any other man on the planet.

If he already didn't like her...what did it matter?

"Yes, I am enjoying myself tonight—at times. Like now...you should always wear this color. And wear dresses cut just like this. Although, it's far more daring than I would have expected. I think there may be a rebel inside you somewhere?"

"This old thing?" She'd ordered it special for this evening. She and Izzie had spent several hours shopping online until they had found what they'd wanted. This dress covered most of the scars she wanted to hide. "It's not half as daring as Izzie's, you know."

"Oh yeah, it is. You, Shelby Grace, are enough to give a mere mortal man like me a heart attack. I think you do it on purpose.

Old Scott thought so. He was looking at you like an angel had fallen right into his arms."

Shelby frowned up at him. She had found nothing offensive about Victor Scott. The older man was just...intent. "He's grieving still. He mentioned his son to me. And asked me all sorts of odd questions. Like how well I did in school and whether I play a musical instrument. He asked almost the same questions of Zoey and the rest of my friends."

His hands tightened. "Stay away from him. Promise me you will."

"Why?" His expression frightened her. All her taunting fell away. There was a look in his eyes she'd never seen before.

He leaned forward until his could whisper near her ear. "He's involved in some seriously shady shit. He's dangerous, and I don't want him anywhere near you. Just keep away from him, period."

She just nodded. "I'll do that."

"Good." He pulled her even closer, until the scent and warmth of him surrounded her. "Because the son of a bitch is watching us now. He's going to want to dance with you again."

"Should I tell him no if he asks?"

"Might be a good idea. I don't want him anywhere near you."

He pulled her even closer. Far too close.

Shelby would never admit it, but having him wrapped around her the way he was almost helped make the evening not seem as overwhelming as it had just a few moments earlier.

Heaven help her, she was using *Jake* for comfort.

The world truly had gone sideways again.

13

SHE'D SURVIVED. SHE'D BEEN PARADED UP ON STAGE like a trained seal, just like she had feared she would. The mayor had "recognized" her bravery and given her a certificate and a medal and allowed her to quietly move to the back of the crowd on stage. Turner knew her well enough now to know she wasn't comfortable on stage. And she greatly appreciated that.

She *had* hidden behind Jake and his TSP friends. They were tall, strong, broad-shouldered men, after all.

They'd made a Great Wall of defense. They and Darrell.

When it was over, she said goodbye to her friends and returned to her original table.

With Izzie...and Jake.

Her ride home.

Great.

To her surprise, instead of dropping Shelby off first and then taking Izzie a few blocks away, back to the house that they'd recently moved into, Jake turned down Izzie's street first. They'd already checked in with the security guard at the north gate.

Allen wanted Izzie behind secure walls, too. Allen wasn't

taking any chances. Not with Izzie. Allen was constantly riding Shelby about adding an actual security team to her own estate.

She wasn't ready for that. She already felt trapped by everything as it was.

Shelby knew the truth—a good portion of paid security guards were ex-cops. Unless she went with an all-female guard staff, which would be extremely difficult to find, she would be surrounded by former cops all the time. Not something she even wanted to think about.

She had one of the best security systems money could buy, though. And the gated community had guards that patrolled.

She was safe.

As safe as anyone could be, anyway.

"Out," Jake said. "Inside."

Just like that, he walked Izzie to her front door, leaving Shelby in the rear passenger seat. She was going to have to get in the front. Be alone with him.

Not exactly something she was looking forward to.

He came back all too soon. She'd already gathered up her courage and slipped into the front seat.

"All set?" he asked, quietly.

No. She wasn't all set. This was the first time she'd been alone in a car with him. She didn't like it. The man unsettled her. No denying that. "Of course."

The last thing she would do was let him know he made her nervous. She had more pride than that.

"Good. You look gorgeous tonight. Have I told you that yet?"

"Yes. But thank you." Her mother had instilled those manners into her, too. "So do you. Look...nice...I mean."

"Thanks. You picked out the tux, remember?"

"Yes." What was she supposed to say to this man?

Shelby didn't have a clue. So whenever that happened, she did the only thing she could. She said nothing at all.

It was just a three-block drive now.

Then she'd be home and wouldn't have to think about Jake MacNamara again. At least, for a while.

"I didn't know you were friends with women from the TSP." There was a question there, and a challenge.

She bristled. Here it started. The jabs about the money. It was his stock in trade. "Why? Different socioeconomic groups prevent friendships? I prefer to pick...pick...pick my friends based on character rather than tax bracket."

"Sheath the claws, kitten. I just was wondering how you met. Choir, your brother said?"

"Yes. Charlotte started a children's choir eighteen months ago. I help. My friend Zoey's sister was one of the first members."

"That's great. I like Chuckie and Madison."

"Of course, you do. They both told me exactly how much you did." They had laughed about it, too. Both had dated this man—within weeks of each other. Apparently, Jake had quite the reputation amongst the women of the TSP. Everyone knew it.

Shelby had learned about a side of Jake that she seriously doubted Izzie was aware of. It hadn't exactly made her think that much more of him. Not at all. She thought about that as he finally turned into her drive.

"What does that mean?"

"Nothing. Thanks for the ride." *See you never again!* Oh, that was what she wanted to say. She never would.

She didn't have the guts to tell him what she really thought about him.

Not really—that would just hurt Izzie, after all.

And that was the last thing she ever would want to do.

Izzie was her family, now.

To Shelby that meant everything. "Thanks again, Jake. I can walk myself in."

"Hell, no. I'm not about to let you walk in by yourself. Any more than I would Izzie. This part of town—you're a walking victim."

"It's not exactly a bad neighborhood. Gated security, and a few houses have private security teams."

"Yes. And millions of things to steal. To a determined thief, that gate wouldn't stop them. Hell, I could get into your place in fifteen seconds flat if I really wanted to."

"That's reassuring."

"You need better security. At least a guard posted on your place, like that house two blocks back."

"Please...don't start. I have my reasons. And you're starting to sound just like my brother. You don't want to sound just like Allen, do you?"

14

OH, SHE WAS *GOOD.*

He'd figured her out tonight. She was deflecting. Distracting him. Playing him. How often did she do that?

She was shooting him a challenging look in the interior light of his SUV as he drove past a few houses in her neighborhood with *For Sale* signs in the front lawns.

Still, she wasn't his responsibility. Jake would have to remember that.

Seeing those damned Barratts with their hands all over her and hearing her story from Izzie had made him feel like she *was* his. At least for tonight. He'd been aware of her standing next to him on that damned stage. He'd practically felt the nerves running through her.

Jake had wanted to grab her hand. Pull her close. Reassure her that the mayor's dog-and-pony show was almost over. To just take care of her as best he could.

He had resisted, barely. The last thing he'd want her to do was get freaked out by him in front of hundreds.

He wouldn't do that to her. Dom had razzed him about staring at her earlier.

Dom had been staring just as hard at Madison. Both men had been well aware of it.

That table of beautiful women had drawn a lot of attention tonight.

From them—and from other bastards in the crowd.

There had been a constant stream of men by that table. Stopping to talk to the women, to try to get their attention. Finally, that sheriff friend of Shelby's had moved to the most accessible part of that table and turned away every guy who'd gotten too close. Except Mike Evers, that was. Mike had been allowed into the inner sanctum to retrieve his wife whenever he'd wanted.

Beautiful women were always targeted.

It just was.

They were all very beautiful, complex, intriguing women. As soon as he got Shelby settled, he'd text Madison and Chuckie. Make sure they made it home ok. Just to be on the safe side.

Daniel would see Haldyn home, but the other two had been driving back to Chuckie's place together. Jake didn't trust the country-club set one bit.

They were as much thugs as the lowlifes he collared in the city at times.

They just had more money to cover up their deviancy. That was a lesson he'd made certain Izzie, Annie, and Josie had learned years ago.

15

SHELBY WATCHED HIM DRIVE AWAY. SHE HAD AN unobstructed view of her driveway from her front parlor. She'd had all the trees removed a week after she'd taken possession of the house. No one had understood why—except Zoey.

With no trees in the way, she could see any threats coming.

For a while there, she had built her life around protecting herself from threats. From *seeing* those threats everywhere. It had only been after an intense round of counseling with a psychiatrist hired by W4HAV to handle trauma related to sexual assaults that Shelby had seen that this was what she'd been doing.

She'd been trapped in flight mode for years and hadn't even realized it.

She could be prudent about her safety, but Shelby wasn't going to let herself continue to be paranoid. She didn't want to live like that. It would be so easy to just build a twelve-foot stone wall around this house. Keep the rest of the world out.

Maybe she'd hire herself a tribe of Amazons, someday. Put one on each corner of her estate.

There was no other word for this place.

It had felt so awkward when she'd first moved in. She had been accustomed to the condo she'd purchased when she was twenty, when she'd stopped wanting to live with her brother any longer. She'd bought it with part of her inheritance from her parents. Daryn had lived with her for a year or so after. Until the night of the party.

Then, Daryn had moved back in with Darrell. And Shelby... she'd moved right back in with Allen. They'd run right back to their big brothers. Where they had felt safe. That was something else she'd figured out recently.

Allen had always protected her. Sheltered her.

Now, she had to find a way to stand on her own two feet.

The first six months she'd owned the house, she had left it exactly as it had been. A blend of Logan and his parents, who had originally built the place years ago.

Logan and his brothers' toys from their childhood were stored in the attic, carefully labeled. Forgotten about. She'd have to go through those things someday. Decide what to keep and what to get rid of.

It had felt wrong to change his house. To erase him. Everywhere she'd looked, she'd remembered him. She'd wanted it that way.

Until Izzie had told her flat out that she wasn't helping herself at all, not making the house hers like Logan had wanted. Izzie had said that if Logan had loved her at all, he wouldn't want Shelby to just waste away behind gilded walls, weeping over his ghost.

Shelby hadn't been *weeping* exactly. She'd just been hurting.

Shelby had let Izzie read his last letter to her.

Izzie had wept with her then, too. The woman had a soft heart. There was no denying that.

Gradually, Shelby had begun making each room hers. She'd started with the kitchen and updated it, even though she wasn't much of a cook.

The biggest change had been to the piano alcove above. It was to there she headed whenever she felt unsettled at all.

She had photos of the people she loved or had loved and lost on the walls there. Her parents, Logan's parents, Allen and Izzie, Logan and Allen together, Daryn and Darrell, and Zoey and Pen. There was a small framed photo of Izzie, Nikkie Jean, and Annie, too. There was another of the children's choir, Shelby, Zoey, Charlotte and Madison. Even Haldyn, Powell, and Daryn were in that one—they'd helped with the admission stand during the last three concerts.

They were a team now.

Shelby sat at the piano that had once been Logan's as she thought about how much she appreciated each every one of them. As she replayed how she had felt seeing her friends there to support her tonight. After she'd left the stage, Zoey and Madison had pulled her right back over to the table. Charlotte, Powell, and Haldyn, too. Shelby had felt like she belonged.

She was getting better. For the first time in a long while, she was finally feeling like she was getting better.

Tonight...had been a success.

She hadn't fallen into a million pieces.

She had survived.

Maybe no one else would understand how a simple evening event could mean that much to her, but Shelby had made it to the end without breaking down in a panic.

She had triumphed.

She was going to take pride in that now.

Even if no one else ever knew.

Tonight, when she played, the music that came from her fingers was happy. Triumphant.

Like it hadn't been in a long, long time.

When she was finished for the night, Shelby laid her head down on Logan's piano.

And wept.

16

VICTOR HADN'T BEEN IN HIS HOME FIFTEEN MINUTES before Kessler was buzzing him with notice someone was at the gate. Victor battled back the annoyance; he had things he needed to do tonight.

Why didn't anyone understand that *time* was of the essence?

He had a list of eight eligible young women he needed to go over. Each one of them was beautiful, intelligent, well-spoken, successful, and intriguing. He had to find the one that *fit* him best.

Victor schooled his features into a calm façade he did not feel.

Kessler and Dave, the two men who had worked for and guarded him for fifteen plus years, knew what he liked and what he didn't. They wouldn't have ever interrupted him unless it was vitally important. They were far too well trained and too well compensated for that. "What is it?"

"John's brother, sir. James."

Victor almost snarled. This was a connection he only tolerated, and everyone knew it. He had known—tonight when their paths had crossed after Victor had danced with a particularly enchanting woman who worked as a sheriff, of all things—that he and James would be speaking again.

He just hadn't expected it to be tonight.

He would end up killing James before he left this world. He was already planning how that would come about.

John had been Kyle's closest friend in the world, until the injury in Houston had turned him into something no one truly recognized now. Kyle had been trying to help John on the road to recovery, even paying for round-the-clock care.

It just hadn't been enough. Kyle had felt guilty for getting John addicted in the first place. Victor had always cautioned Kyle to play responsibly, if he was going to play.

Apparently, that message hadn't been given to John in time. Victor honored John still because it was what his son would have wanted, seeing that the man was kept gainfully *employed* in certain ways.

It was John's brother, James, who was the real problem. He was also the one who had the real connections within the TSP that Victor needed.

The man responsible for keeping John moving forward at all was such a despicable bastard that he sickened Victor. Oh, how Victor hated him. The cold, slick, good-old-boy charm was so grating that Victor had called him on it a million times before.

James had the connections that Victor needed now. That was all that kept Victor from taking care of the problem he was becoming.

The reins were tightening on Victor's own connections within the TSP.

With the diagnosis from Victor's doctor, he didn't have *time* to build new connections. He was tying up the strings of his life now. Finding resolutions.

Finding someone to leave his empire to whom it would matter.

He wanted that so badly.

He wouldn't be around to see his next child grow to adulthood. He had to have that child soon. Or everything he had worked for would pass out of pure Scott hands forever. That sickened him to even consider.

The bombing of the TSP and destruction of the TSP building by the storm had played in his favor. He couldn't get complacent. Someone could find out more than Victor wanted known. Victor had to continue playing the cards he had drawn when his world had been so different.

But he had eight names now. He had hope.

James entered the room, strutting like the cocky bastard he had always been. Victor had always despised him.

Victor wished he could just put a bullet between the man's eyes and get it over with. But patience...he could not rush this. Not...yet. "What do you want? I have things to do."

His plan to find a young woman to carry his next child had to take precedence over everything else right now. Victor was not getting any younger.

Nor was his health improving as rapidly as the physician had indicated it would.

The drug he had been given—one he backed and sold through eight of his own private, off-the-books enterprises—was supposed to be close to a miracle cure for the condition threatening him now. At worst, it would delay the condition long enough for him to do what he must. Victor reminded himself to just give it more time. The drug could heal him, buying him another year or so on this earth, if he was lucky.

That time would matter.

Even if it wasn't a miracle cure exactly, it was so damned profitable, he was completely in love with it. He loved it when his empire just grew with a little bit of nurturing. That was the true testament of wealth, after all.

"We have a problem. Someone has been digging into some of

what Johnny and Kyle did. Years ago. I thought you'd want to know."

"Well, take care of it. Isn't that what you are supposed to do?"

"I'm already on it." James smirked at Victor. "I just thought you'd want to know. Keep your boy's ghost clean, after all. Isn't that what matters?"

It did. It *had.* Until he'd learned what was to become of his own life. Victor had more pressing priorities now.

Kyle was dead. Victor was not. Yet. If he didn't act fast, the Scott name would be next. He was never going to let that happen.

He would kill to see that didn't happen.

17

SHELBY WOKE EARLY. SOMETIMES, SHE HAD nightmares and couldn't sleep.

Sometimes, she woke far too early. This morning was apparently going to be one of them.

She forced herself to get out of bed. She could always nap in the afternoon, if needed. She had before, when the nightmares would become too much.

She'd take a few hours to sort through things in the far guest room. Then she'd hire a crew to paint and recarpet that room. It was a good-size room.

Although Shelby had no clue what she was going to do with it.

What was a single woman supposed to do with a twelve-thousand, eight-hundred-ninety-two-square-foot home? It wasn't the largest in her neighborhood—there were a few Barratts up the road, including Powell, who all had bigger homes than she did—but it was still way more than Shelby was used to. It sat on a five-acre parcel of land, too.

A parcel she spent a small fortune on to have the housing association maintain for her. Sometimes, just managing Logan's estate felt like a full-time job. If it weren't for Powell and Allen helping, she would feel totally out of her depth. Not with the house—but with all the rest. The money, the investments, the charitable donations...it all added up to stealing her time in so many ways.

Shelby headed into her kitchen to grab breakfast. And coffee. She hated coffee, but sometimes, it was needed. Insomnia was a frequent companion lately.

She flicked on the light. The sun was rising, but it was still dim in the kitchen. Her eyes landed on the back door.

She froze.

All five locks.

Open.

Her door stood open four inches.

Her gaze slid to the security panel by the door. It had a bright red light flickering.

Only Allen and Zoey knew the code. Had keys.

Movement out of the corner of her eye had her jerking around.

A curse rang out.

The man lunged toward her.

Shelby screamed. He grabbed her as she tried to run, slammed her back onto the kitchen counter. His hands closed over her throat, cutting off her next scream. She clawed at his arms.

It did no good.

She kept fighting.

It did no good.

The coffee maker beeped. Right next to her ear. Right there, next to her ear.

Shelby didn't think. She just grabbed it.

She crashed it into the side of his head, scalding her palm and sending hot coffee everywhere. She screamed.

He bellowed. His hands went toward his face.

Shelby lifted the heavy fruit bowl next.

She swung it into his skull as he screamed *bitch* at her.

And she ran. Straight toward the open door.

She didn't make it.

Shelby sprawled to the floor as the intruder rammed into her with a rock-hard shoulder. He was big and strong, equally as big as her brother. So strong. And he was right over her.

"Damned bitch! What in the hell do you think you're doing now? You're going to ruin everything again."

Hard hands went around her neck. She didn't hesitate—she jammed her knee into his crotch as hard as she could. Then again. She just kept kicking, kept fighting.

It wouldn't do her a bit of good to scream. She was just too far away from her neighbors for that to ever be effective.

She had worried about that before.

The security system should have engaged. It should be shrilling right now.

It wasn't. It should. Somehow, he'd gotten past it. How?

She squirmed beneath her attacker. And twisted.

Shelby got lucky. He was still pulling in a gasping breath when she pulled herself back to her feet.

And ran.

One hand gripped the doorknob.

It hadn't been locked.

She *knew* she had locked the back door before she left for the benefit. She always did. And she'd asked Allen to check them once, as well. They should have been locked. No one but Allen and Izzie, and Zoey had keys to her house. No one. Shelby yanked the back door open and ran. She just kept running until she was on the street.

Mrs. Kelley, her nearest neighbor, was walking her schnauzer up the road. Something so normal had Shelby falling to her knees, right next to Meatball. The dog tried to crawl into her lap as Shelby fought the panic, fought to catch her breath. "Shelby, child, what on earth is going on? You're still in your night clothes. And you're sopping wet."

"Someone was in...in...in my house. My house. He grabbed me. Tried to choke me."

Mrs. Kelley yanked out her phone. "I'll call the police and security."

Shelby bit back the terror. That was what someone did when there was a break-in. She knew that. They called the police. The idea of strangers... No. She couldn't...

The TSP...no...

Dark eyes flashed into her head. Eyes just like Izzie's.

"Ask...for Jake MacNamara. He's...a...friend." Not exactly how she would describe him, but the thought of some stranger in her house... "Just ask for Jake."

Mrs. Kelley screamed. Shelby jerked around.

There he was, a ski mask pulled over his face. No more than thirty feet away. His eyes locked on Shelby's. He had blue eyes. Really blue. Shelby would never forget that blue. She couldn't look away, couldn't even *move*.

Meatball went into full aggression mode. Lunged against the leash.

The attacker stopped when Meatball barked and Mrs. Kelley screamed at him to get away from Shelby.

He pointed at Shelby. "Bitch! You'll pay. Just wait! I'll come back for you someday. Mind your own fucking business or I'll come back for you!"

Meatball barked and snarled, and the man ran off. He looked over his shoulder at Shelby, shooting her a rude gesture. Her eyes met blue ones and she knew...

It wasn't over yet.

18

JAKE HADN'T BEEN AT HIS DESK FOUR MINUTES
before an officer he vaguely recognized from the nightshift patrol
team for Boethe Street stopped at his desk. "This came in for
you. Came to me by mistake. Friend of yours called. Had a break-
in that got physical at her place. Requested you specifically, and
considering the part of town it was in, I kept it from Callahan.
Guy was going on about how swanky that area of town is."

Jake took the paper quickly. He recognized the address—he'd
just been there the night before. He swore and stood back up.
He looked at the other guy, quickly. "How long ago was this?"

"Two hours ago. I was just about to head that way myself in
case you weren't available. Figure they've been waiting long
enough, even though a unit was dispatched in that area." He
held out his hand. "Jack MacGregor, don't think we've met."

"Nice to meet you." He shook quickly. "I'm going to roll.
This is family."

"Need a tagalong? I have a light load today. If I stay here
much longer, I'm going to be on death row for taking out Callahan. With a pencil."

Jake didn't give a damn who rode along with him. The only thing he cared about was her. "Let's go."

It took twenty long minutes to get from the precinct to the lower Finley Creek area where Shelby's house was located. Hughes Heights. The most exclusive, expensive neighborhood within city limits.

They had a local unit on sight now. Jake had radioed them himself to let them know he was on his way and would want answers when he got there.

He'd needed to know that she was safe.

Shelby was terrified of the TSP. Izzie had made that beyond clear to him last night. This...this wasn't good. He swore again when he saw the squad cars blocking the entrance to her housing development.

"You close to this woman?" MacGregor asked. He was looking around like a seven-year-old at the zoo.

"Something like that. She's my niece's sister-in-law. This woman...has some anxiety stemming from a previous attack when she was in her early twenties. She knows me. It's why she asked for me."

That was all he was saying.

"That stinks." MacGregor was a quieter kind of guy. Jake found he liked him ok enough.

It beat being stuck in a car with Callahan—something he had experienced only twice and didn't want to repeat. "She's got to be terrified right now."

He parked the car and climbed out quickly. MacGregor would just have to follow. Jake stopped, studied the scene. Looking for her.

There was Shelby, next to an older woman and a dog. Three TSP officers surrounded them, including Dom.

Some of his tension lessened. Shelby knew Dom enough to not be so frightened. Dom was one of the few men Jake trusted at his own back. More—he'd trust Dom at Izzie's. And Shelby's. That mattered.

"Heard the address over the radio. Recognized it. I was close enough to swing by," Dom said by way of explanation for why a Major Crimes detective was on scene for a random break in. Jake didn't care. He was just glad someone he trusted had been with her when Jake hadn't.

"Shelby!" Jake stepped closer to her. His hand went around her elbow quickly. "I'm here, baby. I'm here."

She jerked to look at him out of storm-blue eyes. That's when he saw it—if he hadn't known her well enough, he would have missed it.

Shelby was holding herself together by sheer willpower alone.

Hell, of course this was a nightmare for her.

Jake didn't stop to think about physical evidence on her then. He wrapped his hands around her shoulders and turned her to look at him fully. "I'm here, now, baby. You're going to be ok."

He kept his words low so only she could hear him. She took in a shuddering breath and then exhaled.

That's when he realized what she was wearing—in the middle of the damned rain. No wonder Dom had been keeping his big body between hers and the rest of the crowd watching.

He slipped his denim jacket off his shoulders and wrapped it around her. Any damned evidence that was on her would have been washed away by now, anyway.

Maybe.

There was a familiar little evidence tech behind Dom. Jake looked at her quickly. At least it was someone Shelby knew. Liked. Would be comfortable with. "Chuck, you got everything you need from Shelby's clothes?"

"Next time, ask before you destroy evidence, Jake," Chuckie said. "But yeah, I'm done with Shel. Let's get her out of the rain."

"I'd just suggested we move back inside," Dom said, quietly. Dom, at six four or so and broad with it, could be very intimidating.

"I...was waiting for you," Shelby said as Jake buttoned the denim in the front. Her damned clothing was too thin and too wet. He knew Dom wouldn't be staring—the man was better than that—but any of the other male idiots out there he couldn't say the same about.

"Thanks, Jake."

He cupped the back of her neck gently. He wanted to pull her close, hold her, help her understand that he was there now— that he would see to it that no one from the TSP ever hurt her again.

She flinched. He dropped his hand immediately. "Did I hurt you?"

"He...he...he had his hands there," Shelby said. "I think he bruised me."

Jake didn't stop to think that she wouldn't have wanted him to do it, but he tilted her chin up toward the sky and looked for himself. There were red blotches on her pale skin. Finger marks. The same on the back of her neck. Where the bastard had tried to choke her.

Jake wasn't stupid. He put things together fast.

He battled back the rage, using his years of experience to contain the anger that threatened to explode. "Tell me what happened, baby. From the very beginning. And then, I'll go find him, and he'll never come near you again."

Her skin was flawless, soft. Delicate.

The marks just pissed him off.

She told him in a halting voice what had happened. "I know the door was locked. I checked it before I went to bed. I hadn't unlocked it. And I had my brother check before we left for the benefit. It was locked, Jake. I know it was."

"And the security system was disengaged? Who knows the passcode?"

"Izzie and Allen and the security company, and my friend Zoey." Zoey Daviess—a TSP sheriff Jake knew well enough to know that she would never give that out. Ice shivered down his neck. "That's it."

"I'll find him, Shelby. He won't hurt you again." Even if he had to take a damned vacation and spend the entire time tracing who had done this. He hated seeing the terror in her big, storm-blue eyes. He pulled her against him and, right there in front of the rest of the TSP, he kissed her forehead. Held her closer than he ever had before. "You want to grab a bag? I can take you out of here."

He wrapped his hand around her narrow fingers. The way she clung to him told him everything he needed to know. He expected her to say yes, or ask to go the Barratt, or Mel's, or another friend's. To run. He wouldn't blame her at all.

She shook her head, firmed her chin. "No. I'm not going to run. I'm not. This is *my* home. No one is going to make me afraid in my own home ever again. I am staying right here."

Then he was staying right here, too.

Because to get into this house that she had locked up tighter than Fort Knox, someone had to target her place specifically. To take the time to figure out a way in. Jake wanted to know why. He focused on the house in the full light of the day, despite the rain.

He could think of millions of reasons why.

She made a damned good target.

SHELBY FELT LIKE A FOOL. OR A CHILD. JAKE WAS looking at her like that was exactly what she was.

The last thing she wanted was Jake invading her space, but

the idea of being alone was ten times worse. The TSP left, leaving a car with Jake. He'd ridden with another detective, but she hadn't gotten close enough to meet that man.

Shelby didn't care. It had taken every bit of her strength to face the three TSP who had responded.

If one of those detectives hadn't been someone she had met before, she probably would have been a quaking mass of idiocy.

Dom had been very kind to her. That had stuck with her. She had spoken with him the evening before, too. He was one of Jake's friends, and Daniel's.

Jake didn't say anything other than questioning Charlotte. Charlotte had said they might be able to find DNA in the hall and the kitchen, and there was a tech processing when Shelby stepped inside.

Shelby was questioning the decision to stay where she was. That way lay only madness, right?

She should grab a bag and check herself into the Barratt or something. Shelby just feared that if she did that, she would never want to come home again. She had enough money in various bank accounts that to just move into a hotel where there were actual *people* was a definite possibility.

She wouldn't have to be alone.

That wasn't what normal people did, though. Shelby missed being *normal*. Before Logan's money, she and Allen had been moderately well off. They'd had a nice pair of condos in an exclusive part of town. What Logan had given her had moved her up the level of wealth considerably.

Changed things. Taken away normal. Made her even more of a target.

She couldn't just go hide away and let hotel security protect her from the world.

For a moment, she just imagined doing that—she could get a suite on the penthouse floor. She would have daily maid service, instant room service, free Wi-Fi, a swimming pool, spa, and restaurants, and every luxury the Barratt offered.

Including a highly trained security staff whose sole purpose was to protect the guests 24/7.

Thanks to Logan's bequest, she didn't have to work another day in her life. She could do it.

She could just hide herself away—until she died.

Decades.

At times, that was a more tempting fantasy than others.

She fought it, every time.

Shelby wouldn't let herself just become a ghost of herself. She wouldn't.

19

Jake took another look around the place, trying to figure out the woman better than he had the one and only other time he had been allowed inside.

It had been after Logan Lanning's death. He'd been with Daniel when they had executed the search warrant on the place.

He'd read Lanning's journals after they had been copied and labeled as evidence. The man had had some serious problems, no doubt about that. But he hadn't been malicious.

Lanning had mostly come across as lonely.

Grieving something. Someone.

Hell, Jake could understand that. The guy had lost both his parents and his brothers. His entire family.

Jake had lived in this country alone with just a rotten kid and her even rotten-er bestie for several years before he'd started making connections.

Jake had friends, people he cared about. Had built himself a decent community here. He did miss his family, though. Going back to visit every few years just wasn't enough, sometimes.

He had Izzie—and eleven other nieces, though he didn't

know them very well. He'd given that all up when he'd come to the United States to be there for Izzie all those years ago.

Who did Shelby have?

Izzie and Allen. A few friends, maybe. That was it, as far as he could tell.

The place looked a little different than it had, though the house was far larger than just one woman needed. Ten women could live there comfortably.

It was filled with arches and columns and neutrals and pastels and flowers. It smelled like a woman lived there, too. She'd lightened it up, and the curtains were open, letting even more natural light pass through. It didn't look as cold as it had the last time he had been there. And the overly heavy furniture was gone. "I like what you've done with the place."

"Thanks," she said quietly. She had that look in her eyes that said she didn't fully trust him. Jake had a long way to go with that.

The back door was standing wide open.

The woman was still terrified. Jake knew it with one look at her gorgeous storm-gray eyes. She stared at her home like she had never seen it before.

Jake knelt in front of her. "You need to go change clothes."

Her eyes burned into his. But they were unfocused. Was she seeing him at all?

Someone knocked on the open front door.

He looked up. Dom stood there, a familiar woman wearing glasses next to him.

For once, they weren't snipping at each other. "Madison is here to take some fingerprints and DNA samples."

Jake looked back at Shelby. "Shelby? Why don't you go upstairs? Change clothes. Grab a bag."

"Why?"

"Because Madison is going to take a while. She's adorable,

but she's real slow on the job. She's probably too nice to say you'll just be in the way."

"Where will I go? Allen and Izzie both have double shifts today. They told me last night."

Jake made a split-second decision. "You're going home with me. To my place. Spend the night there in Izzie's room. That should give Madison just enough time to get things done. If she gets off her ass long enough."

"I can't go...go...go...to your place. I can go to the Barratt."

To hide away in the damned hotel? Hell, no. Besides, he had questions for her.

Lots of them.

To see her looking so damned defeated nearly destroyed him.

There was a worried look in Madison's eyes, too. So it wasn't just Jake seeing it. "Then what about your sheriff friend? Can you stay with her?"

"She's leaving today. Visiting her family in St. Louis. She's taking Brynna Marshall and her daughter with her. She can't babysit me today." Shelby closed her eyes and pulled in a ragged breath. "I-I-I don't need a babysitter. I...can take care of myself, Jake. I'll go to the Barratt."

"No. I'm not telling Izzie I let you go to the Barratt alone. She'd skin me alive. Worse, Annie would march into the Barratt to get you, that damned mayor trailing after her like always. They'd even bring her sister, Josie. *Josie* would cause all kinds of hell, and I'd get blamed for it. So..." He knew he was about to piss her off, but so be it. He wanted her where he could see her—where he could figure out what was going on. "Either my place—or I call your brother and tell him you're up to your eyeballs in something he doesn't know about." It was a gamble, but it paid off.

She jerked, eyes flying back up to meet his. Yes. Shelby had secrets she wasn't sharing. He'd bet his next paycheck on it. "Get upstairs. Get changed. We're leaving in fifteen minutes."

The glare she shot him was full of fire. Exactly what he'd wanted. The defeat was gone.

Now, he had her exactly where he wanted her—going home with him. Now he could be certain she was absolutely safe.

When she finally disappeared up the staircase, there were two pairs of eyes—both brown—staring at him.

Madison stepped forward, her forensic kit slung over her narrow shoulders, a digital fingerprint scanner in her hand. "I don't know what you're up to with her, Jake, but Shel isn't your normal kind of woman."

He heard the warning. "No kidding."

"I'm not. She's...she won't even know the kind of game you are trying to play. Not until it's far too late. She's not sophisticated enough for the likes of you. Not experienced enough at all. Do not do anything to hurt her."

"Jake can handle himself just fine, Madison. Don't you have work to do? Chuckie is already inside. I called you in to help her, get this done quickly for Shelby."

"Stuff it, Acardi. This is important." Madison stepped closer to Jake and away from Dom. She put one hand on Jake's chest, as if she could keep him from moving. "Don't *mess* with her. Don't play games with her. Don't yank her around at all. It won't even be a fair game from the start. All you'll end up doing is hurting her. I think that's the last thing she needs right now. Just leave her alone."

See, everyone saw it and knew the truth—Shelby wasn't the kind of woman Jake should ever even look at.

They were of two different worlds.

Damned if he wasn't going to do his best to protect her from the wolves of the world that he could, though.

20

She'd just gone along with him. Shelby berated herself for doing that on the entire drive to his apartment complex a mile south of Main Street. She had been manipulated. And he'd done it on purpose, the ass. "Are you proud of yourself?"

He glanced at her for a brief moment. "I usually am. Why?"

"You basically f-forced me."

"Nonsense. I gave you reasonable options, and you chose the best one. Me."

"Hardly. So…now you have me. What do you want now?"

"Baby girl, if I had you, you would know it. And, if you would let me, I'd be up for it. In a heartbeat. Except Izzie would probably kill me. And she terrifies me. Far more than you. Or that brother of yours."

"His name is *Allen*. You should be scared of him. He doesn't like you much." Some fire in her heart made her continue. Snipping at Jake was far easier than thinking about what had happened this morning.

Her throat still hurt.

And the exhaustion… it was almost debilitating.

She wasn't about to let him know that, though. Give Jake ammunition, and he'd use it. In a heartbeat.

That was a lesson she'd earned with him early on.

"First, I am just helping out family. Second, you'll be fine with me. Unless you're afraid? Maybe you're thinking you want to jump me, and I'll tell you I have a headache? I can guarantee that if you jump me, I will be more than willing. In whatever you want to do to me."

"Clobbering you?" She was used to him sending little barbs her way. But not like this, not sexual. And not with that kind of heat in his eyes.

Something was different about him. And it had changed last night.

She couldn't quite figure out just what it was.

It had her on edge with him in a completely different way. She didn't say anything until he had led her into the apartment that smelled like him.

The cat came running to circle around her ankles.

"It's not much, but it's been home since Izzie was sixteen. Her room is through there. Well, what's left of it. She cleared it out pretty fast once your brother brainwashed her into moving in with him."

"Once they fell in love, you mean."

"Sure. If that's what you want to call it." He shot her a beautiful smile, revealing perfect teeth. *Grrr.* "Brainwashing, love—same thing."

The man was just too good-looking for his own good. No wonder he had such a big ego. Women probably fell right at his feet.

Well, Shelby wasn't interested in being a number.

Not on Jake MacNamara's list, anyway.

21

THERE WAS A BEAUTIFUL WOMAN SOUND ASLEEP ON his couch, his damned cat Earl curled up on her stomach, when Jake disconnected the status call from Dom several hours after he'd led Shelby into his too small apartment.

There were bruises on her neck. Bruises that pissed him off and had his fists balling. If the bastard was in front of him, Jake didn't know that he wouldn't kill him.

Money didn't buy safety. Not truly.

It often did the exact opposite.

He perched on the arm of the sofa for a few minutes, just watching her.

He wanted to touch her. He couldn't deny that. He spread a blanket over her, adjusting it around the cat. Mostly to hide the temptation from his eyes.

What was it about this woman that burned him so much? Maybe it was her eyes. Maybe it was the way she spoke. Maybe it was the way she eyed him like he was a cobra sometimes.

Maybe that was part of it.

Pounding came on the door. He checked the peep hole

quickly and opened it before it could wake her. His nephew by marriage stood there, Izzie right next to him.

There was a wild look in Allen's eyes. "Where is she?"

"Quiet. She's sleeping on the couch. I offered her Izzie's old room, but she didn't make it that far. She was so tired she just crashed after I finally got her to eat something."

"What happened, Jake?" Izzie asked, always the voice of reason when her idiotic husband was around. He hoped their baby took after Izzie and not the doofus next to her. Although... maybe the kid would get Shelby's eyes. That would be cool—Shelby's eyes in Izzie's face. Or Shelby's face and Izzie's wild dark hair. He'd get a kick out of either—but he hoped the kid got Shelby's eyes. "All we heard was that someone broke in and Shelby was hurt."

"Just a few bruises. She managed to get outside to her neighbor. She clubbed the guy in the head with a fresh pot of coffee. It had to hurt him, burn him. She's got a few burns on her arm, but they are superficial. We've put out word to the EDs about a guy with scald marks on his head. She had the neighbor call me, and I went to her." A bit more simplistic than it had been, but hell—he understood the fear in her brother's eyes.

He'd felt it himself for Izzie.

Allen had been there to pull Jake's niece out of the fires every time. Jake owed him for that. Jake would repay that favor with Shelby, no questions asked. No hesitation. "She's going to be ok, Allen. Dom and I will find the bastard responsible. First thing in the morning, I'm going to talk her into letting me stay with her for a few days. Until we know more."

Allen was at the couch, kneeling by his sister. Up close, it was easy to see the resemblance. And the worry.

Hell, Jake didn't really despise the guy.

"Thank you for getting to her," Allen said. "When she wakes, we'll take her home with us."

"Nope. Not going to happen. If there's something more

going on with this, I don't want it near Iz." Or the baby she carried. The idea that she was pregnant was just now starting to sink in. He didn't want anyone getting near his niece ever again. "Shelby's going to stay here tonight, until we know more. Callum is two apartments down now, so I have backup if needed."

"You think it was more than just a random burglary?" Izzie asked, fussing with the cushions on the chair like she always did when she was upset with something. If he didn't stop her, she'd be getting out the vacuum cleaner or duster next.

She always cleaned when she was nervous, feeling out of control. It used to drive Jake nuts—but he'd always had a clean house. He had drawn a line when she'd folded his underwear and lined them up like little soldiers in his top drawer, though. A man needed his privacy sometimes, especially from his niece.

"I doubt it, but after the last few years, no sense in being stupid or complacent."

"No offense, Jake, but I can't see Shelby being comfortable staying here with you," Shelby's brother said. He'd straightened, stood cross armed in front of his sister.

Like he wanted to protect her from Jake. Like the guy knew exactly what Jake thought when he looked at Shelby. Hell, maybe Allen did. Jake had drooled over her quite a bit whenever their paths crossed. Someone was bound to have noticed by now.

Jake shrugged. "It's up to her. I don't think she needs to be staying with you."

Hell, the odds of it being something that would endanger Izzie or anyone else around her were slim, but they did exist. He just didn't want her brother barging in and making decisions for all of them. Perverse of him, but Jake never had done well with the rich and spoiled telling him what to do.

He wasn't paid to follow this man's orders.

Allen was looking at his sister with worry that Jake understood.

He wasn't lost to the parallels between him and Allen. They'd both ended up raising teenage girls through no fault of their own in their twenties. Practically alone—though Jake had been more alone, in a foreign country—and muddling through it with no road map.

Traumatized young girls, at that.

It couldn't have been easy, and Allen could have said no. Sent Shelby somewhere else—even boarding school—but he hadn't.

It was obvious he loved her a great deal. Would protect her, just as Jake did Izzie. "She'll be fine here for a while. No one is going to know she's here, except us and Callum. And since she's the one who pulled his wife, A.J., out of the rubble, Callum's already building a shrine to her. Even gave his baby girl Shelby as a middle name. He's not going to do anything to put her in danger."

They moved into the small kitchen. He and Izzie had lived in this apartment for years. It had been just the right size for the two of them.

It wasn't exactly huge.

A man's place said a lot about him. About what he valued.

Jake wasn't quite the housekeeper his niece had been—she had control issues that Allen was welcome to, actually—but he kept it reasonably neat. He wondered what Shelby had thought about it. "Now, get out. I don't want you waking Sleeping Beauty up."

"I'm not leaving until she tells me to go herself," Allen said.

Well, hell, he could have predicted that.

Jake didn't have the heart to argue with Allen tonight. He was damned tired, and Izzie was looking pretty exhausted herself. She confirmed that by curling up in the armchair—once her favorite spot in the place—and falling asleep. So pretty, his little Izzie. She'd make a great mom.

Too bad the baby's father was going to be Allen Jacobson.

She could have done so much better than a wealthy, highly successful world-famous trauma surgeon who supposedly worshiped the very ground she walked on, after all.

He snorted at that.

Every mama's dream husband, there.

But as he looked at the two women sleeping in his living room...maybe he understood the other man just a little.

22

Shelby woke with an achy body and a cat draped over her stomach, digging his claws into her side. For a moment, she forgot where she was, and then memory came rushing back.

She had had no business just letting Jake bring her back to his apartment.

He hadn't given her much choice. She felt a bit railroaded, actually.

"Hey, sleepyhead."

Shelby turned to see her sister-in-law in a chair nearby. Izzie's hair stuck up all over her head, and there was a blanket around Izzie's shoulders, too.

"Welcome back to the land of the living," Izzie said.

"Hey, what are you doing here?"

"I am refereeing, of course. It's been my biggest pastime since marrying your brother." Izzie leaned closer, looking at the bruising on Shelby's neck. "Yep. Those are going to hurt for a few days. And, heaven help us, the boys are on the balcony together. Trying to figure out Jake's grill. Together. Did I mention they were trying to do something—together?"

"Seriously?" Just one big, happy family. That was not good. "Yikes."

"Yep. I figure it's good for them. Will build character. Or maturity. Which I think they both need. They've been needling each other for hours. I'm starting to think they enjoy doing it."

"I think you're right. I think they may even be bonding."

"Jake says you aren't going anywhere. Allen says you are. I say you get to decide. How do you feel?"

"Scared. I'll admit that. But...but...but Jake was very kind to me today."

"Yeah, he has his moments. I personally think you should come home with us."

Shelby shook her head. "I can't. If I do that, Iz, I'm afraid I won't ever leave. I'll just hide myself away and let Allen protect me...like ...like ...like he always has. Keep the big, bad world at bay. Until it becomes me just fading away completely."

She would just disappear. Become more invisible than what she already was.

Shelby just couldn't do that. She'd been fighting for herself since the storm.

Since she had laid in a storm drain with Darrell's arms wrapped around her, knowing they were most likely going to die.

She would have died, when she'd barely lived first.

She'd attended Logan's funeral. There had been ten people there, counting her and Allen. *Ten.*

Logan's entire life had just been forgotten.

He had left two legacies behind—one as a brilliant surgeon whose work would save the lives of countless ill children for generations to come, and one of pain and terror as a man who had nearly killed several women and injured others.

He'd been the villain to a select few. To so many others, he had been the hero.

His work had saved thousands. Would go on to eventually

save millions.

Logan had changed the world for the better for so many people.

Ten people, that was all who had cared he had died.

Shelby probably had around that—Allen, Izzie, Zoey and Pen, Powell, Darrell, and Daryn. *Maybe* Charlotte and Madison. Mel, maybe. She'd thought about each one of them as the storm had raged around her.

Shelby wanted to make an impact on more than ten people in her life.

She couldn't do that hiding behind walls.

If she let Allen have his way, he'd build those walls around her to keep her safe. Shelby would be right back where she had started. Coddled and protected—and silenced.

Always somehow fighting for herself. Just like Logan had written to her in the letter she couldn't bring herself to burn. Logan had wanted her to shout to the world.

To live.

"I-I-I need to go home in the morning, Iz. I can't let someone run me out of my home. If I do...I don't know that I will ever go back."

Fear robbed you of the future.

Those were the truest words Shelby had ever heard. She was tired of not even having much of a present. "I have to."

Izzie wrapped her arms around Shelby. Shelby hugged her back, thinking again how perfect this woman was for her brother. Izzie just sort of fit their little family.

Even if she did have a Jake attached.

Shelby looked for him. He was on the balcony, shirt off beneath the late Texas sun, muscles rippling, spitting fire at her brother, who was trying to light the grill.

"I think they just like having someone to fight with, to be angry at," she said. "They both love you very much."

"Yes. That they do," Izzie said. "If it wasn't for me, they

wouldn't ever cross paths. Which I'm almost certain would be a good thing. Jake is getting pretty cranky in his old age, though."

Jake was six or seven months older than Allen. That was it. Not exactly elderly. There was less of an age gap between Shelby and Jake than Izzie and Allen.

Shelby didn't point that out. Not that it mattered.

Jake was close to the same age Logan would have been. A few months difference.

Logan had said he was too old for Shelby, multiple times. She hadn't believed him then, either.

"Jake seems very alone."

"Yes. I'm trying to work on that. He is made for a family, Shel. A wife and kids would be perfect for him."

"Only if she was willing to wear...wear...wear battle armor. Carry a pitchfork to bed every night."

Izzie smirked. "He isn't that bad. Usually. He just...with you..."

"He doesn't like that I was given Logan's money. Probably thinks I should give it all away or something. Since Logan was the devil, and I didn't earn it or anything." She had given quite a bit to charities around Finley Creek. Even if she gave a million dollars a year away, she'd still have far more than one woman could ever need. Just off interest alone. For probably the rest of her life. Logan had been good at investments, too. He'd set everything up for her after his parents had both passed away, just in case he died early, too.

She was still trying to process that idea.

The money just kept...earning more money.

She intended to leave it all to Allen and Izzie's children someday. Or her own. She would love to have a family of her own someday.

Once she wasn't so afraid of the world, that was.

She had to fight her fear first. To do that...she had something to finish first.

23

Izzie had left some of her things in the bathroom a year or so ago when she had been carried off by that asshole husband of hers. Jake heard her telling Shelby to use them. And she'd changed the sheets for her sister-in-law, as well.

Izzie asked Shelby if she wanted Izzie to stay with her so she didn't have to be alone with Jake. He'd snorted at that.

Izzie was extremely protective of Shelby. After what she had told him, Jake understood it a bit better.

Shelby brought out the caveman in him.

It was probably time he admitted that. As they ate the hamburgers Jake had grilled, he studied her and Izzie. The two women liked each other. That was obvious.

Izzie was more confident, but Shelby had a quiet, slightly sarcastic humor someone could easily miss.

Jake had.

He was starting to figure out that he had greatly misread the woman. Had let preconceived ideas of her cloud his judgment to the real woman she was.

Jake had learned something tonight. Something he'd been

stupid to miss since meeting her. Well, maybe he'd been blinded by other…characteristics. And made a few stupid assumptions.

Shelby spoke slowly with everyone, but he suspected now that it was because of the speech impediment. Most times, he hadn't even noticed.

His brother Bennie's daughter, Camelia, had had a slight stutter. Probably still did, though Jake hadn't seen her in ten years, since she had been all of twelve. It was time he headed back to Italy for a visit. Maybe he could convince Izzie and that albatross of hers to go with him.

They could take Allen's sister with them. Jake would enjoy showing Shelby around his homeland, introducing her to his brothers and Izzie's eleven cousins.

He would like showing Shelby all the beautiful places he came from. Help her see that the world didn't have to be such a scary place after all. That not all men were total assholes like the ones who had hurt her and Daryn all those years ago.

He'd like that very much.

Maybe someday. When she didn't think he was the cave dweller he sometimes was.

Jake had been watching her all night. Shelby had caught him multiple times.

Like she was a puzzle and he was trying to figure it out.

She supposed that was something a good cop did. Tried to solve things. She just didn't want him trying to solve *her*.

After she'd finally convinced her family to leave, she busied herself cleaning up the small kitchen while he took care of the grill. And the cat.

"You didn't have to do that. I'd have done it."

"I wanted to help. I know you didn't count on a houseguest. And I'm sorry. I could have called Detective Evers..." It would have made more sense. Considering that Mike Evers was married to her best friend now. "Or Darrell."

"You ever have need of *anything* from the TSP, you are to call *me*. Only if I'm not available do you call Callum or Evers. Better yet, you can't get me, you call my commander right away. Daniel and I have been good friends for a decade. I'd trust him with my life and with Izzie's. Him and Dom and Gunnar Erickson and Charlotte Fields's father, Charlie. I'd trust any of them with yours. You got me? You call me or someone from Major Crimes, and I will come running. All you have to do is yell. And I will be there. Always." Jake scowled and stepped closer. He pulled the plastic cup out of her hands. To her shock, hot male hands cupped her cheeks. Then, just like that, like he wasn't causing her heart to pound out of her chest, he dropped a casual kiss right on her open mouth. "Stay inside. I'm going to take the trash to the shoot at the end of the hallway. I'll be back in a few minutes."

Shelby just scooped the cat up and watched the enigma that was Giacomo MacNamara as he walked away.

24

HE WANTED TO DO THAT AGAIN. IT HAD BEEN AN impulse, but he wanted to repeat it. Jake would admit it. He'd liked touching her, even for something as simple as a peck on her perfect lips.

She'd looked so real there, cleaning his damned kitchen, the cat circling her ankles for attention. He'd had to do it.

Just like he had had to find an excuse to meet Callum in the damned hallway.

He tossed the trash down the shoot and turned to the other man, who had been waiting with his own bag of trash in his hands. "Hey, how's A.J.?"

"Sleeping. They are both finally asleep." There were rings of exhaustion under his friend's eyes. His three-week-old daughter was a bit of a howler—and a night-owl. "I never thought it would happen."

Jake had sat with the baby a few nights back when Callum needed to make an emergency diaper run and A.J. had been too exhausted to sit up straight. He hadn't minded. That was what friends did for each other.

He did have twelve beautiful nieces, ranging from Izzie's

almost twenty-six all the way down to Caledonia's six. Last time he'd been in Italy, Caledonia had been all of three months old. He'd taken a turn walking her around during the night, too. "So what's up?"

"Daniel called. Wanted me to let you know they collared a guy for Shelby's break-in a few hours ago. Went into the ED. Nikkie Jean treated him herself, became best buddies with him —then turned around and called him in to Daniel."

"Why the hell didn't Daniel call me?"

"He didn't want Shelby overhearing."

Jake tensed. There weren't many reasons for that. "What?"

"The guy's just a hired thug. Idiot was bragging about it at the bar—after the waitress asked where he'd gotten the burn. It started to hurt him too much, and he decided to try to use it to get some painkillers. Shelby got him good. Permanent scar. He was paid for by some big shot. Daniel has him in interrogation now. He thinks it might tie into that Kyle Scott angle from last year. Guy was a known associate of Scott Junior."

"Shit." Kyle Scott had been the only son of one of the wealthiest men in Texas. Victor Scott. A man Jake and McKellen had been investigating for almost three damned years now. What in the hell did Shelby have to do with any of this? "Why Shelby?"

Callum shook his head. "I have no clue. The only thing— Charlie is working a kidnapping ring angle. Considering Shelby's net worth..."

"I'll call Daniel once she's asleep for the night. Whenever that will be. She slept for three hours this afternoon."

Hell, if it came down to it, Jake was going to talk to her brother. The two of them together might be able to convince her to get out of the damned country for a while.

He knew exactly where he wanted her to go, too.

Right smack in the middle of his brother Benveluto's living

room. Where she'd have six strong MacNamara brothers to protect her.

While Jake took care of any threat to her here at home.

Hell, maybe he'd just send Izzie with her, too.

Just to be on the safe side.

25

SHE APPRECIATED THE LOAN OF A BED FOR THE NIGHT, but she woke the next morning filled with resolve. She was going home. She had hidden for one night and that was it.

Even if it made Allen angry.

Even if it made Jake angry.

Shelby wondered what the two of them would do if they realized that the words they had said to her were nearly identical? Maybe Jake didn't sound quite like her brother—Jake still had a faint Italian accent, even though he'd been in the States for around fifteen years—but the words were almost the same. The order certainly was.

Shelby found that ridiculously amusing.

At heart the two of them were too much alike. They just refused to admit it.

She looked at her host as she held Earl.

Shelby ran her fingers over his soft fur, loving the feel against her skin. Maybe she'd go get herself a cat. To keep her company at night.

First chance she could, she'd consider it. A sweet little

kitten, a dainty girl, that would keep her company. She'd never had a pet before. Maybe it was about time she did.

"I need to go home soon." Best to get started exactly as she intended. To not let him get the upper hand. "Thank you for bringing me here."

"You are ready to go?"

"Yes. I...it's my home, and I don't want to stay away for too long."

She wasn't about to let herself hide.

Because once she got started, she probably would keep hiding forever.

"You're not going." He had a skillet of eggs in his hand. He'd set the table. Had two glasses of juice poured. Toast was sitting in the toaster.

Well, wonders never ceased. Jake was almost domesticated.

"I'm not?"

"No. You're going to sit down, and you're going to tell me what you are all tangled up in. So that I can help."

"Uncle Jake, there comes a time when you have to cut the apron strings and let your little birds out into the world." She shot him a level look. "If I won't let Allen boss me around, why do you think I will let you?"

"Because Allen doesn't have the power to cuff you and force the answers out of you. In various...ways."

"Is that why you became a cop? To cuff unsuspecting women? To get the badge bunnies? Figures."

"Something like that. Women do like a guy with a badge."

"Some women, anyway. Not all of us."

"You are definitely not one of them." He put the skillet down, and then turned to her. Just like that, he was in her personal space.

"J-J-Jake?" He slipped one hand around her waist. Pulled her close. Until they were closer than they had even been when they were dancing before. "What... what... what are you doing?"

"I'll tell you what...you tell me what *you* are involved in and why someone found their way inside your inner sanctum, and I'll let you go."

"If I don't have that answer, what happens then?"

His hand slipped up, cupped her cheek. He gave an almost feral grin. "Then I'm going to kiss the answers right out of you."

Shelby froze right there, pressed almost chest to chest with the devil. Stared into his dark eyes as she finally *got it*.

Jake hadn't been joking.

The little sexual innuendos and jabs. He'd meant them.

She was totally out of her depth here.

Shelby didn't know where the courage came from. But she acted. She twisted. Drove her elbow into his solar plexus.

He gave a satisfying *oomph*. And dropped his hands.

Shelby stepped away with a smirk. "Hands... hands... hands to yourself, Giacomo. Or I'll file a complaint."

"With Daniel? He won't blame me for what I think or feel. He wants you himself. Told me so after you danced with him and got him all twisted up."

"Don't be a jerk. I'll go one better. I'll tell Izzie you're a sick pervert who can't keep your hands to yourself—and tell her and Allen you hit on me when I was so scared and defenseless. You made me really uncomfortable. Then, I'll spend a few days with Allen so he can protect me from you. I'll play it up. Big time. He'll never forgive you."

"You are harsh, woman. And you win." He rubbed his stomach with one hand. "Your brother teach you that?"

"And a few other things. Don't try me."

"Guess he's not such a pansy ass as I thought."

"He's a brown belt in tae kwan do." Another year or so, and Allen would have his first black belt.

"He's a wuss. Guy's got soft hands."

"He's a brilliant surgeon. And look what he did to protect Izzie. My brother isn't a wimp. You just don't like him because

Izzie likes him better than she does you." She was only half joking on that. Sometimes, she suspected Jake *was* jealous, or feeling a little displaced.

"Hardly. Eat your breakfast and quit beating me up. I can't defend myself against a woman like you."

Shelby ate her breakfast while he asked her things.

Made noncommittal responses while he interrogated her.

Helped wash the dishes while he badgered her.

Cuddled the cat while he listed what she needed to do to correct the security *deficiencies* he'd spotted at her house.

And she bit back a smile while he complained on the entire drive back to her place.

She'd won.

The only thing she didn't like?

Jake had packed a bag for himself.

And threatened—he wasn't going anywhere.

To her own shame, and she would never admit it to anyone, knowing she wasn't going back to her house alone was all that had her going back at all.

She hated this, hated being so weak.

She thought she had gotten past this.

Maybe she hadn't healed as much as she'd thought.

26

HE WAS *IN.*

Jake resisted the urge to crow. For a while there, he'd thought he was going to have to physically pull the woman over his shoulder and carry her away. He didn't know where he was going to carry her to, but he was going to do it.

She pushed his buttons. No denying that.

Jake was absolutely convinced that she was hiding something from him.

Something that wasn't good. And just might have gotten her into some serious trouble.

Either that, or Logan Lanning had been involved in more than what Jake had originally thought. Which was entirely possible. Jake had been floored when he'd learned the man had had close to eighty million dollars sitting in offshore accounts.

Forensic accountants had gone over it—every penny of it had been accounted for. The money had been legitimately earned or inherited and invested, by either Logan Lanning or his parents before they'd died from natural causes. Leaving it to the next in line.

It had been turned over to Logan Lanning's heirs. Finally.

With the majority going to the woman right next to him.

No one knew why. Why *her*?

Jake wanted to know all her secrets. Not just because of some damned case. Because the woman absolutely fascinated him.

"So how do you like living here in Lanning's place?"

She almost flinched. For a moment, he regretted his question. "It's fine."

"That's it? The guy left you millions of dollars and a small mansion, and it's fine?"

"Is this an interrogation?"

"It could be. You want to play with my cuffs? We could take turns cuffing each other. And then getting the answers out of each other. We can call it strip interrogation."

"Pervert."

She led the way up her sidewalk reluctantly. Jake stepped in front of her, reached for her keys. "I go in first. Part of my guard dog duties."

"Yeah, you do have the whole junkyard thing down, don't you?"

"So snippy. Very sexy. Remember that. When you snip at me, it turns me on even more. I think that's part of our problem over the last year or so. You burn me. Every time you looked at me or spoke to me, I'd be ready to go off like a rocket."

"Yeah… yeah… yeah…right."

Jake unlocked the door. Shelby entered the code.

And then he was inside. Shelby's domain.

Finally.

JAKE MACNAMARA WAS HER HOUSEGUEST. SHELBY shivered as she thought about what that meant. This was not what she'd intended at all when she had told him she was going home.

But he had insisted.

The man was hiding something from her. She'd seen it in those devil-dark eyes of his. She'd have to call a new security company in the morning. After what had happened the night before, she just didn't trust the system she had now.

Or her cleaning crew.

She wasn't lost to the fact that her alarm hadn't sounded. That somehow, someone had been able to get inside, and that someone had been hired to break in...terrified her completely. She had no idea why someone would do that, except Jake had told her they were about to tie up a kidnapping ring case in the next two days.

Someone was grabbing wealthy victims and ransoming them back—sometimes alive, sometimes not—in a ring spanning everywhere in between Indianapolis and Phoenix.

The TSP was working with the FBI to crack it.

They suspected someone had seen Shelby as a victim.

Maybe.

She half thought Jake didn't believe that.

Jake had come inside with his gun ready. Shelby tried not to freak, just seeing it. She would never forget what it had felt like to have that man point a gun at her so many years ago and tell her she was going to make him feel *good* that night.

Jake holstered it quickly when he saw her looking at it. "I think we're good."

"You don't have to stay with me." Shelby almost flinched at his words.

"If I didn't, Izzie would show up with just that damned dog and a large stick to defend you from the big bad monsters out there. We both know that."

"Yes. Probably. Izzie can be fierce when she cares about someone. She's great. She's going to be a wonderful mother."

Shelby smiled softly, imagining her future niece or nephew. The baby would be absolutely gorgeous, of that she was one hundred percent certain. Her brother was made to be a father. He'd had plenty of practice with Shelby. "She and Allen are perfect together. It's so beautiful."

He snorted.

Shelby glared at him. "You know, most women would be lucky to have a man like my brother love them the way he loves her. He'd willingly die to protect her, you know."

"That is one thing I can't argue with there. I think he's more than proven that. Tell you what—truce where the family is involved, ok? You got a TV in this place?" He shot her his most charming grin. "My shows are on tonight, you know."

She wondered if Izzie had ever wanted to strangle him as a teenager.

He'd say the most butthead things, and then grin like he thought he was cute or something. It was enough to drive a woman crazy.

"I-I-I have multiple spare rooms upstairs. You can have your pick. There is a TV in the guest room at the end of the hall."

"I want the room closest to yours."

Shelby jerked around to look at him.

"It just makes sense. I'm here to protect you. I need to be as close to your body as I can be in order to guard it properly. Especially in a place this big. Hey, I don't make the rules. I just live by them."

"Probably only when it suits you."

"But of course. I'm old enough to get my way whenever I want it."

"Doesn't anyone ever tell you no?"

"Sometimes. I just don't listen."

He was the most exasperating man on the planet. Hands down. She was going to order him a trophy with that engraved. One made of solid gold.

"Hey, look, kid...I'm sticking with you until we know for certain this is part of that kidnapping ring. No one is taking you away from us—not on my watch. Might as well get used to me. Just consider me your...annoying...live-in boyfriend?"

"Hardly!"

"Well, I was going to say uncle or big brother—but considering that I want to kiss the hell out of you right now, neither of those felt right."

Shelby's mouth dropped open and she stared at him. "You are insane."

JAKE HAD BEEN NEEDLING HER. HE KNEW THAT, BUT what else was he supposed to do? She was wearing jeans and an old FCU T-shirt. The jeans cupped her ass perfectly, and the red shirt looked soft as it draped her breasts. Shelby had perfect breasts that his fingers practically ached to touch.

He was a real cave dweller, after all.

For a moment or two, he'd forgotten she was Shelby, and he was her mortal enemy. All he could think about was that, if she'd let him, he'd willingly scoop her off her feet and carry her through Logan Lanning's damned house to her bed.

Where he would show her that not all men were bastards.

He wanted the right to do that so damned much.

But...he'd been attracted to women before. And had controlled himself before.

She was looking at him with a wary, untrusting look in the storm-blue eyes. Like he had unbalanced her—broken the unstated rules between them. He supposed he had.

Adding physical attraction had changed the game.

"Hey, just relax. I'm a caveman, but I'm reasonably civilized. You tell me what room you want me to have—I will be all set."

She just nodded.

"Maybe we can order from that Chinese place Izzie likes so much?" Shelby liked it, too. He'd seen them eating lo mien before.

"That sounds good."

"Great. I need to make a few phone calls. Then we can argue over the menu and what Chinese we are willing to share. I'm an eggroll hog. Izzie is used to it, but I figured I'd warn you now."

"As long as I get the egg drop soup."

"Perfect."

He couldn't think of much more that would be perfect than spending an evening with a woman he found beautiful and fascinating and utterly maddening.

Except if that woman allowed him into her bed.

That would be one perfect night.

He would settle for the scraps he could get. Jake knew one thing with utter certainty.

Shelby might be the most beautiful, fascinating woman in his world—but he was the last kind of man a woman like her would ever need.

27

Victor studied the young man dispassionately. Victor had had forty-four years in business. He had worked with *hunters* before. The man before him was exactly that.

A hunter.

The man was hunting information now. It was why he was at Victor's place at six p.m. asking questions. He would need to be dealt with eventually. "What is it that I can do for you?"

"I'm here about a property you own on North Jude Avenue. I have credible information that, five or six years ago, some... assaults may have occurred there. And I was wanting to ask a few questions. The registered owner at the time was your son."

"Yes. I sold...those...properties recently."

"I heard about the loss of your son. And I am sorry. A father shouldn't outlive his child. I've lost a child of my own. I know that hurt well."

Victor bit back the sudden emotion. The man was sincere. He could see that. "Thank you. Kyle was...my hope, of course. What kind of assaults happened there?"

"Battery and sexual assault. There were reports after at least one party," the private investigator said.

"I'm sorry to say that my son enjoyed alcohol and wild parties a few years past the time he should have outgrown them. But he stopped around his thirtieth birthday or so. I'm afraid I was never present at any of his parties. I greatly disapproved. It was one of the few things my son did that I didn't like."

"I'm basically looking for a place to start. To give one of the victims closure. A list of people your son may have invited? That could help me a great deal."

"It's been years. What is she hoping to gain now?"

"The ability to walk down the sidewalk without fearing the men who attacked her are watching. She doesn't even remember all of their names."

Victor understood—either he gave the hunter what he wanted...or the man would stalk him for answers later. Victor couldn't afford *later*. He ordered Dave to compile a list of names from Kyle's old contact list from years ago. It should hold this hunter off long enough.

Then, after the younger man left, Victor promptly forgot about his request.

Victor had some hunting of his own to do now. He still had several names to research.

He wasn't stopping until he found the perfect woman. Then...he wouldn't stop until he had her.

28

SHE'D SNUCK ONE OF HIS EGG ROLLS WHILE HE'D BEEN upstairs checking in with the rest of his team. That little thief.

Jake went hunting for her, disconcerted that it took longer than he had anticipated. He checked her favorite family room, the dining room, outside on her back patio overlooking the swimming lagoon—no other word for the odd-shaped, crystal-clear, aquatic monstrosity—and then back into the uppity ritzy parlor he doubted Shelby spent any time in at all.

Nowhere.

He finally found her in the marble and heavy wood office that she had frillified up with thick white rugs and soft peach accents everywhere.

She stood over her desk, a file open before her, an egg roll half-eaten in her hand. Evidence of her perfidy. Case solved.

"You stole my favorite thing in the world."

"Sorry, not sorry. There are eight in there for you. I grabbed the nineth. Why did you order so many?"

"It's an addiction." Jake sidestepped the white rug. He wasn't about to step on that in his damned boots. "Got to pay the fine. Or go to jail."

"I think Elliot will let me out on this one. Gabby will make him."

"So what do you do in here all the time? Tell me what rich ladies do in their home offices. Make nail appointments?"

She shot him an irritated look that cleared up when he smiled at her. "I...I...I...work."

"Oh?" He stepped toward the desk. "On what? I'm curious about you. Every aspect of you." Every delectable inch of her.

She finished off the stolen egg roll, and then scurried around, stacking up a small pile of manilla files, envelopes, and photos.

Interesting.

He wanted to see them.

Especially after the way she tried to hide them from his gaze.

"You do like to stick your nose in people's business, don't you?"

"Yep." To get a rise out of her, he started poking around the shelves before making his way toward the desk. He pulled a small leather-bound book free, a journal of some type. She snatched it from his hands with wide eyes and tossed it back to her desk.

One of the large envelopes slipped to the floor. Jake picked it up.

She shocked the hell out of him when she jerked it out of his hands next.

He hadn't missed the letterhead in the top left corner. *Lassiter Private Investigations.*

"Hands off, Jake." There was real bite in her tone now.

Well, he took that as the challenge it was.

29

Jake hooked one arm around her waist and yanked. She practically landed against his chest. To his satisfaction, storm-blue eyes widened, and that perfect mouth opened. Oh, he wanted her. So damned bad. "You have been driving me crazy for almost a year, woman. Do you know what you do to a man like me?"

"A man like you?"

Her fingers spread on his chest. Hell, he wanted those fingers on every single part of him. "You taunt me and torment me until I want you so damned much, I can't breathe."

"I don't do anything to you." Her chin rose. "You're the admitted caveman. Can't you control your base urges? I know it's just proxi—nearness making you act this way."

"My urges are very base where you are concerned. And, believe me, I have tried to do just that. I just can't get you out of my head, or my dreams at night."

"Because of the way I look? Rather shallow, aren't you?"

There was a look in her eyes that said she was still irritated with him. Was taunting him.

"Your eyes. It's because of the way you look at me. I've seen beautiful women before—been with my fair share. I won't lie about that or hide it, but you... It's the way you look at me. Drives me crazy. You drive me crazy and the only reason I'm keeping my hands to myself is because of my niece and your asshole brother."

"What about what I want?" Her hands tightened on his shirt. "Don't I get a say?"

"All you have to say is kiss me, and I will forget all about Izzie and that husband of hers. I could want you forever, damn it. Forever."

To hell with it. He wanted to kiss that perfect mouth.

So Jake did.

JAKE MACNAMARA WAS KISSING HER. SHELBY TRIED TO process that while his hard arms tightened around her and his mouth practically stole her soul.

She had been kissed before, of course. She wasn't a virgin, though it had been six-and-a-half years since she had been sexually involved with a man, five-and-a-half since she had willingly even kissed one.

Jake's body felt hotter, harder, bigger. His arms were more certain.

He was obviously far more experienced than her ex, and far, far more intense.

She couldn't do much more than hold on.

She trembled, uncontrolled shaking.

Every nerve in her body did seem to be on alert now.

He pulled back. She didn't want him to. She half wanted him to continue kissing her forever.

Which was utterly crazy.

This man didn't like her at all. One truce called between them at the benefit shouldn't lead to *this*.

Far from it.

Shelby forced herself to step away.

He pulled back with a curse. The harsh word snapped her out of whatever fog or spell she was under for a moment. She deliberately put some space between them. "Towels are in the hall closet."

She got out of there before she did something completely stupid.

THAT WAS THE DUMBEST THING HE HAD PROBABLY ever done. Jake thought about that as he took a long, cold shower in a bathroom nearly as big as his entire apartment. He'd kissed her, and he was damned certain that, just for a minute there, she had kissed him back.

He wished he had the right to kiss her as much as he wanted.

No sense lying to himself about that anymore.

Jake had wanted women before. Even intensely. Hell, if Chuckie or Madison—who he'd taken out a few times, as well—had been up for more than the kisses they'd shared, he'd have been all about it. He liked them that much.

Well, maybe not.

Chuckie was a friend's daughter, and there were unwritten rules about that—and Madison, well, everyone knew she was Dom's girl.

Except maybe Madison, anyway.

Kissing them hadn't held a candle to that brief kiss with Shelby.

The one woman he couldn't have.

Maybe that was a part of it? He wanted her more because his head was telling him he couldn't have her?

He always had been a perverse asshole at times. This was no different.

Even if she had tasted perfect and sweet. Even if holding her against him had felt right.

Like that was exactly where that woman was supposed to be.

Hell.

30

SHE WORKED LIKE A FIEND. HE LEARNED THAT OVER the next day. Jake sat back in the waiting room of W4HAV in street clothes, so he didn't frighten anyone in the charity. He'd made a point of never making a big deal about being TSP when at W4HAV.

He'd volunteered a bit at Izzie's request. Sometimes, they had clients who needed someone to walk them through the legal system. He'd also spoken for about an hour with a twelve-year-old boy who wanted to be a police officer when he grew up—Nikkie Jean had thought the boy needed a mentor.

The kid still emailed Jake now and then. Jake made a point of keeping in touch.

W4HAV was a good place, and he'd also had a long discussion with the heads of the charity about the need to provide services to male victims of major violence. It was needed.

Men were victimized, too. Even sexually.

Jake felt strongly that that shouldn't be covered up or ignored. Far from it.

One of his brothers had been jumped and beaten when Jake was fifteen. He'd never forgotten the impact that had had on his brother, who had only been twenty at the time. Just because he'd walked down the wrong damned alley in an unfamiliar city.

That had led to Jake's decision to become a cop in the first place.

People deserved to be safe.

People felt safe with Shelby. She had a way of connecting with the women around her.

W4HAV was run eighty percent by volunteers. From what Izzie had said, Shelby was one of the handful of paid social workers. She organized therapy groups with the two other women on duty. They were licensed social workers, as well. And there were two women volunteers at the desk.

A few of the women had brought their children—six of them —with them. The kids had happily settled into the playroom nearby.

It was a good place.

That there was a plaque on the wall a foot from where his niece had nearly been killed was just something he was going to have to overlook. It dedicated the room to the women who had been hurt in that space—Izzie, Nikkie Jean, and Shelby.

Shelby had been seriously wounded by flying glass when someone—a damned cop Jake had worked with a dozen times before—had shot through the window, aiming for Izzie that day. He'd missed killing Shelby by millimeters.

Jake still had to push down the rage when he remembered carrying Shelby across the street to help.

It had been far too damned easy for Jennifer Henedy to get that cop to do her bidding. Someone had to stop that.

To clean up the TSP.

It was going to take them a long time to find all the snakes in their house.

Corrupt cops had targeted his niece for money. They had nearly killed her, that jerk of a husband of hers, Annie and Turner, and Shelby.

He would never forget that. Or forgive.

Jake took it on himself to order a lunch delivery. Shelby barely ate enough to stay alive; sometimes she just forgot to take care of herself.

The woman needed a keeper. He wished he was brave enough to volunteer.

Shelby seriously intrigued him. He had been hoping that spending time with her would help him get past that. The exact opposite was happening.

When the delivery boy arrived, Jake cautioned Shelby to stay inside the building and away from the windows. There were security guards in the building now, and metal detectors, but he wasn't stupid. He knew just how ineffective they could be. A determined criminal could get anything past.

She nodded and shot a worried look toward the playroom, where the children were watching a movie. "Should I come with you?"

Jake shook his head. "No. Stay in here. It's the safest place."

He hurried outside to where the delivery boy was waiting. Impatiently and with a familiar scowl. Dom—who had Italian roots, as well—said something completely unflattering about Jake's ancestry. Dom held out the bag of foam containers. "Now, you have me running your errands? Shit, MacNamara. I feel so important, now that you've moved up in the world."

"Just tell me what you found."

31

Jake had it bad.

"Someone is a bit pissed," Dom said, as Jake kept shooting looks back at the entrance of the women's charity.

"No wonder." Jake smirked, but there was irritation in the man's eyes.

Dom got it—Jake had worked for months to break this particular counterfeiting ring. Only to have the first bust come last night when Jake was otherwise occupied. That had to smart.

It was Jake's case. Jake and Dom and Fields's. That would matter. Credit would be given where it was due. When the time was right. "Still, I thought you'd want to know what we've found in initial interviews."

"Anything helpful?"

Dom just grunted and nodded politely at a woman entering the building. She saw him and Jake and scurried in the other direction.

Yeah, Dom supposed the two of them could be a bit intimidating. "Ties to Victor Scott. I just need to connect the dots."

"We've been working to tie those knots with Scott for three years now," Jake said, almost growling.

"Impatient? Have other things taking precedence? Shelby welcome you with open arms? You need a vacation to spend all cuddled up and cozy?"

"Shut up. I don't have time to be distracted by this right now."

Jake always got grouchy when things heated up. Especially when he couldn't go out there and get the bad guys himself.

Dom was used to it by now.

"Well, it might interest you to know—we're going over Wallace Henedy's journals again."

Jake grunted again. "Anything that matters?"

"Yeah. Gunnar and I started in on Logan Lanning's, too. To collaborate information we found in Henedy's. Found them fascinating reading, considering where you are staying right now. Lanning wrote that he suspected Henedy was involved in some seriously illegal shit—and Lanning was going to go to his pal Allen Jacobson. He never got to that point. Thanks to the shooting in the FCGH parking lot. Lanning was asking questions before he died, by the way. Truth is, if he hadn't ended up going over that roof, Scott's people might have took him out anyway. He was asking a lot of questions. Questions about Henedy's son's closest friend. Kyle Scott. You might ask your girlfriend what she knows about good old Kyle…"

"Lanning? Shit. Not him again. I thought we were finished with him. Guy is haunting me."

Dom thought about exactly where Jake was staying. They probably weren't finished with Logan Lanning at all. "Lanning wrote that he had finally found something. He'd been searching for something for a few years by that point in the journal. Said he hid it in the house, in a place no one would be able to find until the time was right. Guess the guy didn't plan to die first. Poor bastard."

"Shit. I need to search Shelby's house, don't I?"

Dom nodded. "Best get to it."

32

Jake knew the answers Major Crimes had been looking for had to be in Shelby's house. Or houses. He thought about that for the rest of the day, until they were sitting at her kitchen island, eating takeout she'd reheated for an early lunch.

Jake had spent all morning watching her. Planning. She'd spent the morning tolerating him.

He needed to keep looking. It was going to completely eat at him.

They had never had enough evidence to secure a warrant to search the other two houses that had once been owned by Logan Lanning and his parents. Just the estate that had been his final residence after he had been shot and released from the hospital. The man had owned a condo and another house in Finley Creek, plus this estate, which had been his parents' home.

They had searched this home twice—as it was where he'd been living at the time of his death—and then it had entered the system to be returned to Logan Lanning's rightful heirs. At the time, he hadn't known it was Allen Jacobson's younger sister.

Jake honestly hadn't cared. They hadn't found what they had needed to find. That was all that had mattered.

The instant she had taken that journal out of his hands the evening before, he had known he had found something.

He wanted to read that journal. Bad.

That was only going to happen if they got a warrant. Which meant...he had to find something that would get them a warrant. "How many of Lanning's journals do you have?"

She shrugged, eyed him like a rattlesnake. "All of them, now. Well, the printed out copies. The TSP returned them to me when the case was finally closed. What was left of the originals, anyway. I...I...I...am reading them when I get time. Why?"

"No reason. Just curious."

"I bet you are." She shot him a pointed look. "Stay out of my office. Logan...Logan...Logan is dead. Whatever he wrote...it shouldn't be processed and labeled by your evidence people. Dead end, Jake, literally. He never was involved in some larger crime organization like your people thought. Can't...can't...can't you leave his ghost to rest?"

"Hey, I just want to make sure whatever your pal was involved in, no one else is going to be hurt by it."

"Logan's been dead a long time. Wouldn't something he was involved in be over with now? If anything, it wasn't Logan, it was Banks." She shuddered after she said it.

"How well did you know Banks Claireson?" Had anyone interviewed her about the third member of her brother and Lanning's little trio? He couldn't recall seeing a statement from her in the notes.

"The man was a monster. And I hate that he was targeting Zoey's sister and Zoey and I never even *knew*. I tended to avoid him. Allen never really let me around some of his friends. Not for a while there. After I...was twenty-one."

"Keeping you away from the party boys?" Hell, he had dug

into Allen so deep even before the man had gotten involved with Izzie that Jake had known what brand of toothpaste his dear nephew by marriage had preferred when he was twelve. While Allen had had a few years of partying a bit hard, there had never been anything suspicious.

All of that had changed almost eleven years ago when he'd taken custody of his teenage sister. The partying had ended, and the man had become almost boring. At least on paper. Allen must have loved her very much.

A look Jake didn't recognize went over Shelby's face. "Yes... He...Banks was a friend of his from high school, but he was more Logan's friend after. Allen and Logan were friends. Banks and Allen really...weren't."

"Neither were you and Claireson's sisters?"

"No. That we weren't. If that's all, I'm really tired, Jake. I'm going to bed."

"Can I tuck you in?"

He would make certain she was all snug in her bed, and then he was going to come take a look at her shelves for himself.

Jake felt mildly guilty over that plan, but they had lost seven cops to this case, in one way or another.

Daniel's younger sister had almost died from rubbing up against a small part of it. He owed it to his friend to find all the answers he could.

Annie had almost been killed because of it, too. Jake would never forget that.

Because the bastard who had nearly killed Annie, who had been in league with those damned Henedys, had just been a small part of a bigger picture. That picture included Banks Claireson and the former lieutenant governor Justin Albright, too.

There were a lot of evil tentacles around Finley Creek. Jake was going to cut them off.

As soon as he found all of them.

The idea that Shelby could unknowingly be sitting on the key to finding all the bastards had his blood running cold. She'd be a target of every unscrupulous son of a bitch involved in this case.

They'd take her out without a second thought.

That was all the justification he needed.

33

JAKE WAS ABLE TO WAIT TWO HOURS AFTER SHE WENT to bed. That was it. He had instructed her to keep her door open so he could hear her—mostly because she had fought the idea so hard.

He had persisted.

He loved making that woman angry. It made the eyes swirl with the storms. Directed right at him. Jake really was an ass sometimes. Messing with her was a bit of a dog thing to do, but he enjoyed it.

Jake would make this up to her someday. Maybe by convincing her to let him take her to Italy, as an apology. He contemplated it for a bit, then decided against that. He got her alone for too long and he would do something stupid.

Sometimes, in the job, he had to do things he didn't necessarily want to do.

He peeked inside her room, seeing the beautiful, curvy lump that was the sleeping form of his Shelby Grace.

Hell, he would give his left arm to have the right to climb in that fancy bed beside her, pull off those satin pajamas in the color of the softest peach, and show her just what kind of storm she built in him.

If someone was after something Logan Lanning had left in this house, Jake was going to find that something first.

And keep the dirt of Lanning's world from *ever* touching Shelby again.

Period.

No matter what he had to do. The end justified the means.

He spent over an hour searching through the books on the shelves in Shelby's office.

She hadn't locked her office door.

Probably didn't even occur to her that she would need to.

He pushed the guilt away and kept looking. He was a fast reader, after all. Jake should have plenty of time to do what he had to do.

He'd found two journals from Lanning's med school days and put them on the desk. They didn't have what he needed, and he knew that.

In the back of one was an added code in ink that wasn't quite as faded. Jake grabbed his phone and took himself a handy little photo of it.

Rory was one hell of a cryptographer. If there was something important there, that little blond firecracker would find it. For kicks, he'd have Charlie drop it off with her—that was bound to create some pyrotechnics. Rory and Charlie really didn't like each other all that much.

He flipped through the next journal, one from about six years or so ago, going by the dates. A letter fell out, right at Jake's feet.

As if the hands of fate were working in Jake's favor. How handy was that? He slipped the letter out of the envelope—that had been helpfully dated—and read.

.   .   .

Keep your nose out of it, Logan. You'll only invite attention your way. Attention you don't need. You'll ruin your career. Victor Scott is the last man you want breathing down your neck because of his son. You don't want to fuck with the bastards at the TSP who are involved. Keep out of it, burn what you've found, or you'll end up in a damned cell. Or dead. Getting involved is the last thing you should do. Find another girl and move on. There are plenty out there. Quit being so hung up on this one. Either marry her and tell her to forget what happened, or move on. Leave the past in the past.

It was unsigned.

Well. That was helpful.

And probative.

Not enough to get a warrant though. He needed more. Like the name of the person who'd written the letter, for a start. Or Lanning's girl. That would be interesting. Jake could think of several questions for her.

Like what kind of taste did she actually have?

Maybe she would know a bit more. He'd find a name eventually.

Jake kept searching.

He found one more journal. One that was exactly what he was looking for. It mentioned Banks Claireson and Justin Albright in the very first entry. And that Lanning believed the two were involved in things they shouldn't be.

Things Lanning didn't necessarily think were *legal.*

Perfect.

He had just about finished reading when a sound had him whipping around.

To stare into storm-gray eyes filled with fury.

To see Shelby standing there, vibrating with pent up emotion.

Oh, hell.

"W-w-what are you doing?"

"Calling Major Crimes." Jake felt lower than pond scum. Shelby stared at him. His hand tightened on the journal when she tried to take it from him.

She looked down at it and paled. Right before his eyes.

"That's...that's...that's not yours."

"No, it isn't. It was Lanning's. We should have found it before. Why didn't we? Where did it come from?"

"It was in a box in one of the safes. It's not yours. That one's not yours. It's mine. *Give it back.*"

"No. That's one thing I am not going to do. Lanning was involved in whatever is going on in this city. And I'm going to know every secret he ever had."

Shelby went white right in front of him. Jake took a step toward her.

What exactly did she know that she wasn't telling him?

"No! If you want to pry into his life any longer, you'll have to get a warrant. Right now. You're not reading it. Ever!"

34

SHELBY WAS LOOKING AT HIM LIKE HE'D BETRAYED her.

She hadn't stopped looking at him that way since he had told her it was happening whether she liked it or not.

It had taken Daniel two hours and a called in favor to get it accomplished, but Jake had known the other man would have his back on this. All he'd had to do was say *Logan Lanning's missing journals* and Daniel had gotten right on it like a good little boy.

A judge had signed off on the warrant without question because of what Lanning had done before. Everyone wanted to get in good with the Barratts and with the governor, considering one of Lanning's victims was now the governor's *wife*.

Now, they stood outside in Shelby's driveway. Waiting.

Jake felt her eyes on him. Storm-gray and filled with the lightning of anger now. He deliberately turned away.

It was the first time in his adult life he was afraid to meet a woman in the eye.

"You've probably screwed up every hope you ever had of

having a chance with that woman now," Daniel said at Jake's side. "I hope this gamble is worth it."

The commander of Major Crimes didn't come out for a simple search/seizure warrant. "Why are you even here for this?"

"For Shelby, actually... This is one of the worst situations a woman like her can face right now, especially after the recent break-in. I wanted to act as a buffer. Make it easier on her, if I can. I want to help her. Protect her. You might try it some time. Just try...being kind to her. Respect her."

Jake was getting the feeling he'd pissed off Daniel here.

Jake looked at the people starting to gather in the driveway. TSP Major Crimes detectives and the top team for the forensics unit. Hell, they'd even drawn a few uniforms who were now busy keeping the crowd of gawkers off Shelby's front lawn. It was a large lawn, but that wasn't stopping people.

They were going to get attention. Especially in a swanky neighborhood like this, with piss-poor security not everywhere they should be.

He cursed. This was not what he'd intended. He'd thought Dom would bring the warrant, he'd grab the journals, and Dom would take them back to the lab. That would be it.

Not this. There would be gossip and speculation and sly looks. Maybe even a news van or two.

It had to be because of the money.

All directed at Shelby. This would be literal hell for her.

Shit.

Jake had been the one to do this to her. He probably could have handled this in a different way. Should have.

He should have searched the damned place by himself. Had Daniel and Dom help. Or quietly called Madison or Chuckie, or something, even though they were her friends. Anything to protect her from the visibility of all of this.

The circus.

He'd invited her nightmare right into her front yard. Into her home.

All because she'd protected that damned journal from him. He'd tried for two hours to get her to give it to him.

She'd stubbornly refused.

"I was just trying to get to the bottom of why she was targeted. What she was hiding. Solve this, fix this. And hoped I'd find something for the Henedy/Lanning connection, as well." He'd gotten impatient. Made a stupid mistake.

He looked toward her, to where she now stood with her brother. He almost cursed out loud when he saw the two women just behind Allen.

Hell. Not the two of them. Izzie and Annie.

Glaring and pissed.

Annie had her arm around Shelby, trying to comfort her. Annie shot a glare in Jake's direction. One that had him wincing.

Annie had a terrible temper when she was riled. A real bad one for such a sweet little thing.

Shelby's arms were over her abdomen, but her back was ramrod straight as the wind toyed with the chestnut brown curls. She had her mask on again.

Trying to hide what this was doing to her.

What *he* had done to her, making a spectacle of her in front of her neighbors. The last thing she ever wanted was attention.

Jake had trampled all over Shelby to get what he wanted. He really was a cruel bastard sometimes. He swore. "I'm going to have to fix this for her."

"Probably. But how? I could talk to her for you. Be your wing man. Try to smooth the way."

"Or help me crash and burn so you can have a shot with her?" He wasn't stupid. He had seen in it in Daniel's eyes at the benefit. Daniel was attracted to Shelby. Just as Jake was. The more sophisticated Daniel knew how to play in the wealthy world's sandbox. Unlike Jake. "Last thing she needs or wants is the TSP staring at her across the pillows. Stay away from her, Dan. She...needs a different kind of guy than men like us. A politician or a lawyer, maybe. An accountant. A surgeon, like her brother, or something. Someone...different...than us."

Allen had insisted not a single TSP employee—including Jake—was to step foot into his sister's home until her attorney arrived.

Allen had said it loudly and right in Jake's face. *Someone must protect Shelby.*

Because Jake hadn't.

The attorney had shown up—with her first cousin, the mayor. Who was good friend's with Shelby's brother. They were all pissed at him, ready to tear him apart for this. And circling the wagons around the woman they thought was the target.

The chasm between them was ever widening. He studied his nephew-in-law and the mayor, saw the suits they were wearing. Just one of those suits cost more than Jake's first car had. No ratty jeans and scuffed work boots on a Barratt or on Allen, that was for sure.

"If she'd say yes, I'd ask her out in a heartbeat," Daniel said bluntly. "I think you might be on the hook for this. Here's Haldyn. I called her in for this one. I figured only women searching her space might be best for Shelby."

"You know what happened to her, don't you? You knew, and you know the bastards responsible. And you've done nothing about it." Jake swung around. Stepped into the other man's path before Daniel could head toward the cool strawberry-blonde. Daniel sent him a challenging look. "Tell me."

"I can't. Because I don't know the names. I just heard about it after it happened. There were nasty rumors going around. It took me a few weeks to figure out who the women involved were. And that was just because Darrell said something to me about it. He...I had to talk him down from doing something stupid. They went after his sister, too, that day. Though Shelby got it worse—she didn't have a brother with the TSP. Someone so helpfully pointed that out in time to save Daryn from being hurt worse. But Shelby? Wealthy, beautiful, shy, naive, no real family but her workaholic brother to protect her? Yeah, she was a perfect damned target. They toyed with her like a mouse for weeks after, just because they could—and she didn't tell anyone until it was almost too late. They ran her off the road in the middle of a thunderstorm, then gave her a damned speeding ticket—and a warning to keep her mouth shut forever. As far as I know, she has. I'm here to see that that doesn't get repeated."

"No one will ever hurt her again." Except what he had set into motion now. She'd never forgive him for this.

"You can't guarantee that. No one can. And that...is at the heart of who she is. Something to keep in mind. Shelby's probably afraid she's going to get hurt again, Jake—that's it just a matter of time. Because it was the TSP who did it last time, she doesn't know who she can trust when it does happen again. You've just proven she can't trust you. Or any of the rest of us, really. Good going, jackass. You've really screwed it up this time."

35

SHELBY FORCED HERSELF TO BREATHE. SHE WOULD not fall apart. Not in front of her neighbors, not in front of these people, and definitely not in front of her family.

Acid twisted her stomach into knots as the forensics team stepped out of their van and came over to where she stood.

Daniel McKellen was there, his hand held out toward Shelby.

She forced herself to let him take her hand. "Daniel..."

"Hello, Shelby. I am sorry about this. This will take several hours; is there somewhere you can go? Get out of the heat?"

She considered it. Considered going home with Izzie or Annie, who had both already offered. Just pretending this wasn't happening.

If she left, knowing strangers were going through her home, she wasn't certain she'd ever be comfortable in her house again. Didn't know if she'd ever be brave enough to come home again.

She wasn't going to let Jake take her home away from her.

"I can't do that. I can't leave. I need to see what they are doing to my home. I have to know." Her home, her safe place. Her sanctuary. Invaded by the TSP. She closed her eyes and took a breath. When she opened her eyes again, she saw understanding in Daniel's. That helped her center herself a bit. "I'm staying right here."

"What in the hell are you and that asshole looking for?" Allen asked, pulling her closer and wrapping his arm around her. "Care to explain?"

Her brother was very, very angry right now. She suspected the only reason he hadn't lost his temper was for her and Izzie's sake.

This wasn't exactly going to do wonders for his relationship with Izzie's uncle at all. She turned to him. It was hot out; Izzie didn't need to be out there right now. Neither did Annie, who was two months farther along. "I-I-I am ok, Allen. Izzie and Annie need to get out of this heat. I can...handle...this. By myself. I...have Powell here now. I'm good."

She could. Damn it, she *would*.

And then she'd tell that ass Jake MacNamara exactly what she thought about him. He never should have gone behind her back to begin with.

She would have let him look in every corner and crack of the house, if he had just asked.

She wouldn't have stopped him at all. Even...she would have let him go through Logan's journals. Even knowing what they contained. If he had just respected her enough to seriously ask, to explain what he was looking for.

The one Logan had poured his heart into about *her* was in her work bag, anyway. Jake would never have seen that one. It was slung over Izzie's arm right now, after her sister-in-law had taken it from her and made her sit down for a few minutes.

She'd have let Jake have access to whatever else he wanted, except what was in her bag.

He hadn't trusted her enough to even ask.

His hang-ups about her and her brother were his own choice. His hatred of Logan was beyond unreasonable. Logan would never be able to defend himself now.

One way or another, Jake MacNamara had just ceased to exist for her now.

She looked at Daniel, and at the man who had just come up behind him.

"I'm staying for this, Daniel. And then...I want you to get Jake MacNamara as far away from me as you can. If the TSP has any more questions from me, send Callum or Evers. I'm never talking to *him* again." Shelby didn't know where the courage came from, but it was there right when she needed it. She looked right at that bastard. "I would have let you, you know. All you would have had to do was ask. You couldn't even respect me that much. Just go away. And stay away. I never want to even s-s-see you again."

She turned away and left them all staring at her back.

Each and every one of them.

Shelby straightened her spine and lifted her chin, dropped the arms she'd inadvertently crossed over her abdomen. *No more.* She would be cowed by the TSP no more.

She would be cowed by *no one* anymore. Never again.

She was tired of other people trying to tell her how to live her life, what to do, and not even trusting her enough to give her a *voice*.

She ignored Jake calling her name, ignored Allen saying something cutting to him. And she just walked away.

36

JAKE TRIED NOT TO WATCH HER AS THE HOURS dragged on. Everyone was sweating, hot. Texas in August wasn't exactly made for cool relaxation. The forensics team were in their paper burritos. They had to be roasting. He and the rest of the TSP were kept outside, to preserve anything they found.

He'd watched as the team had stepped inside Shelby's house and gotten started. Only women. Daryn Evers had shown up, hopping mad, with the sheriff of Garrity. Both she and Daryn had hugged Shelby, then followed it up with an intense conversation amongst the three of them. And lots of hate-filled glares Jake's way.

Then the Garrity sheriff had approached Daniel and given him a piece of her mind, too.

She had flayed Daniel loudly, and Jake heard the terms *abuse of power* and *harassment charges* and *illegal searches* and *scum of the earth*. That had just been directed at Daniel. What she'd had to say about Jake had been far, far worse.

Until Daniel had winced and stepped back, both hands raised in the air, almost in defeat.

That woman was a bit on the scary side.

Now, the only one anyone from the TSP could talk to was that sheriff. She would relay information to Shelby, only. Her glare could dissolve lead at ten paces.

As the sister-in-law of the governor of Texas, no one was truly willing to piss Zoey Daviess off, either.

She was rabidly protective of Shelby. Daniel had learned that when he'd mistakenly gotten too close a few hours earlier.

Shelby had completely shut Jake out. He'd tried twice to get her to talk to him, when her friend was distracted. Shelby wouldn't even look at him. Wouldn't let him explain or apologize.

She'd cut him off completely. Like he didn't even exist in her world.

And it stung.

Izzie hadn't said a word, other than that she'd talk to him later. It had been a definite threat. She'd left a few hours in, with the mayor and Annie.

Shelby's attorney was still hovering over her. Keeping everyone who wanted to talk to her at bay, unless the attorney was right there next to her. For such a small woman, she was just as terrifying as Zoey Daviess.

Good. Jake understood how this all worked, and he wanted her protected, too.

She was just collateral damage.

Because he'd made that call.

"Jake?" A soft voice said from behind him. He hadn't realized he'd just been there staring at the house. He turned. Chuckie stood there, an evidence bag in her hands. "We found some files and journals and a few zip drives. They were in a hidden panel in one of the guest rooms. I'd say they've been there for a while, from the sheer amount of dust. Several years. There are hidden safes everywhere. We found a good fifty thousand dollars just socked away. Madison and Rory are documenting it. Then the house is Shel's again."

"Thanks, Chuckie."

"Shelby doing ok? I hate this for her. Doing this to her." There was worry in her green eyes when she looked at him.

"You know her. Will this be a problem?" A good DA could make a case, if they found something important. It was too late for that, now.

"It won't be a problem with chain of evidence. She's a friend, yes. We've documented it, full disclosure. It's not like she's a suspect, right? It's just her house's previous owner who is under suspicion. Haldyn is aware, too." She hesitated a moment. "Shelby's experience with the TSP before was bad."

"It was."

"I bet she feels violated right now. Betrayed. Her house...her safe place has been invaded. For a woman with a total of forty locks on eight doors, this is a massive blow, coming just days after it was broken into. Don't be a big jerk to her. She needs and deserves respect. Zoey has said she'll be staying with her for a while, at least. Get her through the first few nights. That should make it easier. Hopefully. I can't stay with her myself, not after today, but I would if I could."

"What are you saying?"

"Simple. If a team of TSP officers were going through *my* underwear drawer and looking under my bed, poking into my life because of things I had no part of, I'd be sick, too."

"Too?"

"She went to the neighbor's fifteen minutes ago, Jake. Zoey said she was physically ill from all of this. I don't think it's just the heat. I think she's hit the limit of what she can take. Something I thought you should know. She's going to be even more resistant to the TSP after this. I hate that I had any part of it. I just hope she's still my friend once this is finished. I don't have many of those here, and neither does she."

He felt lower than a slug when he searched the driveway for Shelby once again.

37

HER NEIGHBOR INSISTED SHELBY COME INSIDE around one that afternoon.

Shelby had to take her up on the offer. Meatball climbed into her lap, and Shelby just let the little dog snuggle there, as she drank the lemonade Mrs. Kelley had given her.

"Now. Talk, young lady. What on earth is going on over there?"

She hesitated, but Mrs. Kelley had been there that day. Could have been hurt, too. She deserved to know—to not be afraid. Shelby had known Mrs. Kelley since she had been a teenager, following Logan's mother around almost lost. Mrs. Kelley and Linda Lanning had been good friends for years. "Logan may have left something in the house that someone else wants to find. The TSP thinks the man in my house was hired to find it. The TSP are trying to find it first."

At least, that was what Daniel had implied. But who was Shelby to believe?

"And they had to do it this way? Making a spectacle out of everything? I'm sorry. The TSP can be a bit of a crude beast, can't it?"

That was a good way to put it. A crude beast.

She could think of a real beast right now.

Zoey had stayed outside to coordinate with the TSP, if it was needed. Daryn's husband had shown up to join Jake and his little buddies. Shelby had reminded herself that he was a nice man that she was actually starting to like a bit. Mike wasn't the enemy.

Jake was.

Even if Mike's questions after Logan's death had been far too harsh. Like they were looking for more from her than she had actually had.

Shelby paused.

That thought had her putting the lemonade down on the table very carefully as she thought about it.

Considered.

The TSP had wanted something from her back then—something they hadn't gotten. Maybe they still wanted it, and the intruder had been a convenient excuse for one of them to get inside?

So they could keep searching.

They had used her. She'd been stupid.

She and Jake weren't close enough for him to be so willing to change his whole world right now to protect her from a simple B&E. If the kidnapping ring had even existed, she'd be shocked at this point.

That had probably been a ruse.

No.

She never should have trusted him.

A simple intruder didn't justify the head of Major Crimes, his immediate subordinate, nor other high-level members of his department, like Mike Evers and Dom Acardi.

Nor did it warrant the supervisor of the *entire* forensics team for the Finley Creek region.

Something more was going on here.

Major Crimes meant something major.

Jake knew exactly what that was.

Shelby was just incidental to him. A pawn in his endgame.

Jake had used her. Daniel may have even put him up to it. They'd probably played on the fact that she'd trust him most because of Izzie.

They may have been coordinating all of this from the heroes' benefit, even before. She didn't have a clue how long Jake could have been plotting against her.

Maybe for months.

His coming home with her to begin with was part of his master plan. It had had *nothing* to do with protecting her from the intruder. Not one thing.

That had just been his excuse.

So he could look for something strong enough to lead to a search warrant. There had been a reason Major Crimes had kept Logan's house as long as they had.

Apparently, they weren't done with it yet.

Shelby had fallen right into Jake's hands—she'd thought he was one of the very few on the TSP she could trust.

Because of Izzie.

That was a lie and a crock. Men on the TSP could never be trusted. Ever. She was never going to forget that again.

She'd just relearned that lesson the hard way.

38

BY THE TIME THE LAST TSP VAN HAD PULLED AWAY, IT was nearly five in the afternoon. He was sweaty and dripping— he had spent most of the time outside with Daniel, Mike, and Dom, keeping an eye on everything.

Watching for Shelby.

Worrying about her. There had been a look in her eyes when she'd come back from the neighbor's—a look he would never forget.

Daryn took her away. Daryn's brother had arrived, off the clock, and collected both of them, to take them back to the Barratt Ranch, where Annie lived with her husband. Behind some serious security.

Otherwise, Jake would have made a bigger stink than he had. She'd be safe with the Barratts' security out there.

Not that anyone would have listened.

Shelby had been ignoring him for hours.

She hadn't even accepted a damned bottled water from him when he'd grabbed it out of the cooler in the back of the forensics van and tried to get her to drink it.

He'd wanted to take care of her for a minute—to check on

her. Make sure he hadn't screwed everything up between them forever.

She hated him now.

Shelby wouldn't be allowed back into the house until they were all done. And it was a damned large house.

Shelby hadn't even looked at him. She'd looked right through him. Physically pushed his hand away. From anyone else, he would have thought it was the silent treatment because of anger, but when he'd gotten a look at the storms in her eyes, he'd known the truth. She was more than just mad. She was shutting him out to guard herself from him. Protecting herself from him.

She'd trusted him, and he'd hurt her.

It probably felt like he'd betrayed her.

Maybe he had.

He didn't know how he was going to fix that.

Mike got off the phone with his wife, having called her to let her know they were finished with Shelby's home. That Shelby could come home now.

Jake took a final walk through the house, with Daniel and Mike.

Shelby had made it clear—Jake was to grab his bag and get out before she got back.

She'd said it loud and clear enough for half the TSP surrounding them to have heard. She wouldn't put it past him to plant something, if it got him what he wanted.

Said some cops would do whatever they had to, even lie, if it got them what they wanted. Use people like the bastards they were.

It was the first curse word he'd ever heard come from her mouth.

She'd said that loud enough for everyone to hear, too. Said Jake was dirty to his toes. Everyone had heard her, too.

She'd cast doubt on his very integrity with that one. His

honor. Of course, she probably thought he didn't have either of those two traits now.

The signs of the forensics team were there, to someone who knew what to look for, but Madison and Chuckie had made it very clear to the four women they'd called in to help because of the size of the house—they were not to make a mess of Shelby's home at all. Period. Utmost respect for personal space.

Shelby was not to be revictimized by the TSP. Chuckie had said that loudly—as she'd looked right at Jake and Daniel—with utter disgust. And that today was almost enough to have her quitting the TSP and going back to Wyoming, where people were respected more than this.

Where innocent women were not targeted by those who were supposed to protect them.

He had flinched, hearing that.

Guilt was not a good companion.

He stayed where he was, in the middle of her dining room, while Daniel made the call to Shelby to update her. While she was hesitant with Daniel, she wasn't flat out pretending Daniel didn't exist.

Hell, maybe they'd end up together. He'd watch Daniel fall for her, and know the other man was the luckiest bastard on the planet. He'd see Daniel kissing her. Holding her close. Making her smile just for him.

Hell, maybe Daniel would end up marrying her.

He'd see Shelby occasionally at Izzie's. They'd be together at birthday parties for Izzie's kid. Maybe Shelby would have a few kids with Daniel. At least three or four, knowing her and Daniel.

He could see that; she'd be a good mother. She'd want lots of kids, too. She'd be a great mother, with little girls who looked just like her. Little boys who watched the world from eyes the color of the storm.

She'd continue to look right through Jake as if he didn't exist whenever their paths would cross. Like he was used up chewing gum on the sidewalk.

Maybe Daniel could help her learn that the TSP wasn't there to hurt her. Maybe Daniel could make things right for her.

Or maybe Daniel wouldn't. Maybe Shelby would fear the TSP even more. Would not trust them at all because of this. Maybe Jake had destroyed every chance of her healing in that regard, maybe he'd destroyed her friendship with Chuckie and Madison, too.

Maybe something would happen someday, and she'd need the TSP, and she'd not even call for help.

She wouldn't even call him if she needed him.

Maybe he was just building scenarios in his head like a damned idiot.

What would most likely happen was they'd keep their distance. She'd be with Izzie and the kid whenever Jake wasn't. When their paths would cross, she'd treat him like he was something lower than the dog poop on the sidewalk.

Like he'd thought she had originally.

Only this time, she'd really believe it.

No.

That wasn't good enough.

She showed up around six-thirty. In a limo. Long after Dom and most of the Major Crimes team had taken off.

To his surprise, Houghton Barratt and his wife stepped out before Shelby.

Mel came up the walkway and waited at the end of the four steps. She turned back toward Shelby. Jake watched from the open door.

He wasn't going anywhere.

"Houghton's man will get it installed tonight, Shelby. And we'll stay until Zoey can get here again."

Jake couldn't hear Shelby's response.

Then, she was there. She'd showered and changed clothing,

into an apple green T-shirt with W4HAV printed on it. She wore jeans. She had a body made for jeans.

She'd pulled the mass of curling hair up into a ponytail. Gorgeous.

Damn, he had it bad. Why wouldn't he admit that to himself?

"Shelby…" He started toward her.

Daniel, that prick, beat him to her. Reached toward her like he had the right. Like he wanted her to look at *him*. "Shelby, we've finished here and have returned anything that was disturbed to its rightful place."

"Did you boys find what you were looking for?" she asked, a bite to her tone. Maybe she wasn't exactly happy with Daniel either. She held her body stiff when Daniel got closer. Aloof. Daniel tried to touch her shoulder, but she turned away. Sharply. "When you were invading my life on your…your…your little quest?"

"We found some things hidden in a wall safe behind a false wall in one of the guest rooms. We found a gun, as well. We'll run it, see if it matches anything open. Same for the money found in another safe in one of home offices. Then it will be returned to you," Daniel said, softly. Coaxing.

Jake wanted to shove his fist down his friend's throat for talking to her like that.

"Keep the gun. I don't want a gun in my house. Allen took all of Logan's father's guns. I think he was talking about selling them. Or donating the collector's pieces."

"We may need to see that collection," Daniel said. "Just in case."

"I thought you already had. When the TSP wouldn't let me have Logan's house for almost a *year* after his death. Because it was part of an active investigation with M-M-Major Crimes, followed by a *major* clerical error. Funny, that, isn't it? The TSP really has a major thing for this place. What were you doing with it all that time you had it before? Using it for your weekly poker games?"

It was hard to miss the sarcasm. The bite and fury when she jerked her head back and looked them straight in the eye.

Daniel took a step back from the fury. Apparently, Daniel didn't know about the temper.

Jake just listened.

Shelby was still beyond pissed. The storm in her eyes was now fire.

"Daniel, I want a list of everything taken and photographed," Mel said, putting one hand on Shelby's shoulder. "I'm here to represent Shelby's best interests with the TSP. It can be given to me, to her attorneys Mac Barratt or Powell Barratt, or Shelby directly. As well as Sheriff Zoey Daviess."

Jake was about to say something when someone else came in the door. A man Jake had never seen before.

"Miles is going to install a new security system and change the locks," Houghton Barratt said. The employee in the Barratt-Handley polo shirt got to work. The billionaire turned to Shelby. "No commercial security company will be involved. If something happens, it will ring right to my private security team. It's manned 24/7. We're further than the TSP, but under the circumstances, that's the tradeoff. Just a few minutes away. If something happens, I'll come to you myself. Me or Chance or one of my guys. We'll get to you and keep you safe. I trust them with Melody's life. They will help you if something happens. I promise. No strangers will have any access to your system again, and you won't ever have to face the TSP without someone with you if you don't want to. I promise that. It's the same system Annie and Tucker are checking out for me. I appreciate you letting my company beta test it here. Unlike your current company, no one will hack my records. They'd have to get past my two sisters-in-law first. And those women are the best with computer security I have ever seen."

He turned back to Jake and Daniel. "It's a new system not yet on the market. No viable way for it to be circumvented, either. In fact, he'll begin installing it—once you are out of the room."

In other words, Jake thought, no one could screw with it again. The technician also had a dozen different locks spread out on the table.

Good. She was changing the locks, too.

Protecting herself. Barricading herself from the world. Behind these walls.

She was afraid. Terrified.

Damn it.

"Shelby, can I at least have five minutes?" he asked, leaning closer to her ear. "Just five minutes?"

She looked at him. Fury passed through her eyes. He almost took a step back. "I asked that you not be here when I came ba —home."

"Well, here I am. Please? Don't make me beg."

For the longest time, he just waited. He would beg.

For her, he would.

Until she nodded. "In Logan's study. Five minutes. Then, if you don't have any official business, I want you out of my house. Forever."

She'd left the phrase *out of my life* unspoken. Jake still heard it. Loud and clear. Something too damned close to grief clutched him right in the gut.

39

HE'D BEEN IN LOGAN LANNING'S STUDY BEFORE. IT was one of the few rooms Shelby hadn't changed anything in. She'd said she couldn't.

Jake hated the dark wood paneling and the heavy furniture. The scent wasn't right, either. It didn't smell like Shelby. Like the rest of the house had—until he'd let it be invaded.

He stepped in and she closed the door behind them both. "Say what you need to say. I am tired and I still need to clean my house back up."

Hell, the forensic team hadn't left one thing out of place. Anyone could see that. Chuckie had vacuumed the carpets herself. "I'm sorry for the way this happened. I should have handled it differently. I was an ass. Should have told you what I was thinking instead of just making the call."

"Yes. You should have. I wouldn't have told you no, Jake. But you were a-a-angry and you reacted. To get what you want. Regardless of my needs. I g-g-get that. I don't know why it surprised me, though." Her eyes finally met his. There was no emotion on her face. Just pure, controlled patience. Like she was waiting for him to say what he wanted to say—so she could shut him out forever. Could forget him.

"I know I was an ass. And I'm just trying to say I am sorry. And see if there is something I can do to make it up to you. I was trying to do my job. I got blinded by how I feel for you, and I overreacted. *I'm sorry*, ok." Then he shut up and waited.

Until she spoke. Slowly. Firmly. With no emotion at all. "I understand you were doing your job. I know the TSP is the most important thing to you. Even over integrity or honesty. Izzie told me that long ago. Your priorities are Izzie, TSP, Annie and Josie, in that order, and that's it. I get that. I'm just sorry you didn't see that *I* wouldn't have stood in your way. I know that it wasn't about that, not really. I was just...in your way. I understand now. I'm a pawn to men like you. I learned that a long time ago, but I started to forget with you. Thought...thought...thought maybe one day we could at least be friends. For Allen and Izzie. I know better now.

"You don't want that with a woman like...like...like me. You don't think I deserve even that. Please leave, Jake. I'm tired. I just want this to end. I want it all to stop. Is that too much to ask? Find what you need to about Logan. Just try not to destroy everything about him I have left. I can't stop you. Call Izzie. She's very angry with you. You...might want to avoid Allen for a few weeks, though. He mentioned something to Turner about shoving your teeth down your throat, and Turner was offering to help him. I don't want the TSP to make more trouble for Allen because of you. He doesn't need that right now, ok? So, just don't. He and Izzie need to focus on the new baby, not taking care of me."

"The TSP won't cause trouble for your brother because of this."

She blinked at him like she didn't believe him at all. "They did before. Harassed him and Logan before. Because of me. I don't want history to repeat itself. We won't go through that nightmare again. Be forewarned. No matter what y-y-you and your friends at Major Crimes are planning. I'll fight you this time. I swear, I will."

The tears in her eyes nearly destroyed him.

"Damn it, Shelby, I am not *them*. You don't have to fight." He stepped closer, wrapped his hands around the soft skin of her arms. "I won't hurt you. I won't let anyone hurt you. Ever."

"Except you? Hands off." She jerked her arms back. He let go immediately. "I trusted you, let you into my home. My *world*. When I was terrified. Do you know what that cost me? Just so you could use me to dig...dig...dig into Logan again. It's not about keeping me safe. It never was. It's about your quest for vengeance against a dead man. Logan's dead. It's time you understood that. You can't stand it that I don't see him as the monster that you insist he was. He kept me from being raped by men just like you. Men who had already broken three of my ribs and my wrist, and almost broke my jaw when they backhanded me so hard I slammed into the curb. With my face. Because I wouldn't give them what they wanted. Do you know what that felt like?"

She stared at him. He flinched. Because he could see it in his head.

"They were having a good time, unwinding with the boys after a hard day. *They* wanted something from me. Just like you and Daniel did today. How long have you been planning th-th-this? I was a toy, a pawn to them. They were using me, too. To get what they wanted. What I wanted or needed didn't matter at all to them. Just like it doesn't to you. Or Daniel, apparently." She barely took a breath, and she was shaking so damned hard. "But *Logan* was there, he faced them all, even though he was outnumbered and they had guns and badges and were drunk— he faced down those monsters just *for me*. To get *to* me. I mattered enough to him for him to care. No matter the odds. How can I ever see him as a monster? Logan loved me just as much as Allen loves Izzie. And now he's gone. Leave me alone. I never want to see you again."

He left her. He didn't know what else he could do.

All the while, he knew that if the guy who had paid the intruder was still looking for something from Shelby—Jake wouldn't be the man there to stop him.

No one would be.

Shelby wasn't going to let the TSP near her anymore.

What in the hell was he supposed to do now?

40

Jennifer Henedy was going to die for what she had done. Victor had set things into motion to see that very thing occurred.

For what she had taken from him.

But today, today was for him.

By eleven a.m. this morning, Jennifer would be dead. Gone. Just as it should be.

He would celebrate Jennifer's death later. And then...when the time was right, when he was certain that bastard Wallace Henedy had suffered enough, Victor would target him next.

Make him suffer the agony that Victor had. Wallace Henedy was the man who had pulled the trigger.

Taken Kyle from this world in a manner so horrific... his son had died on Wallace Henedy's bedroom rug, like an animal.

He'd been naked and had bled to death in Jennifer's arms.

He hadn't had his father with him when he'd died. He hadn't known he was loved in his last moments.

Kyle had just been brutally taken from the world. Like an animal.

Victor would never forget that.

Everyone who had allowed Wallace Henedy to get away with his crimes for so long would pay.

Had Wallace been stopped earlier, Kyle would still be alive.

He would be avenged.

But now... Victor had to see to his replacement.

Kyle wouldn't have wanted the Scott fortune to just disappear into the hands of someone who wasn't a true Scott.

Kyle would have understood.

Today's visit to the TSP was two-fold. He needed information from that bastard James.

And he needed to observe the next few women on his list.

He kept his eyes open as he toured the facility with the head of public relations.

They were here. He had confirmed their schedules with one of his TSP sources.

Haldyn was right there, dressed in a sedate business suit. Her red-gold hair was swept up off her graceful neck.

He had always enjoyed holding a woman by the neck. Keeping her vulnerable beneath his hands while he did the things to her he wanted.

He could see doing many, many things to Haldyn Harris.

She had been quiet and reserved, but so graceful and intelligent two days ago at the benefit. He would love to see her stripped bare beneath him. To know everything about her.

He had seen the intelligence in her eyes.

That was remarkably attractive.

Yes, she was staying on his list.

Another woman crossed the hall in front of him. It took him a moment to recognize her.

She looked far different in the bulky lab coat than she had the dress she'd worn at the benefit. The dress that had revealed quite a bit of her small, but exquisite body.

Charlotte Talley, daughter of that Major Crimes lieutenant, Charles Fields.

That had given him pause. There was a high likelihood the daughter of a Major Crimes lieutenant might be resistant to a man with Victor's past, but she had been so damned engaging, he had kept her on the list.

Now, though, she was verbally flaying into a young officer.

Apparently, he had contaminated her crime scene.

No. He quickly crossed her off his list the instant Daniel McKellen joined the discussion—and the woman started arguing heatedly with him.

Daniel McKellen was the man in charge. She had no business speaking to a superior like that.

She had a temper. And was quite vocal, demanding.

That would never do, even though he admired her passion. Charlotte was off the list, but Haldyn... yes, Haldyn was staying.

There was one more woman he needed to see today.

Madison. Daughter of a firefighter and a nurse, he believed.

Quiet, not nearly as flashy as her close friend Charlotte.

She had been articulate and humorous, understated in a way he'd found intriguing. It took him fifteen minutes, but he found her on the last portion of his tour. She was quietly working, diligent in her task. She smiled at the blond woman next to her. She had a beautiful smile, and when he overheard what she spoke about, her intelligence impressed him.

Yes, she could remain on the list. For now.

For now.

Victor was still in search of the perfect one.

Time was running out.

41

This was something he certainly hadn't expected. Dom stared down at the woman's body on the metal table. Not by a long shot. He'd been called away from going over what had been found in Shelby Jacobson's home two days earlier, to drive to the prison and see *this* before it was even seven a.m. "How did it happen?"

"One quick jab to the area between the ribs here. It was fast. She was dead within fifteen seconds. Leaving whoever did it almost holding her body."

"And who was that?"

"I don't know. You'll have to talk to the warden. Someone caused a massive disturbance. When it settled, her body was found in the middle of the courtyard." The attendant looked at him, dispassionately. No wonder. He probably saw dead inmates on a routine basis. Even here at the women's prison.

"She make any enemies inside since she's been here?"

"Once again, you'll have to talk to the warden."

"I'll do that."

Fifteen minutes later, Dom was escorted into a utilitarian office no bigger than ten by ten. With a ruddy-faced man a good ten years Dom's senior bent over a stack of files. "Detective Acardi."

"Warden, thank you for your time. We are both very busy men, so let's get straight down to business." Dom had things to do. Messes to clean up.

The warden nodded. "At ten-fifty-two, a massive argument broke out in the courtyard. At ten-fifty-eight, once it was contained, the body of Jennifer Henedy was found next to a picnic table. Of course, everyone was questioned. No one knows anything or saw anything."

"Of course not."

"I'm a military man, detective. Whoever did it—they were trained on how to do it efficiently. That will narrow down the possibilities. I have investigators coming, and other than removing the body, have preserved the scene."

Dom leaned forward. "I'm not that interested in who did it here, other than I have a few questions. I want to know who ordered the hit. You find me the killer, and I'll ask them a few questions. And I'll owe you one."

"Noted."

As Dom left the prison, he took in a deep breath of the hot morning Texas air.

The free air.

He couldn't imagine ever being locked up in a cage like that.

Jennifer Henedy had gotten off easy last year for what she had done to Izzie. Far too easy in Dom's opinion.

Criminally easy.

As if she'd bought her sentencing.

Dom suspected she had.

That was just one angle he was following.

Well, she had paid for her crimes now. In the ultimate way.

Wallace Henedy's wife. Wallace Henedy's first attorney—who had been killed around a month ago.

Dom wasn't stupid. He was starting to see a pattern here.

One he definitely didn't like.

He grabbed his phone. Dialed that asshole, Jake. Jake had been in a damned evil mood since he'd screwed up with Shelby over that warrant.

Everyone had. Madison had lit into Jake, first chance she had. As had Bailey and Chuckie and Haldyn. Even Rory had told him what an idiot he had been to do that to a sweet girl like Shelby.

It would probably be best not to expect forensics to treat Jake all that favorably for a while.

"Meet me as soon as you can. We have a problem. A big one." He listened to the guy bitch for a minute before he delivered his final salvo. "Jennifer Henedy was killed this morning. A professional hit. What do you want to do about it?"

Of course, Jake would meet him there.

The shit was finally about to hit the fan. It was time to call in the task force. It couldn't have happened at a worse time now.

42

Izzie's biological father, Jeoffrey Stockton, was waiting for Jake after he stepped into the damned precinct.

Jake hadn't slept all that well for the last two nights. He'd found himself driving around her neighborhood, just making sure she was safe.

Shelby had Houghton Barratt helping keep her safe. She really didn't need Jake now.

He'd finally crashed in his own bed around three that morning when it occurred to him that she had the sheriff of Garrity in there with her—an armed guard. It was the best he was going to get.

Jake got the joy of listening in as Jeoffrey explained to Gunnar about the rock thrown through his home window with the words *You should have let Henedy die! Now, you'll pay!* printed on them at seven-fifteen a.m. that morning.

The rock, the size of Jake's fist, had narrowly missed hitting Jeoffrey Stockton's youngest daughter where she had been playing with a baby doll. A five-year-old child who looked so much like her big sister Izzie it was almost eerie. The only thing the kid didn't have that Izzie did was the wild curls.

Jake felt raw and edgy after the interview with Jeoffrey ended, and the guy's five children filed out behind him like little ducks—all resembling Izzie in some way or another.

He had forgotten how much his Iz resembled the bastard who had fathered her. She was a real blend of Stockton and Jake's sister. But mostly Stockton.

He didn't know what he'd expected. The guy had summarized what had happened. He'd been irritated Gunnar had had him come in. Jake had just shrugged that off.

Gave the guy a warning to watch his back.

Then he'd reconsidered and gone into further detail. Told him that anyone connected to the Henedy case might be facing threats. Stockton did have five kids he had to protect. Kids that were Izzie's half-siblings.

Kind of hard for him to overlook that. Even if Izzie hadn't even agreed to meet those kids yet.

Jake stopped by Dr. Macomber's office on his way to meet Dom. The other surgeon had been the one to do the majority of care on Henedy that day.

Gunnar and Fields were meeting Jake soon. They very rarely discussed task force business within the walls of the TSP.

Too easy to be overheard there.

"We need to get the list of everyone involved in the Henedy case. From...Wallace all the way down to the last juror," Dom said by way of greeting. "Just to be on the safe side."

"We don't have enough manpower to put someone on everyone involved," Jake said tersely. "I can get Izzie out of town, though. Her and that husband of hers."

"What about Shelby? Far as I can remember, she testified against the wife regarding her injuries when the wife hired that guy to take out Izzie."

If it was someone Wallace had hired doing this—he could be wanting to take out all of those who had put him in prison. Or put his precious wife in prison.

The man had been obsessed with his wife, after all.

It was a weak connection to Henedy—but it was a weak connection between Henedy and Jeoffrey Stockton, too. Izzie's father had just done emergency care to stabilize Henedy after the guy had tried to kill himself and failed. Someone who could threaten a doctor for doing that wouldn't think twice about going after a woman who had testified.

It could be the reason someone had found their way into Shelby's home in the first place. He'd seen thinner excuses before.

And if someone was determined enough...they'd get to her. Maybe not on her property, but as soon as she stepped off it.

She needed armed guards. At all times.

"I'll handle Shelby."

"I just bet you will," Dom said. "I'm going to meet up with Daniel. We're going to go visit good old Wally. Give him the news that his wife was killed this morning. And ask him a few questions."

"You think he had something to do with this?" Jake asked. It didn't add up for him. The guy adored his wife. Worshiped her. Jake didn't think he would have ordered a professional hit.

Now, the wife...she would have been a cold-blooded enough bitch to have done it in reverse.

Jennifer Henedy had targeted Izzie before.

Shelby had ended up in surgery instead. She'd been in surgery when Wallace Henedy had taken Izzie hostage for a second time. The entire damned ward had to be evacuated. Shelby had still been sedated at the time.

Shelby was connected. He felt it in his gut. "I need to get to Izzie. And Shelby."

"Go," Dom said. "We'll split the rest of the list between us. Izzie and Allen and the Alvaros are at the top of the list for obvious reasons."

And that terrified Jake to his toes.

43

"You're serious?" Izzie just stared at him. She'd let him in, even though her husband had very vocally ordered him to get his ass out before Allen ripped his head off his shoulders and fed it to Oliver for dinner. The dog had seemed up to it —going after Jake's boots like he always did. "This is real?"

"Hell, yes. It's real. Jennifer Henedy was killed this morning, two of his attorneys have been killed, and others involved in the case at all are being threatened." He looked at Izzie. "Including your father. A rock went through his window this morning, almost hitting your youngest sister. Terrified the kid and she ended up with stitches from a shard of glass. She showed it to me herself. Kid looks just like you, but with lighter brown hair. I promised her I'd catch the bad guys for her. I'm keeping that promise."

Allen's anger was in his eyes as well. He wrapped his hand around Izzie's arm and pulled her closer. "We're not going to be stupid about it. I'll talk to Rafe, clear my schedule for a few days. Lay low until you find out more."

"I can talk to Wanda, too." Izzie's fear was so hard to miss.

Jake wanted to be the one to comfort her. But her husband already had his hands on her, pulling her closer.

"What about Nikkie Jean?"

"We've already called her," Jake said. "Gunnar spoke to Sheriff Daviess. She was with Nikkie Jean at the time. She's taking Nikkie Jean and her basketball team of kids to Mel and Houghton Barratt's. They are going to stay there indefinitely. They are waiting for Caine to join them now."

"Annie? She wasn't really involved with the Henedys, but she was a part of things with Dennis Lee Arnold and Turner was a part of all of it," Allen asked, quietly.

"Already behind guards at the family ranch. Turner has doubled the numbers, and both his brothers are sticking close. You two are my first priority."

"And my sister?" Allen asked. "What's happening with her case now? Is the so-called kidnapping attempt just getting dumped while you and your friends deal with cleaning up after the Henedys? Now that you've found what you wanted of Logan's? Was there ever really a case opened for Shelby's intruder to begin with? Shelby thinks one of the intruders was one of you guys."

Hell, did they really think that? Could his own family think he would do that to Shelby?

"We would *never* do that to someone. Especially her. I'm going to take care of Shelby." Jake meant it, no matter what Allen thought. Allen had snarled at him when he had walked in. "I'm headed to her place after I make sure Izzie is safe."

"Like hell, you are. You stay away from my sister, or I'll rip your head off your shoulders." Allen actually straightened like he meant to come at Jake right then. Jake tensed. He almost wished the guy would.

Izzie's small hand on Allen's chest was all that stopped him.

"Like to see you try. You won't stop me. You just take care of your *wife*. I'll see to your sister now."

"Like I'll ever be able to trust that."

Fifteen minutes of arguing and yelling later, and Allen and Izzie were packed up and shipped right off. The arguing had only stopped when Izzie jacked up the waterworks—and he and Allen turned into total putty.

Jake strongly suspected he and Allen had just been played. Izzie was a tough little bird—she didn't *cry* like that.

Of course, it could have been hormones.

They headed to the Barratt Ranch where Annie and her husband and the kids lived. And two dozen well-trained ex-military guards.

That was two of his girls taken care of.

Now...he just had to make certain Shelby was as safe as she could be. He didn't think she'd be as high of a target, not with just her testimony against the cop who had shot her—another reason she had to despise the TSP—and Jennifer Henedy being dead.

He wasn't going to take any chances. Not with her. He'd get her, and get her to either her sheriff buddy at the Barratts', or out there with Annie. Get her behind armed guards and thick stone walls, if just for his peace of mind.

Then Jake would be free to do what he needed to do.

44

SHELBY OPENED THE DOOR AT THE HARD KNOCK. SHE half suspected it was her brother—anyone else and the security guard would have had to alert her someone was there. Allen had been there checking on her twice a day since the search.

When she saw the dark-haired, broad-shouldered man standing on her front porch with a look of fire in his eyes, she wished she'd ignored the knocks.

Of course. Just when she could breathe again, it would be *Jake*.

He would have been buzzed right through security to get to Izzie's. Once he was inside the gates, he had access to wherever he wanted to go. "What do you want, Jake? I thought I told you I'd rather eat worms covered with pond scum than have you in my sight ever again."

"Tough." He pushed his way past her. Walked into her house like he had the right. "I need to talk to you."

"Of...of...of course you do. And what Jake wants, Jake gets. No matter who he hurts. I think Jake has proven that already."

"No. If Jake got what Jake *really* wants, Shelby would be bare-ass naked beneath him right now. Jake would be showing her in intimate detail what she does to him. Has always done to him. Trying to get her to forgive him for his dumbassery in the only way Jake knows how."

Shelby gawked at him like he was an idiot. Well, that was a totally new one. "Stop it with the stupid jokes. We both know you're not really attracted to me. You were just trying to trick me into letting you fight with Logan's ghost again. Why are you here? Forget to check in my dirty laundry for some of Logan's deep dark secrets? Want to check my underwear drawer? Under my pillow? Want to read *my* diary next?"

Well, yes. To all of that. He'd rather just see her undies after they were washed. Seeing them when they were on her would be even better.

"Simple. Jennifer Henedy was killed today. In her cell. A professional hit. Some others involved in the case have been threatened. You testified in Jennifer's trial."

Seriously? Shelby had never even met Jennifer Henedy. Talk about a weak excuse to try to get back in. He probably *hadn't* found what he wanted, after all. Now, he was back. Persistent.

To see if she'd be stupid again.

Here he was, stretching things again. He wanted something. Maybe he'd left his favorite pair of undies in her guest room and thought that would be a good excuse to get him back in her house? "So? All I did was tell what happened to me. I never even saw the man responsible. Why are you really here?"

"I just left Allen and Izzie's. They are under guards from the Barratt Ranch. They are going to stay with Annie until this is over."

Fear pushed the anger at his presence aside. Just for a moment. Then she reminded herself—never trust a Jake in front of you. That way only led to heartache. "You're serious? You think someone will try to hurt them again?"

"I don't know. I'm not taking chances with Iz. You have two

choices: I take you to Annie's, or I take you to Mel's, where your sheriff friend is taking Nikkie Jean's family. What will it be?"

Did he seriously think she would believe a single word he said?

"I'm staying home. Here. I'm not running from my home just because you think something may happen. I've run enough. *Enough*, Jake. Zoey and I talked about it, anyway. We strongly doubt there was ever a need for you to stay in the first place. It was all part of Major Crimes's plan. If I needed to be worried about this, *Zoey* would have already called." She shot him a look. "And I don't necessarily know if I believe you, anyway. Proven track record and all. Thanks for telling me. Goodbye. I have a new security system now. It's a lot more reliable than Uncle Jake the Liar. If something happens to me, Houghton's men will get here in time to run...run...run them off. Or at least catch them and send my body to Daryn in the morgue. Houghton's guards are better than any TSP ever could be. It's amazing what having money will buy."

Jake swore. Stepped toward her.

She couldn't help herself. Shelby stepped back, immediately.

"I don't have time for this, Shelby. I have things I need to *do* right now."

"You've done your duty. I now know to watch my back. Surprise, I've known that for years. I'll be fine." Maybe she wouldn't. It wasn't Jake MacNamara's choice what she did ever again. "Go away, Jake. I can take care of myself. I'm used to looking over my shoulder for the TSP. Bye, bye, now."

"Like hell, I'm going anywhere. I told Izzie I would see that you were safe. If you are too stubborn to see that, then I'm just staying right here."

"I'll call security."

"I'll call Allen. Have him come back here, just to tell you that you are making a stupid mistake. And Shelby—the rent-a-cop on the golf cart that drives around thinking he's the shits around here—I'm not exactly afraid of him. Not for a minute. You want me gone, you're going to have to go way up the chain of command. You think Elliot's going to take your side against me now? Over Daniel? Daniel's ego is still bruised from your pal going off on him over the search warrant. The things Zoey said to him would shrivel a man's shorts for years. I don't think so. I'm not going anywhere."

Shelby just stared at him for a long time. She had no idea what to do now.

"Stay," she ordered. She hurried back to the kitchen and shoved the open files back into the bag she'd kept them in.

Files her PI had provided and those two journals of Logan's that meant everything.

Things she didn't want Jake ever knowing about.

She grabbed her phone. Called Zoey. Explained what was happening.

Zoey didn't say anything Shelby wanted to hear, but at least she made sense. Zoey was worried about Nikkie Jean and Caine and their family.

That was what did it for Shelby.

Zoey was afraid for her family. Zoey felt she needed to be there to protect Nikkie Jean and Caine—and five innocent kids. Six kids. Pen was there, too.

The last thing any of them needed was to be concerned over Shelby. Shelby didn't even ask if she needed to worry about herself. Zoey had enough to worry about now. They were going to go about their daily lives, but cautiously. That was the best they could do.

Shelby would have to do the same.

When she disconnected with her friend, Shelby looked at Jake.

She'd just have to deal with him herself.

He sent her a cocky look that made her want to slap him. Did he even know what it felt like to have your hands tied like that, to feel forced into something by events out of your control?

Somehow, she doubted he did. Not big, strong, dominant Giacomo who thought he was top dog in everything he did.

"So? Do I have to call Daniel and give him a heads up that you are having me arrested for trespassing? Or what?"

She put her phone back on the table, next to her bag. Shelby wasn't getting rid of him. Not anytime soon. Not without a bigger fight than she had time to give right now.

Her shoulders slumped in defeat. She fought angry tears.

She had no clue how to deal with this man. Not at all.

She'd lost.

Again.

And right now—the last thing she needed to do was go somewhere and hide.

"You stay out of the way. You don't go poking around my house ever again. As far as *my* family is concerned—you and I have agreed to a truce. Until you have the intruder in custody. That's it. Because you don't think I'm seriously a target. I-I-I can't be. I don't want Allen's focus split right now. He'll want me with him and Izzie. And I am not running back to my big brother every time something scary happens. If I catch you getting into my stuff, my life, again, I'm going to make you pay. However I have to do it. Even if it's a personal lawsuit that keeps you in court for years—just because I can. I'll tie you up so bad in litigation, I'll even take your cat in the settlement. Earl would probably like it better living with me, anyway. I'm not a dog like you."

And she would. Well, maybe not the cat, but everything else. Her attorney Powell had already made noises about suing him for illegal searches or something.

Shelby had been too mad and hurt to even focus on what Powell was saying. There had to be a way to keep Jake under control in some way.

If she kept him where she could see him, she could work her way around him.

That would be better than being blindsided. The last thing she needed was to draw the attention of the TSP right now.

She had too much to accomplish first.

"You don't need to be going anywhere. You need to stay behind locked doors, with guards, armed guards, and a security patrol around the place. You need that all the time, not just now, anyway. We'll talk about that later. I'm already making a list. We'll go over it when we can. Real soon."

Seriously? Shelby just stared at him. "I *need* to have a life. And I have to be there tonight. I have people counting on me. I don't ever intend to let them down. I'm determined to be someone people can trust. You might try it sometime. It could help you actually build character. Of course, you may be too old for that, at your advanced age. Old dog, no new tricks."

"Damn it, Shelby. Don't you get it? I just want you *safe!*"

She sniffed.

The man was one hell of a good actor. He almost looked like he meant it.

"O-o-of course you do. I'm your ticket to defeating Logan's ghost, after all. I know exactly what you want from me, Jake. I'll never forget it again. You can count on that." But...there would be rules, until she could get rid of him again. "This is my house. You stay out of my room and my office and out of my face. And...I think it's best if we don't talk to each other if we don't have to."

"Still sore over the warrant? Ever going to forgive me?"

"It's a bit more than sore." She felt betrayed, for lack of a better word. Add in the way he'd just run roughshod right over her now—why would he ever think she wanted him there? "You should have known that I'd have let *Izzie's uncle* search wherever he wanted to. I don't have a lot of family, you know. I treasure Allen and Izzie more than anything, anyone, else in the world.

I'd have done it for Izzie. I'd do anything for her. In a heartbeat."

"Hell, you're just going to have to forgive me. You want me on my knees begging? I can beg for you in that heartbeat. Tell me what you need in order to forgive me; I can't stand it." The words were cocky, but the look in his eyes...almost made her think he meant it.

She wouldn't be that stupid.

"Stand what?" The man never made a moment of sense to her. Maybe that was her problem—she just wasn't savvy enough where men were concerned to ever figure this one out.

"You hating me. It was different before. We didn't like each other, but we respected each other. I didn't do it to hurt you. I was just so damned sure I'd find something."

"And did you?"

He hesitated. That's when she knew... "You did. What was it? Is that why you jumped at the chance to stay with me after the intruder? Is that why you are here again? I...probably would have been fine with Detective Acardi. He...I know him. I would have been just fine with him." Possibly. Charlotte had said Dom looked like he'd be a big brute, but he was one of kindest hearted men Charlotte had ever met. She'd genuinely liked him. As did Izzie. "I like him."

"Like hell I'm trusting anyone else with you."

"Control issues? Can't stand it that I don't want you here? Think you're so great that I'll just be begging you to stay with me?"

"Look, I'm sorry. I do regret it." He shuffled impatiently. Frustration was clear. He didn't like that she wasn't just stepping aside.

"So what did you find, and where was it? In my bedroom, maybe? My office? Where? Don't I, as the owner of the house, deserve to know whatever was found in my property? Disclosure of evidence or something? You find something naughty in my panty drawer, Uncle Jake? You forcing your way back in to find my bras next? My thongs?"

"We're not accusing you of anything. And we're still processing it. And for my damned sanity, stop talking about you and thongs. My heart can't take it." He sank into the black leather chair that her brother favored whenever he visited and glared at her. He and Allen had a lot of habits in common. She wasn't stupid enough to point that out.

She'd potentially take away his favorite enemy if she did that. She was so tired.

So tired of the back and forth. The tension. It took everything she had to fight the defeat. "Whatever, Jake. It's done. If you found anything that pertains to me specifically, rather than just whatever you think Logan was a part of...send a copy to my lawyer. I left Powell's card on the fridge, but she's rather easy to find. I'm going to be in my office for an hour or so. Clean up after yourself, ok? I fired the cleaning company. They are the ones who leaked my security code. So...deal with your own messes."

She turned away and started out of the door. She didn't want to be in the same room with him. Not if she could help it.

She was so over it, her teeth hurt.

45

JAKE SHOULD HAVE THOUGHT THIS OUT A LITTLE better. Instead, he was happy he had made it into the house to begin with. She could have had him hauled in for trespassing.

Thankfully, she hadn't. He never would have lived it down if she had.

He'd have to have Dom bring him by some damned clothes to wear, for one thing. For another, Shelby had some seriously weak safety measures here. Even with Barratt's high-tech security system.

Someone on the cleaning crew had sold her security code—and copies of her keys—for ten thousand dollars in cryptocurrency. Charlie was still pressing for answers on that.

If she was on the list of Henedy targets, Jake was going to have to be ready. He busied himself checking every window and possible entry point, making certain they were locked, and the system armed appropriately. And looking for potential ways an intruder could get in to her.

She ignored him, working in her office with a bunch of files and print-outs. He'd check on her through the windows on the

French doors she'd closed against him. He wanted to get his hands on those files. To see what she did with her time that had her frowning like that.

Jake understood the concept of shaky ground.

He took a moment to poke around her house again, reacquainting himself with the layout from a security standpoint. It was close to thirteen thousand square feet, he thought. With at least eight bedrooms and two master suites.

Why did a house need two master suites? He would never understand that.

There were nine doors, points of main entry. Each one had at least four locks engaged. And there were far too many windows.

It was a showplace, no denying that. She was updating it. The colors were different, he thought. Before they were all dark wood and dark blues and greens. Now, there were light-colored walls, gauzy curtains on the windows to let light in and some of the walls had intricately designed silk wallpaper now. A few rooms were even more feminine. Those were where she spent most of her time; he'd lay good money on it.

They smelled the most like her.

At the top of the landing, in an alcove that he swore had marble tile, was a beautiful grand piano. Jake kept his hands off. It was polished so thoroughly he could see his reflection in the black.

There were a pair of pink slippers beneath it.

There was a framed portrait of her brother and Izzie and that goofus dog of theirs on one wall. A photo of her family dominated the opposite wall. The little girl in the photo wasn't any more than twelve. He smirked.

She really had been the ugly duckling. But wow. What a swan she had turned out to be.

There were a few more photos—Shelby and her friends, mostly. One with Shelby, Zoey, and Daryn, smiling and young, with rock-climbing gear on, Daryn's brother standing proudly over the three of them in the background. He wondered if she still went out and did that, or if that wasn't something the rich lady enjoyed any more.

This little nook smelled like her. Felt like her.

This was where she spent her heart time. Just like Izzie used to curl up in the big armchair with a notebook, writing stories she didn't think Jake knew about, Shelby came here.

With the opening to the house below, the sounds of a piano would echo everywhere.

He wanted to hear her play.

Wanted that deep in his gut.

"You finished search...search...searching the place once again? I told you not to. No surprise you didn't listen."

Jake turned, and there she was. Fifteen feet from him. How had she managed to sneak up on him?

"Yeah. Just getting a feel for all the entrances. Weaknesses. That kind of thing. I didn't come up here last time I was here. You play a lot?"

"Yes." She shot him a narrow look. "But *this* piano was Logan's. Allen has the one we learned on. It was my mother's. Going to search it next? Take it apart looking for secret compartments?"

"I didn't realize it was his. Or that Allen played."

"Yes. He enjoys it. So do I. So did Logan. It was something the three of us had in common. The first duet I ever played was on that piano right there. With L-L-Logan."

Jake felt like a total asshat, seeing the pain in her eyes. Storm-gray now. He wondered what color they really were. And wondered what he'd have to do to get close enough to her to find out. "I'm sorry.'"

"Sure you are."

"So mistrusting you are."

"You'd better believe it. I have a few rules. My bedroom—off limits. My office—off limits. My piano—off limits. Me—definitely off limits. The rest of the place, poke around as much as you want. I'm sure you are still looking for something. Why else are you so insistent you be here? And, while you're at it, make certain that the forensics team didn't leave so much as a smudge, won't you?"

"Hey, Chuckie and Madison are the best at it."

She shot him a look of disgust. "*Chuckie?* Hmmm. Guess you don't know her as well as you thought. The great MacNamara charm isn't as great as you think it is."

"Maybe not. But she wasn't complaining when I was kissing her. Madison, either, when I kissed her. I'd be happy to let you test me out yourself?" Seeing the judgment in Shelby's eyes irked him. She turned on the steps a bit too quickly for his peace of mind. "Be careful, woman. You're going to crack open your skull on these fancy steps of yours. Allen might think I did it, and then Izzie would get mad at me."

She just kept going.

Jake watched her.

Hell, he wanted that woman. So damned much.

More than he wanted breathing.

Just to mess with her, he waited until she was at the bottom of the marble staircase—and played the only song he knew.

The opening bars of *Twinkle, Twinkle Little Star* echoed through Logan Lanning's mausoleum.

"Leave my piano alone, you troglodyte!"

Her call was just as loud.

Jake laughed.

Perfect. The woman was absolutely perfect. And she probably knew it.

His gaze landed on the sheer expanse of windows that practically surrounded the house.

Perfect.

And currently his to protect.

He was going to make sure he did just that. Especially from himself.

That was what he'd failed at the last time he was here with her. No more. He was going to keep Shelby safe.

Jake just concentrated on doing that until Dom called with the latest update.

46

JAKE COULDN'T HELP HIMSELF. HE FOLLOWED THE
woman around like a puppy—even more so after he realized he
was irritating the hell out of her. To his surprise, she did her
own laundry and ran her own dishwasher. She even cooked—by
heating up takeout. He'd never seen her with anything other
than takeout.

"Can't cook?"

"Not really. Never had to learn."

"Of course not." Jake had. He'd learned out of self-preservation when Izzie would stay the night with him as a kid. Then
when she had moved in with him and he got a true picture of
how it had been with her mother, he had made damned sure she
had a hot meal every single night, breakfast in the morning, and
made certain she, Annie, and Josie had had lunch money every
day. And hot food on the weekends, too. Annie and Josie had
shown up on his doorstep every Friday at four p.m. for years.
He'd send them home by eight on Sunday nights.

No questions asked.

"Allen hired a housekeeper, once he figured out I couldn't

cook for myself. She was a bit territorial about the kitchen, so I just stayed out of her way."

There was a look in her eyes that told him the story was more than what she was saying. Jake wanted to poke deeper. "Poor little thing."

"Don't be a j-j-jerk, Jake." She shot him a look from those storm-blue eyes. "What is it you want here?"

"Attention. Love. Satisfaction… Leftovers."

"Not going to happen, not going to happen, not going to happen. And find your own food. Call one of your buddies to deliver. I am not stupid. I know why you are here. And the only reason you *won* your little game and got back in here is because I don't trust the TSP one bit. Better a devil I know, and don't trust, than one I w-w-won't even know to watch out for. I don't want strangers from the TSP in my house ever again."

"You have more bite than I expected." That, she did. She was quiet, undeniably, but beyond that—she wasn't easily cowed. Not at heart.

"You mean I'm not a pushover. I get that. You think just because I have a stutter, I should sit back and let…let…let people walk all over me? That I should be voiceless."

"It has nothing to do with that. More like…you've had it good, and now you don't even need your big brother. You have everything you could ever want here."

"T-t-things. Yes. I can… can… can buy whatever I want. Whoopee."

There was such a look of sadness and bitterness in those eyes that Jake just stopped and watched her buzz around her ridiculously large kitchen for a moment. She slammed a plate on the counter and turned toward him.

"It doesn't seem f-fair to you, does it?"

"What?"

"That Logan gave me all this, and I really don't deserve it. Probably think it should have gone to someone else. Someone who didn't have it so cushy already." She sent him a look so full of irony, Jake winced. "Someone who actually worked for it far more than I ever did. Logan…Logan got the money by putting in the time to invest, the time to invent the patents for lifesaving technology and then to know what to do with it. I-I-I got it because you think he had no one else. I'm…just Logan's leftovers. Second best. I just lucked into it."

"You're deserving. Just as deserving as anyone else."

"Am I? Just as deserving as Izzie or Annie? Allen? They do good things. Help people. What do…do…I do?"

"You have a degree in social work," Jake said slowly. He had stumbled onto a landmine, apparently. A war wound she didn't even realize she was sharing. He hated that she hurt.

"Yes. I can teach sociology now. I un…un…understand how groups work. Yay."

"You work at W4HAV."

"I'm easily replaceable."

"What do you do with Mel Barratt, then?"

"Find ways to spend Logan's money. So I don't have all of it sitting on my conscience. As *undeserving* as I am."

"You shouldn't feel undeserving." Jake felt like a first-class heel. He'd told her point-blank she didn't deserve her pretty lifestyle, more than once, when they'd been snipping at each other.

He suspected she'd remembered every stupid barb he'd shot her way.

"He should have given it to Allen. That would have been fair. Better than giving it to me. Allen would have deserved it far more. Allen does good things."

To the hells and back, she *believed* what she was saying. Fully believed it.

She felt guilty for having the man's money.

"Why Allen and not you, baby girl?" She looked so young. There wasn't a hint of makeup on her face, her hair was pulled up in a simple ponytail. She wore jeans again. And a T-shirt with FCCCC and a bunch of musical notes printed on the front. Some of those notes were printed in very intriguing places. "Why do you think Allen is better than you?"

She just stared at him. "Isn't it obvious? Allen saves lives. He's going to go on to save thousands. He's...special. My parents *always* said that about him, and it's true."

"And you're not? That's just crazy." Holy hell, did she seriously think her asshole of a brother was more special than *her*? No way.

"Is it? I know you don't like me all that much, either. Probably because you've never liked Allen, and I know you despised Logan. The thing is...you've never told me why you feel the way you do about me."

"I don't dislike you or despise you." Nothing could be further from the truth. He rounded the kitchen island until he could almost touch her.

"Maybe not. You apparently have no problem using me. I didn't matter enough for you not to. People don't use those they like, those they care about. At least not my kind of people. And definitely not family. Family is important—family matters. Of course, you and I aren't family and never will be, but we will share family very soon. We already do. They've asked me to be the baby's godmother. I know they asked you to be the godfather."

"Yeah, they did. And we do. I already feel lower than pond scum here. I was irritated with you—you push my buttons faster than anyone on the planet—and I overreacted. For that, for what happened, I am sorry. Sorrier than you can ever know. I never intended to hurt you like that. Can you forgive me? Give me another shot?"

"Do I have much choice? You are here, aren't you? Lesser of two evils. The thing about you, Uncle Jake, is that now...now... now I have no real expectations. You know I'm not good enough for you to even think about not hurting. So I'm prepared. Do what you have to do so Major Crimes can finally let Logan's spirit rest in peace. Because the man is haunting me. I swear, he is." She just stared at him with a wild, *haunted,* look in her eyes. One that had Jake's breath catching. "I don't know if I'll ever get *me* back, anyway. I'm almost ready to give up trying."

"Shelby?" Jake just looked at her, at the storms forming in the eyes he loved so much.

She shoved the plate of leftovers toward him, fresh from the microwave. "Here. Eat it. I'm not really hungry. Hate to see it go to waste."

All he could do was watch her as she walked away.

What in the hell had that been all about?

Jake was afraid he wouldn't like the answer.

47

VICTOR LOOKED AT THE YOUNG MAN IN FRONT OF HIM and wanted to shred him. Years in business had taught him how to keep himself under control in all things.

When you killed someone—it was best to plan ahead. Less mistakes were made that way.

Even when he was hearing things he didn't like to hear. He didn't have time for this kind of an issue. "What do you mean, it was intercepted?"

"What I said. Someone from Major Crimes was there. Our men had to abandon the truck and run for it. They almost didn't make it. Now...the women may be talking."

Victor's hands clenched.

Major Crimes. They had been fucking with his business for almost three years now. And it was just getting worse.

Now...they were interfering in the biggest project of his life. In far too many ways.

"And Jake MacNamara?"

"Not involved. Rumor has it he's been assigned a protective detail on some woman in the Hughes Heights neighborhood, about a mile from here. From what sources are telling me, it was

Erickson and Acardi and some of the patrol officers tonight, plus that sheriff of Garrity."

Her again. Victor was quite conflicted about her—but after learning of what she did, he had quickly crossed her off the list of eight possible choices. She...would be too difficult to manage. Of that he was certain. Even if he had found her fascinating. "Check with better sources. I want to know if we need to do some clean up."

"And the sheriff who's been digging into...other...things? She was there tonight."

"That is not my problem. Talk to your boss about her, if you must. I want no part of that." He did not wish her harmed, but if that was what was necessary, than so be it.

Victor always did what was necessary.

"Will do. Strange coincidence, isn't it? That she'd be such good friends with that woman who intrigues you so damned much? Yet be causing so much trouble for *us* now? No surprise though, that woman...she's got all the boys at the TSP talking, too...And Jake MacNamara, wow, is he drooling over her."

Victor bit back a snarl at the underling in front of him. He wasn't stupid. He recognized the threat for what it was. Someone on his payroll was talking—no one should be spreading information about Shelby Jacobson now. No one.

Shelby was on his list. Of course, she was. But no one should know that. That they did, was just another problem Victor would have to overcome.

Jake MacNamara—that worthless fisherman's grandson from Italy—was becoming a problem, as well. A big one. MacNamara had been digging so deeply into Victor's son's doings that he'd found something. And used that something to taint Kyle's name for the world to see.

Victor could never forget that. Forgive.

Now, all of Kyle's secrets were resurfacing. Victor couldn't

get them buried fast enough and still manage his most important task.

Victor never liked to admit failure.

It was coming to the point where he might have to let Kyle's
secrets resurface and focus on what was coming next.

He wasn't getting better. He probably never would. Maybe it
was time he accepted that.

"Find out about this woman he's protecting. If something
significant is going down in my town, I want to know about it."

"Yes, sir."

Victor looked around the office he'd built years ago. Looked
out the window at the city before him. It was a very small city—
but it was where he had chosen to build his world. From there,
it had just expanded. All over Texas. Into Oklahoma and
Louisiana. Mexico.

He was proud of what he had built.

He would not sit back and watch years of hard work be
destroyed because of someone with fish guts in his blood.

It wasn't going to happen.

48

As the hours passed, Jake thought about what she'd said. He thought about it well into the next afternoon. Dom called. Kept him busy, even remotely.

Jake wasn't used to sitting on the sidelines like this. Not for the biggest cases Major Crimes had handled to date.

Jake knew how the game was played. He had to follow the rules. He could do background research, could study Logan Lanning's journals, could try to decipher Wallace Henedy's and compare them to files they'd found from Dennis Lee Arnold, the city councilman who had tried to kill Jake's Annie.

Arnold had been enmeshed in the whole nasty web, but he had been just one tentacle. There were so many more. Through Wallace Henedy, they had discovered a billing fraud ring. Henedy hadn't been the only surgeon involved.

It had originated in a small, now-defunct clinic in Garrity. Cooked up between Henedy and still as yet unidentified physicians who had profited.

The Garrity sheriff was investigating that angle. Going deeper.

Shelby's scary little friend was causing a lot of waves right now.

The call Jake was waiting for came just as a freshly showered Shelby grabbed her keys. Where did she think she was going without him at—he checked the clock—four p.m. on a Tuesday?

He hooked one arm around the woman of his dreams' waist and held her still. "Wait, woman. Quit squirming around."

He answered the call.

"Don't call me woman!" she hissed. Jake shot her a look.

"If you are finished playing with Shelby…" Dom said through the cell. *"I have something you might be interested in."*

"What?" Oh, he wished he was playing with Shelby right now. She smelled good, like flowers. Like all woman. He bet she'd smell that good all over. "What? Sorry, Dom, I'm…distracted."

He tightened his arm around her when she squirmed. He pulled the phone away from his face for just a moment. "You aren't going anywhere without me. So, stay."

"You…you…you need a dog instead of a cat. Something you can train."

"You, Shelby Grace, are far from trainable."

"That's what makes women like her fun. Now, are you paying attention, son?'

"Sorry, Dom, I have Shelby in one arm. Literally."

"I can call you back. Half an hour? Hell, take an hour. And enjoy."

"Not necessary. But I believe she thought she could sneak out of the crypt without me. Bad girl."

"Aren't you…you…you here to search the house? With me gone, you'll have all the time in the world to do that. Best get started; it is a big house Logan left me, you know."

"Quiet, woman."

He almost swore the woman in question growled. Actually growled.

Jake loved aggravating her. She reacted so beautifully to his teasing.

"We've connected Victor Scott to two more incoming shipments. Gunnar and Fields are organizing a few...interceptions for tonight. Just like last night's. What's on your schedule?"

"Not really sure. But I think I'm about to find out."

"I bet I know. It's four o'clock on a Tuesday. You've got choir practice, pal."

That was what was printed across her chest. *Finley Creek Community Children's Choir.* Under the larger FCCCC. Two of those C's curled in interesting places.

Jake had to stop spending all his time staring at Shelby's chest. She was going to catch on. She could be so distracting. He listened to more details from Dom, keeping his arm around Shelby just for shits and giggles.

Then he knew what he had to do. As soon as he had her tucked away safe tonight, he was going to go over everything *he* had.

See if Logan Lanning had any tie to what was going on with actual human trafficking. It was a long shot, and Jake doubted he'd find anything—but you could just never really know.

Lanning was dead, but that didn't mean anything he had started was. There was something going on at that hospital where Izzie worked.

He was just going to have to find the *who* and the *how*.

SHELBY *ALMOST* LEANED OVER AND BIT HIM. RIGHT ON the neck.

She'd bet he'd like that.

Or take it as a challenge.

He was the most physical man she had ever encountered.

He'd thought nothing of putting his body in her space countless times. Over and over again.

He never did anything too inappropriate, and she'd bet a million or ten that he did it just to disconcert her.

Every time he did, she swore her skin would burn for hours after.

It was better to just avoid him.

That was what she was going to do.

Stay far, far away from him.

She took two giant steps back, away from the devil in her kitchen. "Hands off!"

"I want to get my hands on you in a variety of so many ways. Over and over again. And over. I could tell you, show you. But first, where are we going, how long will we be there, and why do you think you are going anywhere right now?"

"It was an intruder, that was it. Someone trying to steal something he could pawn. Or he was one of your cronies trying to trick me into letting *you* in. I haven't ruled that out, either. Nothing more. We both know you are here under false pretenses."

"Whatever I am here for, I need to at least do it a little so I appear to be earning my keep in this swanky place. So bodyguarding. I love the body I am guarding, by the way. It should always wear T-shirts that fit just like that."

"You are a pervert. Does Izzie know?"

He shot her an unrepentant grin. "Probably not. And remember, no one likes a tattletale. Now, give me a kiss, baby girl, and I'll drive you wherever you want to go."

She wanted to argue. Shelby honestly did. But she couldn't be late—she was the one with the keys to the auditorium. The kids were counting on her. "It's on the corner of Jude and Ninth. And you...you...you can't cause any trouble. Not even for a minute, got me?"

"If I'm a good boy, you'll give me a kiss when you tuck me in tonight, right?"

Shelby couldn't help herself—she had to do it.

She kicked him. Right in the shin.

The man brought out more animalistic urges in her than anyone ever had before.

Anyone.

She'd never kicked anyone in her life.

Not even her older brother, who at some point or another had probably deserved it.

No. Just Jake.

Probably because she couldn't care less what that man thought about her at all now. And the braying ass deserved it.

49

THERE WAS A TINY GIRL OF NO MORE THAN FIVE OR six sitting on the piano bench. Shelby was leaning over, showing the little girl where to put her fingers on the keys. *Twinkle, Twinkle, Little Star* rang out.

It took him a moment to realize—that little girl was his Izzie's younger half-sister. Sitting right next to Shelby, staring up at her adoringly.

Shelby patted the girl on the back, smiling down at her—the most open, beautiful smile he had ever seen from her.

Jake just stared. He swore he felt himself falling sideways for a moment there.

The woman burned him. Made him want everything he knew he couldn't have. Not long-term, anyway.

He wasn't made for this kind of life. Not this.

The closest he'd ever gotten to having kids was Izzie, Annie, and Josie. Annie and Izzie had been young teenagers when he'd gotten Izzie, and Josie had been six years younger. Hell, when he thought about it, *he* was the only real father those three had ever known.

He'd been there every time they'd needed him, he'd

protected them, made sure they had food. Taken them to the doctor when they were sick. Ridden Annie's mother's ass when it had been needed. He'd even made certain they all three did their homework every night. He'd practically raised all three of them and not just his Izzie.

The little girl hugged her. The mini-Izzie. He wondered if his great-niece or nephew would look anything like that kid.

Shelby would hold a kid just like that. The little girl had wrapped herself around Shelby's neck and was clinging like a monkey. Shelby laughed, looking like everything a decent man could want. As he watched, she dutifully inspected the little girl's bandage, and kissed the air above it. She hugged the little girl tightly for a long moment. Comfortingly.

For the first time in his adult life, Jake imagined it. Imagined finding a woman he could do the whole family man thing with. Imagined a woman loving him enough to want to have his kid.

He imagined Shelby as a mother. Pregnant, like Annie and Izzie currently were. Annie was already starting to show.

Hell, Shelby would probably be the most gorgeous pregnant woman in the world, too.

He wanted to see her that way.

That shocked the hell out of him, just imagining it.

She'd have that whole earth mother sex appeal thing going on some women got.

Jake bit back a curse when it sank in that he probably would see her like that someday. Some guy way better than him would eventually convince her to marry him. Maybe even a damned Barratt. They were of the same social class. Had the same circle of acquaintances. People like her, who lived like her.

She'd find one of the manicured man-hand set. They'd marry and blend their considerable fortunes seamlessly. Probably be able to play beautiful duets on her piano that cost more than some people's houses and cars combined. Hell, he had no idea how much it cost—he'd never heard of a *Blüthner* piano in his life.

Shelby would have the guy's kids. Build a perfect family, complete with the latest designer dog that wouldn't ever consider pooping on the damned sidewalk and a pedigreed cat who would turn its nose up at the brand of food Jake bought for Earl each week.

Jake would see them occasionally whenever their paths would cross at Izzie's. Shelby's kids and Izzie's would be cousins, family. Shelby would have perfectly beautiful kids who were difficult for him to be around. Because they'd all have Shelby's eyes.

They'd think he was just the weird uncle their mother refused to talk about—or to. She'd usher her kids away from him whenever he got too close. Her pretty boy husband—probably close friends with Allen—would watch Jake like he was a snake getting too near her.

Ready to snatch Shelby away and protect her—from Jake.

Of course, the guy would—Shelby would be *his*, after all. Not Jake's.

Never Jake's.

It would be damned awkward. Especially if he had to interact with the guy.

If he was lucky, Jake would find another woman of his own, one from the TSP maybe. One who would feel out of place hobnobbing with Allen and Shelby and their families. With Izzie, even. Because Izzie's world had changed, too. *Izzie* would eventually change, too.

Become more a part of Allen's world and less a part of Jake's.

It wouldn't come to that, because Jake wouldn't be able to get serious about some random woman. He just knew he wouldn't.

He doubted he'd be serious about any woman. He didn't even know if he ever could.

He sank into an auditorium seat midway back from the kids. He didn't want to intimidate anyone or cause a distraction—and the guy near the back row working furiously on a cell phone and laptop was Izzie's biological father. Not something Jake had missed.

Guess the guy was doing the whole single father gig tonight.

Jake wasn't getting near that guy, not if he could help it.

Jake was there to guard Shelby, after all. Not screw with the guy who had abandoned Jake's sister years ago. Abandoned *Izzie* years ago. Unlike the other five kids he had, Stockton had just tossed Izzie aside and moved on.

Jake focused on Shelby and not Stockton, before he did something impulsive and stupid.

This was the first time he'd seen Shelby outside of their family and W4HAV or her own home—without Izzie around. Got a clearer picture of who she was.

Shelby looked good with kids around her. Relaxed. Far less uptight and reserved.

A woman called out from the left of the stage. He recognized her—Shelby's good buddy, the sheriff of Garrity. In street clothes, now. It took him a moment, but Jake spotted it.

She was armed. She didn't let the kids climb all over her like Shelby did. There was a watchfulness about her. An air that said she knew danger existed.

That she expected it.

Jake understood. He had lived that way for fifteen years now, ever since he'd decided what he wanted to do with his life in this new place, enrolled at the TSP academy in Wichita Falls, and left his plastics factory job behind forever. It had been the first job he'd been able to get in the States. He'd needed that money the factory brought in, and he'd worked hard for it. That money had helped raise Izzie after Stockton had abandoned her and her mother.

Jake had never forgotten where he'd come from, either.

Jake sat back in the chair, not wanting to draw her attention. He wanted to see her with her friends, doing *this*.

Working with a children's group was not something he would have ever expected her to do. Two more women came in, with a herd of preteens. It took half a second for him to recognize them, even though he'd suspected they'd be there.

Chuckie and Madison. They didn't look like lab geeks now. Far from it. The two headed straight toward Shelby and her sheriff friend.

He watched them talk for a good five minutes. After the first few moments, Shelby seemed to relax. Shelby was at ease and comfortable with them. Madison hugged her. Apologizing for searching her house again, maybe?

At least Shelby wasn't holding it against them. They were friends again.

A bit awkward—considering he'd dated both in the past. Maybe he really was the dog Izzie had accused him of being before. He'd kissed three-quarters of the women on that stage, after all.

If the opportunity had ever presented itself before, he would have kissed the sheriff, too. He would have guarded his man goods—but he would have kissed her.

It shocked the hell out of him to know Shelby was friends with the kind of women Madison and Chuckie were, though. Even the sheriff was more blue-collar than the wealthy Barratts of Barratt County—connection of the governor, or not.

Shelby was far more relaxed right now than he had ever seen her.

Even more than when she'd been with her brother. Far less guarded. She wasn't holding herself back the way she sometimes did with Allen.

Interesting.

He wondered why. Why did she hold herself back from the

only real family she had? The woman was more of an enigma than he had ever realized.

He suspected she'd somehow put that brother of hers up on a pedestal, and now found herself unable to live up to his perceived greatness. That was just bullshit, in his opinion. Extreme bullshit.

Shelby was perfectly fine just as she was.

He wouldn't change one thing about her—except the fear that was sometimes in her eyes.

As practice began, as she started on the piano, he was floored.

She was gifted. There was no other way to describe the way she played.

Extraordinarily gifted. Even he could see that—*hear* that.

She should be in a concert hall somewhere, playing for the wealthiest of the wealthy. Her fingers flew. Never had he heard someone play like that.

Chuckie led the choir, throwing her entire pint-sized body into it with a fire and passion and skill that was totally being wasted buried in the TSP lab.

Madison assisted, taking the smaller kids off to one side at one point to work on harmonizing or something. They romped all over Madison, just like little puppies. She looked damned adorable up there.

Zoey took the dozen teenagers off to the opposite side of the stage, including one with blue-streaked hair that looked just like her. Josie's buddy, Penelope or something. Had to be Zoey's sister, the resemblance was that strong.

Just as he figured that out, someone tapped him on the shoulder. Two kids ran past to join the rest of the horde on stage.

He turned to see one of his favorite women on the planet staring at him from thick glasses with plastic musical notes attached to the sides. "We charge admission to sit and gawk at the piano player, you know."

"Hey," Jake leaned back, to put a bit of space between them. Nikkie Jean had had a raw deal thanks to that bastard Henedy. She was still real leery when a big man got too close. "Shouldn't you be behind closed doors and guards?"

"Guards are all around. Outside. Luc kind of insisted. Caine is tolerating them for my sake. The kids...they didn't want to miss this, and we aren't going to let their lives be impacted any longer. Zoey had to come get Pen, anyway. And check on Shelby. Me, too, on that one." She settled into a seat in front of him and unstrapped the baby from the carrier as her older twins—she'd adopted her husband's three children after she'd married, and then they'd had twin girls a few months later—joined the rest of the herd on stage, after they hugged the sheriff.

"So your kids are part of this mob." Which meant...a ready source of information. He'd have to play his cards right—this woman was one of the sharpest he had ever met.

Nikkie Jean nodded.

Jake had always found her as fascinating as he did Chuckie and Madison. She had depth, this woman. And a wicked sense of humor.

He'd been attracted for a while there. *Really* attracted.

Her fear...it had kept him at bay. He was too rough of a man for her, Jake had known that easily enough. It was the same kind of fear he'd seen in Shelby's eyes before.

And no wonder.

Considering their histories.

"Pen has been a member for a year and a half. She convinced Keller and Everett to give it a try. I told Dr. Stockton about it when he asked about activities for his children here in the city. His three youngest are up there. Pen's about to age out, though. Nineteen is the limit; she has another year and a handful of months."

"How long has this been around?"

"Around a year and a half. Charlotte and Madison helped organize it. With donations. The Jacobsons donated quite a lot to help get it started. And Shelby...well, we wouldn't be in this place if it wasn't for her. She organizes our venue—and I suspect she pays for it, too. So...truth. Why are you here? I heard about the search warrant. Is Shelby ok? That was a pretty low move. Not your most gallant. I'm surprised you're still here with her. Surprised Allen didn't introduce you to Mr. Scalpel, actually. He has quite the collection. And they'd probably all like to meet you right now."

"So I've heard." And he was going to hear about it from just about everyone who knew, apparently. "I needed answers. Shelby and I have come to a deal. It's either me, or another armed guard for the foreseeable future. I don't think she's a high target, but I'm not taking any chances with her."

"Be careful how you go about getting those answers. You don't want to destroy people in the process. Shelby...she's far more vulnerable than she looks, you know. People don't always see the real her. I'm not even certain Shelby always does, either. She's done rather well at building her disguise. Probably has been her entire life, growing up in the shadows of "greatness" like she did. Fear probably eats at her each and every day. I know what that is like. I still feel that way. And I probably always will."

"I didn't mean to hurt her. That...that is the last thing I would ever want to do."

"I've seen how you look at her. And I get it. Because she scares you down in that primitive man-soul of yours. That doesn't mean you should hurt her to drive a wall between you. Trust me. Caine can be the same way—or he could, before he realized that he adores me, anyway. Because I'm just totally adorable; everyone says so."

"I've already apologized." Did Shelby believe him? That was the question.

The sheriff tapped Shelby on the shoulder, drawing Jake's attention. The woman's hair was down—straight, dark, and almost to her waist. She looked nothing like a sheriff at all.

"The sheriff...tell me about her. I have questions."

"Don't go getting any ideas there, pal. She won't help you out at all. That's Shelby's bestie, and Caine's younger sister. I'm a bit protective of my in-laws, you know. She had a pretty rough deal as a kid, too. Kind of the theme for his siblings. She has legal custody of Pen for a few more months, until Pen hits eighteen. Pen's already a college senior, that kid. She'll have her first degree by the end of summer term. Scary smart. Like all my husband's family."

"How did she and Shelby meet?"

"Well, Shelby and Daryn knew each other in high school. Daryn..." Nikkie said, as she rocked her fussing daughter back to sleep expertly.

"Evers. I know her."

"Figured you did. Daryn and Shelby met Zoey at FCU, when Zoey was taking a few undergrad classes. The three of them stuck together. Zoey started off in Wichita Falls, then took Garrity when it was offered—to get Pen out of the city, I suspect. It surprised all of us when Shelby was at Zoey's when we swung in to visit one day, considering how far away Garrity is. Garrity is great for rock climbing and those kinds of adventures. Zoey had offered to take Everett with them one day. Shelby has a bit of an adventurous outdoor streak, just like my oldest son; she and Zoey used to go all the time, Allen told me. Mountain climbing was mentioned at one point, heaven help me. Doesn't get much time to indulge it now, though. With all Shelby has to do with Mel and things. Zoey is very protective of her. Best not to get on Zoey's bad side, by the way. She looks like Ariella—but she can act much more like Rafe when riled. That clone of my husband has some serious bite with his bark. Zoey doesn't have the bark—but she has far more of the bite. Bit of a contradiction, my baby sister-in-law."

"No kidding. I thought she was going to carve out my insides. With a silver soup spoon, if she could have found one."

"She's quiet, but fierce. And very, very protective of those she lets in. Everett and Keller just absolutely adore her."

They got all the kids back together on stage.

Shelby played a few bars on the piano.

"Oh, this is my favorite part. Those are my kids up there, and my sisters-in-law. My family." She shot him a totally besotted grin. "I never thought I'd get the chance to say that. Considering the whole miracle baby thing—and the whole men terrify me thing, something I share with our piano girl up there, by the way, something you should consider—but those are *my* kids up there. Just like this one is mine, too." She patted the sleeping baby on the rump. "Caine has her twin and Dalton over at FCGH. Doing the pediatrician-slash-well-baby thing. He'll take this one and the elder two in for checkups and boosters tomorrow. We divided, so we can conquer today. Who knew five kids were so much work? I wouldn't trade even a minute of it. Life is a horrible thing to go through alone, you know. You should get you a good woman and a couple of these things, too. They can be very entertaining."

Shelby went into a piano solo that had Jake's attention captivated. "She's so damned good."

"Shelby is far more than good—she is the best I've ever seen or heard. And I come from Philly, Jake. Music is kind of a *thing* there, after all. Shelby is a massively talented woman who can do great things. She is equally as brilliant on the piano as her brother is at surgery—if not more so. Far more so. It's...she breathes it. She used to compose, Allen told me once. I don't know if she still does, but I would love to listen to something she's created from her soul. She had a real, tangible gift. An extraordinary one that should have been nurtured when she was younger, but wasn't. I'm not sure why. Allen's gifts were; hers weren't. Far more gifted than her brother, which is extraordinary, considering who Allen is and what he has already accomplished.

"She is so locked in her own fear—something I am intimately familiar with, by the way—that she doesn't let herself see exactly what she is capable of. I think some of that came from growing up in Allen's shadow, with parents who most likely compared her to him far too often, and missed the depths of Shelby's own, less obvious and far quieter, gifts, in my opinion—and some came from...other...things."

The baby fussed; Nikkie Jean looked down at her with an expression of pure love. "Would you mind? I need to run to the restroom. Peeing with a baby attached can be a bit difficult, you know. When the babies were first born, I had reoccurring nightmares that I dropped one or the other—or both—in the toilet and couldn't fish them out. Caine laughed at me for a month after I first shared that. But, hey, we were all a bit sleep deprived back then. Then the dork put one of those dancing fish plaques above the toilet in the master bathroom. It took me a while to forgive that. It started singing in the middle of the night."

Just like that, he found himself holding a sleeping baby.

Just like that, Jake fell totally in love.

And he didn't even know which baby girl it was he held.

She opened big dark blue eyes and looked at him. Gave a sleepy dimpled smile that would one day steal men's souls just like her mother's did, and settled back into sleep. Capturing his heart completely.

Jake had never considered having kids of his own. He didn't even have any friends that were fathers—with the exception of that dork, Callum. He hadn't even held Audrea that night he'd watched her. He'd basically just sat in the kitchen and listened to the baby monitor. He'd held Annie's boys before, though.

Had played uncle many times. He was good at *uncle,* anyway.

But he'd never even what-if'd the idea. After his sister's death, he'd inherited Izzie by default. As her only relative in the US—her father's family hadn't counted, Jake had made that very clear to the social workers back then.

His sister had left guardianship papers, thankfully. The social workers hadn't looked for her father that hard at all. Jake had already known some of them through the TSP. That had helped a great deal. He'd taken Izzie home with him, and that had been that. They'd muddled through.

Then again...he hadn't done half bad with Izzie. She was happy, healthy, not in jail, and had a good career. She was settled; she and that husband of hers had bought a house eight blocks from Shelby's just six months ago, after staying at the Barratt for two months once Allen's condo had finally sold.

Izzie had turned out all right. He hadn't done a bad job at all and was her father in every way but legally. He'd survived Izzie's teen years. Nothing could really faze him now. Survived Annie and Josie, too.

Maybe someday, when he'd found a woman who truly "got" him, he could consider a kid. Or two, maybe.

He wasn't going to discount the possibility. If that ever happened, and he wasn't too old...maybe.

As he cuddled the baby, he looked up. At a woman he found far more fascinating than he had any other. He wished he was the kind of guy meant for her.

Jake never would be. But a guy could dream once in a while. He just held the baby, feeling like a fool.

50

JAKE WATCHED HER FINGERS FLY OVER THE KEYS, SAW the look of pure pleasure on her beautiful face—and he felt himself fall for her harder than he ever had before.

He so wanted those beautiful fingers on him.

"You're staring. Hell, I'm staring, too. Different woman, though," Dom said, as he took the seat in front of Jake's.

"Stalking your stepsister is a bit creepy, you asshole."

"Don't call her that. Only I'm allowed to. It pisses her off when I do. The last thing I feel is brotherly toward her. And I saw her long before her mother cast a spell on my father."

"When are you going to do something about it?" Dom didn't shout his attraction to Madison to everyone, but his friends knew—namely Major Crimes. Jake looked at the woman in question.

Madison stood in front of a bunch of kids in the ten- to twelve-year-old range. Half of them were bigger than her. She had thick glasses, warm cinnamon-brown hair, and a sweetly classical prettiness that did catch a man's attention quickly. Quiet and bookish, she was the exact opposite of the rough thug that was Dom.

He suspected that was half the problem. The two were like oil and water. And Dom was afraid because of that very thing.

Dom just grunted. "Not the kind of guy who appeals to a woman like that. She likes Daniel much better."

"Hell, she and Dan got a thing now?" Jake would admit it—he didn't keep up with that shit. He didn't think Daniel would do that to Dom. Not when Daniel was too busy sniffing around Jake's Shelby. "Daniel needs a woman of his own. It's too easy for him to go around poaching."

"Not that I know of. She's said it before. To her mother. Didn't even realize I was listening, I guess." Dom shrugged as if it didn't bother him, but Jake knew his friend well enough. "Thinks he's hot or something, apparently. Sophisticated, unlike the rest of us. We're no better than cavemen, I guess."

There was a sour look on the man's face. Dom had it bad for Madison. Real bad. And he had long before the woman's mother had fallen for and married Dom's own father—a pure coincidence that Jake thought was hilarious.

It just complicated things for Dom. Dom kept bringing Madison closer and closer, even though he wasn't brave enough to do anything about her.

"This surprises me."

"I think Chuckie is the actual head of the choir. Apparently, her mother started a similar choir up in Wyoming before she died, and Chuckie wanted to honor her memory. Madison helps because the two of them do practically everything together now. And, of course, there's Max."

Chuckie broke into a solo to illustrate something to the teenager she was talking to. They watched for a moment. "Daviess is good."

"Shelby's best friend." Jake winced. Zoey had nearly taken his head off. He didn't think he'd impressed her much, even though they'd worked the task force together for almost two years now. They'd been on the same team, but their paths hadn't crossed frequently. He hadn't even spoken to her that often. Of course, she rarely said much in the meetings at all. Just sat and watched, absorbed. "There are Nikkie Jean's two right there, too. The Garrity sheriff is her sister-in-law."

Nikkie Jean had gotten all curled up around that doctor from Barratt County right before Annie and the mayor had hooked up and then Izzie and the bane of Jake's existence had gone on the run together. Now, they were all married off, and the Alvaros' younger twins were a least four or five months old. He looked at the baby in his arms. How was he to guess how old she was? She was barely bigger than Callum's three-week-old.

Izzie and Annie were both pregnant now. His girls, who had once needed him to give them lunch money and teach them to drive, were now married and pregnant by wealthy, successful men. Men more than capable of taking care of them just fine.

And Josie was ensconced at FCU and doing just fine on her path to veterinary school eventually. She'd probably find a guy of her own, too. Marry and have half a dozen children, and just as many pets. Some of the Barratts were already sniffing around her, too.

Jake wasn't needed anymore. He almost felt replaced.

Hell, the world just kept turning too fast. He kept missing things, somehow. When had Izzie and Annie gotten old enough to have kids? Annie had adopted three boys, but this felt a bit different.

Allen and Turner were about the same age Jake was—Annie and Izzie weren't girls anymore. They were women. Adults.

Hell, they were around the same age as Chuckie and Madison and Shelby and that sheriff.

He hadn't realized that before.

He liked the mayor well enough for Annie, he supposed. Turner was a nice guy, a bit idealistic, and he adored Annie and her boys. They had become a family.

Jake was getting old. At least, it was starting to feel that way.

Like he was just on a damn hamster wheel, getting older and older with every ride but never really getting anywhere.

Maybe it was time he stopped to consider if there was *more* to life than the hamster ride?

More to life than the damned TSP. Hell, that was about all he thought about any more. Especially since Izzie had gotten dragged into whatever was going on a year ago.

When was the last time he'd done something like go to a choir concert to watch someone's kid sing? At least eight years ago when Izzie had been a teenager.

Jake had been in the US for almost sixteen years now. How had that even happened? It had never been his intention to stay forever, but that was where he was now. What he really wanted. Here in Finley Creek was *home*.

He missed having family everywhere he turned. Maybe it was time he admitted that.

"This is a good group," Dom said. "Max enjoys it. I'm here to get him, take him to basketball practice in a few minutes. He's going to spend the night so we can talk about women, heaven help me."

Jake turned to the kids on the stage. He could see a few familiar faces—Nikkie Jean's older twins, Jason Buchanan, who had stayed with Annie and the mayor for several months, Dom's stepbrother Max, and there were even a few kids he'd met before whose parents worked at the TSP. Not to mention two or three of Izzie's half-siblings were up there, too.

There had to be fifty or sixty kids on that stage, ranging from around the age of five all the way up to eighteen or so. "Chuckie and Madison do this themselves?"

"As far as I can tell, they have, with help from Sheriff Daviess and…Shelby. Surprised you didn't know."

"She didn't exactly share details of her life with me until recently." He turned back toward the piano. "She's barely talking to me now. She's ignoring me. Just pretending I don't exist. Unless she demands I take out the trash like she did this morning. Like I'm the butler or something."

"She'll get over it. You just keep her out of trouble, and I'm sure she'll be fine. Women can be damned grateful when a guy shows up to save the day."

She looked perfect up there, with a bunch of kids surrounding her. There was a little girl with almost white blond hair sitting on the piano bench next to Shelby now, a fascinated look on her tiny face as she watched Shelby play. Shelby smiled down at her.

"Damn, she's absolutely gorgeous up there."

"Yeah. She still despise you for the search?"

Jake just nodded. Their last conversation in the kitchen was stuck in his head, too. She hadn't been angry—she'd been hurting. Soul-deep hurting. He wanted to make that better.

"It was a total dumbass move. Effective for Major Crimes, but dumbass on the personal side of things."

"So I've been told." Even Izzie was giving him the silent treatment. She only did that when he'd done something totally stupid. "I hurt her. Bad."

"No kidding. But what else were you supposed to do? Would she have let you search, if she'd known what you were doing?"

"I didn't bother to ask. Logan Lanning was her damned hero, Dom. And with good reason. She accused me of having it out for his ghost, of all things."

"Lanning always has been something of your white whale. Do you have it out for his ghost? Something to ask yourself." Dom was damned insightful at times. They understood each other, Dom and Jake. Caveman recognized caveman, after all.

Dom always asked the tough questions, though.

"Hell, I don't know. The guy who caused so much shit at the hospital for Izzie doesn't sound like the same guy Shelby talks about. She misses him. Grieves him. Deeply. I'm not happy the guy died the way he did at all. He was a bastard who hurt people I know personally. But Shelby loved him. What am I supposed to think?"

"That, like all of us, there was both good *and* bad in the man. And let the man rest in peace. See what he was up to, but look to the living for the rest of the answers we're looking for. Don't do anything to lose out on a relationship with one of the hottest, nicest women I have ever seen because of it."

As Dom spoke, Madison stepped over to Shelby. Chuckie was on the other side. They were discussing the music between them, Shelby making notes on it with a pencil while the kids talked and wiggled and even jumped on the stage.

Zoey joined them, her niece next to her. Zoey was just as beautiful as Shelby, tall and thin and almost ethereal.

She was of his *kind,* when he thought about it. She was TSP. She understood the life. Yet she...did nothing for him. Not like Shelby did. Jake watched them for a moment. "The four of them together are enough to give a man a heart attack if they'd just look at him for a minute."

"Isn't that the truth? One of those women looked at you like you matter, just for a little while there. It might not be too late to get that back. What are you going to do about it?"

That was a question Jake didn't have an answer for.

He'd always hated unanswerable questions.

This was no different.

51

IT HAD GONE WELL. SHELBY FELT MORE RELAXED playing piano for the kids than she did any other time during her weekly schedule. She loved it. Adored every minute of being a part of something so special. She could create emotions with sound when she touched the piano. Could communicate exactly how she was feeling without words to slow her down. Every single time.

Shelby didn't have to worry about speaking when she played —something that had been her biggest cause of anxiety as a child.

Shelby was just...free. She could just feel the music as it coursed through her.

The moment Allen had sat her down on his lap—she'd been five and he'd been almost sixteen—and started teaching her the basics while he'd been babysitting her one night had been the greatest gift her brother had ever given her.

She'd begged for lessons after that. Her brother had taught her all he knew for the next two years whenever they had been together. Then she would find herself at the piano, practicing for hours. He had convinced her parents to get her real lessons, and suggested that her mother start teaching Shelby like she had Allen all those years earlier.

Her mother had wanted Shelby to earn the lessons—by stopping her stutter. She had refused to even consider piano lessons for an entire year. And she'd wanted Allen to stop teaching Shelby. Demanded it.

Shelby had been devastated. To lose her freedom like that... to have her own mother tie it to something so hurtful, and to deny Shelby the one thing she truly enjoyed and felt good at— Shelby had never forgotten that moment.

She probably never would, even though she had loved her mother and father to the bottom of her soul.

Allen had stuck up for her, had known how much the piano had meant to her, and gotten their father involved. Together, her father and brother had convinced her mother to allow her to learn, though her mother had refused to be the one to teach her.

Her brother had given her the piano lessons, paying for them for her eighth birthday. *Allen* had given Shelby her first voice. She had adored him for that.

He had always been her hero.

But...she didn't think her mother and father had ever even listened to her play. They just hadn't seemed all that interested, as busy as they were—with their careers and prepping Allen for his. They had expected great things from him.

The sound of childish voices singing around her gave her hope. Punched her in the gut each and every time. Reminded her that the world just kept going. That there were good things out there.

She and Zoey had gotten dragged into the choir by Zoey's little sister, when Pen had been almost seventeen and still recovering from the trauma of what had happened to their sister, Ariella. Pen had been there that day, right in the middle of it. She could have been killed.

Pen still had nightmares, too.

Shelby just wanted the nightmares to go away—for all of them.

She pushed those thoughts away and played, just played, as the kids sang.

When practice was over, she, Zoey, Pen, Charlotte and Madison made certain the community multipurpose center was clean—that was part of the deal to get their security deposit back each time—before grabbing her bag.

Leaving was the last thing she wanted to do. She still had to deal with Jake.

Talk about a buzz kill.

She didn't know what she wanted to do with him. She found him in the entrance to the building, flirting with Charlotte. She knew the story. They had gone on two or three dates before Charlotte had called it off. Charlotte—not Jake. Charlotte was beautiful, funny, outgoing—and TSP. She and Jake had that in common.

Charlotte wasn't covered in the evil, offensive *money* that Shelby was, either.

No one but Charlotte, Madison, and Zoey knew it—but Shelby used some of that evil green stuff to pay for this multipurpose room twice a week so the kids could have a place to rehearse. She also provided the snacks and drinks for after and paid for the technical crew to handle lighting and sound during the concerts.

No one but her friends knew that.

She was going to keep it that way.

It was no one else's business what she did with Logan's money. Ever. No one was ever going to make her feel ashamed for him having left it to her again, either.

She slung her bag over her shoulder and pulled in a deep breath.

Time to deal with her own personal albatross.

She was stuck with him until he got whatever it was that he wanted. She wasn't going to let him see how that hurt.

Jake turned toward her. There was surprise in his eyes when she stepped closer. Why?

She wanted to ask, but she kept her mouth shut. She had to get that man and everything to do with him out of her head.

Worse—she had to get the man out of her house somehow.

Maybe it would be worth giving up her independence for a little while, going to Mel's or to Annie's.

She honestly didn't think someone associated with Wallace Henedy would be after her. It would be Izzie and Allen they were after.

That terrified her—Jake needed to be watching over Izzie, not her.

This was Jake's latest excuse to come digging into Logan's business again. She was almost certain of it. The bruises on her neck from the man who'd been in her house were real. Hard to forget that.

What if someone *had* been after her because of what Jennifer Henedy had done?

Someone like Dom Acardi would have been a better guard than Jake. She knew Dom's father and stepmother, for heaven's sake. She could trust him.

Instead...Jake. He'd probably drawn the short straw and gotten stuck with her or something. Maybe she could trade him in on a better model with the TSP. The big, blond guy who had been super nice and funny the few times she'd met him would work.

He had seemed kind. Unthreatening—well, as unthreatening as a gorgeous guy who looked like Thor could. She thought about that for a moment.

Maybe it was better to stick to the devil she already knew.

Shelby honestly didn't know.

She could do this. She just would remind herself over and

over again not to let her guard down with him. Ever. He couldn't be trusted. That was a lesson she would be best served to remember.

"You ready, *bambina?*"

Bambina? Not likely. She shot him a look of ire. He just smirked.

"I'm ready, *honey*. Madison... Charlotte... I'll see you all later." Sometimes, saying their names was more difficult than she wanted to let on. She forced herself to get the words out. She would always stutter. Some people never outgrew it, and speech therapy didn't fully work. She was good with that—and her real friends didn't care.

Shelby was so tired of feeling alone. Even with Allen, she'd felt alone.

Sometimes, she didn't feel like her brother truly understood her at all. He had a view of her that he expected her to live up to —but sometimes it wasn't *her* at all, either. It had been their parents' view and expectations. Set long ago.

Allen had accomplished everything he'd ever wanted to succeed at. Shelby hadn't.

Her parents had been so proud of him—and so perplexed by her. She had always known she hadn't met their expectations. At least, her mother's; her father had always been so busy he hadn't had a whole lot of time for just Shelby. They hadn't even wanted her, she suspected. She'd been an accident when Allen was ten.

Her father had spent more time with Allen, of course. Shelby had frustrated them at times. They just hadn't understood her. First with her stutter that they'd tried so hard to erase with therapy and medication, and then just telling her not to speak in a group if she didn't have to, and then with her just slightly better than average grades in school and her inability to make friends as fast as her much older, extremely popular, brilliant brother.

She hadn't always lived up to Allen's expectations, once her parents had been gone. Allen had a view of her that she didn't always feel *fit*. Even now.

It had gotten better since Izzie had come into their lives. Shelby adored her sister-in-law. Izzie had changed Allen's world for the better completely. And gotten him out of Shelby's business all the time. Thankfully.

Izzie's arrival had brought the man currently staring at Shelby like she was a Rubik's cube he just couldn't solve—and was ready to toss out the window. Everything came at a cost. Shelby knew that.

Shelby turned away as Zoey and her younger sister walked out of the multipurpose room. Bickering.

"Shel, can you please explain to my sister how I'll be perfectly safe. It's not like I'm going to do something stupid. We'll even have bodyguards," Pen said. "Like armed ones with guns."

Zoey had gotten a two-year degree before joining the TSP. Because of what had happened to Shelby and Daryn that night. Zoey had had to attend a parent/teacher conference for Pen that night, or she would have been with them. Would have been hurt, too. Shelby thought her friend felt guilty about that.

Zoey always had been super protective of Shelby and Daryn. It had just gotten worse after that night.

That night had changed them all.

Now, Zoey was extra overprotective over her baby sister.

Shelby still hurt when she thought about how one night had had the power to shift their world. Just one night.

Shelby looked at Zoey, who rolled her eyes. "I told you, Pen, you are free to do whatever you want. I just want to know where you will be so I don't worry."

"I don't *know* what we'll be doing. I just don't want to hang around the house all day tomorrow, and it's only eight-thirty. And all my friends are in Finley Creek now. Since college."

Shelby looked at Zoey again and saw it. The knowledge that a seventeen-year-old girl just hadn't had time to learn yet. Shelby just shrugged.

Pen was right—she had bodyguards and an armed driver who took her everywhere, thanks to Zoey's extremely wealthy brother. She would be safer than Zoey, Shelby, and Daryn had been at that age. Far safer.

"I'll even be with Syd. So two guards instead of one. Which is a real pain in the ass, I might add. I mean, they watch everything we do now."

"Fine, go. Text me when you get back to wherever you are staying though."

Pen whooped and hugged her sister—then she was gone, skipping to her three friends who waited outside, next to a limo. Syd Beck—Mel's youngest sister—was driven just about everywhere, thanks to her own extremely wealthy brother-in-law. And guarded.

It was a strange world in Finley Creek sometimes.

A lot of money moved through such a small city as Finley Creek. It didn't always make a lot of sense to her. But economics weren't really her thing—people were.

She'd studied different groups of people for years, trying to understand how they all fit together.

Probably because Shelby had never really *fit* anywhere, herself. Not too hard to figure that out.

"She just doesn't get it," Zoey said, a look of sadness in her eyes. "Of course, I'm going to worry. I remember us at eighteen and twenty and what happened soon after. Why wouldn't I worry about her, when she's ten times more impulsive than we ever were?"

"Because she has a bodyguard watching out for her? She'll be ok, Zoey. We...were. Eventually."

Maybe.

They had the nightmares to show for those years. She said a

fervent prayer to herself that Pen never faced any nightmares of her own.

At least not any more than she already had.

"Why don't we go out? Pen's right. It's not even nine yet," Charlotte asked after the awkwardness was over. "Hit Mamaw's? I am addicted to diner food, after all."

"That's because you eat like a long-haul trucker, Char," Madison added.

"Hey, I burn it off. Shel? You in?"

Shelby wanted that. She almost thought she needed it.

"I'll take this out back, and we can take off," Zoey said.

But...Shelby had a tagalong she had to consider. "Jake?"

He shrugged. "I'm good with that. I'll even grab a table of my own, far, far away. So you can all have girl time. Chit-chat about the men in your lives and how imperfectly idiotic we can be. I'm sure Mads has a lot to say about her boy-toy, Dom. He pants every time she walks by."

Madison just glared.

"Gee, thanks," Shelby said, fighting back the sarcasm. She wasn't exactly too thrilled with him following her around—and he knew it. "I-I-I'm sure we'll have plenty to talk about in that regard."

Jerk.

This...whatever it was couldn't end fast enough, as far as Shelby was concerned.

When it did, she was going to erase the memories of Giacomo MacNamara out of her head completely. And then... she was going to put herself out there. Start meeting people.

Including men. Attractive, available men.

Allen had a partner in his practice—a pediatric surgeon, she thought—who was good friends with Izzie. Izzie had been trying to get Shelby to date him for months. Izzie said Dr. Ralstone was funny and kind and loved kids.

Well, Shelby was going to do it. Even though she suspected

any brilliant surgeon would be far too much like her control freak older brother, at least he was a good place to start.

No more hiding herself away, just like Izzie, Daryn and Zoey always said she did.

She was going to live. It was time to stop just sitting back and watching life pass her by. Starting tonight. *She* was going to hang out with her friends like she hadn't in years.

Jake was just going to have to deal with it.

52

It always took Zoey a day or two to get her head back on straight after a night like what happened with Dom Acardi's human trafficking bust. Zoey would never forget those women's faces, those girls, as she'd spoken with them a few nights ago.

That little boy who had been only eleven years old and taken outside a homeless shelter to be used and abused. Thank God they had found that truck in time to prevent that from happening to him.

She didn't know what was going to happen to him now.

She would keep an eye on where he ended up, and if she needed to intervene...Zoey would. Somehow. Even if it meant getting the governor of Texas or her brothers involved.

She wasn't going to let that kid just disappear. She'd seen too many do just that.

There had been kids all around her tonight, too. Happy, well-cared for, *loved* kids that she adored. She needed this choir, probably more than any of the kids did.

Practice had gone well, but Zoey was worried. About Shelby.

She had known Shelby long enough to know that Shelby was

getting herself deeper into trouble. Shelby had always kept secrets too well, but Zoey knew.

And it worried her.

It couldn't be good.

Ever since the final inheritance from Logan Lanning had been discovered, Shelby had been different. Furtive, determined, secretive. Hurting.

Even more of a target than she had been before. Every time Zoey had mentioned that to her, Shelby had refused to listen.

She'd been too afraid to.

Zoey wasn't stupid. Wealth like that brought with it more problems than it solved. Even if no one would come right out and say that.

She'd argued with her eldest brother until she was blue in the face about that very thing. He had casually suggested she quit her job and find something to occupy her time in a way that he could somehow keep her safe. Working for him.

Be kept by him was more like it. Because he had enough money that none of his sisters should ever have to work again. Nothing was ever mentioned about Caine or Rafe quitting. Just her, Ariella, and even Paige.

That hadn't exactly gone over well with any of them—or Luc's wife, Payton. Luc had a bit of a sexist streak, apparently. At least, where his sisters were concerned. He wanted to protect and coddle.

Well, he was the rich guy, not her. And she wasn't ready to give up her way of life and her goals for someone she saw maybe once every two months, when he'd fly down from his mansion in St. Louis to "make the rounds" with his newly discovered Texas relatives.

She was happy with the life she had built for herself—and for Pen, though Pen seemed to be accepting being the sister of one of the richest guys in the world rather easily compared to Zoey —and Zoey wasn't ready to just throw it all away.

Zoey could protect herself just fine.

The familiar weight of her weapon comforted her. She took *this* one off for only two things—sleeping and bathing. Even then, it was well within reach.

Luc's money had made Zoey a target. She would never forget that.

Shelby's money made Zoey's best friend a target, too.

Shelby refused to even have a single bodyguard. Even though Zoey had told her time and time again that she could help Shelby find a woman she trusted.

Shelby still refused.

That worried Zoey every single day.

She grabbed the bag of trash and waved to Shelby. Shelby nodded. She'd stay right where she was until Zoey came back in.

Shelby had some questions to answer.

Like why there was a sexy dark-haired, dark-eyed cop watching every move Shelby made again. And just how long he had been following Shelby around like that.

And if there were any leads on who had broken into Shelby's home.

Zoey was half-tempted to put in for some time off and move right into Shelby's guest room. Keep an eye on things herself, for the time being.

She thought about that as she tossed the trash in the dumpster after practice had ended.

A dark sedan drove by, slowing down near the head of the alley.

Zoey tensed, her hand resting an inch from the .38 she carried.

A window rolled down. A flashlight beam hit her in the face.

"Can I help you?" Zoey asked coolly. She wouldn't overreact, but she wasn't stupid either.

"We're with the TSP," a male voice said. "Just checking things. Saw you moving around a bit."

"Who is your commander?" She knew the entire hierarchy at the Finley Creek post. "I'm Zoey Daviess, sheriff of Garrity."

"Ma'am, sorry to have bothered you. You rather blended in, in the dark clothes. Sorry to have bothered you."

Well, didn't their tone change after finding out who she was? Imagine that. "Yes, I suppose I did. Have a good evening, gentlemen."

"You, too, ma'am. And...be careful out here alone. A woman alone, even a sheriff...just can't be too careful. Not in this part of the county, after all..."

Zoey resisted the urge to shiver at the guy's tone. Something about it chilled her. As the car drove away, she made a mental note of the license plate. Someone had targeted her best friend again—she wasn't going to take any chances.

There were very few people in the Finley Creek post that Zoey would say she absolutely trusted. History had just proven that was a good policy to have.

53

Jake watched Shelby's friend as she stepped back inside the building, an odd look on her face.

Every month, like clockwork, they met at the governor's task force meeting, at the governor's Finley Creek home. Her sister, the governor's wife, was usually there. He had studied them together before—two highly beautiful, if somewhat reserved, women with tall, thin builds, big, dark eyes, and long, straight dark hair that fell down their backs almost to their waists.

The kind of women men didn't ever forget.

She looked nothing like the dedicated TSP sheriff that he knew her to be.

Larger cities had a hierarchy of the chief of the post, commanders of each division, lieutenant commanders, the detective division, and patrol officers, forensics and support staff. Outlying areas had local sheriffs and their deputies. The sheriffs reported to the regional chiefs at the nearest posts.

Elliot Marshall was her chief as well.

The cases the task force worked, which officially didn't exist, covered Garrity. Covered the entire state of Texas.

He didn't even know if the co-sheriff of Garrity even knew

about her *activities* with the task force. Jake wasn't one hundred percent certain she was the right choice for the task force. He hated to say it, but she didn't look capable of doing the job at all. Especially in the thin jeans and the choir T-shirt that made her look like anything but a TSP sheriff.

She was armed. He hadn't missed that. Another armed cop protecting Shelby. He could handle that.

Shelby and the rest of her little buddies were finishing up in the auditorium itself. He could hear them laughing and talking from where he was in the main lobby. He hadn't been too keen on the idea of the sheriff outside by herself this late at night. Not in this particular neighborhood.

They were just four blocks from Boethe Street, the worst place in the city, after all.

"What's going on? Why are you really here?" she asked. "And don't tell me it's you doing Izzie a favor. I'm not stupid. Cops like you—always have an angle. What are you after with Shelby?"

Well, so she was a bit more direct than he would have expected. He mentally shrugged. He could respect that. "The only thing I'm after is finding the bastard who hired her attacker. That's it."

"That doesn't mean a TSP lieutenant commander follows around a burglary assault victim for days. I'm not stupid. You're wanting something from her. Like every other guy on the planet whoever gets near her. So what is it? Money? Connections? Sex? They've been after all of that. Just in the past six months alone—a good dozen. I've run most off myself. Powell handled a few, too. Every guy always wants something from Shelby. But none ever want to give her something of value in return—even respect."

Well, someone was a bit cynical. Jake looked into dark eyes that he could almost swear saw straight into a man's soul. He didn't think he'd ever gotten that close to her before. Intense.

He made her a promise. "I'm going to make certain no one hurts Shelby. Period. Believe it if you want."

"Nobody *else*, you mean? I don't trust you, MacNamara. I know too much about you and your kind. I definitely don't trust you'll have Shelby's best interests at heart. I've seen you work, remember? The only thing you truly care about is the TSP. You've already proven that. You are not the kind of guy she needs in her life. You'll be the one to hurt her. Then I'll have to tear you apart."

"Yeah. You and what army?"

"Everyone who knows the two of you. Hurt her, and I'll find a way to destroy you." A threat, delivered in the voice of an angel. Scary, this woman.

Well, yeah. He could almost see that happening. Everyone wanted to protect Shelby. Even Jake.

He held his hands up and took a step back. "Like I said. I'm not going to let anyone hurt her. Even me."

"See that you don't. And, while you're at it, find out if the TSP in this patrol car had any business driving down the alley behind the auditorium tonight." She rattled off a license plate number. "Something felt off about them. Like they were looking for something specific. Someone. If they're looking for Shelby…I want to know about it. And you…you need to earn your keep again, MacNamara."

"Yes, ma'am. I'll get on that right away. Whatever you say."

As he watched her walk away—she had a very nice walk, that woman, and Jake was a healthy red-blooded male, after all—all he could think was that he didn't envy the Garrity co-sheriff for even one moment.

Guy probably had to have balls of titanium to work with that woman every single day. Jake felt for the guy, he really did. Some women had the natural ability to destroy men with barely a flick of their delicate little hands.

Inside that auditorium were four women capable of doing just that—five, if he counted Nikkie Jean, which he certainly did.

Jake would protect each one of them with everything he had. He called Gunnar and rattled off the license plate like the good little boy his mother had always told him he should be.

54

To his surprise, Charlie Fields was in the diner already. Jake joined him, needing reinforcements with Shelby's crowd. He texted Dom and Gunnar his location.

Now was as good a time as any for updates. He wanted to hear about Charlie's kidnapping ring investigation, anyway.

"I'm doing guard duty. The girls wanted something to eat, so here I am."

"Lucky you," Charlie said, sarcastically. "I hate guard details. So boring. Of course, I somehow doubt you are bored at all with this one."

"Hey, I put in for a few vacation days to watch her. Since I've been sidelined from the Henedy case and all." He was guarding her on his own time.

Shelby and her friends showed no signs of just finishing their damned dinner and taking off their separate ways. They just kept gabbing and laughing. Drawing attention their way effortlessly. Even Shelby, though she spoke far less than the other women.

Shelby had been joined by Mike Evers's wife when Mike had

brought her in for dinner. Daryn had promptly abandoned her husband for her besties the instant she saw them.

Leaving Mike pouting at Jake's table. Guess he'd had other plans for the night than staring at Jake's ugly face.

Dom and Gunnar tracked them down a few minutes later.

"What is this, our version of a hen party?" Dom practically grunted. "Max ended up going home with a few friends tonight instead of hanging with me. He's in love with his best friend's little sister, apparently. She's a year younger and hates his guts. Poor kid. It's Stockton's middle daughter, Jake."

"Do they still call them that? *Hen* parties? I don't really like the sound of the male equivalent." Gunnar asked, grabbing a nearby chair and carrying it over, ignoring the waitress's blush when he smiled at her absently. "Where's Dan at tonight?"

"He and Haldyn had an "engagement" at the Barratt tonight," Dom said. "Tuxedo time. Still, bet she looked damned hot, wherever they were going."

"Just bet she did," Jake said.

"Damned TSP is a soap opera lately. Heard that Jack MacGregor has been sniffing around Madison this week, Dom. You might want to go all *brotherly* and give him a warning. Seems the ladies all have a thing for him. Almost as bad as they do the Naylor brothers. It's the blue eyes, apparently."

Dom gave a truly vicious smile. Jake just waited for the man to start cracking his knuckles. "Already taken care of. I like the guy, but he has no business looking at Madison that way. Now he knows."

"You know, she's eventually going to file a restraining order against your ass. And I wouldn't blame her. I'll even take the report," Jake said. MacGregor wasn't the first guy at the TSP Dom had had a talk with about Madison. Jake suspected he wouldn't be the last. "By the way, she's right there in the back booth with Shelby. In case you want to talk to her about it. I'll call her over, if you'd like."

Dom swore and turned—just like Jake had known he would. The guy had it really bad. Jake had been watching that table most of the night himself. He was supposed to be doing guard duty tonight, after all. Watching them wasn't a hardship.

Shelby was the least outgoing of her group, followed by her friend Zoey. When she smiled, every inch of her lit up.

"Beautiful women back there," Gunnar said, eyeing them with interest. "All of them. Charlie, you still beating them off Chuck Junior with a stick? Think I'd have a shot with her now?"

"Keep your eyes off my kid, you shit. You're not good enough for her." Charlie was around ten or twelve years older than Jake and the rest of the guys. He didn't look old enough to have a daughter who was only three or four years away from thirty. He did. Even if neither one of them were too happy about it.

He'd told Jake the story once. Charlie had met a much older woman when he'd been twenty-one and visiting family in Wyoming. It had lasted three weeks, and they'd never told anyone. Nor had he ever seen her again.

Then he'd come home to Texas, leaving her behind in Wyoming. With a little gift—a gift she hadn't bothered to track him down to tell him about.

Chuckie had tracked him down using a family DNA service after her mother's death. She'd literally shown up on Charlie's front steps, saying, "Hello, I believe you are my father. What do you want to do about it?"

He suspected Charlie had told her *nothing*. But Chuckie had stuck around.

"Heard she was going out with that Barratt guy from the prosecutor's office now," Gunnar said. "That true?"

"Those damned Barratts get around. Madison had a date

with one two days ago," Dom almost snarled. "Damned poachers."

Jake snorted. *Those damned Barratts* was a good way to put it. Sniffing around where they shouldn't be. They should stick to their own pond. The mayor had already scooped up Jake's Annie, and his cousin had grabbed Jake's former partner in Homicide a while back. And if he wasn't mistaken, the forensic supervisor Bailey had married a Barratt first cousin.

Why did the Barratts keep fishing from the TSP pond? They should stick to their own kind.

Then again...their own kind would be Shelby. He didn't like that idea at all. His scowl deepened just thinking about it. "What in the hell are we doing here, talking random women's love lives?"

"They aren't random," Dom said. Dom was watching Madison, like a fool. The guy should just go for it already and stop being such a coward.

The worst she could do was tell Dom to go jump off the pier at the Value Reservoir. Which she did on a weekly basis as it was. So not much difference there.

"I'm not discussing her love life. I'm just making sure she doesn't get involved with some asshole," Charlie said, shortly, dumping his half-eaten plate into a to-go box. "As far as I'm concerned, she should marry a rich guy instead of a cop. Be set for life. Get out of the business completely. Maybe even out of the city. Go back to her *family* in Wyoming. Where she belongs."

"Fields here is uniquely positioned to recognize assholes, since he is one himself where women are concerned," Gunnar said. "Apparently, that extends to his daughter."

Charlie practically snarled. Well, someone had his shorts in a bunch.

The women finally stood to leave. Jake straightened. He turned to his friends. "That is my cue. Time to go babysit the pretty lady."

Gunnar leaned forward. "I will trade you places with her in a heartbeat. Hell, I'll give you every penny in my savings if you suddenly develop appendicitis and I need to take your place. Right now. That woman is worth it. Totally worth it. How about you put in a good word for me? I'll marry her and carry her off into the sunset. We'll live happily ever after and have twelve kids, six dogs, and one cat to lord over them all. We'll...name the cat Earl. And two kids can be Jake and Jacob. Just let me have her."

Jake barely resisted the urge to ram his fist into Gunnar's face.

"Can it, Erickson. Shelby is Jake's girl," Dom said, quietly, leaning forward. "He's just too stupid to see it yet."

"Oh, I see it. And I want her. I'm the last man that woman ever needs screwing up her life. She's not made for a man like me. Like us. Best just keep that in mind. She's better off with one of those damned Barratts. Same world and all that shit."

Jake tossed his share of the tip on the table. And waited. Shelby and her friends had to walk right by where he stood.

He watched her as she looked up at him. As their eyes met. She had a smile on her face as she listened to Madison. Jake could almost fool himself into believing she was walking toward *him* willingly.

Like Daryn had just walked right into Mike Evers's open arms.

That the smile on her face wasn't just a leftover, but was meant for him. Just him.

Because Shelby did belong to him. And he belonged to her equally as strong.

That was just him being stupid. Shelby was never going to be his. That was never going to happen.

55

ZOEY HAD OFFERED TO SPEND THE NIGHT, BUT SHELBY told her friend no. She needed to deal with Jake herself.

Zoey nodded, and then took off. She was going to camp at Nikkie Jean's to help with the kids in the morning, while Zoey's brother had a meeting with the head of the hospital board. The plan had been she'd stay with Shelby and drive to Nikkie Jean's in the morning, but...plans could change.

Zoey lived far away, but she visited when she could. Her friend worked long hours as the sheriff of the small Garrity region of the TSP. The only real personal time she'd been able to carve out was the nights of the choir practices. She did that mostly for Pen—and her twin niece and nephew, who were almost nine now, Nikkie Jean's children. Plus, she loved visiting with Nikkie Jean's infants and preschooler. They were handfuls. Beautiful, but handfuls.

Zoey loved spending time with the kids, even if building relationships with her half-siblings had been very difficult for her. Zoey was closer to Nikkie Jean—thanks to Nikkie Jean's relationship with Shelby—than she was any of her brothers or her other sisters.

Zoey was used to being alone. With the exception of Daryn and Shelby and Pen, that was. Tonight had been a good night —for all of them. Sometimes, Shelby thought Zoey needed to get out of her shell just as much as Shelby did. To enjoy the world.

They both had their fears, apparently.

She didn't say anything as Jake drove through the streets to her neighborhood. She'd ridden to the diner with Zoey. Jake had tried to protest, saying he was supposed to be protecting her.

Well, he was just a lieutenant commander—Zoey was an actual sheriff. Her friend had just as much ability as he did to do guard duty. Zoey was higher on the hierarchy—Shelby rather liked that fact.

He hadn't liked that when they'd pointed it out. But he'd backed down. She sensed he was playing nice. Jake was wanting to get back in her good graces, after all.

She wasn't stupid. He would do whatever he needed to win whatever game it was he was playing.

Well, surprise. Shelby wasn't playing with Jake ever again.

She didn't bother talking to him even once on the ride to her home. Jake wouldn't admit to anyone how much that stung.

"So is this the way it's going to be?" he asked as she unlocked the five locks on her door. It took her a minute. Then she disengaged the new alarm system from Houghton Barratt's company. Jake fought the impatience.

She turned to him in the entryway.

Damn, she looked good.

He wanted to lift her off her feet and carry her to the nearest flat surface. Show her what she did to him. Apologize to her with his entire damned body.

He wasn't that stupid, though. He'd meant what he said. She wasn't the kind of woman a man like him messed with. She needed someone…better.

At least, better for her. Someone less rough around the edges than him. Someone more refined. Maybe a doctor or a lawyer. Or one of those damned Barratts that were always everywhere now.

He could see her as a rich man's wife. Why not? She was a rich woman. She'd wear silk and pearls as easily as women like Izzie and Annie wore denim and cotton T-shirts.

She'd host dinner parties in this mausoleum of hers. They'd laugh at refined jokes while drinking specialty wines. While the kitchen staff served them the three- hundred-dollar-a-plate dinners.

A man like him had no business in a life like that.

The house around him echoed what he was thinking. Jake knew that was stupid, but he felt it.

Even in the children's choir T-shirt she wore and the jeans that cupped the most feminine ass he had ever seen, it was obvious.

Hell, Shelby was just too *good* for him.

They both saw that. A sharp pain went through him at that thought.

There was no point in him looking at her like he was.

Nothing would ever come of it. He had to stop fooling himself.

Before he did something else stupid that hurt her more than that damned search warrant ever could have.

"What will what be?" She dropped her bag on the armchair in the family room she seemed to favor. The house was more than twelve thousand square feet, but she used very little of it.

He had figured out her habits quick. There were some rooms that just felt more like *her* than others.

The front family room was one of them. The furnishing in there was of high quality, like all of that in the house, but it was obviously a little more welcoming.

More comfortable.

She had books everywhere in the room. Fiction, mostly. Shelby liked to read. A lot. Though she hadn't since he'd started tagging along with her.

Mostly, she disappeared into her bedroom and left him to his a few doors down.

He wanted to get into that room with her.

He wanted to have the right to pull that T-shirt right off her and just let it land where it landed. And every other stitch of clothing that covered that beautiful body from his sight.

He wanted her so bad he hurt. Deep down, where only a man's soul could ache.

He wanted her. He would never have her. It was time he accepted that.

Somehow.

Jake didn't think he could just let her walk away tonight. Not after seeing the soft part of her, the part he doubted she let others see that often. Jake pulled in a breath, and then stepped closer to her.

He wrapped his hands around her.

"J-J-Jake?" She looked up at him, those stormy eyes of hers gray tonight. "What are...are you do...do...doing?"

He'd made her nervous.

Good.

He needed to know he made her feel something for him. Even just a little. Something that wasn't just disgust and anger.

"Just let me kiss you tonight, Shelby Grace. I need to...more than I have ever needed anything ever."

He knew he wasn't making any damned sense.

Her hands spread over his chest. She didn't shove him away.

Damn, she felt perfect in his arms.

Perfect.

This woman was as close to perfect as he had ever seen. Making his sorry ass the furthest thing she would ever need. "Just one kiss. I need to kiss you, Shelby. Please, let me..."

Hell, of course he would beg. He wanted her enough to throw all pride away.

Did she understand that? She just kept staring at him. Jake stayed where he was. Waiting. Watching. Wanting.

Her lips firmed. His mouth went dry.

And then, she destroyed him.

She shook her head. Stepped back.

"No. I don't think...that's a good idea. Not...I just don't. You'll hurt me again, Jake. And I don't deserve that. Ever. I...am going to my room now. I suggest you go to yours."

The hardest thing he had ever done was watch the woman he wanted more than he wanted breath turn and walk away. From him.

Because she was afraid he'd hurt her.

Again.

Hell, he knew the truth.

He wouldn't mean to—but he probably would.

56

SHE CRIED. SHELBY CURLED UP IN HER BED, KNOWING he was just a few walls away, and she cried. Because for one moment there, it had felt right to have his arms slip around her.

Jake's.

That…that was so insane.

She had almost said yes. Almost let him kiss her, against her better judgment.

He wanted to have sex with her. She wasn't stupid. She knew when a man was seriously attracted and when he was just flirting around.

Jake wasn't just joking around now.

Well, Shelby wouldn't be a number in his que. That wasn't going to happen.

She wasn't going to let herself be hurt by Jake again. She had to remember that. She just had to.

She finally drifted off well after midnight.

She didn't wake until harsh pounding sounded on her door.

SHELBY WAS DRESSED IN THIN, PINK PAJAMAS THAT had to be silk. Jake's mouth went instantly dry. Her hair was tangled around her head in a way that made him wish he had been the one to tangle it. With his fingers, while holding her still for his kiss. And other things.

He had always loved long hair on women. Not for any antiquated cultural beliefs that women should have long hair and men short—far from it.

It was because, as a man, he loved touching soft, silky hair.

He really was a caveman at heart. And he owned it.

"What... what... what has happened?" she asked, around a yawn. Her eyes were wary when she looked at him.

"I got called out. A case I've been working on for years. I got to go. Just for a while."

"Ok...Just...I'll lock the doors after you leave."

"Not happening. I'm not leaving you here alone while I go out and chase bad guys." He couldn't help himself. Jake found his hands going to each side of her waist. He turned her slightly, pulled her closer.

She wasn't resistant.

Shelby wasn't fully willing, either.

He couldn't help himself. He liked to touch.

Still, he dropped his hands immediately. "I've called someone I trust to come stay until I get back."

Her storm-blue eyes widened. Her pink lips trembled. "Jake..."

"I know. Not what you want. And I am seriously sorry about it. I would have called your little sheriff friend, but...well...she scares the hell out of me. I think she'd fry my balls with barbecue sauce if I wake her up."

That got the smallest of smiles out of her. "Probably. Zoey is a bit overprotective."

He cupped her cheek, just wanting to feel the softness of her. "I can understand why. You inspire that in people."

A look he couldn't interpret passed over her face. "I don't want to. I can take care of myself just fine."

"I know. Anyway...as much as I'd love to stand right here and see if those jammies are as soft as your skin, I got to go. Dom is waiting. He's the crankiest sonofabitch I have ever known when he doesn't get his eight hours. Eight o'clock bedtime, I swear. Should probably warn Madison about that eventually."

"Who...who...who did you call?"

"Callum. He owes me a favor. And since he thinks you are the Goddess of All Things Not Autumn Jane, and you are the most wonderful woman in the world after his precious Autumn Jane, he was more than willing to come help me out. He'll be here in about fifteen minutes. I didn't want to just leave and him be here if you wake."

She nodded. "I'll...put on a robe."

"Probably wouldn't hurt. A really thick, old, unattractive one would work. You are tempting me."

"You can stop the innuendos."

"Why? Aren't they just innuendos if they are on the sly? I mean what I say."

"We've known each other for how long? Since before the storm, at least? And now you are suddenly attracted to me? I don't think so; you are just trying to play me. I'm not going to be stupid anymore."

"Oh, baby girl, I was attracted to you from the first moment I held open the door for you that day at W4HAV. Bad. I just know that I am not the kind of guy meant for you."

She gave a delicate little snort. "Please...what you mean is that I am not the kind of woman who is good enough for *you*. I know what you have always thought about me. Why sugarcoat it?"

Jake just gawked at her like an idiot.

Her...not good enough for him? Hell, that was the furthest from what he felt.

He didn't have time to go into why.

Not now.

Still, he couldn't let her think that. Not even if it made things easy for him.

"Hardly. It's that I am not ever going to be good enough...for *you*." He brushed a soft kiss against those perfect pink lips.

Just because he had to.

He wanted her more than he had ever wanted any other woman in the world.

That was something he would never tell her.

"Grab your robe. That doofus Callum is usually early for everything. He'll probably be here at any minute."

57

VICTOR HATED WAITING IN CARS, BUT THIS WAS something he wanted to ensure happened as it should.

The body would have to be left in the right place. Victor couldn't afford to be found on security cameras, either.

But the woman had to die.

No one would ever be left alive to help Wallace Henedy, even from behind prison walls.

The man would have no *woman* connected to him alive.

That the attorney in question was just a young woman assigned to Henedy's case mattered little to him.

She was perfectly expendable. And would send the exact message he intended.

Wallace Henedy would never be safe.

No one connected to him would, either.

For a moment, he imagined Wallace's face as he learned his beloved son Reggie, Wallace Reginald Henedy, Junior, was dead.

Victor imagined doing it himself.

Watching as his son's old friend, his son's closest friend, died on the damned rug like an animal. At Victor's feet. In his early grief over Kyle, he had planned to do just that.

Kill Reggie.

Dead by Victor's hand.

Not with a gun. No. He would want Wallace and Jennifer's son to suffer.

A knife, perhaps.

Victor always had enjoyed using a knife for close work.

The first man he had ever killed had died from blood loss.

Victor still had that knife in his collection.

He thought about the people he had hurt through the years, wondered if their loved ones' pain was anything like his own.

Maybe it was fate paying him back now for his sins of before?

Maybe he should just kill Reggie and move on. Then take out Wallace as he intended to take out Wallace's bitch of a wife.

And then move on to the next world himself?

But no.

Kyle had loved Reggie in his own way. And that mattered.

He would not do that to his son, even now. Harming Reggie would be something Kyle would never have condoned. It would have hurt Kyel to lose his friend like that.

Victor would not do that.

He would stick to his plan. The future of the Scott family depended on it.

The front passenger door to the Lincoln opened. Dave looked at Victor and Kessler, who was driving.

"It's done. She's dead."

"Good," Victor said. He said a small prayer for the woman's lost soul to himself.

He had borne her no true ill-will. It was just bad luck or fate that it was this young woman assigned to Wallace's case.

But this… this was exactly what Wallace deserved.

"Home, Kessler. I have plans for the morning." He had two more women to evaluate.

He needed to stick to the plan.

58

DOM STARED AT THE WOMAN'S DEAD BODY, KEEPING A flashlight pointed on her as he waited for the night shift crime scene techs to arrive.

It wouldn't be Madison. She worked the eight a.m. to four p.m. shift every Tuesday through Saturday, taking Sunday and Monday off each week. He knew her schedule as well as he knew his own.

The woman dead at his feet bore a resemblance to Madison.

They were of the same age range, the same build. Same hairstyle. She wore a blouse similar to the one Madison had worn this evening while out with her friends. White with little ruffles around the sleeves. Ruffles that made a man want to touch.

It was the glasses that had struck him first. The victim had glasses lying next to her. Glasses very similar to Madison's.

He bit back a curse.

Someone out there would be missing her soon. If they weren't already.

He wanted to be able to give them the answers to the questions they wouldn't be able to not ask.

Dom had recognized the name when the ID had been made.

He'd heard of her before. A *defense* attorney. For Wallace Henedy.

His newest.

Since the death of his previous attorney under suspicious circumstances four weeks ago. She was the third female attorney of Wallace Henedy to be killed.

Hell, if she'd made it to her thirtieth birthday, he'd be surprised.

There was an engagement ring on her left ring finger.

Someone...loved her.

Dom was going to destroy some other man's world tonight. Or woman's. What mattered was someone had lost someone they loved—and Dom would have to tell them.

Why? Why would such a young woman be tossed aside like trash?

She'd been found inside the courthouse next to the damned custodial closet.

It looked like a professional hit, too. Neck twisted just right, and she was dead instantly. Too damned small and vulnerable to have put up a fight.

Damn it.

This was the fourth such hit in two years, just in Finley Creek County. There had been a few in Wichita Falls and Brownsville as well.

If it was connected at all.

Jake finally showed up. He'd had to get someone he trusted in to babysit Shelby. After this—no one was taking chances with anyone involved with the Henedy case. Period.

Jake's weak excuse to be with Shelby had just gotten a hell of a lot stronger.

"Who stayed with her?"

"I woke Callum's ass up. He's off the clock, but he owed me a favor. And she reasonably trusts him."

"Good." Dom got down to business. "Think you are back on

the clock after this."

"We sure this is connected?"

"I wouldn't have called you out away from Shelby if I wasn't. We just got to prove it."

This was just another shit show in their quest to bring down the men bent on using Finley Creek as the heart of their organized crime activity.

It was just a matter of time.

Shelby didn't know what else to do with Sean Callum.

So she served him coffee. Callum would always make her nervous—he'd been one of the main interviewers after Logan's death, and he'd been pushy and rude—and had terrified her. Flat out terrified her.

It had taken her a while to get past that.

Shelby had made herself a vow.

She was going to stop painting every member of the TSP with the evil brush. They weren't all that way. There were good ones out there. Callum and Mike had just been doing their jobs.

Mel had been TSP, and she was one of the nicest, kindest, funniest, most *trustworthy* women Shelby had ever met.

And then there was Zoey.

Shelby had to stop seeing everyone the same. Friend or threat. That made her no different than Jake and his disgust for everyone with a bigger bank account than his. She wasn't going to keep being like that.

Not all apples were rotten.

Shelby knew that. Her biggest issue was that *she* just wasn't good at telling who was rotten and who was not. It wasn't everyone else she didn't trust—it was her own judgment.

Jake was proof of that problem.

"Thanks, Shelby. I will admit it: I'm exhausted. I don't know how Autumn Jane keeps going, but that woman has more determination and energy than anyone I've ever seen. Shouldn't she be like all crashed out? It hasn't even been a month. I'm exhausted just thinking of all the things that woman has done. After she gave birth."

"Probably autopilot." Shelby loved the way he looked when he talked about his wife. He never called her A.J. like everyone else. And when he talked about her, his eyes lit up.

He loved her. Down to his soul, loved her.

It was a beautiful story that she'd heard before. Callum's partner was A.J.'s brother—Daryn's husband, Mike—and best friend. Callum had had a thing for A.J. for years. And didn't act on it until the storm. He was one of the biggest players in the TSP, Daryn had told her.

A.J.—his best friend's baby sister—had terrified him. But he had loved her.

They had been trapped under a table in the annex together during the aftermath of the storm. Shelby had dug them both out herself.

Callum had made a point of trying to connect with Shelby since then. She'd been reticent—but he didn't scare her nearly as much as he used to. She was making progress.

Shelby didn't *want* to be afraid of every man connected to the TSP.

She wasn't going to be.

He showed her photos of his daughter, Audrea Shelby Callum. She was a homely little thing, who looked a bit too much like a cross between her father and her uncle Mike. Hopefully, once she lost the newborn look, she'd look more like her mother. Shelby *really* hoped that happened.

Callum was definitely a proud, besotted daddy, though. Envy shot through her. "She's so beautiful."

"Really? I mean, she's my kid and all so I think she's perfect.

But she looks like a wrinkled old man. Or that thing in the *Lord of the Rings* that kept saying precious. I told Autumn I thought she looked a bit like a troll or an orc with the wild hair everywhere and the scrunched up face like that. No matter what I do, the hair keeps sticking straight up. I tried slicking it down a few times so it doesn't grow that way forever. I mean, she has a Mohawk already. Autumn wasn't amused by anything I said."

He was absolutely serious.

"I can't wait until my niece or nephew is born."

"Yeah, Jake mentioned Izzie is pregnant. Tell her congrats for me, ok? She'll be a great mom."

"Yes. They didn't want to wait too long. Said they want several." February. Her niece or nephew was due on Valentine's Day. Shelby thought that was absolutely perfect.

"Yeah, Autumn Jane says at least one more. I'm thinking four or five years down the road. When I start sleeping again at night. I do want at least one more, too. There…when they put her in my arms for the first time—there is never another feeling like it. And now…I have a baby girl. With the woman I adore. Life doesn't get any better than this."

In that moment, all her nerves and anxiety associated with this man just evaporated. Yes. She'd never be leery or afraid of Sean Callum again.

He had a suspicious spit-up spot on his left shoulder. The shirt he wore was buttoned wrong. She didn't have the heart to tell him it was inside out, too. Shelby didn't know how he had even managed that. His hair probably hadn't been combed in the three weeks since his daughter's birth. And he looked utterly content with his life.

She envied him that, too. She would find that for herself. As soon as she possibly could.

"So what do you do in this place all day?" Callum asked, looking around. "I do like the changes you've made. Makes it seem brighter."

She wouldn't touch that with a ten-foot pole. The last time he'd been there had been after Logan's death. He'd been one there to give her the keys when it had *finally* been released to her.

Callum and Daniel.

She'd had to get her attorneys involved. Make threats. The TSP had held Logan's estate as evidence of a crime—with no reason to back it up. For well over a year. Only to tell her "clerical error" once she'd pushed hard enough to finally get attention.

They'd said it had been automated—with the wrong date entered. Yeah, right.

She'd had to confront Elliot Marshall herself, right there in Mel's dining room in front of her brother and his and everyone else. To put Elliot on the spot, with just Powell next to her, demanding answers.

Shelby had gotten possession of the house within the week after that. One month before the storm. Elliot moved mountains. That was for sure.

Logan hadn't been involved in Banks Claireson's drug manufacturing or trafficking organization. She'd read all of Logan's journals. He had barely mentioned Banks at all. Just in passing.

He hadn't mentioned Lacy McGareth even once, either. Not even in passing. Even though he'd almost killed her the day he had died.

Mostly his journals had been him venting and rambling. Being lonely. Logan had been so lonely.

Guilt shot through her.

Some of that...some of that was her fault. Most of it.

That was a secret she and Logan had shared. Something intimate between them that not even Allen had known about. Would *never* know about.

"Mostly, I try to stay busy. I do...do...do a lot of work for

W4HAV charities outside of my hours on the clock there. I have a home office here that I use."

"It's a good place. It's helped a lot of people."

"It has. And thanks to Logan, I have enough money now to help in a significant way. We're branching out into services for male victims, and children. I work with Mel Barratt for almost twenty hours a week, deciding what charities we can help. Until this week. She wants me to take this week off and deal...with this."

Mel had gone one step further. She'd asked Shelby if she wanted to go to St. Louis and stay with the man who had first bankrolled W4HAV; Zoey's brother, Luc. He had offered her a place to stay instantly. Said his siblings' besties were always welcome with him. No questions asked.

Mel had promised Shelby would be safe there. Just like Mel's husband Houghton had promised she would be if she chose to stay with him and Mel for a while.

It had been tempting. She'd be safe. All she had to do was say yes.

She had to face things. It was important that she did just that. Her counselors through the years had reiterated it and reiterated it.

No more running. No more hiding.

Face her problems. No matter what.

"How did you get into search and rescue? I am beyond grateful that you did."

Shelby put down her soda. She didn't ever drink coffee past ten in the morning. "I...had...had...something bad happen to me. When I was twenty-one."

"I've heard parts of the story, Shelby. I'm not going to lie to you. Daryn ripped into me one day and spilled. I know what happened to her. And that you were a part of it."

There was no judgment in his hazel eyes. No pity. Just understanding. In another life, maybe she could have considered this man a real friend. Like she did Darrell. "It's Daryn's story, too."

"I'm sorry that happened to you. I wish I could have been there. I would have stopped it. When I think that it could have been Autumn Jane there that day. Or any woman I care about. Or heaven help me, if something like that happened to my little girl...they shouldn't have done that to you. And I'm sorry it was the TSP that did it."

"I...thank you. We didn't even know what we were walking into." Maybe it was the lateness of the hour, or the coffee and almost intimacy of having him in her kitchen. Or maybe it was that there was no judgment, and maybe she was just finally able to talk about it without hurting so deeply. The words just came out. "Daryn and I were the classic nerds. Geeky, awkward. I had braces and pimples until the year before. Daryn wasn't much better; always face down in books. I had never been to a party with alcohol before, either. I was completely naive about every-thing like that. Allen...kept me sheltered. Logan...I knew he was close. We'd passed this house on our way there. I knew he was home. I'd seen him pull in. And...he became my hope. My hero. I know he got involved in things he shouldn't have after. And I will always hurt for Jillian and Izzie and Lacy and the others that he hurt. But..."

"I am sorry you lost him. I'm sorry for the whole damned situation, for everyone involved. I'm not sorry he was there that day for you when you needed him. And if you ever want to tell me their names, I'll find them for you. Find out where they are. So they won't ever hurt you again."

Shelby stared at him. Judged. Made a decision. "I hired a detective once I inherited Logan's estate—once the TSP finally released it to me, anyway. He's...he's going to find them for me. At least, find their names. They may be out there right now hurting someone else. And I don't even know their names. I gave a report and it just...went away. Disappeared like it never existed. Logan started hunting for them right after. I have what he found...and...my investigator is looking for more. They are a part of the TSP—who is ever going to stop them? Except someone with money and power because of it? I just want their names."

Callum sat his coffee on the table. "Does Jake know you have someone looking into this?"

Shelby exhaled slowly. "No. It's none of Jake MacNamara's business. Please don't tell him. I don't think he'd care anyway. He's on a quest to destroy Logan's ghost right now for revenge for what Logan did to Izzie. He won't care about anyone living—or anything *good* Logan might have been trying to do. At least... he doesn't care about anyone not Izzie or Annie. I have people I trust who can help me. Charlotte and Madison and Haldyn, too. Powell, my attorney. They are all helping me. I'm not doing this alone. And Zoey, she is helping me, too."

"I think you should still let Jake know. He'd want to. Want to help, for one thing."

Shelby just shook her head. "Jake...and I... no. I'm not telling him anything. Not about Logan. Please don't tell him yourself."

"I won't. What do you plan to do with the information if you find it?"

"I have someone looking into them. And when or if I find something important, I know who I am going to give that to. It won't be the TSP; I know that. No offense." It would be Paige, Zoey's older sister. Paige was with the FBI. Paige would know what to do with it. It would be finished then. "If I find them... maybe other women will come forward. I have to do something. I should have done something sooner. Something to make them stop. They may have hurt others in the years since."

That was what hurt her the most. She had just...frozen. For far too long. Become useless. *Voiceless.*

"It's not your *job* to stop them, Shelby. It never was."

"I just want to know their names, Sean. So that I don't have to constantly look over my shoulder. That's it." Once she knew who they were, Shelby would put it behind her forever. "Once I know that, I...can sleep at night again. I barely sleep at night now, you know. I can't. I can't stop seeing ghosts in every corner. I haven't slept a full night in almost six years."

She'd finally be able to *move on*.

She had to take control of her life again. That was the one thing Logan had asked of her in the letter he'd included with his will.

To start living again. To not be so afraid she missed out on real life, love.

Logan had wanted her to have a life filled with *love*.

He'd wanted her to have that kind of love so much she had ached reading his final words to her.

This was how she'd chosen to start. She needed to finish this. For her—and for Logan. It had robbed him of something vital, too.

He had changed after that night. Became darker. Far more broken.

Shelby was probably the only one in the world who had ever known why.

It had been because of *her*.

She had no doubt those monsters had hurt other women. Five years ago, she had not been emotionally equipped for the fight to stop them.

If she would have even been able to. The TSP was a broken organization in many ways. Especially then. Mel had told her that herself—Mel, whose sister's brother-in-law was the Finley Creek chief.

He was trying to fix it.

There was hope on the horizon.

There hadn't been five years ago.

Callum stood, then knelt down a bit in front of her. Shelby

forced herself not to shy away. He was still a big man, and in her space. She would never be comfortable with that.

"Jake...there is nothing that man won't do for you, Shelby. I know you're angry with him, but remember that. You can trust him with this. I promise. I think you should tell him. You don't have to do this alone. He can help you, better than anyone."

She shook her head. "It's none of his business. At all. Please don't tell him. And I'm not alone. I have my friends now."

He hesitated. "I won't. But...if you need me, all you have to do is ask. I promise you that. Just ask, and I'll come running; Mike, too. We're your friends, too. Don't forget that. Tell Jake. Promise me you'll at least consider it."

Shelby just nodded. There really wasn't much else to say.

The last thing she was going to do was tell Jake MacNamara anything.

59

Someone had targeted Wallace Henedy's defense attorney. Jake stared at the woman's case files spread over her home office, but kept his paws off them. Client-attorney privilege was a damned real thing. And with Henedy's association, he wasn't going to be allowed to proceed on this case either.

Damn it.

They'd have to turn it over fully to Homicide. That was the last thing he wanted to do, but it was the way the game was played. MacGregor was taking over now.

She had been twenty-nine and engaged to a man in her office. Jake had been there when the fiance learned of her death.

Devastation. Utter devastation.

The man had lost his world tonight. Jake would never forget that.

They had a little girl together. Two years old, big dark eyes and dark silky curls. Hell, she'd reminded him of Izzie at that same age.

Her father had taken her out of the house tonight, back to

his parents'. Because the baby's mother would never be coming home again.

It had been the love in the man's eyes that stuck with him the most.

He made it back to Shelby's near three a.m.

Jake parked, then hurried up the sidewalk. He wanted to see her. Needed to.

He just needed to, tonight. Make sure she was ok, where she was supposed to be. Safe.

He'd sneak in and check on her while she slept. She'd never even know he was there. Just...he needed to look at her just once tonight.

Callum met him at the door at his text.

"She's curled up in her study. Fell asleep about an hour ago. I think I made her nervous being here," Callum said. "You good?"

"I'm off the case now. The woman was Henedy's newest attorney. So I can't officially touch it. Over to Homicide."

"Shit. I've met her a time or two. Nice lady. Nice family."

"I know. Saw them tonight myself."

"I'm sorry. That sucks. Any leads?"

Jake shook his head. "I think it was contracted. Homicide is going to have to find out why. Major Crimes is off it. Back to... what we need to do." Jake headed down the hall.

He needed to see her. Just look at her and know she was safe tonight.

"Pretty swanky place here," Callum said quietly behind him. "Pretty quiet, too. I think it would drive me crazy. The quiet. I don't even think there's a TV on this floor. Piss-poor security, though. She needs a full-time security team, Jake. An actual bodyguard. Hell, that piano upstairs alone probably cost well over a quarter of a million. The paintings on the wall could finance Audrea's full college education at an Ivy League. You might convince her to get a personal guard soon. Besides you."

Jake barely listened to him. She had the doors to her office closed, but there were windows in the French doors that separated her from the rest of the first level. He could see her. Right there. Her arms pillowed her head.

Her hair was spread over her shoulders and hid her face from him.

Hell, she was gorgeous. Real. So damned real.

"She has fought some tough odds. Don't do anything else to hurt her. You'll have me—and Mike and Darrell—to answer to if you do. I'll stomp your face in."

Jake just grunted. "I never wanted to hurt her to begin with."

"You sure about that? She's convinced you are lashing out at Logan Lanning's ghost, and using her to do it. Her words, by the way. You screwup."

"It probably does seem that way to her. I've screwed up. I'm doing the best I can." Didn't people get that? The last thing he wanted was to hurt her, and he was the kind of man who inevitably *would.*

"No kidding. But...so is she. She's a stronger woman than I think even she realizes. Don't destroy that. And I think you probably can. Have already started to with that dumbass move of yours. That was stupid. Any guy after a girl should have realized that."

Callum always had liked to bust his chops. "Well, I had to do what I had to do. Who are you to talk? You waited on A.J. for years. Coward."

"Bullshit. That's all I am saying." Callum looked at Shelby, an odd expression on his face.

"What?"

"She's more determined than I think you realize. Keep a close eye on her. And make certain that whatever she's doing doesn't get her hurt. Keep her safe, Jake. No matter what."

"What in the hell are you talking about? What is she doing? This have anything to do with the case?"

Callum shook his head. He followed Jake into the massive kitchen. Jake grabbed a soda from Shelby's stash for himself and handed one to the other man. "No. That doesn't change the fact that some assholes hurt her. And they are in the TSP. It's waited this long, but it won't wait forever. The idea that my sister-in-law and my *wife* go to work with some of those assholes every day? It makes me sick to think about it."

"Tell me."

"I can't betray confidences, man. Don't hurt her again, Jake. Or I'll break your face myself. That woman in there—hell, if I didn't have Autumn Jane, I'm not so certain I wouldn't be fighting you for her now. She's too good for the likes of you— even if she does catch fire when your name is mentioned. Although not exactly in a good way."

Like that was something he hadn't heard before. "No shit. You think I haven't known that from the moment I first saw her? A woman like that, who has a life like this? Hell, I was born in a three-room cottage with holes in the roof and thirty-year-old carpet. That's part of the problem. I'm no good for her."

"That's the dumbest thing I have ever heard you say. I think she just needs a guy she can trust more than anything else. You just need to decide if you can be that kind of guy, really."

After Callum left, Jake stood in the door to the study where she was sleeping, and just watched her.

60

THERE WERE HANDS ON HER. SHELBY JERKED AWAKE and bit back a scream. She stared right into the dark eyes less than a foot away from her. Her heart settled back into her chest.

Oh. He was back. The devil. "Jake. What time is it?"

She sat up straighter and rubbed one hand over her eyes.

"Around four. I just sent Callum home. Figured you'd wake up sore if you stayed here much longer."

There was an odd expression in his eyes. Somehow, his hands were on her, and he was pulling her to her feet. "Jake?"

Hard arms wrapped around her. She was pulled to his chest. He squeezed her. Tight. Almost too tight. "What are you doing?"

"I...just...don't bite my head off, baby. I just need to touch you tonight."

"What for?" She wanted to wrap her arms around him and hold him back. Shelby knew that about herself. She needed someone to hold her sometimes, too.

The middle of the night, especially.

She didn't trust Jake—or his motivations. Not for one moment.

She hated being alone, too. Shelby almost softened against him.

Almost.

This was the last man on earth she was going to trust. She just couldn't.

He could hurt her too much if she did. "What are you doing?"

He brushed a kiss against her forehead, then sighed. Stepped back.

"I screwed it up completely, didn't I?"

"What did you expect before? That I was just going to fall into your arms? What? You decided you were wrong about me so you'd just kiss me a few times and everything would be ok between us? Or...or...or you thought you'd kiss me and I'd let you tear right into whatever Logan left in this house that you didn't find the first time? I'm not all that experienced with guys, Jake. We both know that, but I'm not that stupid. And I'm not that easy. The next man I get involved with will be one that I can trust. Absolutely."

"You planning on getting involved with anyone soon?" He almost taunted. Becoming the old Jake again.

Yes. That was what it was. He'd thought she'd just fall for his charm, give him whatever he wanted. This man didn't really know her at all. Or he was accustomed to women who did fall for it.

Shelby jerked her chin up. Gave him as cold a smile as she possibly could. "Actually, I have a date in a few days."

"Who the hell with?" A look of fury on his face had her stepping behind her desk quickly. She hadn't seen him truly angry before. She wasn't eager to, either. His arms crossed over his broad chest. "Who? And when the hell did this happen?"

"Turner's cousin, Powell's brother. He confirmed with me while you were violating my privacy and my trust. There is a benefit auction for a charity I'm involved in, featuring his mother's sculptures. He asked me at the storm benefit, and I said yes." Of course, she'd said yes. He'd not wanted to go alone— and she believed him when he'd said he was in love with Charlotte's cousin in Wyoming.

Powell's twin brother was *safe.*

He'd be her first real date in almost five years.

She fully intended to enjoy that. And maybe it would be enough to get her brother and sister-in-law off her back about "getting out there" and all that stuff she was so tired of hearing.

"Like hell you're going."

"Like hell I'm not." No. This growling jerk was not going to intimidate her in her own home. It just wasn't going to happen. "I've given my word. And more than that, I like Brandt. He's a wonderful man—who respects me."

"Brandt Barratt? He's a damned playboy. Everyone knows that. He's in the *Snotty Garlic* all the damned time. With a different woman. You want to be just one on a list?"

Playboy? Well, Izzie had called Jake a player. What was the difference? The amount of money in their bank account? Maybe Jake would be so kind as to enlighten her on the subtleties.

"Please, who are you to talk? Izzie told me you've dated at least five women just since the storm. Madison, Charlotte, a woman named Rory, and at least two others. All TSP. You like fishing from the company pond, or so I've heard."

"Because those women get it. Get me. They aren't wrapped up in their ivory tower. They are the kind of woman a man can be himself with. My kind of woman."

And she wasn't. He hadn't said it aloud, but Shelby wasn't stupid.

She got the picture.

"I think you mean *green* tower, Jake. Why lie about it to me? I'm not going to be on your list—because I'm too...too...too rich for your blood. That's what's got you so angry. You want me, but you don't think you can afford me. Because all you ever see is how much money someone has in their pocket. Well, there are good men out there who want to be with me. Respect me. Men that I can like, can care about. I don't care if they are rich or if they are the poorest on the planet. Who are you to tell me that I can't?"

She smirked at him, pushing her tangled hair out of her eyes. She knew she was hitting him right in his ego.

And it felt good. "What are you going to do about it? I don't even want you here to begin with."

61

HE HURT FOR HER SO BAD HIS TEETH ACHED. NEVER had he wanted her more than he did in that moment, with her hair tangled around her shoulders, and the soft pink pajamas and silk robe clinging to her breasts. He wanted his hands on her, his mouth on her. Everything.

He wanted everything with her. The hunger was so strong. His hands were actually trembling. The idea that she had had a date with another man already planned—that just pissed him off. Made him more of an idiot than he should be. "I'm going to kick his ass—that's what."

Storm-gray eyes widened. "What?"

He tensed, readied himself to make his move.

Jake was going to get his hands on her. If just for a little while. "Brandt Barratt, that damned pansy-assed rich guy, can't have you."

"Pansy-assed? He's a black belt in tae kwan do—he and Allen go to the same dojang—and he's bigger, stronger, younger than you. Not everyone has to be 'me warrior, you all bow down before me' like you to be a good man. Maybe you've spent too much time with your poker buddies. And your precious TSP..." Her eyes snapped fire at him. Lightning. "Because the TSP is inviolate, after all. Nothing more p-p-perfect on the planet."

Oh, so she was mad. Letting it out at him with everything she had.

This woman in front of him was real. In every way that mattered.

He would make damned sure Brandt Barratt didn't put his hands on her. If any man was going to get his hands on Shelby anytime soon—it wasn't going to be that wealthy asshole Barratt. It just wasn't going to happen.

"Better than sticking with all the snail-eating set. You looking for a wealthy husband, baby girl? Ready to settle down and make little trust fund babies of your own?"

"Wh-wh-why shouldn't I be? At least, we would have something in common. My kids can play with Izzie's and Annie's, go to the same prep school, even. If I get started quick enough. Maybe he's looking for a wealthy wife? Maybe Brandt and I should compare bank account statements first? His sister Powell could draw up our prenup. That would be con...convenient. What does money have to do with anything? With human decency? Mel and Houghton are richer than anyone I've ever met—yet they are the nicest people on the planet. They do good things. Yet they should be looked down on because of their money? You're a snob, Jake. You judge people by how much money they have. And that's disgusting."

Oh, she was enjoying this.

She hadn't yelled at someone since she'd been a teenager chafing under the restrictions put on her by an overprotective big brother who hadn't truly *known* her at all.

She'd yelled at Logan, too. Yelling, talking, had just been far too difficult when she'd been young.

That had carried over into adulthood. Apparently not with Jake. With him...oh, she wanted to yell so much. More than she ever had before.

Jake was smirking at her. She'd always hated when he looked at her like that. Like he was so superior to her because he had to work for a living. She had never treated him or anyone else as *less* than her because she had Logan's money and they didn't. Ever. "You are nothing but a conceited, arrogant, snobbish ass. And I'd rather be stuck with anyone else right now. I'd rather have Dom...Dom...Dom Acardi or Daniel here. Much better men than you! Why don't you go get one of them for me instead? Maybe I'll date them next. Go slumming like Brianna Claireson wants to with you. When I'm finished working my wiles on Brandt. Daniel has already asked me to the theater, you know. And not the kind with popcorn and Milk Duds. I'll just work my way through Major Crimes, starting with Daniel and going all the way through Charlotte's father!"

"Not going to happen. No mere mortal man gets to deal with you—but *me*." Jake stalked her around her desk. Shelby scooted around it. Behind it. "I'll kill Daniel myself. He can't have you. Can't put his hands on you again. No matter what that nerd wants."

He'd taken her move, her words, as a challenge.

He was *enjoying* himself.

That was not what she had intended.

Shelby moved partially around the desk again. He echoed the movement. She kept going, making almost a full circle before she realized it. Realized what he was doing now.

He was toying with her. Like she was the mouse. The prey.

That was exactly what she was. The Cro-Magnon man's quarry.

He smirked at her. Feinted left. Feinted right. Then he kept coming.

Shelby yelped and took off.

It didn't matter.

She still ran, still tried.

He caught her by the door.

Hard male arms wrapped around her before she got even three feet away. Next thing she knew, they were tripping over the rug, going straight down.

He cursed. His arms went around her, and he lurched to the side.

They landed hard. His hand curved beneath her head, protecting her from striking the floor at the very last minute.

Shelby looked up at him above her. His body was pressed to hers. The scent of warm, spicy male surrounded her. "What... what... what are we doing?"

"I think we're having our first makeup after a fight. I'm not a damned snob." His finger brushed against her bottom lip. "Pretty."

Her mouth went dry immediately. Her lip tingled where he touched. "Jake?"

"If I could have any woman in this world just for me—any, ever—it would be you. I'm old enough to know that I can't always have what I want. And...I'm not the kind of man that's good for you. Everyone can see that. Especially me."

Shelby just blinked up at him. She wished she could believe him. That was at the heart of her anger. She understood that. She'd started to let her guard down with him. And then he proven that she shouldn't have.

Made her doubt her ability to see a man for what he was all over again.

"Why, Jake? What would be in it for you? What would you get...get...get from me?"

Hurt went through the eyes just as dark as Izzie's, so fleeting she almost thought she'd imagined it.

"Is that what you really think of me?"

"You're *always* after something. The end game. I've learned that quick enough. The only times you've ever been decent to me, you've wanted something from me. How do I know you're not just after a little fun in the sack with the rich lady now? That...that you just see me as a prize to win before you move on to the next? Bragging rights or a notch on your belt?"

"You really think I see you that way?"

Shelby shrugged. "Why not? You wouldn't be the first—and you've despised me for Logan's money since the moment we met. What am I supposed to think?"

One hand slipped down to cup her cheek. She couldn't help it—she flinched.

"Oh, baby, I will never hurt you."

Her next words came in a whisper, from deep in her soul. "You already have. I'm not going to let you hurt me again."

"Then push me away. Because I'm not strong enough to let you go of my own free will. I want you too much right now. The things...the things I've seen tonight. I just can't let you go. Not tonight."

It was real pain now. Wild grief in his eyes. His hands were still holding her cheeks. Shelby lifted her own, cupped his left cheek. She just wanted to touch him for a minute.

It was stupid; she knew that.

What was it Nikkie Jean had said once? You were entitled to one stupid thing each decade.

Maybe...maybe this was it.

Jake was her stupid thing.

Shelby just had to decide how much stupid she could live with. "Jake?"

He closed his eyes. His head dropped slightly. To rest against hers for the most fleeting of moments before he pulled back.

She almost thought his eyes were wet when he looked at her again. "She...she was twenty-nine. Had a toddler—and a fiancé who adored her. She was targeted and killed. Just left like trash, like she didn't matter. And...I can't do anything about it. Even go after the men who did it. Because she was Henedy's attorney and it's connected to Izzie's case. And it connects to everything I've been working on for years, and I can't see it destroyed. I can't *do* anything to stop it. But most of all, I can't forget her little girl and how much she looked like Izzie did as a baby."

"Oh, Jake." She could almost reach out and touch his pain. She couldn't stand it. Her arms slipped under his, and she clasped her hands behind his strong back. Her arms almost didn't reach—he was that muscled; she was as close to him as she could get—at least with their clothes still on. She shifted her knees slightly; he was pressing her into the hardwood floor. He settled between her knees.

They just held each other. Silently.

For she didn't know how long. Shelby just...felt he needed to feel a little less alone tonight, too.

That maybe...maybe he felt powerless, too. Her right hand slipped up. Cupped the back of his head.

She just held him close.

62

Hell, he had to be crushing her. Jake couldn't make himself move. Not now. He needed to be right where he was just too damned much. She felt perfect beneath him. If he was a true asshole, he'd pull one knee up and settle himself closer.

It wasn't what he was after. He just stayed where he was, breathing her in. Just for a moment. "Hell, I have to be hurting you."

He rolled to the side, dislodging the arms around him. He ended up next to her on his side. Looking down at her. They were on the damned rug that probably cost more than the first car he'd bought Izzie had. Just lying there.

At least, it was soft. Provided some cushion against the hardwood beneath.

She was looking at him with those eyes designed to steal a man's soul. Questioning.

He felt like an idiot. He hadn't meant to knock her to her damned floor. Not tonight. Her cheeks were red. Her eyes hesitant. Jake wished he was a different kind of man. "I just...sometimes this job gets to me worse than others."

"I can understand. Allen...he's hurt sometimes too. He sees people at the worst times in their lives—just like you do. That changes a person's soul."

That was a good way to put it. He trailed one finger down her cheek again. She shivered. She had the softest, most perfect skin of any woman he had ever touched. His fingers circled her neck. Her pulse raced against his touch.

"Yeah, I suppose he does."

"I'm sorry, Jake. About that woman tonight. And...I didn't mean to yell at you." The fire in her cheeks intensified. He laughed, low.

"You did yell at me, didn't you? I love when you do that. For a moment there, I expected you to start throwing things. I love playing with you. There is a fiery, passionate side of you that you don't show the world. I would love to be the man to enjoy that. Just me."

"You won't be." She said it quietly. "We both know that would be a stupid idea. And I...I...I don't...I can't..."

"I know. I am the last man you need in your life. I am genuinely sorry for the ways I've kept hurting you. That is the last thing I intended. Sometimes, I just get so caught up in the hunt that I don't realize I'm trampling people I care about. And you...I could care about you more than any woman on the planet."

"Because of Izzie."

"Hell, no. Because of this." He took her hand and pressed it against his heart. Where it raced. For her. "Because you are the only woman who makes it beat like this. I knew that within weeks of meeting you for the first time. Definitely when I carried you across the damned hospital parking lot that day—I think that's when it started."

"Why?" Her hand was hooked behind her head, exposing her side. Pulling her shirt tight in all the right places.

He wished he had the right to touch.

He didn't. Jake would force himself to remember that.

Jake didn't have a right to this woman. She wasn't *his*. She never would be.

Some other man would get to free her fire. Would stand next to her forever.

"Why? Because of this." He said to hell with it.

He had kissed her before. But never had it felt like this.

An actual stab of grief went through him. At what he'd lost. What he'd never had. She would never be his. He would have to remember that.

But he would have this moment.

His lips covered hers. His hand slid to her waist. He gripped her there, just to keep his hand from touching places he didn't have permission.

And he kissed her.

Pretended. Lied to himself for just a moment.

Told himself this woman was *his*. That he had a right to her now. He couldn't convince himself, even temporarily.

She would never be his. He was just going to have to accept that.

Somehow.

Never had any woman hurt him more.

63

THE HAIR HAD BEEN WRONG—THE WRONG COLOR, anyway. Madison's was the color of cinnamon. Just like her mother's.

Dom liked to tease her about the red. Madison's curled a bit, where her mother's didn't. Made a man's fingers itch to touch.

He'd wanted to touch Madison long before her mother had captivated his father.

The first time Madison had smarted something off at him when he'd invaded her precious lab, he'd imagined pulling that white lab coat off her and everything beneath and just kissing the sass away right there on her workstation.

Considering he'd literally just met her, that would probably have shocked her.

He'd woken tonight less than an hour after finding his bed, that woman's face in his dreams and Madison in his head.

The dream victim had turned into Madison. He'd seen her lying there in the floor, covered in blood. He'd been helpless to help her. To protect her.

His phone beeped with an incoming email.

He checked it out of habit. Just for the hell of it.

He wasn't going to sleep tonight. Not without knowing Madison was safe and tucked into her little bed in the apartment he'd been to twice. It had smelled like her. Had been decorated in bright, happy colors. It had felt like a home.

Unlike the one he occupied now. He had white walls, tan carpet, and a few football jerseys on those walls. That was it. He didn't even have a damned cat.

There was nothing "home" about it. Not like her place.

Maybe that was why he found himself at his dad's more and more lately. Because his dad, Cherise, and Max were a family.

His family.

Sometimes, Madison was there. Snarking at him while helping her mother peel carrots or something innocent like that. Those nights when they were all there were his favorites.

There were some nights he just had to see her more than others.

Tonight was one of those nights.

The killer had stepped on the victim's glasses. Just crushed them.

Madison wore glasses like that sometimes. Little round wire-rimmed glasses that made her look...cute. Real.

He swore, yanked the blankets back. He wasn't going to lie there in his bed at four a.m. and think of Madison for hours. He'd been there, done that. Madison drove him crazy in his dreams at night. Far more nights than Dom wanted to admit.

She burned him. Straight to his gut.

He would have to find a way to get her out of his head somehow. Eventually. He couldn't go on like this forever—he was getting almost as bad as Jake.

He checked the email. Saw the attachment had finally started downloading.

It was apparently a large one.

He wouldn't be able to read it on his phone. He hated damned cell phones and tolerated computers barely a bit better.

Still, he functioned adequately. Even if Madison did laugh at him occasionally.

Damn it. He wasn't getting her out of his head.

Not tonight.

He might as well get some work done. He opened the first attachment—and began to read.

The photocopied final journal of Dr. Logan Lanning.

Shit. He'd been looking for this for months. Since well before the storm had destroyed a quarter of the city.

From the dates, it was the one written in the year and a half before his death. The period when Banks Claireson, Logan's close friend from high school, had begun his drug manufacturing and trafficking enterprise. An enterprise that had almost gotten the governor's young wife killed. Zoey Daviess's sister.

Everything was connected in Finley Creek—Dom just hadn't figured out how yet.

Dom's heart raced in excitement. Gunnar and Jake would want to see this, as fast as possible. This could be exactly what it was they had needed.

He just kept reading.

Learning about the man who had given Shelby Jacobson everything.

Learned exactly why *her.*

Answered that question.

Hell. Now it made perfect sense.

64

Victor studied the woman in the photos closely. His breath caught. She was physically flawless. Five eight or so, curved beautifully, and excellently groomed. Healthy, intelligent, well connected, wealthy in her own right.

Yes.

She would do nicely, if they found they were compatible.

Her unusual blue-gray eyes were quite riveting. Captivating.

She wore a common cotton T-shirt.

It had the words *Finley Creek Community Children's Choir* emblazoned across a most perfect set of breasts.

She had a half smile across her face. A shy expression that had him wanting to scoop in and rescue her from whatever made her feel insecure.

It had been a long time since he had wanted to protect a woman from anything.

"I didn't realize it before, but she's the woman who is in the photos published after the storm. The one who crawled through the rubble and pulled Chief Marshall free," Kessler said. "Her sister-in-law was the woman Wallace Henedy shot, sir. Izzie Jacobson. I have prepared a file on her. She is also a connection of Jake MacNamara. I thought that would eliminate her from your...plan."

"I know. I have seen him with at her." Victor battled back the rage. "Dinner. I want to have dinner with her. How soon can it be arranged?"

"I am not certain, sir. A week seems sufficient. She is not the type of woman you'll want to rush. I will contact her staff, see if we can arrange something. At the Barratt, perhaps? From all accounts, she's rather reclusive and reserved. Her activities for a typical week are listed in the file as well. From what we can find on social media—she doesn't have an account, other than an email—and news reports. I do have someone waiting on word to continue gathering what they can find."

"Kessler, get me everything you can on her. And do it quickly. By end of today."

The hunter in him stirred to life. A good hunter knew when the *right* prey was before him.

"Yes, sir. I'll see it done."

Victor studied her beautiful face, her sweet expression, the perfect mouth. Yes, he wanted *her*.

Anticipation filled him, like it hadn't since he'd been a young man hunting the woman who had become Kyle's mother. She had suited her purpose adequately until he had learned she found his business partner far more appealing.

Victor hadn't had a business partner since. Nor had he had a wife.

Only this time, it would turn out much better for all involved.

This time...he would get it right.

65

LETTING JAKE KISS HER HAD BEEN STUPID. SHE should have known better. He had been hurting, and Shelby couldn't leave anyone hurting. Not with that kind of pain.

She just couldn't.

They had kissed in the middle of her office rug for what had seemed like hours, but was probably less than ten minutes. It had felt different. Far different than the kisses they'd shared before. She didn't think she had mistaken that.

There had been a connection this time. And that was what scared her the most.

She didn't *like* Jake MacNamara. She certainly didn't trust him.

And she had no business kissing him.

Not even for a moment.

Certainly not sprawled out on her floor beneath him.

Until she had jerked herself away and basically run to the safety of her room.

Shelby had run. That didn't surprise her at all—running from her problems was rather what she did, after all.

His curse had rung out behind her.

To say she hadn't slept well last night was a complete under-statement.

When she finally had drifted off, he had been in her dreams, too. Never had had a man confused her as much as this one.

She was starting to think that he was unique among men in that regard.

She had given him his space that morning before she had told him where she was supposed to be today.

Now he sat at the desk next to the window in the front lobby, his cell phone and laptop in front of him, with one eye pointed toward the door.

Guarding her.

Izzie was there. She'd bought lunch for all of them at the diner up the road. She seemed to sense things were tense between her uncle and Shelby. She hadn't questioned. Shelby knew her sister-in-law was just brimming with those questions.

Izzie didn't ask them, thankfully.

Shelby didn't know what exactly it was she'd say. *Your uncle kissed me like I mattered, even though I know it was just an interlude for him? I'm never going to be the woman for him. Why? Because he thinks I'm not good enough...And I'm tired of never being good enough for the people I care about, no matter how hard I try.*

Yeah, that would go over well for family unity.

Allen showed up a few minutes later, a personal security guard trailing after him to stay in the lobby. Her brother was just in time to finish off the rest of Izzie and Shelby's lunches. He looked haggard. Shelby watched as he quietly wrapped his arms around his wife and held her. Just held her.

They looked so beautiful together. So perfect.

It must have been a bad day in the surgical department so far. Shelby didn't ask. If he needed to share, he would.

With Izzie.

That thought echoed as they gathered Izzie's things to leave.

They were going away now. For a few days. To Houghton's place in Mexico.

Allen had Izzie now. He didn't need Shelby as much as he had before. Not that he ever really had *needed* her, exactly. He'd just been...stuck with her, really.

That was something else she had always known—no one had ever really *needed* her before. Not so much that it mattered. Not her parents, not her brother.

That was a life lesson she had learned long ago.

66

Jake was always uncomfortable when Allen let the emotion show.

Still, he'd only ever seen the guy like that with Izzie. And with his sister.

The other man was wrapped around Izzie, eyes closed, just holding her. Izzie's arms were around him, and she looked as if there was nowhere else she'd rather be than pressed close to that doofus.

Hell, the guy did make Izzie happy. So far.

It was the look on Shelby's face that caught him the most.

She looked broken. Alone.

As if she didn't know where she belonged any longer.

Hell, he half understood that. His whole world had shifted when Izzie had moved in with Allen, too. Dynamics had changed.

For all of them.

Izzie had been his family for so long—just her, with Annie and Josie and Annie's boys. Then she was just...with Allen.

Jake came home to an empty apartment every night. Izzie hadn't *needed* him any longer. Everything had changed.

He strongly suspected Shelby Grace Jacobson didn't handle change all that well. She probably felt unsettled.

And alone.

He bit back a curse.

He'd spent the entire damned morning immersed in Logan Lanning's final journals Dom had sent him.

The ones they'd been searching for since Banks Claireson's death.

Grief and loneliness were the predominant themes. Deep, soul-breaking, heart-wrenching grief and loneliness.

Not something he had particularly enjoyed reading.

Jake had found himself feeling bad for the guy. Even after what the other man had done. Rooting for him to find something to make him happy before he died. Anything. Anyone. He'd hoped the guy had had *someone* at some point in his life that had truly mattered before he'd fallen off the deep end.

Then the entries had turned to...Shelby.

One thing had become extremely clear.

Longing. Pain. Guilt.

Shelby was Logan Lanning's truest heartbreak.

If there was anyone Lanning had ever *truly* been in love with...

Well, Jake was looking at her now.

Shelby had been Lanning's heart and soul. Something Lanning had apparently never told anyone. Ever.

From the journal entries, he had never even told Allen. He'd been afraid it would destroy the relationship between the two men if Allen had known what Lanning had felt for Allen's much younger sister.

Shelby hadn't even been twenty when Logan Lanning's feelings for her had first started.

Now it made sense why Lanning had left everything to his best friend's younger sister instead of anyone else. Hell, it would have made more sense for him to have left it to Allen, not

Shelby. Allen would have understood how to manage it, how to leverage it—and Lanning could have left Shelby a bequest that Allen managed, as a token, if he'd felt obligated.

That was what Izzie had implied when Jake had asked her once why Lanning had left his house to Shelby. He'd wanted to help his best friend take care of his friend's sister. That was it. The house had just been a gesture.

Wrong.

No. There was so much more to it than that. Far, far more.

Lanning would have known Allen could manage it, and manage whatever small bequest Lanning made to Shelby.

Except for one thing.

How Lanning had felt for *her*.

Bone deep, head over heels, in love with his best friend's much younger sister. It had eaten at him, destroyed him, that he could not have her.

She'd been nineteen when Lanning's feelings had first changed for her. Lanning had been almost thirty. And fighting it. Hard.

There had been the same age difference between Lanning and Shelby as there was between Jake and Shelby. He hadn't missed that at all.

Would Jake have fallen so hard for her back then if he had been in Lanning's position? If she had been right there in front of him? Looking at him as if he was a hero? As if he mattered to her?

Lanning had always felt guilty for not protecting her when she'd been assaulted. Though he had never come out and written that in his own private journals.

Jake didn't even know if the other man ever even realized it.

It was there, right between the lines.

Lanning felt he should have protected her or should have stopped her from going out that night to begin with. They'd had plans for the next night—he'd written that he should have changed their plans to the night before, then Shelby never would have been hurt. Would have been with him instead.

Lanning had hated himself for that one decision for years. Blamed himself.

The guilt had nearly destroyed him.

Jake didn't know if that was something he should ever tell her, either.

How in the hell could he?

67

It was awkward. There was no other way for Shelby to describe how she felt. Jake watched every move she made, an odd look in his devil eyes, until she was so jumpy she felt like screaming. What was he hoping to accomplish?

The man...sometimes she thought he was doing it just to disconcert her.

He had to know how he made her feel. Had to.

"Get away from the window, baby girl."

She turned toward him. There he was. Staring again. "Don't...don't call me that."

Jake stood. Came closer.

Shelby forced herself to hold her ground.

"Baby girl?" His smirk made her want to slug him.

"I'm...I'm...you...you use it to make yourself appear older, wiser than me when you...you use it. Not as an endearment, but an insult. I know the truth."

Jake stepped right into her space. His hand slipped up to cup her cheek.

He was careful not to touch her in front of people, but they were alone now. Glenna would be there in about an hour. She took the evening shift four nights a week, until nine. When she'd take her three little girls home and put them to bed.

For now, they were alone.

Of course, he would take advantage of that. She suspected whatever he was working on in front of her had bored him. He seemed restless. Hurting.

She was about to become his entertainment.

Shelby forced herself not to look at him, instead focusing on a point just outside the window.

There were guards there.

Wearing polo shirts with *Barratt-Handley Enterprises* on the breast pocket.

Armed guards. There was a patrol car with TSP printed on the hood, the doors. She could see it from where she was, in front of the window. Jake had said the plainclothes detective doing a ride-along was named MacGregor. She couldn't remember what the uniformed woman with him was named. She just knew they were out there. As she watched, they pulled out, their light on top now blazing. Jake's phone buzzed with a text. She figured it out pretty quick.

Jake was her sole guard from the world now.

She was never fully safe.

"Just don't call me that. I know you don't mean it."

"Maybe I do." His hand dropped to her back, and then he pulled her closer. Then she was almost pressed against him. "I... don't want you to look at me like you hate me."

"I don't...hate...you. I just will never trust you again. Never believe a word you have to say. I know...you are reading those journals now. I looked." Her eyes met his. Why try to play peacemaker with a man like him? Shelby never would again. Open, blunt honesty was all she would ever give him from now on. Until she never had to deal with him again. "You are just toying with me. We both know that. So just stop it, ok?"

"Excuse me? May I get some assistance, please?"

Shelby jerked around at the unfamiliar voice. To stare into irritated blue eyes.

The eyes of Victor Scott.

What was he doing at W4HAV?

68

VICTOR FORCED HIMSELF TO REMAIN CALM AS HE eyed the man he had first learned about during Wallace Henedy's trial sentencing for what Henedy had done to Kyle.

Why was that bastard standing so close to *her*? They had a familial relationship, according to his sources. And even that was tenuous at best.

Henedy had accepted a plea agreement. Victor had wanted to be there for the sentencing. He'd greased a few wheels in the system to ensure that agreement was as strict as it could be. Henedy would never get out of prison.

Neither would that bitch wife of his. Victor fought a cold smile thinking about Jennifer Henedy's final moments.

He had paid well for them, after all. After he was certain Wallace suffered as much as he could, Victor would end him as well.

It was Jennifer that Victor truly despised. He'd considered her a friend once.

She had betrayed that. Sleeping with his son for more than eleven years. That had been disgusting.

She had been far too old, too worldly for Kyle then.

Jennifer had taken advantage of him. It was no wonder Kyle had always refused to come work for Victor—even though he would have inherited everything Victor had built.

No. Kyle had been happy making his own way being Jennifer Henedy's lapdog. Her sex toy.

It still disgusted him when he thought about it. Right here— in this very room, was where Wallace Henedy had almost killed two young women, and *Jennifer*'s action had led to Shelby almost dying.

It must have taken a lot of bravery for Shelby to return to this place. But there she was.

Looking absolutely perfect and real before him.

The woman he was there to inspect studied him out of eyes the purest gray he had ever seen. "Can...can ...can I help you?" she asked in a cool, cultured voice that sent shivers down his spine. He would love to have her speaking to him with nothing between them but the sheets.

She would be the last woman he slept with before he died.

Victor studied her. She wore cream trousers and a W4HAV polo shirt. Her personal interests involved this women's charity, search-and-rescue training, and a children's choir. She was a woman with a degree in social work and had a brother who was a world-renowned trauma surgeon.

She was accustomed to helping people. He found that intriguing. He wasn't exactly considered an altruistic man, after all. Far from it.

Perhaps their child would do great things for the world, and not just the business sector. Could make the Scott name mean something other than money as well.

"Hello, my dear." He continued to catalog her. Graceful. Poised. In control. Highly intelligent, as her college transcript had indicated. Victor's people were extremely thorough at ferreting out the information he needed. He paid them well to be just that.

He was impressed with what was before him now. He had seen her before. Had danced with her at the benefit.

Why had he not put her at the top of the list that night?

It took him a moment to remember. She'd stuttered at the benefit, and he'd thought it meant she was uncomfortable among the people around them. Out of her depth in *his* world.

She had stuttered while speaking with him and had been thoroughly uninterested in what he had to say—more intent on returning to her table than learning about him. That's what it had been.

Now he wished he had been a bit more persistent. They could have been several days further along his path if he had.

Brianna had flashed her way into his attention then—and been derogatory about the younger woman dubbed the "heroine of the storm."

Brianna's obvious flash had distracted him, Victor would admit. Brianna had been jealous of course. How could she not be when compared with Shelby?

This woman in front of him was stunning. Flawless. Perfect.

Victor turned slightly as she stepped closer.

Jake MacNamara was right there, looking like a smug bastard from his ink-black hair to the scuffed workman's boots on his feet.

He had a good two inches on Victor and was broader through the shoulders.

The big brute belonged on a foul-smelling dock somewhere. Wasn't fit for much more than hard labor, like his ancestors before him.

But there MacNamara was.

Next to Shelby. With one hand on her shoulder, holding her close. Possessive? "Scott, you need something from W4HAV?"

There was the challenge. For her.

Her. Victor's Shelby.

Victor fought the rage boiling within him. He stumbled

through saying he was there to give a donation in Kyle's name, to honor those Henedy had harmed.

Shelby gave him an information packet and told him to get in touch with Melody Barratt. That was it.

So calm, so cool. So sweet in her perfection.

And then he left. He needed to strategize. Something had been made extremely clear to him.

Jake MacNamara wanted her. Desired her. There was nothing pseudofamilial about it at all.

So did Victor. And Victor wasn't about to lose. He would never lose someone who mattered to him ever again.

He definitely wouldn't lose to that bastard.

This woman was at the top of his list now. Where she belonged. Perfection.

Victor *needed* her.

And he would have her.

69

Jake was pissed the rest of the afternoon. He kept her as close as he possibly could until she was just as pissed—at him.

Victor Scott had no business getting near Shelby at all. The idea that he had been right there close to her—Jake still burned. He didn't buy that the man was there in memory of his son. Not for one minute. Guys like that had personal assistants and entire charitable donation departments to handle that.

No, they didn't come themselves.

Not just days after they'd met the most gorgeous woman in Finley Creek.

Jake had done his best to run the guy off.

He succeeded too.

Only to have Shelby light into him as soon as the older man was gone. "What were you doing? You were incredibly rude to him! You'll get me fired."

"So? Not like you need to work." He watched the eyes go from blue to storm-gray in a heartbeat. Jake loved it when her eyes changed like that. He stepped closer. He wanted his hands on her again. So bad his bones ached. "Why do you work anyway?"

"Why wouldn't I? I wasn't raised to be a blight on society or anything. Look at who my parents were—my brother. He's... going to be great one day. I can't just sit there every day wasting what I've been given. What kind of person would that make me?"

Well, ok, he could understand that. "Didn't mean to push a button."

"Sure you didn't. Isn't that what you do? Push people and push until they break? Sean and Mike tried to do it to me. Think I'm stupid? You probably have been a cop so long you don't even know how to talk to real people."

"Real? You are as real as it gets. I talk to you all the time." Jake couldn't help himself. He wrapped his hands around her. And pulled her closer. "That's part of my problem. I look at you, and I lose all parts of my sanity. Have from the first time I saw you on the sidewalk right outside this very building. I walked behind you and just wished you'd look around and see *me*."

She looked up at him. "I don't believe you. You lie. It's kind of what you do."

"Stay away from Victor Scott. He comes near you again and I am not here, you tell me. Instantly. I don't want him near you ever again. He can't have you."

"He...I can't control where he goes. And if I'm working and he shows up—"

"Hell, woman. You need a security team every minute of the day." It was just too easy for someone with nefarious purposes to get to her.

Jake had counted a hundred ways just in the last two hours.

That was enough to double his nightmares now. He was just about ready to say something when the glass doors swung open.

A man, a pregnant blond woman, and a redhead—plus a wildly shrieking redheaded toddler—stepped inside. Elliot

Marshall jerked his head in Jake's direction, anger in his eyes, as his wife and sister-in-law greeted Shelby.

"Jake, we need to talk. Outside. Now. Immediately."

Jake knew when not to argue.

He followed the chief of the Finley Creek TSP region outside.

"Where the hell are MacGregor and Isen?" Elliot asked. "I confirmed they were to be posted here, personally. I assigned MacGregor the detail to teach the cocky jerk a lesson this morning after he mouthed off to Rodriguez."

Jake pulled his phone out. Checked the text again. "Called off. By the TSP dispatch."

"Well, isn't that convenient now? Gave someone time to do *this.*"

He looked right where Elliot pointed.

Jake cursed.

Jake fought the fury, seeing the words painted in garish chartreuse paint across the rear of Shelby's small luxury SUV.

You're next, bitch! I'm coming for you! Keep your mouth shut!!!

Someone cried out behind him.

Jake knew. He turned.

And there she was. She'd followed.

Why had she followed? "Shelby…"

He saw the terror in storm-gray eyes, and he reacted. Wrapped his arms around her and pulled her close. She needed the comfort, and he was damned well going to give it. Jake looked at the other man next to him while Jake tried to tuck her head against his chest where she couldn't keep staring at it. "It's ok, baby. You're safe now."

Elliot Marshall shook his head; the anger in his eyes was hard to miss. It echoed that filling Jake. "I'm getting the forensics team here as soon as they can get here, but I'm not holding out hope. Unless the security cameras can give us a lead. Where she's parked, I don't know."

The bastards had been right outside W4HAV. Too damned

close to her the entire time. Jake hadn't even realized it. That was a lesson he wasn't about to forget.

"I have you, baby. You're safe with me now."

She looked up at him, the doubt written right there for him to see. It etched itself into his soul forever.

70

Jake watched Madison and Shelby and wondered what it was the two of them were talking about so quietly. Madison sent a furtive look toward Dom. When she should have been printing the rear of Shelby's SUV.

Shelby looked just as secretive. He watched them have another intense round of conversation. That didn't look normal. "What are the two of them up to?"

Dom just grunted. It was one of his favorite responses. Jake was used to him. Dom didn't talk all that much—his partner, Gunnar, talked too damned much.

Elliot was on his cell a few yards away.

Jake stepped closer to Shelby, wanting to be nearer. Just in case.

He wasn't about to risk anything happening to her out here.

"Got a little close to her today," Dom said. "I don't like this. What could Shelby be involved in that has grabbed the wrong kind of attention?"

"No clue. We can't even be sure it was intended for her."

"What do you mean? Pretty clear message."

"That's the steed I rode in on today. And we had an afternoon visitor you might be interested in."

"Well, don't keep me waiting. Spill."

"Victor Scott. Walked in bold as you please. To talk to Shelby."

"Well, well, well, guess the rumors are true." Dom turned to look at Shelby and Madison.

"Which ones? That he's a sociopathic asshole?"

"Scott is looking for...a lady friend. I heard other rumors that the man has less than eighteen months to live. Seems he's in a bit of a hurry. Been visiting every pretty lady who was at the ball. Probably made himself a nifty little list, with all the *right* ladies there in one place, thanks to Mel Barratt. Our Prince Charming is going around to the corners of our kingdom, seeing if his particular glass shoe fits one unlucky lady. He showed up at the TSP building itself. Asked for a tour of the forensics lab he donated to after the storm. Reintroduced himself to Haldyn, Chuckie...and Madison. Was quite charming, Haldyn said. In a way that gave her the creeps, apparently."

"He can move on past Shelby. Maybe Banks Claireson's sister is more his cup of tea."

"Still, if Scott wants Shelby for his macabre mating dance— and who can blame him, there—then *this* probably isn't his doing." Dom nodded toward her SUV. "Isn't exactly Mr. Suave-and-Debonaire's style."

"He's connected somehow. I'd bet money on it," Jake practically snarled. There was no way he was going to sit back and watch an asshole like Victor Scott get anywhere near Shelby again.

He looked at her. Madison should have been processing the vandalism—but there was something else going on. And if he wasn't mistaken, Shelby had just slipped Madison a piece of paper or a business card. "What are the two of them talking about over there?"

71

THE NIGHT WORE ON. JAKE WAS PRACTICALLY ALL over her. Watching her. Questioning her. Constantly. Until Shelby was about ready to scream. After he ordered dinner from a diner that delivered, and she quietly ate what he'd ordered for her, she tried to escape into her office.

Madison had given her a secure website where she had uploaded copies of what she had found for Shelby.

Shelby had given her Naelin's business card in return. They'd dial him in on what Charlotte, Haldyn, and Madison had found.

Then she and Zoey were going to talk about it. About what the next step would be.

One of the men's names was Jon. They had that now.

They just needed to figure out his last name next.

Naelin was trying to find a list of people who had attended that party five years ago. But parties like that...they were informal. Just random people hanging out. Not exactly the kind one sent invitations.

Someone had seen something. She had been aware of eyes on her. People had watched. Daryn had confirmed it, too.

Someone had to have a conscience and be willing to talk now. They would find them.

It was just a matter of time. When they did, she would see this finished to the very end. And then she was going to move on.

Make her life worth something again.

"What's in your bag?" Jake asked when she stood up to go into her office. She'd kept her workbag next to her while they'd eaten. It wasn't like she trusted him or anything like that. "That you keep it so close? And what did you give Madison today? Did it have something to do with what happened?"

"Practicing your interrogation skills on me tonight? Bet you were a b-b-barrel of laughs for Izzie as a kid. 'Did you do your homework? What color ink did you use? Did you sit next to Annie? Did one of you copy off the other? Who did you sit with at lunch? What is that boy's last name again? What do his parents do? Does he have a record? Do they?' and all of that."

"Hardly. Iz and I—we just stumbled along together for about four years. Until I got her to go to college. She was a bit resistant. Her and Annie both. Troublemakers, the two of them. Bet you didn't give good old Al even a moment of trouble after he had you, did you?"

She winced as the memories flooded her. "That...that...that is none of your business."

"You did? Do tell, baby girl." He raised a brow at her, obvious challenge on his face, at the endearment. "What did you do? Not get straight As? Run around with the wrong crowd? Get caught making out with the quarterback of Finley Creek Prep? What?"

She lowered her fork and stared at her personal albatross. Then jumped to her feet and began clearing the table, carrying the containers to the kitchen. He grabbed his own and followed. "I stopped going to school at all, if you want to know. I didn't see the point."

"What?"

"After my parents died, I stopped going to school for a few months. Just kept skipping. The school would call Allen, and he'd come find me. Make me go. Carried me in bodily once."

"Bet that went over well with the country-club set at FC Prep."

"Maybe. I didn't care. We got through." She gave a sad smile as she remembered. "After that, the only one who could get me to go was Logan. He would come and drive me in. And we'd... talk. Every day for my last year of high school. He was there of the morning. Allen would be there to get me of the afternoon. Logan *always* listened to me. Always. Sometimes...sometimes I thought Logan knew me better than Allen ever would. And he did. So go ahead—say something about him. I know you have to be done reading the journals you found by now."

Shelby looked right at him and crossed her arms as she issued the challenge.

72

HARD HANDS WENT AROUND HER. SHELBY FOUND herself pulled into his arms. His broad chest was pressed up against hers. His breath was hot on her left ear. "Lanning was in love with you. Did you know?"

Shelby froze. Trepidation shot through her. "What do you mean?"

His scent surrounded her, overwhelming her with *Jake*.

"I mean that the man was head over heels obsessed with you. More than that, he was in love with you. But thought he was too old and just not good enough for you. I have to agree with him there. Logan Lanning would never be good enough for a woman like you. No mere mortal man could be."

Shelby didn't stop to think about it—she just acted. Like Darrell had taught her and Daryn and Zoey years ago. She shoved her nails into his wrist and twisted as she spun around.

He cursed. Then laughed. He actually laughed at her.

Reducing everything down to a joke. Like Logan's entire life was nothing but a punch line. To him and his buddies. She could see that—could see them all sitting around the TSP Major

Crimes bullpen, laughing about Logan while they dissected his journals, his private thoughts and wishes. And made notes.

"*Yes.* I know he loved me. Was in love with me. *I* loved him, too. Bet you didn't know that, did you?" Now he looked at her. Really looked at her. She saw the shock in those devil-dark eyes of his. The disbelief. "And...and...and we were supposed to have our first date the evening after I was hurt. Instead of him taking me to the opera like we'd planned, he was holding me while I cried from the three broken ribs and broken wrist I needed surgery on to fix after the surgeon told me I might never play piano again. I didn't want a relationship with *any* man after that night. Logan promised he would wait for me. But I never... If I had...maybe Logan wouldn't be dead right now, Jake. Maybe he wouldn't have hurt all those people. I'd have a family of my own running around in this stupid mausoleum. Maybe...maybe Izzie would be keeping my kids sometimes for an auntie sleep-over instead of just Annie's boys. Maybe...maybe *I'd* have the kind of life I'd dreamed about when I was a kid, with the one man who has ever actually loved me for *me.* Who saw *me* exactly as I was. Instead of this life. Where I am too scared to even get a puppy of my own because I may have to take him outside in the dark and that thought absolutely terrifies me. I'm afraid of the dark now, too. Because there could be monsters hiding in the darkness. Do you even realize that?"

He reached for her, but she pulled away. "Baby...no... baby...Shelby...I..."

"Did you...you...you notice that when you were spying on me? When I had Logan, I wasn't so afraid. Even a-a-after what they did to me. When he was with me, I felt *safe.* I haven't felt safe since I lost him. No. Before. Since...since I lost *me.*" Her hands were on his chest, and she pushed. Not enough to hurt him, just enough to get him out of her space. He was the last man she wanted in her space right now. "I have ghosts of Logan that haunt me, too. Of the Logan *I* had before. The Logan no one else ever saw. Not even Allen." She let out a sob that nearly destroyed her. "Ghosts of me, too. Because I don't even have me anymore. I lost me that night, too. And I never got me back. I'm not sure that that *me* didn't die that night five years ago, too. So go ahead, Jake. Dig into Logan all you want. Destroy all that I have of him left. Why does it even matter anymore?"

73

Jake stayed right where he was.

He hadn't intended to make her cry. That had been the last thing he had wanted to do. Ever. He had just...the words had slipped out.

Because he had understood the man for the first time. The moment Lanning had written how he felt about her Jake had understood him.

About not being a good enough man for her.

Logan Lanning was a world-renowned physician who had patented lifesaving medical technology at the advanced age of twenty-eight.

He'd been damned brilliant. Successful, wealthy, fit and healthy, reasonably attractive, and right there in Shelby's sphere. He had known her since she'd been a young girl and had her trust. All the cards were aligned for him and Shelby to have formed a relationship. Marriages among their set had been built on far less.

But Lanning hadn't thought himself good enough for her.

Because he hadn't been able to save her that night.

That one night had started to consume Lanning. Had changed him, too. Jake hadn't missed that in the journals at all.

Lanning had obsessed about what had happened to Shelby. For years. Lanning had been so filled with regrets, it had been written on almost every page between the lines.

As had the love.

Deep love. Real love. The kind Jake had never felt for a woman before. The kind he envied.

Lanning's worry that he'd hurt Allen by being with his sister had been strong, real, too. Lanning had truly cared about Allen, admired him, and respected him. Wanted Allen's respect in return.

He'd felt Allen was a better man than he was, too.

That Shelby would never heal from what had happened to her had warred with Lanning's need for her, constantly. And with his need to find the bastards responsible.

None of Lanning's private investigators had been able to build a case either. Lanning had felt useless to her.

The one woman he had ever truly loved. Lanning had succeeded at everything he had ever done—except for her.

Lanning had wanted to make the world safe for Shelby and had failed. Three hells, Jake understood that.

He had read every other journal that Logan Lanning had written—they had been found after Lanning's attack on Lacy McGareth, now the governor's sister-in-law.

After Lanning had become addicted to prescription pain killers and other drugs—to numb the pain.

This most-revealing journal had been written several years earlier. Chuckie had found it in the guest room wall—between Shelby's room and that one.

It started just before Izzie had even hired on to the hospital by a few months. Long before Jake's niece had been come a victim of Lanning's particular brand of harassment at the hospital where they had both worked.

The journal had been the one most hidden. Because it showed the real Logan Lanning. The man who he had kept hidden.

The man who had loved Shelby.

The end of the journal had just shown Lanning's bitterness. His loneliness. His hatred of himself for his failure. Lanning had built a shell around himself. Changed.

The man who had never failed at anything had failed at protecting the woman he adored.

His writings showed his worry for Shelby. The fear that she'd hide herself away forever until she just disappeared. More than anything else, Lanning feared what would become of *her*.

He had set up his estates for her, then. So that she would be taken care of if anything ever happened to *him*. So she would have a place to be safe.

That was where the journal had stopped.

With Logan Lanning regretting that he had not been able to chase her demons away. He had failed. And it had destroyed him.

Jake understood that all too well, too.

Maybe he and Logan Lanning weren't all that different from one another, after all.

74

SHE CLOSED HER BEDROOM DOOR BEHIND HER AND stripped down, changing into pajamas before falling onto her bed. It had been Logan's bedframe. She'd just changed the mattress, and the paint color of the room around her.

Made the room more hers. The bedframe was the only furniture she had kept.

She'd kept his pillow after he'd been killed. Even though she hadn't gotten possession of the house for almost fourteen months after his funeral, thanks to the TSP. She had just almost convinced herself that she had been able to smell him. Which was ridiculous.

Logan had been gone far too long by the time she'd gotten the house for that.

She'd moved his pillow to the guest room next door six days after she'd moved in. It was still in there.

They hadn't been in *real* love. Not like Allen and Izzie were; she didn't think. She had been far too young and inexperienced for that. Too hesitant and naive.

They had both known that it could have happened, and they had started taking that first tentative step toward it after a beautiful surprise kiss between them in the moonlight one warm September night after he'd given her a ride home from class at FCU where he'd been giving a lecture.

Just like that, one sweet kiss had changed everything.

The next day, he'd found her in his pool and proven that one kiss hadn't been a fluke at all.

They could have been that in love, could have grown that way. If they'd gotten the chance. They had been going slow, because he'd thought she was too young and because he hadn't wanted to ruin his relationship with her brother.

Logan had been thirty-four years old when he died.

He had pulled away from her long before that. Told her that it hurt too much to be near her. To even look at her sometimes. That he wasn't the same man he had been when they were younger. That being around her just reminded him of that.

Of his failures.

That had hurt, too. Almost destroyed her. It had been her fault.

Her failure. No one else's.

The one man who had ever truly needed her and she had been too consumed by what had happened to her to have really seen that. To see that Logan was hurting, too. To see that he had needed her.

If she had…

Why was it that she was the only one to have ever seen Logan for how he was, how he could have been?

She would never forget the moment Allen had come to her, told her what had happened.

That moment had almost completely destroyed her.

Logan had become addicted to pain killers after being shot during a TSP cold case investigation that had involved another doctor at the hospital.

He had been in the wrong place at the wrong time and had wanted to help.

That had been the final change.

The addiction had started his spiral to destruction.

He'd started mixing drugs and alcohol, according to the personal journals that had been returned to her after the TSP were finished with them. The forensic team had sliced off the bindings and processed each page. Desecrating them. She had them now, laminated and preserved. In a box in the study.

She had read them once, in a particularly weak moment when the loneliness had risen up to choke her. She had needed to hear his voice again.

Allen had just disappeared somewhere to protect Izzie, but she hadn't known that. All she'd known was that he was gone and she couldn't find her brother.

She had had no one to tell her what was going on. Just a cryptic message saying Allen was ok—from one of Mel's connections.

She hadn't known what was going on—Allen would never have left her like that if he had a choice. Shelby had been terrified to call the TSP. It had taken every bit of courage she had to do just that. If Mel's brother-in-law hadn't been the chief's brother, she never would have been able to make that call at all.

It hadn't been enough.

The TSP hadn't told her a damned thing.

She had read Logan's journals all through that night, looking for something to point her to the *why* behind what he had done.

All she had found were the remnants of a broken man.

One she understood so deeply she grieved for what *her* fear had caused between them. She should have forced herself out of her shell after the attack. Instead of mentally running from every problem. She should have made herself *see...*

Kept on living.

Maybe she and Logan could have had something then.

Maybe he wouldn't have been in the hospital parking lot that late the night he'd been shot. Maybe they'd have had a child or two of their own by then and he would have been at home with her. Safe.

Or she would have been at his side after he was hurt, would have kept him from taking the drugs and drinking.

The addiction would never have happened, then.

He would have been the good man she would *always* remember him to be.

Instead of the monster Jake kept painting him.

If she just hadn't been so afraid, everything could have been so different. Instead, she had, and he had died, and now here she was.

In the shell of what Logan's life had once been.

That was the real reason she'd started remodeling the house.

So she wouldn't have to be reminded of him everywhere she turned. Wouldn't remember that if she hadn't been so afraid to live, she wouldn't be living *here* now.

Jake was right—she didn't deserve any of this.

But Shelby didn't know what to about it now.

She lay there a long time, thinking just that. Until she cried herself to sleep once again.

75

JAKE FELT *ITCHY* NOT BEING WITH HER. WATCHING HER.

Daniel had called him in to deal with yet another bust by Gunnar and Charlie—reminding Jake he couldn't just stay with Shelby forever. He had work to do, had a career he cared about. A life of his own, even if it was wrapped up in that career now.

He couldn't stay with Shelby forever. Even if he wanted to.

She had agreed to a guard from Mel Barratt's stash of handy-dandy ex-cop security staffers. Enthusiastically.

She didn't exactly want him around—she'd made that clear.

She should be safe at W4HAV now. The chief had made it clear to the officers he had patrolling that area that if anything happened to Shelby on their watch, Elliot would pluck their eyeballs out through their ears. That only *he* or Daniel or Jake could pull them off the patrol detail.

It should do for now.

She should be safe.

After what had happened to Izzie, Nikkie Jean, and Shelby in that building—and in front of it—Houghton Barratt and that Davis Lucas guy out of St. Louis had assigned two security guards to watch the charity specifically, and added metal detectors at the front and back entrance.

Both guards were retired military, and Jake had vetted them himself. Just to be on the safe side.

His niece spent a lot of time there—and was married to a man now worth close to twenty million dollars. Jake wasn't going to take any chances with Izzie, either.

Or Annie, for that matter.

Now, though, he was wondering if a third guard wouldn't be a good idea.

Just to be on the safe side.

Three armed guards to keep Shelby safe would make him feel a hell of a lot better.

Someone slapped him on the back. "So have you tapped the rich lady yet?"

Jake turned, fist ready to slam into the leering face. Jody Callahan was a nasty-ass snake in the water—especially where women were concerned. And a brown-nosing punk where the TSP was concerned. Jake saw right through him.

"Say one more word about her, and I'll rip your face off."

"So it's like that? You really have a thing going on with her? For real? Man, you are so fucking lucky. So are you going to marry her? Put in your papers early and go live the high life? I so would. I would. I would put this place behind me forever. Spend the rest of my days keeping her naked. Or covered in all that dough. A blanket of one hundreds, man."

"Shut up, Callahan," Jack MacGregor said from his desk. Major Crimes was across the bullpen from Homicide. "You're being damned insulting to MacNamara's woman."

The open bullpen.

Hell, Homicide could hear everything Major Crimes discussed. He'd always hated that.

"Shelby is not up for discussion." Jake looked at Callahan then grabbed the little punk's shirt, pulling him closer. "*Ever.*

She's a good woman who doesn't deserve to be bullpen fodder, got me?"

"Still, you got an in with the hottest woman I have ever seen. One worth tens of millions? No way I would keep working the desk here. Of course, maybe you're not good enough for her needs? Maybe she needs a real man? One a little younger, with a better attitude? More go-to power in the sack? Wouldn't mind her lowering herself to my level. Even if just for a week or two. I could make her scream, I bet. You break her in for me, ok?"

Jake's hold tightened, and he growled. Callahan's eyes widened. Gunnar chose that moment to yell Jake's name and for him to get his ass in gear. That was probably all that saved Callahan's life. Jake lowered the asshole back to the ground. "We have an understanding, right?"

Callahan nodded. "Didn't mean nothing by it."

"Come on! Let's roll. Now," Gunnar said. "I'll help you knock the shit out of him just for fun later."

"Sorry, Callahan, the job calls. You might try doing yours sometimes."

Gunnar waited impatiently.

He didn't say a word until they were outside the parking lot. The new building, just finished in the last four months, towered above them. The lab was in the basement now, instead of an annex. The evidence vault was warehoused behind them. Under guard at all times.

So much had been lost in the storm. In the bomb before.

Including so much of what Major Crimes was looking for now. That made a man feel a little hopeless at times. "What's going down?"

"Got a call in from Shelby's neighbor, Mrs. Kelley. Said she saw a man prowling around Shelby's windows. We thought you'd want to know."

76

DOM BIT BACK THE WHISTLE THAT ALWAYS WANTED TO escape when he saw the opulent luxury that characterized Shelby's home.

They had an unobstructed view of her place from the road.

Jake knew the security code, and he tapped in it quickly. The other man was cursing like a sailor as the gate swung open. Saying the woman needed armed guards and better security. An entire three-person team at all times—all women if that's all she'd do, but it needed to happen sooner rather than later.

Round-the-clock security that Jake was going to hire himself, if he had to take out a second job to pay for it, if she was too stubborn to pay for it herself.

Dom didn't disagree. He was going to suggest that to her, or her friend Zoey, when he could.

People would look at this place and want two things—either to steal from her or hurt her for having what they didn't.

It was just human nature where money was concerned. Want it for themselves—or despise those that had it.

Shelby didn't deserve to be hurt because of Logan Lanning's money.

Far, far from it.

All she had done was be the woman Lanning had loved.

No one deserved to be hurt because of being loved like that.

He pulled up to the parking area in front of the garage. No tame driveway for this place.

Not at all.

He would bet his next paycheck Jake felt damned out of place here. Dom would. Did. Movement out of the corner of his eye had him jerking around the instant he stepped out of the vehicle. "TSP! Freeze!"

Jake gave a vicious snarl and took it one step further. Going right at the guy when they realized he wasn't holding a weapon. The guy was armed, but it was holstered.

Dom didn't stop Jake.

He understood.

Jake's woman was threatened. That was all it would take.

77

JAKE SHOVED THE MAN TO HIS KNEES ON THE concrete, taking the gun from the holster.

Gunnar tossed him the flex cuffs. Jake cuffed him quickly. "Don't move."

"I'm a private investigator. My license is in my back pocket. I'm friends with Marshall's brother, Chance. Why don't you guys let me up, and we have a little chat?"

At the familiar name, Jake paused. "What the hell are you doing here?"

"I'm doing my damned job. Check for yourself." The man's ID was right where he said it would be. Naelin Lassiter, *Lassiter Private Investigations.*

Gunnar ran it through the system fast.

When he looked at Jake and nodded, Jake and Dom got the man back to his feet and sat him in the passenger seat of Jake's SUV.

Jake had questions—lots of questions.

"What in the hell are you doing digging around here?"

"I've been hired by the owner of the house. Been working for her for over a year now. Ask her yourself. We're supposed to meet here in an hour. Nice lady—and I won't have you shitheads from the TSP hassling her again." Fury went over the man's face. "Damned bastards, you can't leave her alone, can you?"

"The woman's name?" Jake asked, ignoring the digs at the TSP. He was damned well used to those. Apparently, Shelby had another valiant protector.

She seemed to be collecting them.

"Shelby Jacobson." He went on to rattle off Shelby's cell phone number and email. "You can check my damned references. Melody Barratt referred me to Shelby the month before the damned storm."

"What the hell for?" Jake believed the guy—and he recognized the name from those damned files she wouldn't let him see. "What's she got you doing?"

"The woman's worth millions. She keeps me on retainer. Some asshole or another is always trying to get the pretty lady to part with her cash. You ask me, protecting her interests is a full-time job in itself. That's all I'm saying. Nondisclosure and all that. I protect my clients' privacy."

The guy's eyes shifted. He was lying. There was more to it than that. Far more. Ice slivered across the back of Jake's neck. She was up to something. And had been for a long while. He'd bet his entire paycheck on it. "You're going to stay right where you are until she gets here."

"Why are three TSP detectives screwing around in Shelby's front yard?" the guy asked. Had he not been cuffed, he'd be a pretty intimidating kind of guy. He was equally as tall and broad as Jake was himself, even though he was a good eight or so years younger. He had that air about him that told Jake he was a dangerous son of a bitch who'd seen too damned much.

And the guy was sniffing around Shelby?

Hell, no.

Not on Jake's watch. "Shelby is a family connection."

The guy's eyes narrowed. "You the sister-in-law's uncle,

then? She's told me about you. And not to say a damned word to you about anything. Ever. Under threat of extreme torture and dismemberment. Those were her exact words. And when she looked at me like that—sorry, dude. Not happening. So...I'm just going to sit here and entertain myself for a while."

Jake wanted to punch the guy. He couldn't explain it. He just did. He didn't want a guy like this anywhere near her. That wasn't too hard to figure out.

Jake forced himself to step away. He nodded at Dom. The other man would keep their new pal company.

He had to walk away for a while.

Gunnar followed him. "Guy seems legit. I called Chance. He vouches for him. Chance was aware he was on Shelby's payroll. We can't keep him cuffed forever. The man hasn't done anything wrong—except know your girl."

Jake just grunted. The guy had been peering in her windows. He hadn't overreacted. "I don't like it. What in the hell does she need a private investigator for?"

"Chance said the guy is good at ferreting out scam artists and grifters. Maybe that's it. Shelby's got more dough than almost anyone in this county except the Barratts and that toadstool shithead Victor Scott. Gold diggers are real, man. A beautiful, insecure woman living all alone with all that money—it's only a matter of time before some asshole targets her." Gunnar talked a lot, but the man always made sense.

"Like hell they will." The idea had the proverbial smoke building in Jake's ears. Her friend had said it had already happened. Now he wanted details. Names.

"What are you going to do? Babysit her forever? Move in and play Igor, answering her doorbell every time it rings? Run background checks on everyone who says hello to her? That sounds a bit like too much work. I mean, unless you're all into that with her? Because that sounds more like serious commitment time, there. That what you are after?"

Jake swore.

It was the truth—why in the hell hadn't he thought about that fact? He had almost forgotten the sheer amount of money she had hidden in her bank accounts.

Money always drew the monsters.

That could be what was behind the break-in and the threats. Someone using terror to eventually extort a ransom.

It was possible; and knowing her, she'd keep it secret—so it wouldn't worry her brother.

The woman had some questions to answer.

The questions list just kept growing.

"It's not like that with Shelby."

"Like hell it isn't. She's all you think about. We all know it. From the moment some punk broke into her place, your focus has been ninety-five percent on her. We can all see that. And there's a damned live wire that runs between the two of you whenever you get within range of each other. I personally think you're stupid to not act on that. Here you are, with a real in with this hot, sexy, intelligent, kind, loving, rich, hot, sexy, loving, et cetera, et cetera, woman that has almost every guy who has ever met her slobbering like a beagle next to a pan of fried chicken. And you are too much of a pansy ass to do anything about it. I just don't get it, man. Go for it. What could go wrong?"

"I hope that's rhetorical."

Gunnar shook his head. "Hell, MacNamara, maybe we are all supposed to find someone who lights us on fire like she does you. I've seen it lately. You ever see Elliot Marshall and his wife when they don't realize someone is watching? Burning fire. Don't you ever think about that with someone?"

Jake just grunted. He knew what the other man was talking about.

He'd seen it when Izzie would look at that dumbass husband of hers. Or Annie when she'd be wrapped around the mayor—

had the mayor wrapped around her, rather. Turner Barratt was rather impossibly clingy where Annie was concerned.

Like the entire world had been narrowed down to just them.

For that one special moment, no one else existed.

He had never felt a connection to a woman like that. He couldn't deny he'd seen it between that asshole Allen and Izzie. And Annie and the mayor. Even Mel Barratt and that penny bank she'd married thrummed when they got too close to each other.

He had never been that way with a woman.

Never felt that alive with a woman was far more like it. Except with her.

He almost snarled at the other man. "If you are so concerned with love and romance bullshit, find a woman of your own."

Gunnar smirked, looking like a stupid blond male baboon. "How about I just take the first available woman to walk across my path and go for it? See what can happen?"

"You're a damned fool, Erickson. No wonder Marshall stuck us with you. No one else could handle your asshat stupidity." Jake watched as Dom spoke with the PI, across the driveway. Questioning him, while the asshole PI just picked at his damned nails. Still cuffed.

"Challenge accepted. First hot woman I see, I'm going for it. Yep. The very first one. Wonder who it will be?"

Jake's eyes narrowed. They were in Shelby's front yard. That would narrow the possibilities considerably. "Not Shelby. Not ever going to happen."

"Not Shelby," Gunnar agreed. A strange look went over his face. "Hell, Jake, it sucks shit being alone all the time. I've not had a serious relationship in years. Maybe it's time I did again?"

Jake cursed himself for being an idiot. A clueless, heartless jackass. He had totally forgotten. Way to twist in the knife. Maybe he needed to take a page out of Dom's book and keep his own damned mouth shut sometimes.

Gunnar had lost his wife of two years to a nasty car accident when he'd been on an undercover case five years ago. The guy who'd caused the accident had been awaiting trial on drug charges. Gunnar's wife had been seven months pregnant with a boy at the time.

The driver had been stoned to the nth degree at the time he'd killed Jamie Erickson. Gunnar had told him that in a particularly weak moment a year or so ago. "Being alone sucks. Being married...doesn't. Something to consider."

In that moment, Jake got it. Gunnar wouldn't admit it, but he was lonely. Bone-deep lonely. "Deal. First available woman *not* Shelby we both see, you go for it. See what happens. See how long it takes her to tell you to shove off."

Not likely anything would come of it, but at least, the guy would be trying. Getting himself out there again. Maybe a bet was the best excuse to get him started. Gunnar hadn't dated anyone seriously since joining Major Crimes. Jake half thought the other man was afraid to.

A long dark limo pulled into Shelby's drive.

It had taken him threatening to get Allen involved to get her to agree to use the car service for a few weeks. Until he could figure out who'd vandalized her car.

An armed-car service, owned by Houghton Barratt. They provided almost instant guarded car rides for anyone Houghton chose to grant that privilege to. Unpredictable, almost untraceable. Houghton's private car service would come in real handy.

He watched as she slipped out of the back seat, followed by two other women.

Women he'd seen before. *Gorgeous,* available women he'd seen before. Well, well.

He looked at Gunnar, who'd perked up considerably. Well, they were both hot. But as for *available*... "Not Madison, either. Dom will rip your head off at the shoulders and use it to teach that brother of hers to play basketball."

"That's an understatement," Gunnar said, grimacing. He was a bit squeamish with talk of blood and guts. "The other woman...I saw her at the benefit. Dating one of the Barratts? The taller one. Brandt, I think. I don't poach."

Jake smirked. "Not dating him. That's his twin sister. The realtor whose face is everywhere. You really need to start paying closer attention to details. As far as I know, she's not dating anyone. Good friends with Madison and Chuckie. She's Shelby's attorney."

Gunnar almost snarled. If there was anything he hated more than he hated drug dealers, he hated lawyers.

The guy who had killed his wife had been a *lawyer*, after all. Whose lover had gotten him out on bail for the drug charges to begin with. Gunnar had had a hard time with attorneys ever since.

"Still on?"

Gunnar grinned. "What the hell? I've always loved a challenge, and maybe she'll consider a career change if she decides she loves me enough. As soon as we deal with our new friend over there, I'm going to get started."

Yeah. Sure he was.

Gunnar wasn't that much of a dog with women. Far from it. Jake thought the idea of a good woman actually scared the other man.

He was struck by a bolt of understanding.

It did scare Gunnar. The other man was afraid—because he knew exactly what he was missing.

78

THERE WERE FOUR MEN IN HER FRONT YARD. SHELBY stopped walking and just stared.

Powell put a hand on her elbow. "Don't say anything. They can't be here for a good reason. Not at all. Let me do the talking." Shelby just nodded. She had no idea what the men were doing there.

Zoey pulled in, parking next to the car-service limo. She stepped out quickly.

Then they were almost lined up—four women against the three men from the TSP.

And... "That's my private investigator. They have him in handcuffs. Why is Naelin in handcuffs?"

Zoey came up to her side. Stepped in front of them all. Protective, like always. "Gentleman, can we help you today?"

Jake grunted. "I'm here for Shelby. She knows why I am here."

"That's a rather obvious assumption," Powell said coolly. "Care to explain why you have Shelby's employee in handcuffs? Or is that just something you do for entertainment?"

"We thought he was a prowler," Dom Acardi said. "If you

could confirm he is supposed to be here, Shelby, we'll set him loose with an apology."

Shelby nodded. "We have a two p.m. appointment."

Naelin Lassiter gave an attractive smirk, eyeing Zoey appreciatively. No surprise; most men saw Zoey first and just... reacted. It annoyed Zoey constantly. "I was a little early. My meeting with Chance Marshall was rescheduled. He had to take his daughter to that pediatrician cousin of his. The little redheaded beastie upchucked peas and bananas all down my good shirt, and I had to borrow one from Chance. Want to do a DNA check on it to confirm?"

Shelby apologized. She looked at Zoey, who had keys to her house. "Can you take him inside and get him something to drink?"

"Of course." Zoey shot the TSP men a look. "And the three of you will behave yourselves. Or I'll bring Elliot Marshall in on this. Shelby is not to be harassed again. Don't even think about it."

"What's going on now?" Jake just grunted. Shelby stared at him. How long were they going to just wait there? Have an odd little standoff in the middle of her front yard? "We have plans tonight. Why are *they* here?"

"Plans you are interrupting," Madison said. "Just go away now. All of you. Shoo."

Shelby looked to her left. His pal Dom was practically stalking Madison around the hedges, trying to get her to talk to him in private. "Detective A-A-Acardi, are you here on official business? If so, Powell is more than willing to speak with you. Outside. Leave Madison alone right now."

A big blond man she'd met before stepped forward and raised his hand. "I'll talk to Powell. She's pretty. Very, very pretty. Please, can I have a Powell?"

"Can it, Erickson," Dom said. "Shelby, it's hot out here, and we're all acting like idiots."

"Big surprise," Madison said, snickering. Dom shot her a challenging look.

"Can we come inside? We have some questions," Detective Erickson said. "And most of us are house-trained. Not Dom, though, he's such a bad dog he should probably stay outside. He likes to jump on pretty Madisons and slobber all over them."

Madison almost growled. "He does not."

Jake and Detective Erickson smirked at Madison simultaneously. Jake reached for Shelby's elbow. She barely resisted jerking away at the last moment. She wasn't about to let him know he had unsettled her last night. He turned back to her. "Can they come in?"

"I don't think that's a good idea." She kept her eyes on Jake. He was the barometer of what was really going on. Shelby wasn't stupid. "You wouldn't all be here if you didn't want something. So spill."

Nope. Major Crimes was there for a reason. She could bet millions on it.

"Why have you hired a private detective?" Was his first demand.

Shelby turned and stepped toward her front door. Madison and Powell stayed with her. Like they were protecting her.

They were her buffer against her unwelcome houseguest, after all.

She had gone out of her way after choir practice to bring people into her world. It hadn't been easy. Zoey was staying the night, like she often did.

Madison and Powell were there to keep talking about the choir. Powell was going to help them turn it into a legal nonprofit entity. Charlotte was joining them in half an hour after she stopped off and checked on a friend on the way. Shelby was going to fund the choir so that it would have all the money for props and supplies that it would need for years to come.

Then they were talking about starting a theater branch of the choir to perform in between choir concerts. Shelby intended to fund that, too.

She had friends over, a purpose, and was actually doing what she had to in order to get on with her life. Shelby was proud of that.

Of course, Jake would be around at the worst possible time to ruin that.

He seemed to be good at that.

His fingers wrapped around her elbow the instant she stepped into the foyer.

"You ok? Nothing happened?"

"I was *fine*. I know you had someone watch practice. Zoey was with me on the entire drive. She's always got her gun, Jake. Always. I think she even sleeps next to it. I was protected."

He nodded. Madison had been there once before with Zoey—not to mention the day of the search. She'd taken it on herself to lead Dom and the blond man away from Shelby.

There was no real shaking Jake.

Powell watched every move he made. "Shelby, do you want me to leave you alone with him? You'll have to remember that anything you say to him can be problematic at a later date. I really don't advise—"

"Gunnar! Help me out here!" Jake called impatiently. "Come get your new little friend!"

His big blond buddy came running. "What? What did I miss? Did Shelby kick your ass? Even a little bit?"

"Take Powell on a walk outside. She's getting in my way."

"Jake!" Shelby protested.

"Gladly. Shelby, do you think Powell wants to go to dinner with me tonight? I'm cute, house-trained, reasonably well mannered, and have had all my shots. I've recently been told that I look good in a tux. I can also provide character references."

Powell just gawked at him. So did Shelby.

The way the man was eyeing Powell, she almost thought he meant it. He certainly looked capable of scooping Powell up and carrying her away. Shelby could imagine him wearing Viking gear, hauling a helpless female captive away back to his furs.

Most women probably wouldn't have minded, either.

They still hadn't answered why they were now in the middle of her living room.

79

JAKE BIT BACK A SATISFIED SMILE AT HOW efficiently Gunnar separated the Barratt woman from the rest of the girl pack. Step one complete. Now…

He shot a look at Dom. The other man nodded, then used his big body to block the private investigator, Madison, and Zoey from where Jake hustled Shelby into the kitchen.

His buddies had his back. Her buddies let up squawks once they realized they'd been outmaneuvered. Jake almost growled with impatience. They needed to stop being so damned overprotective of her. They weren't doing her any favors.

"The deal was, you worked today being Mr. Big Bad TSP. And I used the car service and took a guard from Houghton with me. What has changed? I have plans for the rest of my day. Charlotte…Madison…Powell…Zoey and I have choir business to discuss, and we're going to do it here over pizza. What do you need?"

"A kiss hello." Jake used her wrist to reel her in. Until he had her right where he wanted her—pressed close. Three hells, he wanted to kiss her. So damned much. "I…was worried about you, after what we talked about. I didn't mean to upset you."

He brushed a kiss over her forehead before she could protest, then he pulled back. Just looked at her. She didn't have any makeup on.

She looked so young and innocent.

He wanted to debauch her, if that was still a word for it.

Jake understood himself. Gunnar had disconcerted him, all that talking about marriage and shit. It had him thinking about having a woman of his own. Imagining what she'd be like.

Realization slammed into him like a Mack truck.

There was only one.

"So you accosted my employee?"

His thoughts darkened. "Why do you need him in the first place?"

"He's looking into certain things for me. And he helps me weed out questionable people after my money."

He could halfway understand that. "That's all there is to it?"

"This isn't any of your business."

"No. It isn't. Except I'm making it my business."

"Why? It's my money, my time. And you have nothing to do with it."

She was hiding something. Jake knew it with one look. She fought him more on things when there were secrets she didn't want him to unbury. "What are you hiding?"

"You want the truth? I don't trust the TSP to have *my* best interests at heart. Mel recommended Naelin back when I had to start fighting to get Logan's estate turned over. Mel and her brother-in-law, Chance Marshall. *They*, two people I trust, told me I can depend on him. So if you find anything else that pertains to me, expect a subpoena for it to be turned over to Powell. I'm tired of playing around, Giacomo."

She stared at him for a long moment. There was a look of determination in the storm-blue today. A look that made him want to gobble her up. Something had changed in her since their encounter last night.

"I've got the money to do what I want. I'm going to start. This is just the first step. Now, like I said, I have business. I'm going to meet with him for a few minutes, while we wait for Charlotte. Then, we're going to talk about better things than the TSP and break-ins and everything poop that you just roll around in every day. We are even talking about going to see the new Hunter Louis Clark movie this evening, too. Th-th-the one where he has his shirt off for half of it. I would love to see that on a theater screen. Up close and personal. Charlotte was in a movie with him. She's seen him without his shirt. No mere mortal man can compete with Hunter Louis Clark. You should know that, Uncle Jake. Even your super-hot blond Viking friend can't. Although he actually comes pretty close. I've always had a thing for blonds, after all. Just like *Logan*. Your friend's hot enough to have me breaking my no-cops rule, too. If I can see him without his shirt, that is. I'll go to dinner with *him* if…if…if Powell doesn't want to. If you'll just unground me from everything fun."

She shot him an exaggerated look and crossed her arms over her beautiful chest. He growled.

He was on to her now. Yes. She was trying to distract him. Little witch. She'd pay for that. She was good at distracting people from what she was up to. Real good at it. Practiced.

He wondered how often she'd done just that to her older brother. How often had she played Allen to get what she wanted? Interesting.

Jake checked behind him. Dom had done a damned fine job of getting Madison and the others away from the parlor Jake had ushered Shelby into.

He could see Gunnar and the lawyer arguing—the lawyer was ranting something right into his face. Gunnar stood with his arms crossed, looking a long way down at the petite woman, an arrested look on his face—they were out of Jake's way, too.

"I'll gladly let you see my chest up close and personal. Let you touch..." He wrapped his hands around her waist and backed her into the wall. Her palms spread over his chest. He leaned down, ready to snag her lips with his own. She pushed against him. "Only if I can see yours in return, though."

She smirked. Dug her little kitten claws into the cotton of his T-shirt. Viciously. Damn. It stung. Her smile was pure evil at his wince. "I call a load of crap. The instant I say yes, you'd head for the hills. Giving...giving...giving me some sort of line about it being 'all for my own good' and 'you're not the man for me' and 'we're from different worlds.' You are too big of a coward. I am just your plaything right now. The latest pawn on your TSP chessboard. We both know it. You are incapable of seeing anyone—especially women—of anything else. At least anyone not Izzie, Annie, or from your beloved TSP. I know you think I'm not good enough for you—so what are you really playing at?"

"Not a damned thing."

To his shock, after her little daggers dug into his skin. she stretched that delectable body of hers up and pressed against him. Full-out pressed against him, having his heart beating straight out of his chest. She gave him a pointed kiss that almost scorched his insides—and then shoved him away from her. "What are you really doing here, Jake? Time you told me the truth."

Falling head over heels with the woman in front of him. No doubt about that.

"Truth? I missed the hell out of you today." Hell with that. He wasn't about to let her get the upper hand. Jake scooped her back into his arms where she belonged.

And kissed the hell out of her. Like he'd been wanting to since she'd climbed out of her hired car and stood toe-to-toe with him in her driveway, her friends looking at him like he was a garden slug.

Jake just kissed her.

He'd been away from her for far too long today. It had felt like a lifetime.

80

It was stupid of her, but she kissed him back. She was starting to think she always would. The instant his lips touched hers, she had a hard time resisting. For even a moment.

Damn him. Why did he do this to her?

Was it because when she was fighting with him or engaged in the duels their kisses most certainly were that she felt more alive than she had in a long, long while?

Jake didn't have any impossible expectations of her for her to live up to—or live down. She was free to be really *her* with him.

Good or bad.

Her imperfections didn't matter with Jake. He didn't like her at all to begin with.

That was surprisingly freeing.

She supposed that was one answer.

The cliché was "he got her blood pumping." That didn't necessarily mean in a good way. But she kissed him back. Like a fool, whose friends weren't just a few rooms away, she let him back her into the wall of her formal front parlor and kiss her.

She had no pride. Dignity was just a ghost, too.

"Well, looks like everyone's doing just fine in here," a female voice said from behind Jake's back. "Except Powell. She looks about ready to commit murder."

He pulled away.

Shelby focused on the woman standing in the open door.

"You really shouldn't leave your front door open like this, Shel. A strange batch of men seems to have wandered right in off the streets. Why is Powell trying to shake Gunnar loose? Something tells me I've missed something."

"Charlotte, you...you're here." Hallelujah. Jake was dangerous to her sanity. She was going to have to remember that. "Jake...go away. I have things to do."

"I'm coming back tonight. To do guard duty. Text me when you get to wherever you are going, or if Daviess has to leave. This isn't over yet. Chuckie, looking good, little devil doll."

Just like that, he was gone. Leaving her a wobbly mass of jelly, almost at Charlotte's feet.

"I hope he takes his goons with him. I heard it's poker night at my old man's," Charlotte said, green eyes peering up at Shelby, concern written all over her face. "Are you ok? I mean, I know he's a decent kisser—Madison and I compared him to a few others—but he never rocked my world like that. I think the two of you were wobbling for a moment there. My expert opinion says those are scorch marks on the wall. Even on your lips. We have so much to talk about. I want details."

"First...I have to talk to my private investigator. We have some business to discuss. And I think I need to apologize to him. He...they had him in cuffs when I pulled in. And he had dirt on him. I can i-i-imagine what they did to him."

"Those guys are total idiots sometimes, Shel. Total idiots. I like Powell's older brothers and cousins so much better." Charlotte crossed her arms and kept watching her. "Come to think of it, she has one for each of us—with a few spares left over. Maybe we should let her set us up with them, after all?"

SHELBY WAS GOING TO ENJOY THE REST OF THE afternoon with her friends. She wasn't going to let Jake or his little buddies stand in the way of that. That just wasn't going to happen. But first...

Naelin was familiar with her office and settled into his favorite chair in front of her desk.

"Are you ok?" Naelin asked. At first, she had been very hesitant with him; she had never hired anyone to do anything in her life before him. While he was a rough man around the edges at times, he was genuinely goodhearted.

He had worked for Shelby since one month before the storm. Finding the answers she needed. Unfortunately, those answers weren't emerging fast enough. For either of them.

"I'm fine. Jake may be with the TSP, but in a weird way, he is family. I am physically s-s-safe with him." That was a lie. The last thing she felt for Jake was familial, but it would buy her some privacy where the man was concerned. "What have you found?"

"Nothing good. I tracked down Joanne Spietzer. Had a little chat with her, right there in her office. She wasn't too helpful; her fourth husband was just on the other side of the wall. She's his receptionist."

"Fourth? In five years? Wow. She's b-b-been busy." Joanne had pretended to be their friend that night. They had trusted her, completely. And when she had goaded and wheedled them into attending a party her brother was throwing, they hadn't seen the harm in it. Because they had trusted her. Joanne had thought it was all a joke-gone-awry and had made a half-hearted attempt to apologize to Daryn two days after it happened.

When she'd seen the bruises.

Neither Shelby nor Daryn hadn't been stupid, Joanne hadn't

been sincere. She'd gotten a kick out of what she had done. Out of having that kind of control of them.

The apology had only come after Zoey had arrived. Zoey was two years older, tougher and scary—Zoey had always intimidated Joanne. If Zoey had been there with them that night, the attack might not have happened.

Then again, it might have, and Zoey might've been hurt as well. That was the last thing Shelby would've wanted.

No, it had just been a random event. One that had changed her life forever.

She had to remind herself to be patient. That the answers would come eventually. So would the moving forward.

"I did get another first name," Naelin said. "I'm running down leads now."

His biggest task was finding witnesses to that night who were willing to discuss what had happened. When it was the very cops who were supposed to be protecting you that were committing the crime, finding witnesses was a little harder than she had imagined.

"Don't give up. I want to keep going."

"Good girl. I'll find you the answers, Shelby. You have my word."

81

He was watching her place. Waiting for her to finish with her friends. Jake knew that was a bit over the line, but he wanted to know when she got home. They'd filed out of Shelby's place and into a limo like a bunch of beautiful little ducks.

He'd done some digging into Naelin Lassiter. The guy wasn't just a private investigator. The man had some serious connections—including some with the FBI. He didn't do just run-of-the-mill background checks like you could buy off the internet. He went deeper than that.

The investigator part of his description meant something. And that concerned the hell out Jake.

She was up to something. He was going to find out what, now that he had her alone.

Except...

She wasn't climbing out of her car alone.

Another, thinner, slightly taller woman walked next to her.

Jake stepped out, where they could see him. "Shelby."

She gave a breathless yelp. Her friend went into a defensive stance. She was armed.

Jake held up his hands. "Sorry, ladies, I didn't mean to scare you."

"MacNamara, you're either lurking or stalking. I'm not sure which," the sheriff said, holstering her weapon. "Shel, I'm going to go into the guest room and call Pen. See what she's up to. Then you and I are going to talk about this sudden impulsive streak you've developed. I like it, but it's so unlike you."

"I'll just be a few minutes." Shelby didn't take her eyes off him.

He was going to get his questions answered. He waited until the other woman was inside, after the sheriff shot him a warning look. Jake just smirked. Too bad Gunnar hadn't seen *her* first instead of the Barratt woman. It would have been entertaining to see the sheriff butt heads with a big blond pain in the ass like Gunnar.

"Talk. What do you want?"

"What is Naelin Lassiter really looking into for you?"

"I told you before. He handles just general security and in…in…inquiries."

"We're going to talk tonight. And you're going to tell me what you're involved in."

"Jake, if I choose to sashay naked through the Barratt every alternate Tuesday, it's none of *your* business. Nothing I do is your business. Period. In fact, I have Zoey here. You can leave. Go home. Feed your cat."

"I'm making it my business. And if there is any naked sashaying, it'll be for me only." Jake stepped closer. "Here's the deal. I'm not going anywhere. You are stuck with me until I am ready to leave."

Shelby kicked him.

Right in the shin.

Again.

Jake wrapped his hand around her wrist and pulled her closer. "You keep kicking and scratching me, and I'm going to spank your ass myself, woman. And I'll make sure we both enjoy it. Now. Decision. Are you worried about your virtue after what happened on the rug? Even with your little pal inside? I'll assure you I can behave myself just fine where you are concerned. It's hard, but I think I'll manage."

It was a lie, but at least, it sounded good.

He wanted to scoop her close and devour her right up.

82

ZOEY CAME BACK OUT, AN ODD LOOK ON HER FACE. Shelby just waited. She knew her friend well enough. Zoey would spill when she was ready to spill.

"Pen's in trouble," Zoey said. "I have to go. I swear, if I have to bail her out again, I'm leaving her in jail overnight. Maybe then she'll figure things out."

"It was just the one time, and an accident," Shelby reminded her as she finally stepped into the house and headed to the kitchen, Jake and Zoey just steps behind her.

"Well, she's having far too many accidents lately." A worried look passed over her face. "It's like she has her own demons."

"Don't we...we...we all? I think she's just trying to find out who she is, too." Like they all were. Zoey had always worried over Pen. She probably always would. For years, Pen had been all she had.

Except for Daryn and Shelby, anyway. When Zoey had had an emergency appendectomy a few years ago, it had taken Shelby and Daryn several hours to get there to the small hospital ninety minutes south of Garrity, where Zoey had been rushed. It had been bad. Pen had been terrified. Terrified and alone and just a fourteen-year-old kid.

Shelby had wrapped Pen in her own arms and held her. Told her that she and Zoey would not be alone ever again. They were a part of her family, too.

But Pen had changed that night. Grown up a little.

Unfortunately, she'd become a little more anxious than she had been before.

Something she shared in common with her older sister. "Wh-wh-what has she done tonight?"

"I'm not certain. But I think there may have been some spray paint involved. And…the mayor's brother's production studio. Mel's sister called Elliot Marshall to get them all out of trouble. I don't know the entire story. Yet. But I will."

Shelby privately wished Pen good luck. Zoey had that warrior queen look in her dark eyes again. The one that meant she was about to go all mama dragon on her little sister.

"Is he sticking around?" Zoey asked, looking straight at Jake. She'd made it very well known that she didn't like him around Shelby at all. She'd told Shelby all her objections to anything between them. Objections Shelby fully agreed with.

Zoey had finally been satisfied when Shelby told her exactly why she was not protesting Jake's presence any longer.

And she'd agreed.

Better the devil they knew in Shelby's house than a demon they didn't.

Shelby wasn't stupid. She was going to keep Jake exactly where he belonged. Shelby yanked her arm free of his. He just smirked at her.

"*He* is staying right here next to Shelby. Wrapped around Shelby, if she'll let him. So go, Sheriff Zoey. Do what you got to do. Watch your back out there. Wear your seat belt, look both ways before crossing the street, don't talk to men you don't know, don't take candy from strangers, don't walk down any dark alleys, use a condom, and call me and your mother when you get there, young lady." Jake gave a cocky little salute in Zoey's direction. "Seriously, though, I'll take care of her. I am more than willing to do guard duty."

"But who is going to guard her from you?" Zoey shot him a glare, then looked at Shelby. It was obvious she was conflicted—but Shelby was firm on one thing.

Pen needed Zoey more than Shelby did. Hands down. Zoey was the only parent Pen had ever had. And that mattered. So very much.

"Guess we'll have to find out, won't we?"

Shelby wanted to kick him again. Why was that so satisfying?

She pondered that as Zoey left. Why did Jake bring out the raw side of her so easily?

Then it was just her. And him. Shelby looked at the dark-haired devil. Waiting for the questions to start again.

"So what did she mean by impulsive? You decide to take up pole dancing tonight? I would love it if you did. Put a pole in the gym downstairs. I'll watch you twist around it all night long. Especially if you take off your clothes while you are doing it."

"You are a total dog, aren't you?"

"I've heard that before. I didn't believe it then. I don't now. So...what's the story?"

Shelby moved around the island, putting the marble expanse between them. He had a look in his eyes...one of hunger.

It had an answering heat practically scorching her.

She needed a distraction. Fast. "I'm going to buy Mamaw's Place. Pay...pay...pay someone to run it for me."

His eyes showed his surprise. "You could run it yourself...if you knew how to cook. Join the working class again."

She shot him a glare at that little dig. He'd teased her about not cooking twice since she'd admitted it.

Well, admitted part of it. The housekeeper had thought

Shelby had been stupid because of her stutter. The woman hadn't wanted her anywhere near her precious kitchen. By the time Shelby had admitted that to her brother, the woman had worked for them for a year, and Shelby had been determined to not learn how to cook from that woman at all. Even though Allen had wanted her to learn.

Shelby had refused.

Shelby could do enough to get by, but cooking was not something she'd ever enjoy. Not like her brother did.

He'd taken over cooking for them after he'd fired that housekeeper the very next day—once Shelby had finally told him why she avoided the housekeeper all the time.

"Well? Why aren't you? I'm very curious here. Why would you buy a restaurant?"

"Why not?" Shelby spread her hands out on the counter in front of her. Faced the devil head on. "Isn't that what we rich women are supposed to do? Buy frivolous things?"

"Diamond tiaras, not restaurants."

"Well. I want a diner, not a tiara. My friends and I like Mamaw's. This way...it'll always be there for us when we want to go there. And the people who work there won't lose their jobs. It was going to cl-cl-close if someone didn't buy it soon. I don't intend to *tell* anyone I'm the owner when I'm there, though. So keep your mouth shut."

"Yes, ma'am." He gave an exaggerated bow.

The man just irked her straight to her toes, sometimes. That hadn't been missed when he'd been staring at her earlier. Him and his little buddies. She stalked toward her office, just knowing the beast would follow her. She needed her space around her now—and her office was where she felt the most like *her*. Her office and her piano, anyway. "I do so love to be your entertainment, you know."

"Now, now, *bambina*. Snotty princess doesn't work on me any longer."

"What?"

"I know it's all an act now."

"Is it? How would you know? You don't know anything about me, Jake. You n-n-never have."

"I see you, Shelby Grace Jacobson. The real you." Jake's tone softened. There was a look in his eyes she'd never seen there before.

One that scared her. "How?"

"I catch a glimpse. Usually when you are kicking me, though. There is a fire in you. I would love to get burned by it."

"Do you see her? I'm glad one of us does. I don't think I've seen that Shelby in a long, long time. Years, maybe. I'm pretty certain she died a long time ago."

Shelby forced herself to hold her ground as she turned to look at him, right there in the hall between her office and the kitchen. She wanted to run. To get to her sanctuary and slam the doors shut. Lock him out.

To hide.

Like she somehow always had. In the five years since that night, she had spent ninety percent of her time *hiding*. And she was so, so, so tired of it.

She wanted out into the light. Was that so much to ask?

"Baby…that Shelby is right here…"

"Is she? How do you know, Uncle Jake?"

"No. No doing that. No deflecting. I know you now. I've caught on to your little distraction trick. And I'm not falling for it again."

Shelby jerked her head back, fighting the warring emotions with everything she had.

Why was it that she felt so much more *alive* when fighting with Jake? He had her almost pinned to the wall in front of him. Trapped and vulnerable.

How was that even fair? She fluttered her lashes at him, even though she wanted to press against him and have someone just *hold* her again.

Have someone to really see the girl she used to be, wanted to be again.

Then again, maybe it was time to say goodbye to that naive, stupid young girl?

Accept the woman she was now?

Actually let that woman *live* for once. Tonight had felt great; she'd had friends with her, a common purpose, and joy in what they were doing. Joy in *life*.

It had been a long time since she'd felt that on a regular basis. Shelby wanted that, wanted it so much she practically ached from it. She was too afraid to go for it.

So she just did what she knew would work. And pushed.

With Jake. Always with Jake. Why was it always with *Jake*?

Why did she feel she could push back with him and no one else? That didn't make any sense to her at all.

"What...what...what...are you going to do about it, Jake? What are you going to do about *me*? Come on. Show me. Unless you are too scared?"

83

JAKE KNEW ONE THING IN THAT MOMENT. HE WAS getting his hands on the woman. Showing her what she did to him. He had reached his limit. "Come here."

Storm-gray eyes burned into his. "Wh-what?"

"I said come here. I can't take it any longer. You have been tormenting me for months. Until I can't stand it. I dream of you at night. Every damned night I hold you in my arms and when I wake you are not there. I can't stand it any longer. I'm a mere mortal man. I can only take so much."

He knew her well enough to know she was going to run. It would be instinct. Basic self-preservation. He would have her. Sure enough, the eyes widened as she yelped.

Just like that, she ran toward the French doors.

Jake was damned faster. His hands went around her waist and he yanked her closer, until they both stumbled into the wall a bit. "I got you now. You're not getting away from me."

She trembled in his hands. He wanted to make her tremble in so many other ways now. He just hoped she'd let him.

He wanted that more than he had ever wanted anything ever. He wanted her.

Needed her.

He told her that. Then covered those soft pink lips with his own.

No one was quite like her in the world. No one.

Jake wanted her so damned much his teeth ached from it. He bent a bit, lifted her.

Her legs went around his waist. He was a taller, stronger than average guy. She felt just right in his arms. Perfect.

The most perfect woman in the world. For him.

What in the hell was he doing?

Jake carried her back into her office. To the sofa there that had taunted him before. He just wanted her on the first available flat surface. He didn't care where, at this point.

Never mind the sofa. The rug would work.

And it was a hell of a lot closer.

Never mind that she deserved better than to be rolling around on the floor with him.

He wanted to conquer her, have her beneath him where she belonged. Showing her who he was and what she meant to him.

He really was an animal at heart.

Especially where she was concerned.

"Jake?" She asked in a whisper. "What...what...what are you thinking?"

Her hands were clinging to him. When he touched her, she let him. She wasn't pushing him away. He cupped her cheek in one hand. "How much I want you. Breathe for you."

She stared up at him, a hurting look in the eyes he loved so much. One hand rose, cupped his cheek in return.

Jake stared down at her for a lifetime. Something was different between them now. He couldn't put his finger on what, but it was there. In her.

Maybe in him, too.

He was ready to beg for this woman. Putting that into words

would damn near destroy him.She had more power over him than any woman ever had before.

That terrified him.

Now he understood Dom and Madison a bit better. The other man had to feel just like this when he looked at Madison. And to know he just wasn't good enough for her? It would destroy a man after a while. To see the woman he wanted and to not have her.

Because he just wasn't good enough.

Hell, for the first time, he empathized with Logan Lanning, too.

To have watched Shelby be hurt so badly, and not been able to stop it—it would have destroyed Jake, too. In ways he didn't even want to contemplate.

"I want you, Shelby Grace. We both know I'm the last son of a bitch on the planet that you need. I...but I can't stay away. You draw me like fire. I think you could destroy me, too."

She blinked up at him with wet and stormy eyes. Just watched him, looking deep into his soul. Then her other hand rose and she held his face in her hands. She leaned up, pressed her lips to his.

As her hands slid around his shoulders as if they were meant to be right there forever.

He'd started off thinking of showing her the man in him that wanted to be her hero, be in charge. Be strong and in control.

The instant she'd touched him, he'd turned into this mess of need.

He *needed* her more than he needed breath.

Jake wanted to show her that somehow. So that someday she would remember him and understand.

He needed *her*.

Jake just didn't have the words.

There was a look in his eyes that burned into her soul. Longing and pain.

Two things she understood on a deeply intimate level. Shelby kissed him. Holding him as tightly as she could.

That was all she really wanted. Someone to hold on to her.

She was tired of being the one that *needed*. She wanted to be needed herself, too.

She had people to stand shoulder to shoulder against the world with. She had figured that out a while ago. She would always have her brother, and now Izzie.

Daryn and Zoey, too. Madison and Charlotte when the chips were down. Powell and Haldyn, too.

She wasn't alone.

But having someone to see *her* deep inside and want to hold her, need her to hold him in return?

She ached for that with every inch of her soul, too. She wanted what Izzie and Annie and Nikkie Jean and Mel had. They had found men who understood their inner fears and needs, too.

She hadn't.

She knew that. Not yet.

Maybe with Jake she could get a little closer.

She did care about him. Jake actually *did* matter to her, even though she'd told herself he didn't, almost from the moment they had met.

That...struck her like a lightning bolt.

She deeply to her soul cared about the man holding her. She didn't even know *why* exactly.

Maybe that was what it was. Shelby saw the echoing loneliness in *him*. Understood it so much.

When he pulled back with regret, she protested. "Jake...I..."

"As much as I want this to continue, I don't have anything to protect you. It's...not exactly something I carry with me."

It took her a moment to put together what he meant. Her cheeks flamed. She had literally never had this conversation with a man before in her life. The last time she had been in this position with a man, he had been prepared and just handled it.

Shelby had been planning to let Logan handle it, if the time had come, too. She had just known he would.

She had been rather naive back then, after all. Just a stupid kid.

She'd been passive about that, too. Well, no more.

It was time she took control of her life.

She wanted this man. Period. One night with Jake wouldn't change her. Not that much. She just wanted someone to hold her tonight.

She stared into his dark eyes as she weighed her next words carefully. "There…in the bottom drawer of my desk. In a bag with W4HAV printed on it. Nikkie Jean hands them out like candy. Sometimes she won't let you leave W4HAV without taking at least two. Sometimes it's embarrassing and quicker to just take them…in the bottom drawer. I wasn't certain what I should do with them, actually."

He stared at her for the longest time.

Everything had changed, pivoted. Shelby had made her decision.

And she wasn't going to run away. "Jake? They are right there, and I…I…I…am not saying no. Hold me tonight. I think that's what we both need now. Just hold me for a little while. Please?"

"I can do that."

84

HE HELD HER WHILE SHE SLEPT, LOVING HAVING HER next to him. Even while he was filled with regrets. It had been the best night with a woman in his life.

It never should have happened.

Because it had been Shelby.

She slept curled up next to him, naked in his arms. He'd slipped his boxers back on a few hours ago. His gun rested beneath his jeans in the chair by her bed. Right where he could reach it.

Just in case. He hadn't forgotten why he was at her place to begin with.

To protect her.

Well, he was doing a damned shitty job of it. She'd told him she'd only been with one other man before. He hadn't asked if it was Lanning.

Tonight, he hadn't wanted to know.

She'd been nervous, so damned nervous as he'd touched her. As they'd explored each other.

Jake had been as gentle as he could, feeling like he'd been given the best gift of his life by being allowed to touch her. He brushed her tangled hair off one cheek. Touched the smooth silk of her skin.

His arm tightened around her. She snuggled closer, pressing against his side. So damned perfect he almost wanted to cry from it.

Hell, it felt right to be exactly where he was.

But just because it felt that way, didn't mean it was true.

The room they were in now was twice as big as his own. More. It had to be half the total size of his own apartment alone.

Even the bed he slept in cost more than the entire furnishings in his apartment. And she wouldn't understand why or how that bothered him.

He couldn't imagine a woman like Shelby living in his white box of an apartment. She was made for this. For the silk sheets and two-hundred-year-old bed frames and he would bet his last paycheck that little knickknack on the bedside table next to his cheap cell phone was real gold.

She was made for this world. He wasn't.

Never had Jake felt that more. Felt just not good enough.

Hell, he'd been born in a three-room cottage next to the sea. His parents' place would have fit entirely in Shelby's front parlor. His mother had worked as a maid until she'd passed away when Jake had been nineteen. He'd lost his father when he'd been eleven, not that he had known that man well. Jake's father had been a workaholic mechanic at the nearby US military base.

Jake had barely known him at all, except as the man he knew to obey immediately and the man who often yelled at Jake's mother. Over money, and that there was never enough of it. Not enough money and too many kids.

His mother would have worked in this place, not lived in it.

Never had he felt the divide between them more.

"Jake?" She asked in a sleepy voice that had his gut tightening with instant lust. "What's wrong?"

"Nothing just can't sl—"

The security alarm cut him off. Jake reacted immediately. "Go."

She had a panic room, just off the back of the bedroom, where most of the country-club-set women would keep their shoe collection. She'd shown it to him reluctantly before. There was even a secret exit at the rear.

She'd had it installed after inheriting the house. No one had known of it until the day the TSP had searched the house. He'd cautioned Chuckie, who'd been with him at the time he'd found it, that it was to be kept out of the official records.

No photos were to be taken of it. It was Shelby's. And she deserved to feel safe in her own home. Chuckie had understood and promised to keep it secret after she'd peered inside looking for evidence of Logan Lanning's crimes.

"Come with me!" Her hands pulled at him. "Please, Jake. Please."

It wasn't in his DNA to hide while there was a threat. Especially when that threat was to the woman he...cared about. He tossed her the nearest shirt quickly. His.

Jake shook his head. Cleared it, quickly. "No. Go. I'm going to go see what the problem is. You go where you will be safe. I need you to do that. This is what I do, Shelby. Protect. Let me do it."

The hardest thing he had ever done was leave her alone wearing only his T-shirt while he went to find the threat.

85

Dom hated driving at night, especially three-hour drives. He followed the forensics van at a decent distance. Anticipation tightened his gut.

The Garrity co-sheriff had called the instant he'd realized what he'd found. He hadn't screwed around. Dom appreciated it. There was another car behind him; one he'd recognized from before.

From Shelby's, of all places.

The other Garrity co-sheriff. Everyone in the TSP had heard about the two smallest regions merging into one. And two polar opposite partners who despised each other getting shoved together—one male, one female—the TSP had been speculating about them for months. Last he'd heard, they'd split the region down the middle informally. She took the northern half nearest Value. Lake took the southern, closer to Garrity, itself.

He knew which sheriff he preferred, personally.

The exceptionally hot one.

He spent a few minutes thinking about that woman casually. She was highly attractive—no denying that—but his taste ran more toward fiery little shrews.

Little shrews who were hiding things from him.

If he had his way, he'd bundle his father, stepmother, step-brother and Madison up and send them off somewhere he could be sure they wouldn't be targeted because of him. His dad could keep them safe while Dom did what he had to do.

That wasn't about to happen.

He would have to talk to his father about making certain they took necessary precautions, though. Soon. Probably sooner rather than later.

"You think this is it?" the man next to him asked. Gunnar was a nonstop talker. It pissed Dom off on a regular basis. The man was good at what he did, and smart about it, too. He just talked too damned much.

There were worse partners to have at his back. Major Crimes had come together damned well over the last three years or so. They all worked well together.

Dom liked it that way. It was easier to get the job done.

They were calling in Charlie and Mike as well. The only ones not going to be involved tonight had other commitments—Callum to the paternity leave he'd insisted he was taking, and Jake watching over Shelby.

Dom frowned again. Something about her entire situation wasn't sitting right with him, especially since the vandalism at W4HAV.

Why would Shelby be targeted *now*? When Jake was about to break the biggest case Major Crimes had ever had?

Jake—the second in command of the high-profile, much-talked-about Major Crimes division. Damned coincidental.

Dom grunted at Gunnar. The man didn't require answers, mostly. Just acknowledgment. With Jake consumed with protecting Shelby and Callum out with the new baby, that spread Major Crimes a bit too thin.

Add the magic last-minute summons of Daniel to Wichita Falls this evening—something Elliot Marshall hadn't even known about when Dom had called to update him about the Garrity bust—something didn't feel right tonight.

Charlie radioed in, confirming it was him and Evers approaching them from behind. Yeah, Dom was feeling itchy. Whenever that happened... "Watch yourselves out here tonight. Something's off."

The radio crackled. *"You, too?"*

"Yeah. Keep an eye on forensics, too." Madison and Chuckie were in the forensics van in front of him, having been called in to take the scene so far away from their area by the swing-shift supervisor.

"Will do."

Of course, Charlie would. Chuckie was his only daughter.

She'd be one hell of a target. Get her—and they'd get to Charlie, too. If anyone knew how much Madison mattered to Dom—well, it wasn't a far stretch.

Bailey Addy, the only other woman on the task force, was also in that van.

That was a damned-high-target van right there. He swore as he pushed his foot to the floor. He wasn't letting that van out of his sight.

86

JAKE CURSED AS THE BASTARD PRACTICALLY VAULTED over Shelby's back fence and took off. The guard from Barratt-Handley wasn't any closer to catching him than Jake was.

He hadn't gotten close enough to see the guy. Nothing defining, anyway. Just a guy around Jake's age or younger, and around his size. Fit.

He'd scaled that fence damned quick.

What had he been after?

Jake looked up toward Shelby's bedroom window.

He suspected he knew.

Her.

He suspected the Barratt-Handley guards' presence had surprised the asshole. That was what had done it. Why? Why would someone risk coming for her again? There had to be a reason. Besides the money.

This was too deliberate.

There were other wealthy targets in this city. With the TSP presence around Shelby, why were they so intent on getting to *her* specifically instead of moving on to another target?

Unless it had nothing to do with her money at all, and had everything to do with *her*.

Just what in the hell was that woman involved in?

Jake called it in. Wanting it on record.

Not that he suspected anything would come of it. A low-level intruder in Hughes Heights wasn't going to be a high priority for the TSP right now.

Unless someone made it one.

Jake wasn't going to take a chance with her.

He stormed back into the house after ordering the Barratt guards to keep watch from opposite sides of her property. She needed guards on all four corners, and her own personal security team. And while they were at it, they needed to replace that chain-link fence with a stone one, with barbed wire and electric fencing around the top. Just to be on the safe side.

No sense being careless.

He was going to talk to Chance Marshall in the morning, see what he had to do to get started on securing her place much better than it was. There were things he wouldn't think of. Jake had never hired employees in his life. But he was going to start.

Someone had wanted to hurt her tonight.

Jake would never take that lightly.

He entered the code into the panel by the back door and stormed into the rear of the kitchen.

Just to come face to face with her. "You should be in the panic room."

"I watched on the camera. I knew it was safe to come out."

"Like hell it was."

"Jake?" She looked at him with a hesitant look on her gorgeous face. She'd pulled on pajama pants. They clashed with his T-shirt.

Hell, he loved seeing her in his shirt.

But he was so damned pissed right now. "You need better security. I'm going to take care of it in the morning."

"I-I-I'll think a-a-about it."

"You'll do it. I can't stay here babysitting you forever."

She flinched. He cursed himself, his tone. He'd seen the nerves in her eyes. Either because of him, or because of the bastard who had snapped them back to reality. "I didn't ask you to in the first place."

"No. You didn't. But I am here, anyway, aren't I?"

He would have said far more but his phone rang. With Daniel's ringtone.

Daniel would only be calling if it was important.

He listened, cursed.

Disconnected. "I'll be back. I have to go. Now."

Storms went through her eyes. He'd been as close to her as he could get, and he still didn't know the true color of her eyes. He probably never would figure it out. Blue or gray—they were perfect.

Just like the rest of her.

"M-maybe it would be best if you just don't c-c-come back? I have guards now. I will be ok." Her chin rose, and he saw the wounded pride. The fear and doubt. "I don't need you, Jake. I never really have."

He bit back the impatience. If he hadn't been there, if the guards hadn't...she would be in a hell of a lot worse of a place now. "Get changed. I'm dropping you off with the Barratts. I don't have time to argue. Go."

He had to get out there and do his damned job. Daniel's call and the damned intruder had just served to remind him of exactly who he was.

And what he could mean to Shelby. Absolutely nothing.

She scurried away in an instant.

Jake checked the clock. Hell, it wasn't even ten p.m. yet.

What in the hell was going on out there? The last thing he wanted to do was leave her again tonight, not after this.

After what had happened between them.

But duty called.

The TSP was waiting.

Like it damned well always was. And like he always would, Jake answered.

HE'D BROUGHT HER TO MEL'S AND DROPPED HER OFF on the other woman like a recalcitrant toddler. At eleven p.m. at night.

Like he had his fill of babysitting and just couldn't be bothered.

He had basically said as much to her earlier. Shelby wouldn't forget that. She suspected she'd given Jake exactly what he had been wanting—in her bed. It wouldn't surprise her at all if he didn't find a reason not to come back to her house tonight after all.

Or any night.

To her chagrin, there had been people at Mel's.

Including her brother and Izzie. They had just stared when she'd walked in wearing old jeans and an even older FCU T-shirt. Jake had barely given her time to brush the tangles from her hair.

Damn Jake.

He had basically sat her in front of Allen, patted her on the head, patted Izzie on the belly, and then told Shelby to stay.

Said she was to behave for her big brother and that he would come back for her as soon as he could. He didn't know when that would be.

Then he'd left. Not telling her where he was going at all. Or what was happening.

There had been questions. Lots of questions.

And a sly look between him and his boss, Elliot, who had been there with his own wife.

Shelby had nodded when Allen asked her if she was ok. She hadn't said anything.

She wasn't ok.

She was hopping mad.

So mad she didn't trust herself to say a word. To anyone. She forced herself to take several deep breaths, to try to regain her sense of control.

Tonight had been an accident. A moment of weakness she would never repeat.

Her one stupid thing.

"He's there, and then he's gone. Sometimes for days at a time. Jake really doesn't stay put all that well."

Shelby turned.

There Izzie was. Holding out a drink.

Shelby took it gratefully. "I—"

"I saw your face when he left. I don't think Allen did, thankfully. If he had, you'd have some serious explaining to do. Plus, I know that just-thoroughly-kissed look. I see it in the mirror quite often. Allen refuses to even think about you kissing a man. If your brother knew you were kissing Jake? Well, Allen would probably blow his top even thinking about it. I'm about ready to myself."

'What...what...what are you talking about?"

"I think you know." Izzie wrapped her hands around the railing and looked out over the city north of them. They were just on the outskirts between Finley Creek and the county south's largest city, Barrattville. Finley Creek was visible five miles or so in the distance. Jake was there somewhere. It felt like an ocean separated them now. "Don't fall for him, Shel. Please. I love him more than words can say, but he holds himself back from anything real and lasting with women. You are the last woman on earth I'd want him to be with. Ever. You deserve more than he can give."

"It's not like that. Jake and I...we're just not fighting any longer. Not really. And…and…I…he's staying to protect me. It's his job. That's it." Weak, and they both knew it.

She seriously doubted he was there protecting her now for her. Far from it.

No. She was a part of a bigger case to him. To Major Crimes. It was just convenient for *them* that Jake was the one watching her now.

She had been the one to decide that there would be more between them tonight. Just for a little while. She owned that, and she would not be mad at herself for it. Not tonight.

She had made that decision for herself. No one could take that away from her.

"He could request any other TSP detective take security detail, and we both know it. Just don't let him hurt you. Promise me."

Shelby nodded. She wasn't really in the habit of lying to her family. "I…I didn't mean it to happen."

"I know. Believe me, I know. When you're alone with a man suddenly for days…I know."

'It's not anything serious like that, Izzie. Not like you and Allen were. I promise. I just think it's time I stopped being so afraid of men…men…life. And…and I wanted my first…since *before* to be with someone I somewhat trusted. I needed that—to feel safe. I know Jake won't hurt me, physically. I fully believe he'd never hurt a woman physically. That matters more than you can know. I won't let him hurt me emotionally again. I do think it needed to be with him. Or someone *like* him, anyway. Maybe because he's…safe? And even maybe because he *is* TSP and so many of my nightmares involve the TSP? I need…need…need… to see people as people, not TSP. Even though all he cares about is the TSP. Maybe that is a part of it, too. He bridges the gap between the TSP and…the rest of the world…for me. For now."

Just for tonight, anyway. But she wasn't about to tell Izzie that.

"I can understand that." Izzie nodded, hugged her lightly. "Sometimes I see you as the little girl Allen still thinks you are and talks about you as. Sorry about that."

"I...I ...I hate what I did to Allen."

Izzie stared at her. "You didn't do anything to him. What are you saying?"

"I changed his entire world. He could have put me in boarding school, Izzie. Continued his life as it was. I would have been fine there, too. Would have made do. He kept me. He didn't have to. I know I wasn't exactly easy to handle. I never could do what my family wanted me to, couldn't live up to what they expected fr-fr-from me or for me—even before we lost our parents. Then I was his problem instead of theirs. I really try not to cause problems now. But stuff keeps happening."

"Problems? You weren't anyone's problem. Aren't. Ever. No. He did it because he loves you. Same with Jake and me. That man moved continents to get to me even before my mother died. Because of love. That's why Allen wanted you with him."

"I..." Shelby thought of the years since her parents' deaths. What had happened, the ups and downs. The knowledge that she had her brother.

"I mean...after I was attacked. Mostly." Shelby faced the woman next to her. She didn't speak of the attack easily. She probably never would. "I caused so much trouble for him back then. I don't know how to say I'm sorry for that."

Izzie's hands tightened on the rails. "You listen to me, Shelby. *You* didn't do that to your brother. They did. No matter how you reacted back then. You did what you had to do to heal. Maybe that meant putting up the walls. You needed them then. Don't be angry with yourself for that. You deserve to forgive yourself for that night. You didn't cause it. They did. And someday karma will pay them back for what they did. It's just a matter of time."

87

THE GARRITY CO-SHERIFF AND THE VALUE SHERIFF, who covered a good portion of the territory between Value and Garrity and had been called in to assist, were waiting at the old silo when Dom pulled in just after the van.

Dom approached the two men quickly. "What do you have?"

Zoey walked at Dom's side. With her dark street clothes, long dark hair, and pale skin, she looked far too ethereal in the light of the full moon above them to ever be involved with law enforcement, let alone a member of the governor's secret task force.

A very beautiful woman with secrets in her eyes. Fascinating, but troublesome. No denying that. If he didn't have it bad for Madison…

He'd seriously want to figure her out.

He turned to the forensics van as the rear door popped open. His little shrew was there, a bag slung over her shoulders and a set of the white burritos in her hands. She worked normal hours, most times, but every once in a while, something like this would crop up, and she'd be called in. It was the nature of the game.

"Dom," she said in acknowledgment. "Imagine my surprise. You would be the one responsible for calling us in on our evening off. Well, you got your wish. I had to cancel with my date."

"It wasn't me. It was your supervising coordinator." He stepped nearer. Wrapped his hands around her waist and lifted her down. She never made a fuss about him touching her—she knew he did it to disconcert her, and she wasn't going to let him know if it got to her or not. He so liked to touch her sometimes. He pulled her a bit closer. He leaned to whisper instructions. "Stay where I can see you at all times. Understand?"

He wasn't going to lose track of Madison out here tonight. He just wasn't.

"I'm here to do my job. Don't get in the way of that."

"Damn it, Madison, something feels off about this. I want to keep you safe."

"What are you saying?" She looked up at him. The light from the rear of the van reflected off her glasses, hiding her eyes from him.

"Just gut instinct."

"Well, that's real scientific there." They'd argued instinct versus science a few times. Heatedly. Until he'd wanted to show her what was going on in his gut for her. Let her explain the *science* of that to him, if she could.

What he felt for her was very instinctive, after all. Primitive caveman had found his mate. And wanted to claim. "Madison—"

"You two done snapping at each other?" Gunnar asked as the rest of the forensics team filed out.

Dom cataloged them quickly. Madison, Charlotte, Rory Price, and Bailey Addy—the sheriff of Value's wife and a supervisor with the mobile forensics team.

The pregnant supervisor with the mobile forensics team.

She and Sheriff Addy were already drawing toward each other. Like damned magnets. Big surprise there.

Lucky bastard, Dom thought, as the man ran one hand up his wife's back and pulled her a bit closer to whisper something in her ear.

Brave bastard.

Charlie said something to his daughter, and she nodded jerkily. "Fine, then, Pops. Whatever. We'll just get started."

Dom stayed back. This wasn't his gig—it was Madison's and her team's. He needed information. He turned to the men who would know. "What do we have so far?"

Murdoch Lake, the sheriff that worked with Zoey Daviess, filled them in quickly. "And we have two bodies in the back. I'm not sure how long they've been there. I'm almost certain they're those Wichita Falls TSP who went missing six weeks ago. Found them about fifteen minutes ago."

Dom cursed. He'd suspected those two men were involved in some serious evidence tampering more than four months ago. He and Jake had questioned them.

They hadn't been seen since.

Now he suspected he knew why.

Madison called out something about taking the bodies, as it was her turn. Until the ME's van could get there. They should have called out the ME assistant on duty—he thought it was Mike's wife tonight—earlier. Now they'd have to wait.

That was the real story of Major Crimes—hurry up and wait.

Nature of the beast.

Dom grabbed his phone. It would be a good three hours or more before an ME could get there. Might as well make the call now. And update the rest of the team, as well as the chief.

He had just pulled his phone free when Gunnar, who had been combing the perimeter with Zoey, yelled out from fifteen yards away. "*Gun!* Everybody down!"

Gunshots erupted around them.

Fire shot across his arm. Dom didn't give a damn. He had only one objective in mind now.

Madison.

Where the hell was she?

They were pinned down. He wasn't going anywhere.

And Madison was too far away.

88

ZOEY STAYED WHERE SHE WAS, WEAPON READY AS SHE checked everyone's positions. Detective Erickson had knocked her straight to the ground at the very last minute. Then they'd crawled to the nearest cover. He hunkered behind an old water tank a yard up from where she hid behind a large tree stump.

Neither one was all that effective as cover.

Charlotte and Madison were the most exposed. They'd been headed to the rear of the farm buildings where the bodies were located. They stayed where they were now, flat on the gravel path, pressed down in two large tire ruts probably made by a milk truck or something, heads covered, trying to make themselves as small as possible.

Totally exposed.

Rory and Bailey were nearly as exposed fifteen feet behind them.

Rory had her arm over Bailey's head, putting her own slightly larger body between the shooter and the younger, pregnant Bailey.

Zoey looked at Erickson in the lone street lamp that had lit their way up the gravel drive between the barns and the silos.

He wasn't going to be able to do anything more than she would. Not without providing a huge target. Especially in the light-colored shirt he wore.

Zoey wore black jeans and a dark-green children's choir T-shirt. And Pen's thin black zippered hoodie she'd grabbed from the car to protect her a bit from the light rain. With it so dark, she would be a lot harder to see. Except for her face. She adjusted the hat until only her eyes were exposed.

That could work to their advantage.

She pulled her thumbs through the thumb holes in the sleeve band, covering as much of her pale skin as she could. Pen loved thin sweatshirts that covered every inch of skin. Her baby sister hated to be cold; leftovers from a nasty foster home where Pen hadn't been given any blankets when she'd misbehaved. When they'd locked her outside in the cold to teach her a lesson more than once.

Pen had misbehaved a lot—hoping they'd just give her to Zoey to be rid of her. One lasting effect of that oh-so-great place was her hatred of the cold.

And apparently, her penchant to misbehave, as this evening's activities had shown. Zoey just hoped she got a chance to see her baby sister misbehave again. And again and again.

Zoey bought her gloved sweatshirts all the time.

She cursed the full moon above as it slipped around the rain clouds once again—at the worst possible time. It reflected off every bit of light color around them. Including the women in the white coveralls now. Perfect targets.

They were all just going to have to stay down until they figured this out.

Murdoch was inching his way toward the closest two women, almost dragging his body along the ground. Of course, he would.

Murdoch had one hell of a strong hero complex going.

He positioned himself in front of the one most exposed.

From the hair, Zoey thought it was Charlotte. Charlotte wasn't moving. She gave a prayer that her friends weren't injured. Or dead.

Her eyes scanned the horizon. She checked the moon—there was cloud cover coming again. That was when she'd move. Zoey waited…waited…waited.

There.

She made sure her line of sight was clear. And aimed. That was when she saw it. Zoey needed to get closer. She stood quietly, crawled a bit more up the hill, ignoring Erickson's curse when he realized what she was doing. His warning to get her hot ass back to the ground and keep it there.

Not exactly HR-approved talk, but she didn't care. Not tonight.

She was now almost flush with his right side.

"There. Movement up the hill," she said it quietly, so quietly only Erickson could hear. "Barrel of a rifle. Moron has a laser sight."

It took a moment, but Erickson confirmed. "I see it. Well, shall we light up this party, pretty lady?"

She took careful aim.

Erickson did the same.

She wasn't going to lose people she cared about out here tonight.

Zoey fired again.

Someone yelled out, a curse, a wail. Something.

It wasn't one of her side. She was sure of it. It came from just over the hill. Their people were behind her and Erickson.

Bailey's husband yelled out. Called Bailey's name with a touch of panic. Bailey called back that she was ok. That he was just to stay put and worry about his own ass.

Zoey heard the fear in Bailey's words. Fear for her husband. Fear for the baby Bailey was carrying. She was only four months along or so. Had the tiniest of baby bumps she was so proud of.

With what hell they'd gone through to be together, the Addys didn't deserve this tonight.

Determination filled Zoey.

She watched, waited. Saw the tiny red dot that signified the laser sight. Almost too far to see. But she saw it. Knew what it was.

Everyone else was pinned down or would be far too exposed. In the white coveralls, forensics were sitting ducks.

She had half a clip left.

She was going to put it to good use.

Zoey did, aware of the men around her doing the same.

Until the gunfire ended. Until the sounds of a truck squealing away had her cursing. They hadn't even seen it in the dark, parked where it was behind the old, caved in house.

There was no way they could give pursuit now. Their own vehicles were much too far away.

89

Jake stared at the destruction of his home. "They could have brought down the entire building. If they had wanted to."

It was obvious they hadn't. But what the hell the ones who'd done it had been after was damned murky at the moment.

"No kidding," Callum said. He held his infant wrapped in his arms, holding her close. "We were all damned lucky I was in your place feeding the cat."

"You were damned stupid. Could have been killed," Jake said. As it was, Callum had a few burns from the damage.

"All I was thinking was that it was a damned bomb and my wife and baby were just two units over. I did what I had to do. Saved your cat, too. You're welcome very much."

"Thanks for that. But if there's ever a next time and it's the cat or you, see to it that it's *you* who gets out safe."

He could have lost a friend tonight. He wasn't taking that lightly.

He could walk away from the contents of his home, but that new baby could have lost her father before she was even a month old.

Jake battled back the fury. Now...now it was just getting personal.

Some asshole had thrown a small pipe bomb through his kitchen window. It had landed in his sink, two feet from where Callum was feeding the cat. Callum had grabbed the bomb and thrown it outside to the fire escape in front of the empty apartment two places down from Jake's on the corner.

Where it had detonated and bent the fire escape and blown out both Jake's windows—and all the windows in between.

The entire apartment building had had to be evacuated. What kind of bastards bombed a single apartment in a building of forty units? More than one hundred fifty people lived in this building.

There were easier ways to kill someone than this.

And far more effective.

If that had even been their intent.

They'd been on his damned fire escape, probably before he was making love with Shelby.

Or chasing that damned intruder through her back yard.

Why had someone come for her the same damned time they'd come for him?

The same time someone had shot out Daniel's front tires as he was driving back from a meeting that had never happened in Witchita Falls.

But this... "They are making a statement. They weren't necessarily after killing people tonight. They're sending a message."

"That's what I figure," Callum said, shifting his daughter closer when she gave a tiny cry. A.J. stood nearby, speaking quietly to neighbors. They were going to keep the specifics quiet. As far as his neighbors would be told, it had been a fire in the empty apartment. Or a gas leak. That was it. No sense causing mass panic. "But what is it?"

Everyone was terrified, and had questions. Wanted to talk to the cops who lived in the building. Wanted to be reassured they were safe.

They had gotten lucky.

It had been a small bomb. Not powerful enough to bring down the building.

Big enough to make that statement to Jake now.

90

ZOEY PULLED HERSELF FULLY TO HER FEET. SHE looked at Murdoch. When had he gotten so close to her? His hand wrapped around her elbow, and he pulled her close, his big chest blocking her from the other men for a moment.

"You ok?" It was asked almost grudgingly. No surprise there.

"I hit one of them. At least once. I'm sure of it."

"We'll see about that."

Her partner always had doubted her capabilities. It drove her crazy. Always did. They'd tolerated each other for over a year now. It wasn't easy. And it wasn't getting any easier.

She was about ready to give up her position as sheriff and transfer to the Finley Creek post. Leave Garrity behind.

Her family was in Finley Creek, after all. Finley Creek was where Pen wanted to be, too. Maybe...maybe it was time for that now.

She wanted Internal Affairs eventually. To clean house at the TSP. Now was as good a time as any.

"I did. Just wait and see."

Half an hour later, it was confirmed. One of the shooters had been hit. They found two bloody rounds next to a massive pool of blood. And tire tracks. Two differing sets of footprints.

Zoey cataloged the wounded. On their side, Dom Acardi had taken one to the outer part of his arm, and Charlotte most likely had one hell of a headache where her head had bounced off the ground when she'd dived for cover. Bailey's husband had also been grazed.

So had Erickson—when he'd knocked her out of the way. Zoey refused to let anyone see how that shook her. Just how close it had been.

Everyone else was fine.

"I told you I hit him," Zoey said, looking at Murdoch in the security light. One light had been hit by gunfire, but they still had the one closest to the barn. And forensics had floodlights. Rory and Bailey were getting them set up now. They'd called in backup to secure the perimeter of the scene, but it would take a while for them to get there.

They'd already tagged and bagged two bloody .38 rounds. There would be DNA.

They'd be on edge for a while, that was sure.

"So you did. *If* that's from your gun. Could have been any of ours." Murdoch, again, of course.

"It was Zoey," Dom Acardi said, patting her on the back. "You're the only one out here carrying a .38. Nicely done."

"It's my backup weapon. I was off the clock and in Finley Creek dealing with my younger sister when I got called in."

Dom nodded. "I know where you were. The son of a bitch won't get far. He'll show up sooner or later. Then we'll get him."

"Don't you think this is a bit of a coincidence?" Charlie asked. He had his daughter by the arm. Zoey checked her friend quickly.

There was a blood streak across the white disposable coveralls that forensics teams used. And over Charlotte's forehead.

Charlotte looked like a kid out there right now.

"Char? You ok?"

"I'm good. Just a graze. And a massive headache. Not how I wanted the night to end."

"She got lucky," Charlotte's father said, flatly. Almost coldly. Zoey would admit it—the man gave her the chills. "We all did. In fact, this seems a little too coincidental, doesn't it?"

"What do you mean?" Zoey asked, mind running a thousand different directions. He was right. It did.

"That we would all be out here just to walk into a firefight more than two hours from Finley Creek? It was a damned ambush," Mike said.

"We need to do a status check for the rest of...us." Dom had Madison up off the ground and had pulled her in front of his massive chest. Madison was subdued and quiet, almost leaning against him.

Zoey knew what he wasn't saying. "Who is missing, status-wise?"

She'd just ignore Murdoch's curious expression for a while.

"McKellen and MacNamara. Elliot Marshall. The rest of us out here, except for Clay Addy, Lake, Price, Madison and Charlotte are all on that...*particular*...team. That leaves...Jake, Sean, Dan, Kevin, Bert, and the chief unaccounted for right now," Mike said, quietly.

The task force was said not to exist. They all knew that it did. No use trying to hide it from the ones around them now.

She'd fill Murdoch in later.

"And if this is an ambush..." Zoey said, slowly. "They are next. I need... MacNamara's with Shelby right now. If they go for him...what do we do now?" Zoey asked as Erickson put one hot hand on her shoulder, almost like he was trying to comfort.

He really was a nice guy. Far nicer than the blond behemoth on her other side.

"We watch our flanks. It's about all we can do until we have the answers," Dom said. His dark eyes met hers. "And hope to hell we find those answers soon."

91

IT HAD BEEN A MESSAGE PURE AND SIMPLE.

To let Jake know it was just a matter of time.

And since it was Jake's apartment that had been targeted, he knew exactly who the message was intended for.

And with what had happened at Shelby's—no. He wasn't stupid.

As if Callum was reading his mind, he looked at Jake. "Where's Shelby?"

"I took her someplace safe."

Behind eight-foot-tall stone fences, with armed guards surrounding her. And security technology that wasn't even on the market yet.

Mel Barratt had greeted Shelby with open arms, and ordered Jake to be careful out there tonight. Jake had spent a few moments speaking with Elliot Marshall and Kevin Beck who were visiting. Updating them on what was going on.

The security system had indicated an intruder in the back garden behind Shelby's home.

Jake hadn't gotten a good look at the man in the dark coat

and ski mask who had stood there in the security lights. But it was the guy's words that he would never forget.

"Keep out of business that doesn't concern you, MacNamara. Period. Or your woman will be the next to pay the price. No matter who else wants her now."

He didn't know what in the hell was going on. Jake was going to find out.

"What do we know so far?"

"Not much. This was expertly done. Someone knew what they were doing."

"No kidding."

"And someone had to know where you were tonight. There are no such things as coincidences like that. We both know that—"

Jake's phone rang. Cutting him off. He grabbed it quickly. "What?"

He listened to Dom's account quickly. "I have her safe, Dom. And can confirm the location of Beck and the chief. They are at Mel Barratt's. Everyone good there?"

Jake disconnected a minute later. Then looked at his friend and teammate. At the little golem baby Callum had passed to his beautiful wife Jake had always liked. "Get your things. You're headed back to where I have Shelby stashed."

"What's going on?" A.J. asked, arms tightening around Audrea.

"There was an ambush tonight on a scene north of Garrity. Superficial injuries, but we got the message loud and clear. Someone's coming after Major Crimes and the task force. Hard. Bert Dillon's truck was run off the road. He's hopping mad, but unhurt—he had his oldest grandson with him tonight. Daniel's tires were shot out. You two are going underground." Jake looked at the baby girl when she fussed. "The *three* of you. And, Callum, while you're there—you are going to keep my girl safe, too. You got babysitting duty. Marshall and Beck are both there, already."

Callum just nodded, pulling his wife and daughter closer. "And what are you going to do?"

Jake gave a cold smile. "Isn't it obvious? I'm going hunting."

92

Jake was just gone. Shelby saw him once, when he showed up with Sean Callum's family at Mel's. They were going to stay with the Barratts for a while.

No one knew how long that would be.

She'd heard Elliot Marshall and Kevin Beck talking. The two men were just like Jake in a lot of ways. Secretive. There had been a lot of significant looks passed back and forth.

Shelby knew something major was happening.

That had just become even clearer when Zoey showed up.

There had been a wild look in her friend's dark eyes. That look hadn't gone away until Zoey had hugged Shelby close, then grabbed Pen as tightly as she could. She'd almost strangled them both before letting go when the teenager had squirmed.

Zoey had disappeared into a room with Elliot Marshall, Kevin, Sean—and Jake.

She had a feeling the men had all been waiting specifically for Zoey.

Daniel had shown up fifteen minutes later to join them. He'd looked...rough. His nose had been swelling, too. He hadn't exactly been happy.

They hadn't reappeared for hours.

Jake finally came out around three a.m.

Came right to her, where she sat at the piano in Mel and Houghton's family room. She was alone, playing quietly when he approached her.

"Can't help yourself, can you, baby?" he asked, softly. "If there is a piano, you're going to play."

"Yes. This...the piano was my voice for years, you know." The only voice she had back then. Well, not now. She had her voice now. She'd finally realized that.

Maybe that was it. Maybe she'd had it all along and just hadn't known.

"I can understand that."

"Can you?" Shelby looked right at him. She'd had several hours to think now. She didn't have regrets for what had happened between them.

If it hadn't happened, she would have always wondered...

But she wasn't going to lie to herself. They really were of two different worlds. Not because of the money—but because of their priorities.

The TSP would always be first for him. No hesitation.

Hers was finding ways to live a full, fulfilled, *life*.

She'd spent the last several hours surrounded by couples who flat out adored each other. Understood each other. *Needed* each other.

She barely understood herself most times. How could she expect someone else to understand her, too?

Especially Jake.

She knew the truth—every time he'd said he was the wrong man for her, there had been an implicit unstated belief: *she* was the wrong woman for him.

Shelby wanted more than she thought Jake could ever give. But she would never dare ask him to choose between her and the TSP.

That would be what it would come to, and she knew she would lose. It was just a given. She would always be second to the TSP. "I'm going to stay here for a few days. Until after the concert Friday night."

"That's a damned good idea."

"I'm going to meet with Chance Marshall tomorrow. We're going to address the security d-d-deficiencies at my place. Hire an all-women team of bodyguards. I can handle that, and it makes sense."

"Do you want me to stay with you?"

It wasn't to guard her that he was asking. And they both knew that.

Shelby stopped playing. And just looked at him.

SHE HAD UTTERLY DESTROYED HIM. NOT BY HER words or even by what she said she wanted.

It was the look in her eyes.

The hurt. The defeat mingled with achingly tender resolve.

Jake didn't stop to think about where they were or that anyone could walk by and see them. He just scooped her up into his arms. "Don't let me hurt you, baby. Just don't let me."

"That's exactly what I'm going to make certain doesn't happen. I need..."

"Need better than me."

"Not better. I just need someone who needs *me*. The way Izzie needs Allen, and the way he needs her."

"I don't understand what you mean."

"I th-th-think that's what the heart of what I am saying is. I need someone who hears *my* voice, who sees *me*—the me I want to be *and* the me that I am. Both. You...you...you have ideas of what you think I am. Like...like...like...some fairytale princess who is supposed to fit a mold. A princess you don't particularly like. I'm not that. I never could be. And you...you...you belong to the TSP. That's the real love of your life. Heart and soul."

"Do I? I'm so certain any longer." He belonged to *her* heart and soul. And he always would. His heart beat more when she was near. Jake could never deny that again. "If that's what you want."

He wasn't stupid. She'd forget him.

He'd move on, too.

Life would get back to normal.

As soon as he found the bastards threatening her, that was.

"You go nowhere without an armed guard. Whether that is your buddy, or someone Chance Marshall recommends. Someone watches over you every minute of every day. Until Daniel or Dom themselves come and tell you it's safe. Or me. You understand?"

"I-I-I will. I'm not going to be stupid. I...Houghton caught me tonight. And Zoey's brother Luc is here. They...told me I had to get...get...get my head on a little better, where the money is concerned. Keep myself safer. Start taking better respons...control of it. They made a lot of sense."

"Of course, you'd listen to everyone but me and Allen, right?"

"You'd better believe it." She rested her forehead against his chest. Jake just breathed her in.

He had never felt like this.

Every relationship he'd ever had had ended—but none of them had felt like this.

Like his heart was being ripped right out of his chest. Like his soul was just gone. Kept tight in her beautiful, feminine hands. And he'd never get it back from her.

If he did, it would be irrevocably changed. Completely, forever.

If Izzie felt even half of this for that jackass she'd married, maybe Jake was finally starting to understand. Just a little.

He lifted Shelby off her feet, until those storm-blue eyes were level with his own.

He fought every instinct he had.

They were screaming at him to carry her off, back to his cave. Keep her there, where she belonged. Give her a dozen of *his* kids to keep her occupied, while he went out and slayed dozens of dragons to make the world a safer place for her.

Jake always had been a total idiot.

Instead, he pressed a quick kiss to her mouth and set her back on her feet.

The lid of the piano hid them from anyone walking by. A little. Not a lot.

If someone looked close enough, they'd see. Shelby wouldn't want that.

"If you *ever* need me, you call. Do you understand? Ever. I will always come for you. Always."

Shelby just looked at him. Then nodded.

"I will *always* come for you. No matter what." He wanted her to believe in that.

To believe in *him*.

Just like that, it was over. Severed. He wrapped his arms around her one more time. Pressed a kiss to her forehead. Silently said goodbye to the woman he had never truly had.

Footsteps came toward them. A woman said Shelby's name softly.

He looked up. Into dark eyes. The sheriff was watching him, them. Jake disengaged and walked away.

He stopped next to Shelby's best friend. "Take care of her. I never wanted to hurt her. Ever. That was the last thing I ever wanted to do. Just…take care of her. She is my very soul."

"I always will." There was understanding in her gorgeous dark eyes, too. Like she got him, too. Understood. Jake nodded at her one more time, resisting the urge to look back.

But Jake was old enough to know that there weren't any perfect answers like that. Sometimes things just stunk.

This was one of those times. Why drag out the inevitable?

He found his boss and Kevin Beck and Callum in a formal parlor near the front of the Barratts' place. It made Shelby's twelve thousand square foot home look like a shoebox.

This was her world now. This was where she belonged. Logan Lanning had made sure of it.

He looked at Elliot. "We need to talk. We need to figure out who is coming for us now."

Shelby would be safe here, with Barratt's people to protect her.

Now…Jake was going to find out who was threatening *her*.

And then he was going to tear the bastards into a million pieces.

It would be a good start.

He risked one more glance at her, just one. Just to see her weeping in her best friend's arms, like what he had done had destroyed her. Like he had always known he would.

93

SHE GOT THROUGH. FOUND HER SENSE OF RESOLVE. Stayed where she was at Mel's until it was time for the real world again.

Tonight was the real world. The *life* she wanted. She was going to take life day by day until she found her footing again. She could do this.

Even if she missed that man so much it hurt.

Shelby bagged the last of the trash and tied it off quickly, for Zoey to run to the dumpster out back. Madison and Charlotte worked together nearby to fold the rest of the display and ticket tables down and carry them back to the storage room. Someone would have to run the vacuum, still.

The end of summer choir concert was over. The kids had been gone for half an hour or so already. Now she and her friends had morphed into the cleaning crew.

The excitement and satisfaction were still in the air. Madison was humming and almost dancing around. Charlotte was laughing, almost giddy like she always was after a concert. Charlotte was like a music vampire—she'd said it before—she fed off singing and music and composing in general.

Music was *life*.

Shelby could understand that.

She'd spent countless hours composing her own works—until Logan's money had required far more of her time to manage than she wanted to think about. She was going to compose again, as soon as her heart stopped hurting.

She made herself that vow.

Zoey was in the rows of seats, checking for lost items. They usually found at least two cell phones after a concert, it seemed.

It felt so normal. So right. The fact that there were two guards from Barratt-Handley out in the parking lot waiting to escort her home, along with Zoey, who had completely taken over guard duties from Jake, then, well...she was just going to have to get used to their presence.

Tonight was for celebrating. Not thinking of things she didn't want to think about.

She wished Jake had been there. Wished he had seen, understood that life wasn't just finding the bad guys or biding time until it was time to hunt other bad guys again. He hadn't been—she wouldn't have invited him, anyway.

Allen and Izzie had been there for her, just like she had known they would be. That mattered. She had people to stand next to her.

She didn't *need* Jake. She would remember that. Life would go on. Just as it had after she'd lost Logan. She would get through this eventually. Come out stronger on the other side.

She firmed her resolve. Shelby could do this, could move on. She'd made the right choice.

She'd had the choir concert tonight. Tomorrow, she owed Powell's brother Brandt a date to the art auction. Then...she was going to start living her life again. She could do that.

Knew she could be strong enough to do that now.

She'd hire the guards everyone was so adamant about, and she'd adjust. And then...she wasn't going to let anyone stop her.

She was going to finally grow up.

Be *Shelby*. Live up to her own expectations of herself, and no one else's.

Thanks to Logan, she could do just that.

"So? Mamaw's Place, after this?" Charlotte asked. "I really want a cheeseburger, diner-style. It reminds me of home. And I want to celebrate. We can talk to Shelby about her plans for the place once the sale goes through. We would always celebrate at the diner after a concert with Mom. We can make it a tradition here, too."

Charlotte had relocated to the Finley Creek area a few years ago to get to know her father and his parents better, she'd said. Shelby didn't think it was going all that well. There was always longing when she spoke about home.

"I'd like that. I'm sure Zoey would, too." Pen had left with her friend Josie's family—the mayor and his wife. They were going to get with a few other friends and hang out somewhere. It sounded so normal.

Shelby wanted normal. So much it hurt to even think about it.

The front door pushed open. They hadn't locked anything yet. Not until they were finished cleaning, and carrying out props and supplies.

Shelby looked up.

94

Shelby never looked at their faces. Just the guns.

Guns.

She yelled for the others to run. But it was far too late. The men said something. The blood was rushing in her head too much for her to understand.

Gunshots echoed. Charlotte screamed an agonized scream.

Charlotte went down against the wall between the lobby and the auditorium.

Madison tried to run, toward Charlotte. Madison went toward Charlotte to *help* her.

Just like Shelby tried to do. Tried to get between Madison and the guns.

Madison went down instead. Right in front of Shelby.

Shelby almost tripped over her. In the blood. Madison's blood.

Zoey yelled out from inside the concert hall. Shelby *knew* Zoey would be coming for them. Would run right into this.

"No! Zoey! Run! Run!" Shelby screamed it as loudly as she could. "Run!"

Shelby watched in horror as two men sprayed bullets toward the back of the lobby, where the double doors were still open. More gunshots.

Toward Zoey.

She screamed her friend's name again.

More gunshots came.

One man fell to the ground right next to her. Blood. Blood covered him. It was everywhere.

His eyes stared at the ceiling. Lifeless. Pale blue. Just dead. How had that even happened?

Shelby tried to run, but the third man already had her. She knew the bullets would come. Would strike her next.

He grabbed her, yanked her off her feet. She screamed, fought.

One yelled, said for him to get her and be done. Or kill the bitch.

But the other said no. Said something about *too much money.*

Then, the other gunmen came up behind her, shoved something over her mouth and nose. Held her so tight she couldn't fight him.

Madison kept screaming, screaming Charlotte's name. And for help.

Begging someone for help. For all of them. Madison was screaming Shelby's name, too. Begging.

But help wasn't coming.

95

SHE WAS GOING TO DIE. ZOEY KNEW IT WITH certainty. She'd dived to the ground behind some chairs. Pulled out the weapon that went with her everywhere.

She'd seen the silhouette of a man right there in the doors. A weapon in his hand. And she'd acted.

Just like she had been trained. Like she had practiced.

Darrell had taken her out to the fields behind his family's old ranch weekly for two years, making sure she could shoot.

He'd said she'd need the advantage over the others on the job. Darrell had made certain she could shoot better than any man in the TSP.

And then, they'd spend the night wrapped up in each other's arms beneath the stars. Every Saturday night for almost two years.

He had probably been the only man she had ever trusted enough to love.

She'd hit one of the shooters; she knew she had. She'd had such a small target area. Just the open doors. She hadn't risked firing more than one shot; not with Shelby and the others out there somewhere.

Screaming.

Someone was still screaming.

It was Madison. Madison was still screaming. Begging someone to help.

Zoey wanted to go to her.

But she couldn't.

Zoey couldn't get to her. She just couldn't. She couldn't move at all.

The chairs were little cover.

Two bullets had struck her.

Just two.

One in the leg; one in the stomach. It was the gut wound that would kill her. She knew that much. She knew what would happen once she was found.

It would be her brother Rafe's hospital they took her to.

Rafe's was closest.

Maybe, before she died, she could see Rafe one more time. See his wife Jillian or her brother Caine's wife, Nikkie Jean, who worked there, too.

Maybe...she would have time to tell them goodbye. To tell them how sorry she was that she hadn't gotten to know them better.

Her fault.

She'd been so afraid...to let them in.

The only ones she'd truly let in for a long, long time had been Shelby and Daryn. Even Darrell she had kept at a distance. It had eventually driven him away, when he had needed more than she had been ready to give.

Rafe could be there now.

Maybe...maybe she wouldn't have to die alone. Maybe one of her brothers would be there with her.

Pen. She wanted to see Pen again. She had loved that girl from the moment she had first held her in a foster home where they were treated little better than trash. She had made Pen a vow to always keep her safe that day. To always let her baby sister know she was loved by someone.

More than anything in the world, that was what she wanted. To see her little sister one more time.

She could ask them to take care of Pen for her. They probably would anyway. Nikkie Jean would take care of Pen. Without Zoey having to ask. If Zoey *couldn't* ask.

Pen would be ok. Pen had people to love her and take care of her now.

Zoey wanted to tell her baby sister how much she loved her. Just one more time.

Just one more time.

Zoey couldn't move; all she could do was lie there.

She pulled in as deep a breath as she could. It hurt. It hurt so bad. Tears covered her cheeks. She tried to get up, to get to her hands and knees.

Zoey fell.

She wanted to get to Shelby. She couldn't hear Shelby, either. She wanted to be with Shelby at the last if she could. To be with someone she loved. Shelby had to be out there.

Shelby was probably already dead. Zoey wanted to know, to see. She tried again. Fell, again.

Zoey couldn't move more than a few inches at a time. She grabbed her cell phone. It was right there, where it had fallen out of her pocket when she'd hit the floor.

She could hear a woman crying. Madison. It was still Madison.

She was still alive out there. Maybe all three of her friends were. She'd seen people survive gunshot wounds before.

Someone out there was still alive.

They needed help. They all needed help. Zoey pulled in what breath she could. She could do this. No matter how much it hurt to breathe.

Zoey managed to dial 9-1-1. "Help...been a shooting. Have

casualties." She gave the address. Tried to not let the pain take her. "I don't know if shooters are still here. I saw the doors open and close. People left…I've been hit. I returned fire. Saw one shooter, but there are more. I hit him. There are multiple victims in main entrance and one in auditorium… We are TSP. We are off-duty TSP. Hurry. Just hurry. Please. Help my friends, please…"

She heard the dispatcher's voice telling her to stay on the line. "Sorry…I can't…I think I'm…dying now. So sorry…"

96

THE CALL CAME TO MAJOR CRIMES JUST AS DOM WAS shutting down his damned computer for the day. MacNamara was across from him, looking like he'd been kicked and punched and then had it start all over again.

The guy was a total goner, and he'd been this way for two days.

Jake needed to be with Shelby. Why didn't he just admit it already?

Jake would be happier with that woman now than Jake ever could be without her. It worked that way. A guy was cruising along just fine, then *wham*! A woman came out of nowhere and ruined a guy's good thing. Changed everything.

So that the only good thing he had left was being with her.

It worked for a lot of guys. He suspected it would work just fine with Jake and Shelby. She was one of those women men just lucked into.

Like his new stepmother. He hadn't seen his father this happy in a long time. Cherise adored his father in return. And his dad was just what Max needed in his life now, too.

It didn't get better than that, in his opinion.

He wished he hadn't missed Max's choir concert. The kid had been working so hard. As had that sister of Max's. Madison had the voice of an angel and the body of a goddess. And the attitude of a pissed off rattlesnake where Dom was concerned.

He would have loved watching her work with the kids in their big production tonight.

But Major Crimes hadn't stopped working since that damned ambush had brought Jake back with real fire in his eyes.

Charlie came running in. "There's been a shooting. We've been called in. TSP was involved. Off the clock. Three wounded. All TSP. Major Crimes was requested ASAP. This may have something to do with what's going down. Let's move!"

Dom grabbed his gear as Jake did the same. Everything else they had going on could wait. The TSP took care of its own. He shot a quick prayer to the man upstairs for the TSP officers involved.

They followed three patrol cars to the scene.

The captain of the Rapid Response team met them outside the perimeter. Rodriguez was a big burly guy a few years younger than Dom and meaner than shit. Damned good at what he did, too.

He turned straight to Charlie and Dom. "Scene's cleared. Acardi, Fields, you two aren't going in there. IA has already been called in."

"Why?" Dom asked. As Major Crimes, they were always allowed on scene when something of this magnitude happened. It was a given. "What's going on?"

"No one has fucking told you yet?" Rodriguez hesitated, then turned to Charlie. He grabbed the other man's shoulders. Physically restrained him. "Fields, your daughter is one of the victims. They are loading her into a bus right now. She's alive, but I don't know how badly she is injured. She...hasn't regained consciousness."

Dom would never forget the sound Charlie made in that instant.

When Rodriguez turned to Dom, Dom just *knew*.

Every drop of blood in his body froze in his veins. He just *knew*. "Madison was with her. Madison was with her tonight!"

Of course, she was. The two of them were practically in each other's hip pockets, along with Powell Barratt and Haldyn Harris.

Haldyn had worked tonight. She was safe. He was certain he had passed her in the hall when they were leaving.

Rodriguez nodded, the look in the man's eyes telling him what he already knew. "She was. Both are alive as of this time, but it does look serious."

Dom didn't hear another word said. He just took off running, ignoring Rodriguez's curse and orders to stop. To at least not contaminate the scene.

Dom hurried toward the nearest ambulance. Looking for cinnamon hair, wire-rimmed glasses and a cranky attitude. Not Madison. Please, not her. Just not her.

The first stretcher he came to had a beautiful dark-copper-haired girl lying so still he would have sworn she was dead. Dom turned. "Fields! Over here!"

At his shout, beautiful green eyes opened.

Chuckie blinked at him. Awake. Her eyes were cloudy with pain. She was so pale. The blood—he'd never forget the sight of her blood. One thin hand fluttered in his direction. Reached for him.

Dom grabbed her small fingers in his, just wanting her to know she wasn't alone. Not alone with just fucking strangers leaning over her. "It'll be ok, kid. You'll be fine."

Then her father was there. One of the toughest, strongest men Dom knew besides his own father. There were tears on Charlie's face. Terror.

That terror seared into his soul forever.

Dom passed her father her hand.

Hell, Chuckie was so small, she looked like a damned kid lying there.

He turned, choking back emotion of his own. He said a quick prayer for that beautiful woman who had half the single men of the TSP turning into slavering idiots whenever she was around.

And he moved on.

To the next ambulance.

Searching for Madison.

That was when he found her. The woman he was looking for. "Madison!"

Big light-brown eyes blinked at him. She didn't have her glasses. They'd have to find her glasses for her soon.

"Dom! Dom! It's *you!*" She reached for him, grabbed his shirt and pulled him closer. "You have to listen. You have to. Right now!"

The paramedics tried to hold her still. But she was insistent. Dom ignored the blood covering her, though he would never forget the sight of it. "What, sweetheart?"

"They took Shelby! Three men. Took her. They just dragged her out of there!"

"Shelby was with you?" Jake's Shelby. Of course, she would have been with them. Why hadn't he realized?

"Yes. They came in and *took* her. They used something. I'm almost certain it was on a blue handkerchief. Find that. Bag it, take it straight to Rory or Haldyn. Not random. This wasn't random. Don't let that evidence disappear like other evidence has been lately. Someone's been stealing evidence out of the vault. I documented it myself yesterday. Told Haldyn what I suspect. This wasn't crazy mass shooters with a grudge. It was targeted. A *hit*. Get that handkerchief to Haldyn. Fast. Make sure it doesn't disappear."

"Hell, Madison, we'll process the scene. You just get to the damned hospital." She was hurting, he could see that. But she was lucid and rational and getting impatient with him as always. Thank God.

Somehow she pulled him closer. Not that Dom resisted. She whispered next to his ear. "They took her. And they...called me by name."

"What?"

"The one nearest me. He shot first. He said to me, 'Sorry about this, *Madi*.' And he looked at Charlotte. He said, 'If your father wasn't such a dick, *Chuckie*, this wouldn't have happened to you. Sorry about your shitty luck.' Before he went toward Zoey. He said...said, 'Damned sheriff got into their fucking business. Deserved what she got. Didn't even have to *pay* him for this one, like they did the rich bitch.' I think they were there after Zoey *and* Shelby, too."

Dom just looked at her. He leaned closer when she almost growled.

Madison got impatient. Looked at him like he was an idiot again as the paramedic guided her back on the gurney. He loved it when she looked at him like that. "Damn it, Dom—*Charlotte* despises the name Chuckie. She always has. The only people who ever call her that work in the TSP building with us but don't know her well enough to know that she hates it. She lets them use Chuckie on the clock because it annoys her father so much. They knew us! Work with us and Charlotte's dad. The shooters have to be TSP. Find them. And find Shelby. They came for her and Zoey. I'm sure of it."

An EMT pressed something against the GSW on her shoulder. Madison cried out from the pain and jerked. Cried.

Dom tightened his hand on hers. She had such damned small hands, too. Fragile.

Her words were clicking through his brain. She was the smartest, sharpest woman he had ever met.

If she was seeing connections, there were connections. Someone they knew had tried to kill her tonight. Someone they worked with, someone she should have been able to trust.

He fought a growl of his own.

He was going to find those bastards. And make them pay.

No one ever hurt Madison and got away with it. No one.

Dom was an animal at heart. He'd always known that.

Now it was time to set it free. Someone had hurt his buddy's only child, someone had hurt the woman who meant everything to Dom, and his best friend's girl was missing.

He kissed her palm once. "I'll get them sweetheart. And I'll make them pay for everything they've done. I promise."

Dom would never stop until he found the bastards responsible.

97

Jake studied the scene, checking every vital player as quickly as he could. His eyes landed on the victims. He recognized the third woman on the gurney almost immediately. He shouldered his way through the crowd of TSP detectives and officers surrounding her. The EMTs.

What in the hell had happened?

"What's her condition?" he demanded as questions flooded him. Shelby's best friend looked dead. If she wasn't, he feared it was just a matter of time until she was. She wasn't moving. He wasn't even certain she was breathing. "Zoey, open your damned eyes and tell me what a shithead you think I am."

"She's critical," the paramedic, Drew, said. "It doesn't look good, Jake. Not at all. She took one to the abdomen, and one to the leg. She's lost a lot of blood."

The woman on the gurney never moved.

"Her brother is the COM at FCGH. She's Dr. Netorre's sister-in-law, and Jillian's. She'll want to go there. I'll follow you in."

Where the hell was Shelby?

Dom and Daniel came running up. Dom had blood on his arm. A handprint. It stood out against the crisp white shirt. Jake met them.

"Jake," Daniel said, quietly. "I need you to come with me. Now."

There was something in the other man's tone. "What?"

"Madison and Chuck—Charlotte were both shot as well," Dom said, quickly. Harshly. "Madison is talking and seems to be doing ok. Charlotte is far more critical. I just don't know what her chances are. Charlie is riding in with her."

Ice straight shot down his spine. Pure, unadulterated fear. Charlotte, Madison, Zoey. "Who? What do we know?"

"The shooters were TSP," Daniel said harshly. "We need you to listen and not fly off the damned handle. Just listen."

Dom stepped into his path. Both men crowded him.

Jake tensed even more. Dom's hand wrapped around his shoulder like he was preparing to hold Jake back. Daniel blocked him from the sight of the ambulances.

Shelby. His first thought would always be for her now.

"Madison told us that there was a fourth woman there with them cleaning up after the choir concert," Dom said.

Choir concert. Jake stopped and looked at Daniel. Panic was an icy knife to his gut. Tonight. The summer concert. Hell, he'd known the date. Tonight. "This was the night of the community children's choir concert, wasn't it? Where's Shelby? Where is she? Was she here? Tell me, now. Where the hell is she!"

Dom turned him to face Dom straight on.

"We don't know. Madison stated that the three shooters came in and then started shooting. They took Shelby, using what we suspect was chloroform. We found a blue rag soaked with it, just like Madison said we would. And Shelby's bag was nearby. She's missing." Daniel stepped right into his way. "This wasn't random. Someone came straight for her. And were ready to kill to get her."

Fear unlike any he had ever felt had him almost hitting his knees.

He should have been here. He should have protected her.

98

SHELBY'S HEAD HURT. FELT SO CLOUDED SHE couldn't get her thoughts together. Something wasn't right. She couldn't remember where she was supposed to be. Her eyes popped open.

She was stretched out on a couch she had never seen before. In a room she had no memory of at all.

She bit back the panic. Bit back the instinctive sound.

Her hands...they were bound. Why were her hands bound? The panic threatened again.

She had been at the choir concert. It had gone well. The children had done a wonderful job. She had been cleaning up the auditorium with her friends when—

A sob escaped before she could stop it. As she remembered.

Madison had gone down right next to Charlotte. Right in front of Shelby. Charlotte hadn't been moving. There had been so much red...and Zoey.

She'd heard Zoey cry out.

Right before someone had covered Shelby's face, choked an arm around her neck so hard she could barely breathe at all.

Right after they had said something about Zoey...about Charlotte.

After one of the men had fallen to the floor at her feet.

Blood had sprayed from his neck to her legs.

This wasn't a nightmare. This was real.

Real.

And she didn't know where she was.

She bit back a whimper. She had to think.

People would be coming for her. Allen would have people coming. Someone would have called in what happened to the TSP. Powell had been going to join them when she was finished with a last-minute meeting. Powell had been going to meet them after the concert. She would have been there before, but her plans had changed last minute.

Izzie and Annie and Nikkie Jean had worked the ticket table for them instead. Because Nikkie Jean was the head of the parent volunteers and she'd organized it.

They'd left fifteen minutes earlier. Just fifteen minutes or they would have been there, too. Powell was coming.

She would find Charlotte and Madison and Zoey and get them help.

They'd realize Shelby was missing. The TSP would be called in.

Jake would be called. Jake would come for her.

Even if they couldn't be together the way she wanted, Jake would come for her. Because she needed him.

He'd promised he always would.

99

DOM WANTED NOTHING MORE THAN TO BE OUT THERE, helping his friend find the woman he loved. He equally needed to be at the hospital with Madison and the rest of Dom's family. Max was going to be terrified. Cherise as well. Dom needed to be there.

Someone needed to be there for Charlie. The man hadn't had much opportunity with his kid. Father and daughter fought and snapped at each other all the time.

Charlie deserved to know her. Charlie had already lost one child to a heart defect when the boy had been all of seventeen. Dom didn't think the man could survive losing the daughter he had found a few years later. Fate couldn't be that cruel. It just couldn't.

Elliot Marshall and Daniel had already told Dom and Jake they couldn't work the scene. No one was stupid enough to think that would keep Jake from hunting.

Jake's woman had been taken. Jake was going hunting. It was the way of this beast.

Nothing would stop that. Dom was going to be there to help him. But first...

He looked at Daniel, Elliot, and Jake. "I'm going to the hospital with Charlie. And to check on my family, see if Madison said anything else on the way in that can help. I'll meet up with you as soon as I can." He looked at Daniel specifically. "Keep Jake out of trouble. He's going hunting. Won't stop until he finds her. We all know that. His mate is missing. Jake's angry, very angry—and holding himself together by a thread made of that anger. We have to keep him from doing something stupid."

Daniel nodded, a look of fury in his own eyes. "We all are. These...these women are *ours*. I don't take this lightly. I'm going to find the sonsofbitches, and I'm going to destroy them. I'm getting Haldyn here, and Bailey and Rory. They'll be under guards we can trust. They are the best we have in forensics."

"Can Haldyn work this? It's her team. Her friends," Dom asked, as they headed to the nearest patrol cars. "This is going to tear her to pieces."

"She's bringing in everyone that she can. Rory will be the official head. She can handle this. We need to work quickly."

"They knew their names. And they took Shelby deliberately," Dom said, watching Jake. "It was a planned attack. Someone wanted her. Wanted her enough to do this. To follow her, to follow them, and attack when they were the most vulnerable. Getting those particular four women alone—even an armed one? No. They stalked the girls like damned prey, waited for the best time to ambush them."

Dom was going to hunt them down like the rodents they were in return. There would be no ambush involved; he was going to just tear them apart where he found them.

If Jake didn't beat him to it.

A detective jogged up to them. "McKellen, I thought you'd want to know," Jack MacGregor said solemnly. He shouldn't even be there. No one called in Homicide until...a homicide had been confirmed. This was Major Crimes's until then. Fear froze

Dom for just a moment. Zoey Daviess or Charlotte... "They've found a body in the alley behind the theater."

All three men froze. *No.* Dom stepped forward. "Female?"

Please, *no.* No. Not that sweet, beautiful woman that his closest friend breathed for.

Just not that.

Dom grabbed Jake's shoulder to keep him back. To hold his buddy up. Just in case.

"No. It's Jody Callahan. Took a .38 hollow point to the jugular. Probably bled out within minutes, if it didn't kill him instantly. He's wearing full body gear and a damned ski mask was a yard away. Looks like he was dumped from a vehicle and kicked behind a dumpster. One of the women—the taller brunette—was found clutching a .38 in her left hand. She said on the 911 call that she hit one of the shooters. I think she got him good. And it was a kill shot."

Callahan. Son of a bitch.

They finally had a damned lead to go on. He was going to follow it.

100

ELLIOT MARSHALL PUT OUT THE APB ON SHELBY, BUT without any clue who the other shooters were, what they were driving, or anything other than a vague description found on a grainy security camera, they had absolutely nothing to go on.

Except Jody Callahan's dead body.

Jake knew it was going to be like swimming through mud upstream to even know where to begin.

He had to *think*. He knew her best of anyone right now. Elliot Marshall was going to talk to Allen and Izzie. He was friends with Allen, Jake thought. His wife was good pals with Izzie. They...Elliot had guards on Izzie now. Jake's family would be ok.

Allen was going to be terrified. Jake was.

And Shelby. He wouldn't let himself think about what this would do to her. He had to focus on getting her back. First of all, most of all, he just had to find her. Do his job, and find her. She would be waiting for him to get to her.

Someone came up to him where he was prowling around the Major Crimes conference room.

Daniel. Shouldn't the other man be at the scene?

Jake asked that.

Daniel shook his head. "I'm working this one, Jake. You can't. Not with your involvement with Shelby. And Dom can't. Neither can Charlie. I don't know...if he'll be leaving the hospital anytime soon. His daughter coded on the way to the hospital. I don't know if she's going to pull through. No matter how hard she's fighting now. I'm better utilized here, finding the ones responsible for this than at the hospital waiting. I just can't stand there waiting to know. Elliot is going to keep me updated on their conditions."

"Madison and Zoey?" Beautiful women he'd seen with Shelby, laughing. The three of them and Shelby had been surrounded by kids and happy. Looking...wonderful. Beautiful. Real. "How are they?"

"Madison took one to the upper right shoulder. She's doing well. They're prepping her for surgery, but she'll make a full recovery. She was able to give a detailed account of what happened. The bastards shot her in the back as she was trying to run to help Charlotte. Madison got lucky. If she'd been four inches more to the right, it would have hit her heart."

"And Charlotte?"

"Madison stated that it was a targeted attack. One shooter apologized before turning the gun on Madison. Another told Charlotte that 'if her father hadn't been such a dick, this wouldn't have happened to her.' Then he shot Charlotte multiple times. I don't know how many times she was hit." Daniel's voice choked up. Jake didn't say a word. "Zoey Daviess...from what initial reports are saying, she heard the first shots and went to help. Engaged with a shooter in the open door of the multipurpose room. One of her shots hit home. Probably the one that killed Callahan. Then the second shooter took her down. She's in critical, and is in surgery now. She's holding on. She had a clear path to the rear exit. She could have gotten away; she had time to run for the doors. She went toward her friends instead. Madison said the shooter said the sheriff was 'getting into someone's business.' We need to figure out which of her cases ties to Shelby to make them both a target, and who in the TSP would be involved. Starting with everyone who ever even pissed in the restroom the same time as Callahan."

"Was Shelby hit? She…she's terrified of guns, Dan. This…I need to find her. Bring her home."

"Haldyn has the security video feed from the concert hall. Shelby wasn't hit. They came for her, and they took her, alive. Now…who would want Shelby enough to do this?"

101

WHEN SHE OPENED HER EYES AGAIN, SHELBY'S HANDS were unbound and her head so cloudy she could barely think. The room she was in was dark, but there was light coming through the bottom of the door.

She didn't scream. That would just draw attention to the fact that she was awake. She wasn't stupid. Someone had done this for a purpose. She bit back the urge to scream once more.

To yell for Jake, which was completely stupid.

Shelby knew one thing—once he learned what had happened to her, he was going to come hunting for her.

Jake would never stop. Not until he found her.

He was a hunter down to his very DNA. She just had to keep herself alive until he got there. She had to *think*. Keep her head on straight and not let panic make her do anything completely stupid.

The first thing she needed to do was figure out where she was. The sheets she rested on were silk. Expensive silk. The room was furnished with antiques. Her brother and Logan had always enjoyed nice antiques. Enough that she could recognize them when she saw them.

The room was of a rather large size, larger than those in her own home. Opulent, extravagant.

She was in an expensive place.

This wasn't just random, she didn't think. No. Someone had taken her for a reason. Ransom? It was possible. All they had to do was send a message to Allen—who would get Powell to issue the money. She and Powell had discussed a plan if a kidnapping ever happened to her.

It had almost happened to Powell once.

Powell knew all of Shelby's wishes completely, and had the legal right to make those decisions if Allen couldn't. Shelby had already put plans in place. Just in case.

They hadn't killed her yet. That was good so far. That meant they wanted something from her.

How that was going to help her, Shelby didn't have a clue.

The door opened. She flinched at the sudden light behind the tall figure there. It was a man.

He stalked toward her, careful to keep light behind him so she couldn't see his face. Shelby tried not to whimper or make a sound. She tried to keep her eyes mostly shut so he would think she was asleep.

He knew, though. He told her so, in a voice she didn't recognize. He slipped one hard arm behind her shoulders. He lifted her. She tried to resist, but she felt so sluggish. "Open your mouth. You are going to take these. They will have you sleeping until morning. Then…we will discuss what it is I wish of you. I am sorry this happened to you. I did not plan this, not this way."

He leaned her against his hard chest and forced her mouth open. Shelby had no choice—when he pinched her nose closed and shoved three pills into her mouth, then held the glass of water to her lips. She had to drink.

His hold on her eased after she complied with what he had ordered. "Wh-who are you?"

"That is irrelevant now, don't you think?"

"Where am I?"

"Do not ask foolish questions. I have a plan for you. That is all you need to know. I will see to it that you are well compensated in your lifetime for what will happen to you. Just rest now. You will need your strength in the months to come."

"M-months?"

One hot hand cupped her cheek. To her shock and horror, he leaned down and kissed her gently on the lips, smelling faintly of mint and old vitamins. When he pulled back she just stared up at him.

Then he left her there.

Alone. Unbound. She heard a key in the old-fashioned lock.

Shelby waited until he was gone and lifted one hand to her mouth.

She spit the foul-tasting tablets out on the pillow. He'd crammed three into her mouth. At least one and a half remained. Half the dose.

She had to act fast.

Her parents had tried to medicate her stutter away when she'd been nine or ten, desperate to just "fix" her, despite the side effects. She'd learned early on how to cheek the medicine and get rid of it in her bathroom sink.

Those early lessons had served her well.

Jake was coming for her—but that didn't mean Shelby was just going to sit back and wait for rescue to come.

Not this time.

This time, Shelby was going to find a way to save herself.

102

HE HADN'T GOTTEN ALL THE BLOOD OFF. DOM STARED at it where it matted the hair on his arm a bit and knew he would never forget this. He didn't know if it was Charlotte's or Madison's, but it didn't matter.

Dom would never forget.

Or forgive.

He knew he had it bad for Madison—but nothing like this. The idea that she was hurting, lying in a hospital bed, while her best friends fought for their very lives sickened him. Hurt him to his soul.

He would find the bastard who had shot her. Find the bastards who had taken Shelby.

And Dom would make them pay.

But first...he had a man to find.

One he semitrusted to give him straight information, and when the text had come from the little shithead, Dom had answered.

Dom slowed his SUV to a stop, not even two blocks away from where Boethe Street met the hospital.

It was the worst part of the city.

Tony met him there, just like they'd arranged.

Dom rolled down the window. "Get in. Fast."

The man he'd come to meet was all of thirty years old, looked fifty, had lost half his teeth to meth, and Dom had booked him a dozen times in the past four years. But they had a deal, him and Tony.

For information. Tony was good at ferreting out information, just when Dom needed it most.

Tony's call had come fifteen minutes ago. Dom had almost hung up on him, until he'd mentioned a *choir*. Full of kids.

Whenever something big went down, someone else started talking.

And a guy like that bastard Jody Callahan had had a big mouth. He'd have talked to someone. Dom was banking on that.

"I knew you'd want to know what I heard, man. I just knew it."

"Depends on what you have. If it's good…"

"It's good. I heard…someone offering some money. To some cops, you see. I know they were cops—they were there the last time you booked me."

"Keep going. I'm listening." They hadn't released information that the shooting was TSP related. Not yet. That didn't mean the information hadn't already gotten out. Dom wasn't stupid. He knew how this all worked. "Who were the targets?"

"What's in it for me?"

"I got one hundred in my pocket now. It's yours. I'll get you another hundred tomorrow if it pans out. Only if what you have is what I am looking for. And…it'll probably knock a couple of months off your probation. But it's got to be good."

"It's good. Some old rich guy wanted some rich bitch for his plaything."

"Go on? Who is the guy?"

Tony shook his head. "I don't know. She must be a really good—"

"Watch it. You know how I feel about you being a gentleman in my car." Dom wasn't going to let anyone talk about Shelby like that. He just wasn't. "Go on."

"It's more complicated than that. Guess the girl had some friends. They've made enemies, too. At least, one did."

"Who?"

Tony let out an appreciative whistle. "Man, you should see her. She's the sheriff of Garrity. My mom lives in Garrity. And the sheriff pulled me over once. I just sat there, hard as a fuck—"

"Watch it. The sheriff of Garrity is a personal friend." One who might very well not make it to morning. "She's fighting for her life right now. Ambush."

"Oh, sorry, man. I didn't know. We respect each other, you and me." Tony always had been a little brown-nosing weasel.

Dom scared him, and Dom knew it. Used it. "We do. And I respect that woman. Greatly."

"Me, too, me too. Anyway, Sheriff Hot Ass has been digging her nose into things, I guess. Someone wanted her out. Her, the rich lady, and her attorney. That Barratt woman who is all over the billboards."

"There were two other women hurt tonight."

"Shame. I hate it when fuckers hurt women like that. Anyway... One of the women tonight? I guess her dad is a cop. He's pissed off some important people, and his daughter is like a evidence scientist like that old TV show. The guy offering this contract? He said it was a big one. More than a million dollars— to off two of them scientist girls so they can't go running their mouths about what they know. Man, it's just like some of those TV shows. I coulda been a for-en-zeek scientist like that, you know?"

Yeah, sure he could have. If he'd have stayed away from the damned meth. Tony wasn't stupid. He was just addicted. Dom had tried once to get him into rehab, but the rehab hadn't stuck. "And the fourth woman?"

Tony shrugged. "Guess the guys who did it are going to ransom her or something. She's worth like millions."

"So the sheriff was digging into something, the wealthy woman was taken for ransom, and the two evidence techs were hit to shut them up? Seems a bit farfetched you'd hear all this."

"Hey, I get around. And people talk. What's it to you, anyway? Other than the sheriff. She your girl?"

Dom shook his head. No. His girl had taken one in the damned back. "One of the techs is...special...to me. But all of them are my friends. The girl taken—she's my buddy's girl, Tony. He loves her. And I owe him a favor. I'm taking this very, very personal. You spread the word—if anyone hears anything else, I want to know. And people want to be in my good graces."

"Can do. Sorry about your lady, man. That royally sucks. She going to be ok?"

Dom shook his head. How could anyone after tonight? After what she'd seen? "Get out, now. And thanks, Tony. I owe you one for this."

"Yeah. Hope you catch the guys." He hesitated. Looked at Dom with an open, honest look Dom wasn't used to from him. "I know I should have kept my mouth shut about this. Someone might come after me next, but that sheriff? She's why I'm really telling you this. My mom really likes the sheriff of Garrity. The sheriff helped her plant flowers in her yard or something a few months ago, even drove my mom around town since her car was broke down to buy them. Bought my mom lunch, too. Spent the whole day with my mom. That lady didn't deserve this at all. She...she's mostly why I called. My mom—she doesn't have many friends, you know. And that cop—she didn't deserve nothing like that."

"None of them did, Tony. They were at a children's choir concert they helped create. Volunteers, who care about people.

They are good women—who never should have been hurt like this."

"Then catch the bastards. Give them what they deserve."

Dom watched him scurry away like the little rat he was, as Dom grabbed his phone.

He punched in Gunnar's number. "Attacks might not be over yet. And rumor has it Powell Barratt may have been an intended target, too."

Gunnar understood. He'd get his ass back to the hospital as fast as he could. It was time to ask that lawyer a few questions.

They just needed the right incentive to get her to open up.

103

HE WOULD NEVER FORGET IZZIE AND ALLEN'S FACES when he told him he was looking for her but had no idea who would do this.

He had let them all down.

Jake could never forget that.

His phone rang. *"Get to the hospital. We need to talk to Shelby's attorney."*

"I'm on my way."

He whistled, grabbing Daniel's attention.

Gunnar had the attorney cornered when they got there. Dom had met them in the parking lot, explained what they were after.

Jake looked at the head of the hospital. Nikkie Jean's brother-in-law. "We need a secure room. Now."

Gunnar had Powell Barratt by the arm. She wasn't about to get away. Not that she looked like she could go far. The woman was pale and practically catatonic. Terrified. Gunnar was half holding her up.

Jake understood.

"This way," Rafe Holden-Deane said. He was pale, and the same fear was in his eyes that Jake suspected was in his.

Eyes identical to Zoey Daviess's.

Jake remembered then. "How is your sister?"

"She's...holding on. Zoey's tough." This man—Jake owed him; he'd helped Izzie and Allen when they'd needed it most. Multiple times.

Now the guy's own sister had taken two bullets.

"And Chu—Charlotte?" They'd never call her Chuckie again. Not after what Madison had told Dom.

"Same. They are with some of the best surgeons in the country now. Virat Patel is leading one team, with Jeoff Stockton; Lacy Deane...Lacy went in with my sister. Dr. Macomber is heading her team. They're the best. Dr. Duvall took Madison McAlister back a few minutes ago. They...they're my best, after me and Allen. The best."

Jake just nodded.

"Allen's sister? Have you found Shelby yet?"

"We...don't know yet." He hoped she knew...he was coming for her. He would always come for her.

"Let me know if there is anything else I can do. Even if it's knocking on damned doors, searching for her myself. At least then I'd be doing something besides sitting here waiting on word."

Gunnar hustled Powell into the conference room in front of him. Wrapped his hand around her arm.

She turned to Jake, trying to shake off Gunnar's hold. "What do you know? Have you found anything to say where Shelby is?"

"Dom?" Daniel asked. "Gunnar, let go of her."

"I don't want her to bolt. She did before. I had to follow her into the ladies' room to make sure she didn't take off."

"I'm not taking off!" The woman practically shook apart. "That's...my friends...my friends. I'm not going to just leave them. I can't just leave them. I should have been there tonight, but I had to go. An emergency with one of my houses I'm buying. I was supposed to do the tickets and help clean up. But I wasn't there."

She looked ready to burst into tears at any moment. Gunnar's hand rose, to cup her shoulder.

"Here's the deal. I heard tonight that Zoey and Shelby—and *you*—were digging into things someone wants kept hidden. And that you might be a target, too." She was still shaking. Jake felt compassion warring with the impatience. He put his hands on her boney shoulders and turned her toward him. Looked into her eyes. "Tell me why."

"I *can't*. It's through my position as Shelby's attorney. Client privilege."

"That's bullshit," Gunnar said. "Just tell us what we need to know so we can find her."

"It has to do with Shelby's past. That's all I can legally say. It's a...project...Shelby and Zoey were working on. She may have spoken to someone else about it. Mel, maybe. Mel *may* have been in the room when we were discussing it. You can ask her. No confidentiality exists between Mel and me, if you know what I mean. I just want to help find Shelby. She has to be terrified right now."

Daniel nodded at Jake. "Mel's in the lobby now."

"Did Shelby find out the men's names?" Jake asked, as things started to gel in his mind. "This is why she hired Naelin Lassiter. Just nod. You don't have to say anything. Just between us, purely confidential."

She nodded.

"They are all with the TSP?"

She shook her head. Held up two fingers.

"Two are TSP?" She nodded. "Where is she keeping this information? In her office?"

Powell shrugged. Jake took it to mean she didn't know.

He hadn't touched her desk. She'd had it locked up tight ever since the day of the search. She'd carried a bag with her every-where after that.

He looked at Dom. "She has a bag. Shelby carries it with her everywhere. It would have been there at the auditorium. She never let me touch that bag. If there is something in there she didn't want me to know about it would have been in that bag."

"First, we talk to Mel Barratt. See if she's a bit more open than Powell, here," Dom said. He patted the woman on the shoulder gently. "Gunnar, you go back to Shelby's. Search for that bag. Search her office as well. Jake, I imagine you have the security codes and keys?"

Jake nodded. "Her brother's set. He gave them to me tonight."

Daniel nodded, phone out, texting. "Gunnar, search her office. Mel's on her way here now. See what you can find. Have Callum or Evers find that damned PI. I'll keep Jarrod here, guarding Powell. And Charlie. He can be here if Charlie...needs...someone."

Jake understood what he was saying. The odds weren't in Charlotte's favor. At all. Nor Zoey's.

The odds that both would survive this?

Jake knew those odds far too well.

Mel came in, worry on her beautiful face.

"Mel, what do you know? What was Shelby and Zoey involved in that got them the wrong kind of attention?"

"Shelby hired Naelin Lassiter to help her identify the four men who attacked her five years ago. So that we could be certain they weren't out there hurting anyone else. She has hit the halfway point on the statute of limitations. She didn't want to wait any longer. She has Naelin Lassiter looking for the evidence from back then," Mel said quickly. She knew enough not to waste time. She'd been a damned fine cop once.

"And what did she find?" Charlotte had found a box of evidence in Logan Lanning's house. Evidence that pertained to

Shelby's case. Madison had confirmed that with Daniel before being taken away by ambulance. That evidence was somewhere in this TSP building. And Madison had made it clear she'd uploaded it to a private, secure server to protect it from disappearing. Evidence had been disappearing for a while. Madison had discovered that fact herself. This week. She'd reported four missing semi-automatics to Elliot Marshall and Haldyn herself.

Jake wanted to see the evidence again, for himself.

"I'm not sure of the most recent information. But she told me two days ago she had a few names now. And...I know she spoke to Charlotte recently. And Madison. About what they had both found."

"She involved Madison and Charlotte in searching?" Dom asked, sharply.

Mel nodded. "People she could trust. She wanted them to get her copies of the evidence and case files from her report five years ago. It had disappeared. They were all looking for it—Madison, Charlotte, Zoey, and Haldyn."

"That information in the bag she carries?"

"Yes. She didn't want to leave it around her house for you to find. Sorry. She never told me the names. We were going to discuss it more Tuesday. I have Pippa calling Naelin Lassiter now. He's sometimes hard to track down. He...he'll want to know about this. He is very fond of Shelby." Mel wrapped an arm around her husband's cousin. Tried to comfort. Powell just shook against her. "You think tonight was a result of that?"

"It's looking that way," Jake said, though he knew it was a little too early to know for sure. Things were adding up.

"Let me know if there is anything else we can do to help. If you are finished with the questions, I need to get back out there with Ariella and Nikkie Jean. There are out-of-town family members for both Zoey and Charlotte coming in soon. I... someone will need to be there to help organize. To get them rooms at the hotel while we wait."

Jake nodded. He looked at Dom and Gunnar. "We need to find that bag."

"I'll check Shelby's place," Gunnar said. Jake handed him the keys.

"I'll head back to the scene, with Jake," Daniel said. "Dom, check in with your family and with Charlie. And find Callum and Mike."

"We need to talk to Daryn Evers as well. She was attacked by the same men. Hell, she might very well be a target now, too," Jake said. "Let her brother know what's happening. He's going to want to know about Shelby, too. If this is something related to what they've dug up...it might just be the beginning."

People would kill to keep secrets hidden. He should have figured it out, should have kept her safe. Instead of pushing what happened to her five years ago to the backburner and assuming it had nothing to do with what had happened to her now. He had been stupid.

"It's time to circle the wagons," Daniel said. "Dom, what did your CI say exactly?"

Dom waited until Powell and Mel were out of the room before he spoke. "That someone older and rich wanted Shelby. Said Charlotte's father pissed off the wrong person, and Zoey Daviess and Shelby were digging into things they shouldn't have. There were also evidence techs involved; I'm assuming that was Madison and Charlotte. It was pretty specific. They were the intended targets. And Powell Barratt."

"Powell said she was supposed to be there tonight. It was sheer coincidence that she wasn't. I'll warn her brothers," Daniel said. "The Barratts are pretty damned good at circling the wagons. And Houghton will assign guards. Like it or not, we can't trust anyone from the TSP to watch over her."

104

"WHAT DO YOU WANT IN EXCHANGE FOR HER?" Victor asked. James did nothing for free. "Why did you do this tonight?"

James smirked at him. Like he knew he had Victor by the balls—and was enjoying it. "Took care of our problem with the TSP. Did a bit of housecleaning with the evidence techs. We're going to ground for a while. Since we lost that dumbass Callahan. We'll be keeping our noses clean. Just to be on the safe side. Rumor has it you were offering a million dollars to bring MacNamara's woman to you next week. We just got a bit ahead of ourselves tonight. Things were found that sped up our plans a bit. So…pay up. We lost one of us tonight getting her. So…we'll take three million to keep our mouth shuts."

Victor thought about killing them both right where they stood.

But that would be more of a mess than he wanted to deal with now. Considering who he had in an upstairs bedroom courtesy of these bastards.

They were getting off on screwing with his plans. Victor

could see that for himself. Had seen it the moment the three men had shown up demanding to be let in.

James had been carrying the limp body of the woman Victor wanted above all others. That was the only reason they weren't dead yet.

But now they were making demands.

These men could have hurt Shelby; probably had, in order to get her.

He would see they paid for that eventually.

No one would touch her and live.

Victor took very good care of his property, after all.

Now that he had her...he wasn't prepared to give her back. But just how he was going to make it work—he needed time to figure that out.

Time he just might not have. Considering what these assholes had done.

It was probably more expedient to just give them the money. It was a trivial amount, as it was. He had ten times that kept in his safe, after all.

He nodded at his assistant. Kessler knew what would need to be done. "This is business. If you get caught...I trust you'll—"

"Keep you out of it," James said, smirking. "Of course, I will. I owe it to my brother to do just that. And to Kyle. God rest his soul. He'll...I've made sure this will never stain their names again. You just see to it that John's care is paid for life, and we're good. I'm going to have to disappear for a while...once I finish some business of my own."

There was fervent fanaticism in the younger man's eyes. He meant it.

Maybe he did care about something, after all.

Some men were born monsters. This was one of them.

A ruthless killer in man's clothing.

Tonight had just proven that.

Now Victor had to figure out what to do next.

Especially with the woman sleeping in his guestroom upstairs.

105

THEY STILL HAD THE SCENE ROPED OFF; IT WOULD BE for a long while to come. He felt sick when he saw the yellow tape around the entrance to the building.

Dom put a hand on his shoulder. Daniel stood next to him. "Remember: it wasn't Shelby's blood. We don't think she was hit."

Jake nodded. Fat lot of comfort that was.

She was out there somewhere. And he couldn't get to her. Yet. But he would. "I want to find her bag. Then I want to find out the names of the sonsofbitches who hurt her. First. Then if they have anything to do with taking her? I'm going to rip them apart. Bones first. Right through the skin."

"We'll help you do that," Daniel said. "Let's just do what we know. And find your girl."

Jake took the first step, grabbed the yellow line, and lifted it.

A woman appeared, dressed in the paper burrito. "Daniel... how are they? We haven't heard anything yet."

"Haldyn, sweetheart...," Daniel said quietly. No one had missed the pain and panic in her tone. Several of her crew stopped working and stepped closer.

Rory put one gloved hand on Haldyn's shoulder.

"Madison is in recovery. Full recovery expected. The bullet was a small caliber, through and through," Daniel said. The rest of the crew moved closer. "Charlotte...I won't lie. She's...bad. But at the last update, she was holding on. There was a lot of blood loss. Both she and Zoey were shot at least twice that we know of. Zoey is also in surgery at this time. All three women are still alive and are getting the best care possible."

"And Shelby?" Haldyn asked. "Any news?"

"We have a few leads, Hal," Daniel said. "We think tonight ties into events from Shelby's past."

"Does it tie into what Zoey asked Charlotte to look into?" Haldyn asked.

Jake's attention sharpened. "You know about that?"

"Yes. Of course. Charlotte had questions. And the two of us went hunting for the buried evidence yesterday."

"What did you find?" Jake asked.

"It took us hours to find it, and it wasn't much. I handed it off to Charlotte. I was called away. I assume it's still in the lab."

"We'll get someone to help us find it once we get back. But for now, we need Shelby's bag."

"I have already tagged it. I didn't think it had any relevance to the shooting, so it's over there. With...with Madison's guitar. I thought someone might want to take it to her brother or mother for now. It was their father's."

"Take it back to the precinct. I'll keep it in my office in case it's needed as evidence," Dom said. "But we need Shelby's bag and Sheriff Daviess's."

"Zoey doesn't carry a bag or purse. She just shoves things into her pocket—or into Shelby's bag when they are together. Charlotte's is over here, next to Shelby's."

"Let's get moving," Jake said. He turned back to Haldyn. "Do you happen to know if they had any names associated with Shelby's case five years ago?"

"Sol Kimball was the original investigating detective, according to what we found. But he wasn't going to do anything. Not going against Victor Scott's son like that. That just wasn't going to happen," Haldyn said quietly. "We all know how Kimball is when it comes to people like the Scotts."

"Victor Scott's son?" Jake asked, zeroing in on the name. "He was involved in the attack on Shelby?"

"From what I can tell, he was the main attacker. His name was the only one I actually saw on the reports, though. And that was just because it wasn't redacted completely. I can have someone try to remove the rest of the ink, see if anything of the original report remains." She turned toward her people. "Rory, take over here. Let me know if you find anything. I'll update the boys on the way."

"You're absolutely certain the file said Kyle Scott?" Daniel asked.

"I'd stake my entire career on it, Dan. It was Kyle Scott. I'm sure of it."

106

JAKE DIDN'T CARE ABOUT PRESERVING HER PRIVACY. Not in that moment. He wanted to know if something Shelby had gotten into had led to this. He had a gut instinct it had.

He thought about what they had. A sheriff digging into things. A private investigator with one hell of a reputation for being tenacious and damned good at what he did.

Two evidence techs—who had been helping the sheriff with a special project. Her attorney and Haldyn's testimonies that Shelby was looking into the men who had attacked her.

Men who would know what kind of a threat sexual assault charges would have on their careers, their lives, now.

Men who would be capable of doing this without hesitation. Would have all the resources to do just that.

He had to know what was in those files. He looked up at the two men next to him. "Somehow, what she has been doing ties into this. She came up against someone she shouldn't have. And it bled into our investigation into the Scotts. It has nothing to do with her connection to the Henedys at all."

"And it pulled the rest of them into it?" Dom asked.

"I don't know." Jake tried to look at all the angles. It still felt off. "Maybe it's the other way around? Or maybe it all ties together. So balled up there is no way to tell where one aspect begins and another ends."

"Maybe someone doesn't want you digging into their business and found a convenient way to stop you? Maybe...what Shelby's been up to and what we've been doing have intersected as a way to keep you out of the way," Dom said. "To stop Charlie, too. He was getting close on the kidnapping ring. Left-hand-not-know-what-the-right-hand-is-doing kind of thing?"

"And you. Half the guys in this precinct know that to get to you," Gunnar said. He'd been waiting for them when they'd walked in. Shelby's desk hadn't had anything useful. "They just have to get to Mads. That's all it would take."

Dom's expression darkened. "They made a stupid mistake."

Jake dumped Shelby's bag on the middle of the war room conference table. Answers were in that bag.

"Anything with Lassiter Investigations on it. That's what we're looking for." Haldyn already had Shelby's phone and the sheriff's. Charlotte and Madison's, too.

She would be cross-referencing all their texts to see just what they may have found. What they had all been talking about.

It would take a while. Shelby had texted her friends all the damned time, telling him that texting was a girl's favorite pastime and to keep his nose out of her business. She had rarely been without her phone at all.

"Shelby's phone. It's her lifeline to the outside world. She is on it constantly."

"We need to find Naelin Lassiter," Gunnar said. "He might have insight."

"I already spoke with Chance Marshall. He has some of his security team tracking him now."

Jake grabbed the files she'd fastened together with a large

rubber band. Files first. He'd let Haldyn go through her phone. Haldyn was the best at that kind of task.

Her bag smelled like her. Like the floral lotion she loved. He ruthlessly ignored the punch in the gut that brought. Her wallet was right there. He flipped through it quickly.

She had a photo of her and her friends and all the choir kids right there. He hadn't realized people still carried photos in their wallets and not on their phones.

"Why do women cram so much stuff into their bags? I have never understood that," Gunnar said, shifting nonessentials into a haphazard pile. "Jamie used to do that, and it would drive me crazy. I actually kind of miss it."

"Not all women. Haldyn said the sheriff doesn't carry a bag. She just shoves stuff into Shelby's."

Sure enough, there was an extra wallet in there, with bank cards and a Texas driver's license. No badge, though.

She'd had that on her, as well as her weapon. Shelby had told him before that Zoey never went anywhere without it.

That weapon had saved the sheriff's life. He had no doubt about that.

If she hadn't taken out Callahan, those bastards would have kept going. Shot her more than they had.

Or gone back and finished off Charlotte and Madison. A very real possibility.

Something clicked in Jake's head. "*Callahan.*"

"What?"

"Why would Callahan go after Shelby?" Jake swore. "I didn't know him well at all. He always annoyed the piss out of me. How is he connected to Kyle Scott?"

"He's been going on and on about her for months," Gunnar said. "Since everything went down with your niece. On and on about her. I told him to shut up a thousand times myself. I thought that was when he first saw her."

"But what if it wasn't? He's been in the area for a good eight or nine years. Plenty old enough to have been one of her attackers," Jake said, grabbing the first file and opening it. "And he was always going on about partying on his downtime. Maybe he was there that night she was hurt?"

Kyle Scott's face stared back at him. He swore. Lassiter's notes painted a damned clear picture.

This was where the intersection between Shelby's past and Jake's organized crime case just happened. With Victor Scott's only child.

"What is it?" Dom grabbed another file.

"Kyle Scott." Jake read Lassiter's report quickly. "Says here that the man who owned the house where the party occurred was Kyle Scott. His father owns it now. Another mark against that bastard."

"We need to find known associates of his," Gunnar turned toward the laptop nearby that was hooked into the TSP system, plus several federal databases. "Five years ago. We need names. We should have something like that. I was digging into what that son of a bastard was involved in before Henedy took him out."

"Screw that. Shelby already has the names. Right here. Kyle Scott, Jody Callahan, and a man named John. The fourth attacker is still unknown."

"Perhaps I can help?" a quiet, feminine voice said.

Jake turned.

Daryn Evers stood there, Mike's hand wrapped around hers. There were tears on her beautiful face, and her dark eyes were hurting.

"Go on." Jake said.

"Kyle Scott was the ringleader. I never saw him that night. I was in the closet, hiding. They had separated us, and I ran upstairs. I hid, and when I got ahold of my brother, he came. There was a guy there who recognized me. I never saw him or knew his name. But it got around fast that Darrell was my brother. And...Darrell has a reputation around the TSP. Him and his friends."

"As someone not to mess with," Mike said. He pulled his wife closer. "That had the guy backing off Daryn."

"By the time Darrell got to me, I had gotten away. I'd climbed the fence. I got off the property and to a house two doors down, looking for help for Shelby. Darrell came to me first. Darrell went back to find Shelby, leaving me with the people in that house. They were kind to me, but I don't even remember their names. I was too scared, terrified for Shelby."

Jake forced himself not to react. They didn't have time for him to react, to hurt. Shelby needed him to be Jake the cop. Not Jake the lover.

Not now.

"By the time Darrell got back to the house for Shelby, it was over, and the party was breaking up. Logan had gotten there, thank God. He was known around that neighborhood, and his father had some serious connections with Washington. Money-making connections. To that crowd, part of it anyway, that was what mattered. Logan went crazy. He was so fierce, Darrell said, that the asshole who'd started everything backed off. Fast. Logan had knocked him to the ground and the guy didn't get back up. Darrell had to pull Logan off of him before Logan killed the guy. I never saw the rest of Shelby's attackers, and neither did Darrell. Allen had taken Shelby away to the hospital by that point. Logan and Darrell came back for me. Logan checked me over physically. I remember...how bad his hands looked and thinking that a surgeon's hands shouldn't look like that. It was another day and a half before I saw Shelby again. I never saw her attackers, and she never saw mine. We never learned their names. But she told me last week—she *knew* it was Kyle Scott now. And she was going to keep digging. Because he had friends. And she didn't want them hurting someone else. Closing someone else off from life the way they have her. Taking that from someone, the way she took it from Logan. She... blames herself, I think. For Logan. And what he did to Izzie and those other women after. But mostly...she blames herself for not stopping *them* years ago. Thinks that if she had been stronger, a better person somehow, she would have been able to keep them from hurting someone else. No matter what Zoey and I have told her to the contrary, she thinks she should have done more than she did back then. And she thinks...what happened to her caused Logan to do what *he* did later. She blames herself for everything. All of it. For just not measuring up to expectations she has in her own head."

Jake flinched. He'd read every word of that man's journals. He'd seen Lanning for what he was—broken and hurting and feeling so damned guilty. The idea that Shelby thought any of that was her fault... "And she told Zoey about Kyle Scott?"

Zoey, who had been instrumental in digging into all the illegal activities Kyle Scott had been involved in for the task force.

Leading right back to Kyle Scott's father.

A man who was already high on the task force's suspect list. "Scott. Shit. The man is everywhere."

Dom practically growled in agreement. "It might not have been anything Shelby did at all. It very well could have been the task force itself. My informant said the sheriff was digging into things. And that there were evidence techs who needed eliminated."

"But why shoot three women and take the fourth?" Jarrod asked, as he came in with Callum in time to catch the discussion. "It would be more efficient to just take them all four out. Especially if Shelby could tell what Scott Junior had done to her. We've all heard how rabidly he is about anything that might tarnish his son's name lately. Shelby could do that. Paint him as a pervert and a rapist. That wouldn't go over well with Scott.'

"Unless he took her to find out what she knew or who she

told," Mike said. "Or...took her just to get at Jake? Since Jake is tied to the Henedy case in the first place?"

"I heard from the warden yesterday before all of this happened. There was an inmate who was paid to take out Jennifer Henedy. Said the one who paid her mother was an older guy whose son Jennifer had gotten killed. Still waiting on the warrant to talk to Scott about that." Dom wrote a note on the board and circled it. "It all ties to the damned Scott family."

"I'm here to help," Callum said. "Autumn Jane is ready to work remotely if we need to tap her as well. Using Mel Barratt's setup. They've guaranteed it's secure."

"We need to get Haldyn and forensics up here," Dom said. "See if anything has been found."

"Jarrod's on to something, though. Why shoot three but take one? She would be a witness," Callum said.

"There are two reasons women like Shelby are taken," Jake said. "Her net worth is almost seventy million dollars. So ransom is a possibility. And men want her. Rich, poor, anything in between. A lot of men want her. Zoey said something to me... said she's run men off away from Shelby. Men wanting money, connections, sex. Just in the last year. But that doesn't make sense here—they are all gorgeous women who men want. We saw it ourselves at the heroes' benefit. Men were all about them."

"It has happened to Shelby a lot more since the money," Daryn said. "People seek her out. Think she'd be an easy mark, because she's quiet and alone a lot now. I mean, guys were into her before, but she kept them far away. Just because Shelby doesn't talk a lot doesn't mean she's stupid. But there are guys out there that think she'd be perfect to add to their collections—or their bank accounts. Zoey...she's always been so overprotective. She's taken it on herself in the last year or so to keep Shelby as safe as she can. Just like she does her little sister—because of their brother's money. Especially since that night."

"Men want her," Dom said, writing Shelby's name in the middle of the white board and circling it. "We all know that. No sense sugarcoating it. So...who would have the means to orchestrate this? To have at least four men on the payroll to do this?"

"Someone had to sneak up on the Barratt-Handley guards in the auditorium parking lot," Jarrod said. "They are both in critical, but prognosis is good."

"Shot to immobilize and get them out of the way," Jake said. "Efficient."

"The attackers have done this before. Had training. Probably military and definitely TSP," Jarrod added.

Haldyn came in, Rory at her side. "We can get you basic descriptions now."

"Go. As fast as you can."

"First, forensics. Preliminaries. Security video reveals one man stayed outside, car running. Late-model Ford van. Printing on the side. We have a tech trying to make out that label now. It was probably maroon or navy in color. Three men took out the guards, then headed inside. The setup of the auditorium made it a perfect setting for this. They probably scoped it out before. Not a lot of windows, open space, but nowhere to run. Not that there would have been time." Haldyn's breath hitched, but she kept herself together. "We saw it all on the video. They went for Charlotte first. Then Madison when she went to help Char. Different shooters. Ballistics reports show that. By this point, the third man was on Shelby. Shelby had tried to get to Charlotte, had tried to shift herself in front of Madison. But she couldn't. The taller man covered her mouth with the rag. He was big and strong. Chloroform isn't instantaneous, but most people don't know that. Even some cops. She fought. But couldn't escape. He dragged her from the building with the rag still over her face. Still fighting. From what we can tell, she was still conscious and struggling when the driver of the car approached and hit her on the head. They loaded her into the car then."

"Then he dropped the rag in the parking lot. This was well after Callahan and the other headed toward the main auditorium. The security cameras in there are not great. But we can piece together what happened. Callahan and another man fired on Zoey. Repeatedly. It's a miracle she wasn't struck more. She returned fire. Just a single shot. She had to know the other women could be in her line of fire. But she struck home, killing Callahan instantly," Rory said. "There were more than twenty-five rounds shot into that auditorium. It's a miracle she was only struck twice. That happened just seconds before the remaining two pulled Shelby out of the building."

"There were only four rounds found in the main lobby. The two that struck Charlotte, the one that struck Madison, and the one that struck Callahan," Haldyn said bluntly. "They hit exactly where they were aiming in the lobby. Efficiently. So why did they fire so many rounds just at Zoey?"

"That's a good question," Dom said. "Possibly because she'd been the intended target all along. And they were sending a message—either to the task force in general, or the governor—considering their connection. Or...with Shelby in the lobby area, and them intending to take her—which we know they were, you don't carry chloroform for no reason—they didn't want to risk Zoey hitting Shelby. My source said Shelby was taken for ransom. That makes sense."

"So how is that going to help us find Shelby?" Jake asked.

"We need to connect a wealthy suspect to Shelby," Gunnar said. "Because if someone ordered this, wanted one woman dead, but wanted Shelby...why not? If they have the money, they have ways to make her disappear forever. Would have the resources to keep a woman hidden away indefinitely. Scott does. And his name just keeps coming up."

Dom grabbed his phone. "I'm calling Customs. Getting an

alert for a woman matching Shelby's description. Keep her from being taken over the border."

"Charlotte and Madison could have just been collateral?" Rory asked. "I mean, if Shelby was the intended target of a kidnapping? And someone knew her habits well enough to know she had an armed sheriff as a guard with her, too. They would want to take out that guard, right?"

"But it doesn't explain what they said to Charlotte and Madison," Dom said. "And this doesn't leave this room. They targeted Char and Madison, too. No, this has both the feel of being personal and professional. Like someone wanted something specific—from each one of them. It's not black and white, not straight-forward. But like every other damned thing in life, everything ties together. Somehow. We need to find the strings."

Jake studied the board. There was only one thing that made sense. "Victor Scott wanted her. He wanted her from the night of the ball."

Haldyn shivered. "There was something in his eyes that night that creeped me out. Fanatical, determined. And he held his dance partners far too close."

"You danced with him," Jarrod said. "What did he talk about?"

"He was asking odd questions. Like how close to my family am I? Do I have a lot of family? Do I spend time with my niece or nephew? Do I like children? How much? Did I want some of my own someday? I sensed he liked my answer a great deal. Did I do well in school? Do I play an instrument or speak foreign languages? Am I dating anyone seriously?" She looked at Jake. "It was very strange. He asked how involved with Daniel I was, repeatedly. And if Daniel was the head of Major Crimes like he thought. The questions were similar to those he asked of all of us."

"All of you?" Jake asked. "Who else?"

"*All* of us. He danced with me, Madison, Charlotte, Zoey,

Powell, and Shelby. We thought it was strange, the style of questions he was asking. No other man there asked those types of questions. And between all of us, we probably danced with just about every man there."

"The Cinderellas at the ball," Jarrod said. "All attractive, all younger, all unmarried. Almost like he was inspecting them, maybe?"

"Or digging for information," Mike said.

"Maybe that was exactly what he was doing," Dom said. "Victor Scott has inoperable cancer. Maybe he was evaluating the available women of Finley Creek—women who apparently could fit into his social circle just fine, considering where we were that night—searching for the right princess for his particular needs?"

"But what is his plan?" Rory asked. "Someone to nurse him in his last days? That's just seriously messed up."

"Simple," Haldyn said, a sick look on her face. "He was asking all the women at the benefit those questions for one thing. He was interested in women who want *children* someday. It's why he kept coming around to our table. Zoey finally told him we weren't dancing anymore that night to get him to leave us alone."

Daryn finished the thought for her, a look of horror in her dark eyes. "He was looking for a broodmare. Victor Scott wants a baby before he dies."

Rory flinched. "I think I'm going to be sick."

"I bet he thinks he's found her," Jake said.

"This is just wild speculation. We need to confirm that," Dom said firmly. "Get eyes on his place as soon as we can."

"Screw that. I'm going to go talk to him myself." Jake started to the door.

Dom and Gunnar blocked his path. Dom spoke. "Like hell you are. If we're wrong, Shelby could just be getting farther away. That is the last thing any of us want at all."

"It's been confirmed," Haldyn said quietly, checking her phone as a text buzzed in. "They used trichloromethane—chloroform. We have both rags now. If not used properly, chloroform can cause fatal complications. It requires specialized knowledge to use effectively. It's not like it is in fiction or the movies. You can't just soak a cloth with it and it work like magic. That man had to hold it over Shelby's face for a long time to get it to render her unconscious. It probably wasn't working well. Even after they got her in that car and with her fighting. And if they used too much because they didn't really know how to use it correctly…"

"Find her, Jake. Just find her," Daryn almost pleaded.

"I'm going to." Now he had a place to start.

107

Victor Scott. Jake stared at everything they had on the other man while Dom and Gunnar were chasing down informants and calling in favors. They needed to know Scott's whereabouts—the man owned multiple residences within Finley Creek and Barratt counties. And they needed to know where all the players were.

Dom came in. "Come on, grab your gear. I have someone willing to talk."

Jake didn't hesitate.

They grabbed Gunnar in the lobby, where he'd been waiting on someone to bring him a message.

The underbelly of the city they dealt with didn't exactly use couriers—or send anything in written form.

Not with the internet being forever.

Jake understood that.

He kept reminding himself that every piece of information they gathered was getting them one step closer to her.

It was three a.m. now. Five hours since the shooting.

Updates from the hospital weren't good. Shelby's friend the

sheriff had been rushed back for a third emergency surgery half an hour earlier.

No one knew what would happen now. Jake was going to find Shelby and get her to her friend. Somehow.

Shelby would want to be there for Zoey, no matter what.

They had just reached Dom's SUV when Jarrod came jogging up. He was going to stay on all the evidence gathered so far—and go over what Lassiter and Shelby and the sheriff had found. Haldyn was getting everything Charlotte and Madison had been working on together. To see what was probative.

In the morning, after the anesthetic wore off, they'd be speaking directly to Madison. She was the one link to this that would be able to talk at all for a long while.

That had him tensing. "Dom, how many guards do you have on Madison now? She's going to be our only witness until we get Shelby back."

"Two. Not TSP. Men we can trust."

"Because right now, Madison is our only witness to everything even close to being able to talk."

"I know." Dom's expression tightened. "I haven't forgotten that for a moment. If they get desperate enough, they'll try for her again."

And Dom couldn't be there with her to protect her. Not yet.

Not until they got Shelby back. Jake had never appreciated his friends more.

Dom's phone rang. He grabbed it quickly. Cursed as he read the text. "We're heading to County Gen right now."

"Did they find her?" Jake asked.

"No. But Lassiter was brought in six hours ago. He finally woke. Someone worked him over and left him for dead in Value. Addy's deputy found him practically crawling up the road. Barratt County transferred him to Finley Creek County."

Jake swore as Dom pressed on the gas.

108

Dom took one look at Naelin Lassiter and got the man's measure.

The man was beyond pissed.

"Give us what you got, fast," Dom said. Jake was hanging on by a thread, more agitated than Dom had ever seen him.

He didn't know how much longer he was going to be able to keep Jake under control. Keep him from storming the damned estate of Victor Scott and demanding answers.

If Scott didn't have Shelby, he might very well know who did.

They would have to find a way to make the older man talk.

"Three men jumped me. Demanded to know everything I had been digging in to for Shelby and her sheriff friend."

"Did you tell them?" Jake demanded, stepping closer to the bed.

Naelin shot him a pissed off look, from two eyes that were black and swollen. It was a wonder the guy was awake at all. Dom was infinitely grateful that he was. "Hell, no, I didn't tell them. I wasn't going to set those bastards on her. I just...

heard…what happened. Her friends going to be ok? Is she doing ok?"

Dom bit back a curse. "Lassiter, Shelby was abducted during the midst of the shooting. We are trying to find her now. We're hoping you have something that can help us."

Naelin stiffened and moved like he was going to get out of the bed and go looking for her himself. Dom got it; Shelby inspired that in a guy.

"Hell, yes, I do. But those bastards took it. I need the internet. There is a secure server set up—that cute little redhead with glasses did it a few days ago. I'll give you everything I've found and then some. That Scott, he's a damned asshole. I've been digging. Gave some things to that sheriff friend of Shelby's to look into. He ordered his men to do this to me after I asked him questions about some of his son's activities. After they worked me over and were dragging my almost lifeless ass outside to dump me, I listened to what they had to say."

"Anything that will get us in to talk to the old bastard?" Dom asked.

"Yeah. One of the guys, they called the whiny little shit Callahan—said they were going after the rich bitch next. Said, see if Scott wants her tonight? Another said that if Scott wanted her so badly, he'd have to pay to get her back and keep it quiet now."

That was good enough cause for Dom. "There's the ransom angle, boys."

They asked a few more questions. Gunnar brought up a shot of Callahan's TSP badge on his phone. "This one of the guys?"

"Yeah, he's the one responsible for the tread marks on my chest. I have a score to settle with him someday."

"You'll have to do it when you've met your maker," Jake said. "Shelby's friend the sheriff took him out with a single neck shot."

"Hell of a woman, that sheriff. I'd love her phone number.

Find Shelby, guys. And kick some serious ass when you do. I'd join you, but I'm afraid they kicked mine something good first. Guess that's what I get for taking on five of them at once."

"We'll be back, Lassiter. See if you can identify some of the others for us. For now, we're going to go talk to Scott. Take care of yourself." Dom was going to order a guard on the man, too. One not TSP.

"Watch your backs. The guy had a least three armed guards I could see out there at his place in Hughes Heights. Watch yourselves. And just get her back. I'd do it myself, but I'm going to be stuck here for a while."

109

Shelby knew she had to act fast. Logan had gone into detail about those little lemon-yellow pills with a serial number stamped on them in his journals.

At first, because he was thrilled with their potential. And how valuable they were going to be. Then...he'd discussed his use of them in exact detail.

She'd never forgotten that serial number.

It had been four digits—and seared into her mind forever.

They'd been the date Logan had first kissed her.

She would never forget that horrible irony.

Victor Scott had tried to give her three doses of Sopalmi-traln. She'd been able to spit out some of that. She knew what that would do to her. Even half that was more than he should have given her.

Shelby had to hurry. Before it was too late.

If she was knocked completely out, there was nothing to stop him doing whatever he wanted to with her.

It took her too long, but she was able to slip her ankle from the rope he had used to tether her to the bed. Was he thinking she wouldn't even try to escape? That was just insane.

Or arrogant.

Or maybe he didn't figure she'd get very far, considering he'd tripled the regular dose of Sopalmitraln. Men like Victor Scott had armed security guards everywhere. She'd seen his guards at W4HAV that day.

He'd had two personal guards, and Houghton had told her that most men like him would have an armed driver as well. Maybe more than that.

There were guards.

She'd have to be careful. Shelby slipped over to the window and looked outside.

110

THEY HAD PROBABLE CAUSE. BARELY. IT WAS WEAK, but they had cause. Jake's gut was telling him this was exactly where they needed to be. He studied the layout of Victor Scott's Hughes Heights property.

The bastard was eight houses down from Shelby, on the same damned road. Six away from his Izzie down a side street.

The same damned neighborhood.

The wolf had been right there the whole time. And Jake hadn't known.

Right there behind the security gates that were supposed to protect the two women who mattered the most to him.

That just pissed him off even more. "Why didn't we know about this place?"

"It was his son's. Under a shell company set up by that bastard and Jennifer Henedy. Haldyn found it in online property records a week ago, tipped off by my future girlfriend. From what I've heard," Gunnar said, using binoculars to study the guards. Gone was the big doofus that he usually was. In his place was a dangerous sonofabitch Jake would always want at his back. "He's turned it into a shrine for that sick bastard.

Complete with statues commemorating the sick creep's life. Let's just hope he doesn't have the security up and going as tight as at the other places."

"We have to assume he does," Jake said. He checked—security lights, gated entry, fence lining the entire property. He'd personally have gone with solid cement, especially around the back wall. But all he saw now was seven feet of chain link, with six strands of barbed wire on top. He didn't even see a posted notice that it was electric.

Of course, it wasn't. That was against the homeowner's association bylaws or whatever they were called. Shelby had told him that herself when he'd been harping on the security measures she needed to take. With that stubborn chin stuck up in the air and the storm-gray eyes shooting lightning at him from her irritation.

So was the barbed wire, for that matter. No one wanted *Hughes Heights* to look like a prison, after all.

"There are security lights. We won't be going in dark," Dom added, tightening the strap on his vest. Jake did the same. Time to prepare for battle. "We could just walk right up to the front door and demand he give her back. Tell the bastard to find another woman for his sick plan."

Jake snorted. That wouldn't exactly work. But it might get them some damned intel they could use. "I'll do it."

"You're an idiot," Gunnar said bluntly. "If you get your ass killed by someone we suspect has killed several cops already, what good would you do her? That woman needs you. She loves you, man. We all could see that. Once we find her, if she learns you didn't make it, getting to her—that'll just destroy her. Especially considering where her best friends are right now."

Jake just shook his head. "It's not like that. She told me to hit the road."

"Yeah, it *is* like that. I know when a woman is in love with a guy. To the bottom of their soul in love. I've seen it directed at me. Once you've had it, you never forget it. I'll go."

"I can't ask you to do that."

"You're not asking. I'm telling you. I'm going. I don't have a woman like that waiting for me anymore, and I don't have a single person I call family. You got Shelby, and whether Madison wants to admit it or not, she's hooked Dom so damned deeply he lives and breathes her. We all know that. Shelby and Madison —they'll need you guys even more after what's happened to them. Especially if Charlotte and Zoey don't make it."

"He's right. You can't go, Jake. So it's either Gunnar or me," Dom said. "I'm ready."

"I'm going," Gunnar said one more time, fiercely. Dom gave a low curse.

"No heroics. Nothing stupid," Jake said. They didn't have time to argue. "Just go up to the gate and tell them you're there to talk to Victor Scott about files found pertaining to his son. I have a feeling anything to do with Scott Junior is an instant pass inside."

Then all Jake could do was wait as a man he considered a good friend walked straight into the lion's den.

To save the woman Jake loved.

111

VICTOR SCOTT HAD MINIMAL SECURITY AROUND THE rear entrance—the staff entrance—of his property in Hughes Heights. Jake didn't know whether that was a good thing or not.

They could damned well be wasting their time.

She could be getting farther and farther away.

Storm-blue eyes popped into his head. He could almost hear her saying his name, pleading with him to come for her.

He wouldn't even contemplate failure.

Gunnar had been right. Jake did love her. More than he had ever loved anyone, anywhere. More than he ever would.

Jake had to force himself to push that out of his head.

He had to focus on his objective.

Getting her back.

He'd deal with how he felt about her then. When he had her back safe where she belonged.

And then he was going to build thirty-foot walls with electric barbed wire on the top. To keep any bastard from every hurting her again. The homeowners' association could kiss his ass if they didn't like it.

He was going to keep her safe. Forever.

Gunnar returned, driving in with the truck's lights off to where they had agreed to meet. They were at the property directly behind Scott's. It had been vacant for a few months. Jake had noticed the *for sale* sign himself, driving between Shelby's and Izzie's the night of the banquet.

It was slightly uphill from Scott's place.

Jake took advantage of that, using the binoculars to stare straight into the rear of Scott's property.

"Bastard has an eight-foot-tall statue of his son back there next to the pool."

"Jibes with rumors of him taking out any...enemies...of Junior. He's wrapped himself up in the grief for his son," Dom said.

"And then to find out that he's dying himself? With no one to leave his nasty legacy to," Jake said as he worked out the angles. "And it sent him over the edge."

"So the bastard went shopping—with *our* girls," Gunnar said. "But why the shooting?"

"Zoey Daviess, I think. She was digging into his son—for Shelby," Jake said. "And that brought Madison and Charlotte and Haldyn into it. And the lawyer—she probably has copies of *everything* anyone found. Coordinating. She seems the type. Probably in triplicate."

"We sure she's safe?" Gunnar asked. "I have a bet to win, you know. I'm looking forward to convincing her to wine and dine me. But first..."

"I saw movement," Dom said quietly. "Second floor, middle window."

"How the hell did you see that?" Jake asked, training his binoculars in that direction. "And I see two guards on this side of the property. Not good old Dave or Kessler, though."

Scott usually had at least one of those two bastards at his side.

"I've confirmed another two on the front side, rent-a-boys,

mostly. From an outside company," Gunnar said. "Scott's limo is out front. Waiting. If the old boy was gone, why is the car there? And why was Tweedledee loading luggage into the back? And where the hell is Tweedledum? Kessler's Tweedledee, by the way. He's not as dumb as Dave."

"I'm going back around," Dom said, grabbing the in-ear headsets out of the bag he'd slung over his shoulder earlier.

He handed one to Jake and one to Gunnar.

"Watch yourselves," Dom warned. "I'm going to get eyes on the front. If I see Scott or anything else, we're going in."

What they were getting ready to do was probably damned crazy.

If Daniel or Elliot were there, they'd be kicked off the TSP for even considering this. But Jake had to know.

If Shelby was in there and he did nothing...

Screw the TSP.

"Let's go."

Jake cataloged every weakness and possible entry point he could see while he waited.

112

THERE WERE HOUSES BEHIND THIS ONE. SHELBY could see their lights. That meant...help. Daryn had escaped that house five years ago and ran to the house two doors down. The couple who had lived there had taken her in and gotten her help. Real help, in the form of Darrell.

If Shelby could get to the back fence, she could get herself out of here.

A fence was nothing. Not really.

She had been rock climbing with Darrell off and on for five years now. Shelby had even scaled the worst, most difficult cliffs in Finley Creek and Barratt counties. The one in Value had even been too hard for Zoey to climb, and Zoey was the most athletic of their little trio. Zoey had told her that Shelby was absolutely crazy for even attempting it. And Shelby was never to scare Zoey like that again.

It had been when she'd climbed the last foot of that cliff that Shelby had first felt she was reclaiming her life again.

It had been thirteen months ago, ninety degrees out, almost dark, and a week after she had hired Naelin Lassiter to find the answers.

She had been taking control. Taking *back* control.

She understood that now.

Darrell and Daryn had been so proud of her. Zoey had cried, standing forty feet beneath Shelby, yelling up at her how proud she was—and how idiotic Shelby was for doing something so dangerous. Shelby had put her head back and yelled to the woman below that she had done it. Conquered her personal mountain.

Grief and fear for her best friend had her making her decision now.

Zoey needed her now. So did Charlotte and Madison.

And Pen.

She wasn't just going to stay there and let Victor Scott do what he wanted with her.

She wasn't.

Shelby grabbed the curtain rod, then slipped the thin material free. She went to work. It was silk. Expensive.

Thin. But if she rolled them and knotted them, she could make handholds.

It was just twenty feet or so down. She just needed something to help steady the trip down. The rope he'd used on her leg was far too short and thin.

But...she could make do.

She could do it.

There was a small ladies' secretary desk next to the window. She quietly pulled the drawer open. Looking for scissors or something, anything, that could make a hole.

The drawer was empty, except for a mass of small, far outdated toiletries. And there, at the rear bottom...a pair of manicure scissors that were just abandoned.

They had almost rusted together, but she forced them open. They would work. She hoped. She just needed to get the fabric started. She'd rip the rest.

She moved as fast as she could. Her head hurt. Probably

from whatever they'd forced her to breathe in on that rag. From the Sopalmitraln. Or that monster hitting her in the parking lot.

It didn't matter.

Shelby just kept going.

Until she had the curtain panel torn into four strips.

The window was going to be her best option. She'd already seen the small balcony outside the window. She'd seen the pool right beneath.

If all else failed, she'd go in the pool.

Shelby was a strong swimmer. Allen had made sure of it by the time she was ten. She still swam almost every day she could in Logan's pool.

She loved his pool, and always would.

The second time Logan had ever kissed her had been when he'd found her in his pool one day after he'd left work early. The day after he'd kissed her for the first time, sitting in his car. In the driveway of her condo. It had just happened.

The pool kiss had been far more deliberate.

She wasn't supposed to be there. She'd let herself in after a particularly rough day. She just hadn't wanted to go back to her condo and sit there alone. And she'd ben torn up about the kiss the night before.

She had needed answers.

Logan had lectured her about swimming alone. He'd grabbed her hand and pulled her from the pool. The new swimsuit she'd been wearing had been cut a little more daring than her previous.

He had liked how she'd looked in it.

Then she'd been kissing him. To this day, Shelby didn't know if she'd made the first move or if Logan had.

Logan...it hadn't been the same with him as it was with Jake.

It had been so different. More unequal. Shelby understood that now.

She had been so young back then. She had needed Logan to

lead. She hadn't been anywhere ready for the type of relationship an experienced man like Logan would have eventually wanted. Even he had said as much.

But Logan had also said he couldn't stay away from her. That he needed her. Obsessed over her.

That had been a theme throughout his later journals, too. Obsessing. Over her.

And Logan not being able to save her.

Jake...she suspected Jake would be the same way if he was looking for her and failed. It would eat at him. He wouldn't handle failure well. Would blame himself.

Just like Logan had.

Shelby just knew—Jake was out there, and he was looking for her.

Coming to rescue her.

She was going to be waiting for him when he got there.

Shelby knotted the strips of silk together, praying they'd be strong enough to hold her weight. If not...

She'd fall into that pool and get right back out.

Maybe a cold pool would wake her up enough, shake the Sopalmitraln from her system enough...

She was going to have to move more quickly. Her hands were already shaking—she didn't know if it was from the drug from before or the Sopalmitraln. Logan had written that he'd been shaky from it.

Especially when used in combination with other things. She had to go faster. Had to hurry.

She was already feeling so sluggish.

Shelby unlocked the window. And pushed it up as hard as she could.

The alarm shrieked around her.

113

After the first warning from the guard that the TSP Major Crimes had come his direction, Victor knew he had to act. It was just a matter of time before someone put it together. Discovered the woman sleeping in his guest room.

Probably that fish-shit MacNamara.

Of course, it would be Jake MacNamara. He wasn't a stupid man, MacNamara. He was just crass. Uncouth. Cocky and animalistic.

The ultimate hunter.

An animal.

Undeserving of the perfection that was Victor's Shelby.

MacNamara was out there. Victor's skin was practically crawling with that knowledge.

Victor would check on her one more time. If the damned Major Crimes was already circling closer like the sharks they were, he might not have much choice.

He would have to make all the evidence disappear.

Including the woman sleeping in his guest room one floor above.

Victor gave orders to Dave and Kessler, almost convinced these would be the last orders he ever gave them.

If those bastards got in to search the house...everything would be ruined.

James had ruined everything. James and his friends. That damned little pissant Jody Callahan who had dogged Kyle's steps practically from kindergarten.

Jody had been a nobody. Shouldn't have been in the same school as Kyle. But he had been, thanks to a scholarship he hadn't deserved. The boy had been too stupid to keep it past junior high. He'd ended up at the public school for high school.

But Kyle...Kyle had had an overdeveloped sense of loyalty to the men he'd called friends. Trusted.

Now Dave had told him that Jody was dead.

Taken down by that Garrity sheriff.

Victor remembered the feel of her lean body in his hands. How his body had actually stirred when she'd looked out at him from eyes so dark they almost looked black. She'd been walking perfection, hot sex appeal in a cool black dress.

If she hadn't been with the TSP, he would have seriously considered her.

Now she was fighting for her life.

So that James and his friends could clean up their fucking messes.

Clean up their messes—Wallace Henedy had screamed that in the courtroom one day. Over and over like a lunatic. When his wife had been brought in to testify against him.

Clean up your messes. And leave the children alone.

Victor hadn't understood it then. He didn't understand it now.

But he was going to check on Shelby one more time.

Before he decided what it was he must ultimately do with her.

If he got rid of her, he could build proof he was in Oklahoma

City and knew nothing about this. Move on to another young woman. He had a few others he could consider who would fit his needs.

That cool strawberry-blonde from the forensics lab had been more than adequate, after all. She was his second choice.

But he had to get away first. Nor could Shelby be found on his property.

He had to make her disappear. Now. There were places he could hide the body easily enough.

He would do it himself. He owed her that much. And then he would begin again.

He was running out of time.

114

THE GUARDS HAD TURNED GUNNAR AWAY, WITH THE information that Victor Scott was in Oklahoma City and would return in two days. They had been nervous and young, and Gunnar didn't recognize them from the intel they had about Scott's known associates and staff.

Dom wasn't stupid. It was time for round two.

"Get inside the building and search for her or Scott ourselves," Jake said. "Lassiter was clear—the guys who worked him over were involved tonight. Scott knows something."

Jake was ready to beat it out of the older man. Dom was there to see Jake didn't do anything stupid getting Shelby back.

But they were damned well going to get Shelby back.

They devised a quick plan. It was risky, but it might work.

They needed to get someone inside that damned house.

He climbed into his truck, ready to do his part. Gunnar had made the first attempt. Dom would make the second.

He drove around the block one more time, pulling right up to the Scott gate.

Dom heard the alarm shrieking inside the Scott property, and he heard the guards shouting. One raised a weapon and pointed it at him through the rolled-down window of his truck. It shook. Damned kid was going to get someone killed.

Dom raised his own even bigger weapon. "Put that down, son, or we're going to have a major problem."

"What the hell is going on in there?" Gunnar asked in his ear.

"TSP! Put the weapons down!" Dom yelled at the guards. Hell, the two kids couldn't have been more than twenty or twenty-one. What was Scott thinking? These were just rent-a-guards.

Why would he leave these kids behind to guard the place? Dom knew the man had at least two highly trained specialized former mercenaries on his payroll.

The two men went with Scott everywhere. And were damned dangerous.

Lassiter had confirmed they'd helped three other men reeducate him on Victor Scott's son.

They were around. Dom would bet his left arm they were around. They just had to find them.

"I see Shelby!" Gunnar said into the mic, urgency in his tone. *"Second story. Rear side. She's climbing out the damned window."*

"She...she's weaving erratically," Jake added, a note of panic in his words. Dom fought the urge to swear. Jake...he just hoped Gunnar could keep Jake from doing something stupid. They had confirmation she was alive. And here. That meant hope. *"There's something wrong with her. Physically. He's hurt her."*

"Victor Scott is right behind her. Jake's going in!" Gunnar said.

Dom looked at the kid he was almost old enough to have fathered. "Open the damned gates now, or it's a TSP bullet you'll be feeling." Damn protocol. Everyone on this damned property was involved in this abduction of Shelby. That was enough for him. "That woman is not in this house by free choice. You do not want to interfere with the TSP getting her back. Let me in, now."

The kid seemed undecided.

"So be it." Dom revved the engine on his truck, then hit reverse.

Exigent circumstances had just made up his mind for him.

Once he was far enough back to accomplish his goal, he floored it.

The boy's bullet struck him just under the side of his vest. His damned left side. He swore at the impact.

And just kept going.

This was a rescue mission, damn it. There were going to be injuries.

It was just a part of the deal.

They had one of their girls to rescue, after all.

115

Someone cursed just as she was slipping her leg through the window. Shelby jerked around.

The door...she hadn't heard the door open over the alarm.

Her eyes met his. Shelby knew...there was no more time to waste. She almost threw her body through the window.

He was coming for her. Yelling at her not to be stupid.

The alarm was still shrieking, tearing into her aching skull.

Shelby just kept going.

He grabbed for her.

She used the manicure scissors still in her hand instinctively.

They weren't big enough to do major damage. But they were enough to make him let go of her. He yelled out when they scraped across his cheek.

His blood got on the back of her hand.

She wished they had done more damage.

He had done this to her—and he had hurt Charlotte and Madison and Zoey. Maybe had killed them.

Shelby fell to the balcony outside the window and scrambled to her knees. Her feet. She fell again as her head swam.

It was only twenty feet or so. The pool was down there.

There was a small patch of lawn. She should have been able to climb that, even drugged.

And if she stretched, she might have been able to reach the statue next to the pool. Climb her way down.

Victor Scott changed all that.

"No. Those fools have ruined everything. You are not getting away from me now. You are not going back to that fish-shit cop who had no business touching you!" Victor had her left arm in his. Shelby just kept fighting. "I will not *lose* to him. Not to him."

She just kept fighting—fighting Scott and the drugs. "Let me go..."

She heard the slur in her voice. Knew what it meant. "Just let me go—"

Gunshots rang out around them. He wrapped both hands around her arm and yanked. Pulled. Until she was pressed into his chest and his hands were over her head.

Shelby fought.

Until she got away.

Her hands wrapped around the rail.

But he was there instead.

Shelby screamed when his hands clamped around her shoulder, her neck, and the man pulled her back against his body.

His fingers tightened around her throat. "I should kill you now just to hurt MacNamara."

"You...you...you are a bastard. Just like him." Shelby clawed at his eyes and missed. "I know it was *him!* I know it was your son who hurt me before!"

116

Jake heard her scream first. Then he saw her. In a blue-gray dress the color of her eyes. Held tight in Victor Scott's arms. It looked like the bastard was choking her.

"Taking fire at front gate!" Dom yelled in his ear. *"Could use some help here. A bit of cover wouldn't hurt."*

Just as two guards spotted Jake and Gunnar as they started to scale the fence.

Jake swore when a round whizzed too damned close to his arm. It wasn't the first time he'd been shot.

Shelby was right there. And those bastard guards were shooting. One stray bullet...

He had to get to her.

"TSP! Hold your fire!" Gunnar yelled, perched on the lowest branch of a twenty-foot-tall mesquite tree.

Jake wasn't stupid; they were both too damned exposed.

Hell, he and Gunnar were going to be exposed until they got over the fence completely.

"Dom's got the truck!" Gunnar yelled.

Jake saw what he meant. There, coming in a like a damned avenging angel in a Black Dodge Ram, was Dom. Dom turned the truck at the last minute. Until it was three feet in front of the fence in front of them.

Jake pulled his weapon and fired at the guards, making damned sure to avoid aiming at Dom's truck.

His friend loved that truck.

It would probably never be the same after this.

Jake wished Dom had just taken out the fence completely. They needed a fast way over it, now. The trees on the edge of the vacant property behind Scott's made decent cover, but as long as they were being shot at, they couldn't get their asses to Shelby.

She was too damned far away.

Someone opened up on the side of the truck with every round they had. Jake swore and yanked off his vest.

"What are you doing?" Gunnar asked through the headset and from fifteen feet away. *"Put that back on!"*

Jake ignored him. He tossed his vest into the barbed wire. It hooked into it. But it didn't spark. Telling him exactly what he wanted to know.

The only thing he cared about was getting Shelby back safely.

Then they'd deal with Scott. Fuck the TSP and protocols, all of it. Shelby was all that mattered. He'd take a thousand bullets if it meant she came out of this safely.

"It's not electrified," Gunnar said. *"Now we have to get over it."*

They only had so much time.

Dom wouldn't last as cover for too much longer. He only had two or three clips with him. Thirty to forty-five rounds. Against what sounded like a damned arsenal.

The other man had slid out of the passenger side and now stood returning fire with the two bodyguards who accompanied Scott everywhere.

Tweedledee and Tweedledum had made their appearance.

Dom had bought Jake and Gunnar time.

The alarm was cut off. The only sound now was the gunfire. And sirens.

Police sirens.

Someone, a neighbor, would have reported this. They were only six damned houses away from Izzie, after all. The damned neighborhood had security guards of its own.

It was just a matter of time now.

"Keep them distracted. I'm getting inside."

Gunnar nodded, returning fire. These rent-a-guards had no business out here tonight.

Firing on the TSP was damned stupid. Suicidal. Scott probably paid them well to do this shit. Either that or the guards were just stupid.

It didn't matter to him; all that mattered was they were what was standing between him and Shelby.

With one shot, he took out the taller of the three guards. With absolutely no regret.

117

SHE CLAWED AT HIM. WHY WAS SHE CLAWING AT HIM? Victor didn't understand why she was fighting so much. He had told her he wouldn't hurt her, if she just did what he wanted.

That made no difference. She still clawed at him and screamed for that lover of hers. He had made the wrong choice with her.

Grief stabbed him straight in the loins.

He would have given her everything, even more than Dr. Lanning ever had. Once Victor had realized that she had been hurt by his son during some of Kyle's worst hijinks, it had just felt right.

He had wanted to make amends to her for what Kyle had done. Give her everything the Scotts had ever worked for. As an apology. Shelby would have had a child of her own to love when Victor was gone.

He had thought that would have mattered to her.

His family had hurt her. It was in his power to give her another family. And everything. To even the scales of life perhaps.

Thou shalt not kill.

He had broken that commandment years ago.

Victor had no real regrets in that manner. Maybe some of those who had died because of their association with the Henedys, but that was on them. Not Victor.

People had to have a sense of morality, of loyalty. Of right and wrong. Principles. People had to have *principles*. Especially in this day and age.

He would have wanted her to teach their child that.

They would have made a beautiful child together. He knew that. Even if he wouldn't have seen that child grown. He might not have seen that child at all.

But he had wanted to die knowing he had given his child everything.

He would have loved to know what Shelby thought about that. To have just spent his last days knowing her.

But it was too late for that.

She wanted that fishmonger's grandson. The son of a maid and a poor American soldier, for heaven's sake.

Victor had just wanted to prove to her he had some *good* left in his soul somewhere.

That was all. To make things right.

Shelby made a man want to make things *right*. Any man could see that.

He had just wanted to show her proof before he died.

Proof he wasn't the monster his son had been.

But he could have made up for what Kyle had done to the world through Shelby. If those bastards had just not interfered.

Those bastards from the TSP, especially James. If they had just not gotten in Victor's way.

James deserved to burn in hell for the things he had done.

She reached out with one hand, slim and beautiful, and sliced across his face again. Almost weakly. But still enough to sting.

Victor just reacted. The way he always did to a threat.

He slapped her. Hard.

Shelby went down, sprawling on the balcony. Victor landed on top of her, the trajectory of her fall pulling him down. As much as he would not like to admit it, the cancer was making him a weaker man than he liked.

Shelby yelled, demanded he get off her.

Victor wanted her to be silent for a moment. While he figured out what to do now.

The gunfire...it was so damned close. "Stay down. Those fools from the TSP might hit you."

"J-J-Jake came for me." She had a look of triumph on her beautiful face. Of hope. "I knew he would. I knew it! *Jake!*"

Anger so strong he almost vomited from it had his hands going to her throat. Squeezing. To cut off her yell. "Just stop talking for one damned minute."

There was terror in the blue eyes now. "No. I'll n-n-never stop talking again!"

"He is nothing. Not good enough for a woman like you. I could have given you so much more." The idea that she'd prefer that work-roughened son of a bitch over Victor. Over what he could give her as the mother of his child...fury had him barely seeing *her*.

Just what she was denying him.

She was ruining everything. Shelby and that damned fisherman.

"I have m-m-more than you can ever give me." Shelby just kept fighting. Her knee rammed him right in the groin. "I have people who love me!"

Victor went down.

The little fool stood up. Wavered.

Fell to her knees. Crawled. Kept trying to get away from him.

Like Victor wasn't good enough for her, even now. Why wasn't *he* good enough for a woman like her? With all that he had accomplished?

"Why do you want a fisherman's shit dropping like *him* over me?"

"I-I-I will *never* want you over *him! Ever!*"

118

DOM WATCHED AS THE TALLER OF VICTOR SCOTT'S bodyguards fell to the ground. And didn't get back up. Dom didn't know whether it was his rounds that brought him down, or Gunnar's.

But the man who had been shooting at them was down. The uninjured rent-a-guards had taken off long ago, leaving their fallen comrade writhing in pain on the damp ground.

Someone yelled out.

There Shelby was.

Fighting with Victor Scott on a balcony a hundred feet away. Dom was closest to the house. Jake and Gunnar weren't over the fence yet.

He could see the woman they were after on the balcony, could hear sirens rushing their way. It was almost over. They just had to get her away from Victor Scott.

He started toward the house, knowing Jake and Gunnar would be right behind him as soon as they scaled the damned fence.

Dom had one more magazine in his pocket. He would put it to good use.

He had gotten maybe two yards away from the truck when shots came his way again. Dom dived behind the front of his now destroyed Dodge.

He'd loved that truck.

He would take the cost of it out of shooters' hides when he caught up to them. "TSP! Hold your fucking fire!"

The shooting stopped.

Dom cautiously checked around the front of the truck. He saw a man in a guard's uniform about his own age running toward the front gate. The property was only about six acres or so, and the house and pool sat near the rear. Where Jake and Gunnar were on the other side of the fence. He should have driven through that fence as well. But all he'd been thinking about had been getting something in place to protect the other two men. His truck had done the job just fine.

They were going to have to move a little faster.

Shelby yelled out. Scott was yelling even louder.

There was more movement to the left of the property.

The damned guards were running. Trying to escape the sirens was Dom's best bet. Damned cowards.

Dom wasn't stupid. They had to get to Shelby fast. She wouldn't stand a chance against a man Scott's size. But he wasn't going to risk running across the yard with no cover, either.

But those sirens...

Help was coming. And it would be TSP.

He just hoped to hell it would be Daniel and the rest of the good guys, this time.

119

SHE FOUGHT. SHELBY WOULD GO DOWN FIGHTING, and she made herself that vow. Her head hurt. He'd slammed it into the marble tile that lined his balcony. How stupid, ostentatious. Her balcony at her house was serviceable, beautiful but better designed for outdoors.

Shelby looked into his blue eyes as his hands tightened around her neck.

Shelby stared at him, her arms feeling like lead against her body. She forced them up, to his face. She scratched again. Digging her nails into his cheek. He howled. Shelby just looked at him, as the words came out. "What did I ever do to your son to deserve what he d-did to me? He r-ruined my life and Logan's. And I never hurt him once. But he didn't care. Just like you. Bastard. Scum, just like you."

"Shut up, just shut up!" He tried to slam her head to the floor again. Shelby brought her knee up between them. She shoved it into his groin as hard as she could, even though it felt like her legs weighed a million pounds.

"R-run, Vickie, run! Jake is coming for me. He's coming. He's coming. You can't fight him. He's too strong. And he's coming for me. J-J-Just like he promised he always would!"

He yanked her back to her feet. Shelby wavered. She strongly suspected adrenaline was all that kept her on her feet now. Keeping her awake.

"He'll have to kill me to get to you."

"He will. Jake is coming!" She was saying it for her benefit, as much as his. And she knew it. Giving herself hope.

She had heard the gunshots. Now she heard the sirens. They were coming here. They would find her.

She just had to stay alive long enough for them to get to her.

Jake was there for her now.

120

He should run. But the anger burning his gut made it impossible. Victor knew he was being foolish. Everything he had wanted, had worked for—it was about to be destroyed.

For forty years, he had been building his empire, making something all who carried the Scott name would be proud of.

Only to be reduced to *this*.

His hands went under her shoulders, and he yanked the woman close. He wished he had a gun. Something.

Those bastards from the TSP would get closer. Would want to take her.

"Shut up!" He wrapped one hand over her mouth, just to stop the words. He never would have imagined she could be like this. So cold, so hateful.

He dragged her across the floor, ignoring how she struggled. She should be out by now. Solpalmitraln in that dosage *always* knocked him out when he took it.

He didn't understand how she wasn't.

The woman was a fighter. Strong. She would have made such a wonderful mother to his son.

For one moment, he considered letting go of her. And just running. Escaping. He could flee. Go south, find a young woman in Mexico willing to help his line continue.

But that was foolish. He could give a child *nothing* now.

It was all her fault.

Shelby's and that fish-sucker Jake MacNamara's.

Victor slapped her, more viciously than he had before.

Shelby landed against the rail, and just looked up at him in the dim security light. He would never forget how her eyes glowed gray fire at him in that moment.

How the expression in them just destroyed him.

This young woman had *destroyed* him.

She had destroyed all his dreams tonight. She'd ripped his entire *life* from him. Every bit of it he had left.

Just like Kyle's mother had so long ago. Just like Wallace Henedy had when he had killed the only person Victor had ever truly loved besides himself.

If Jennifer Henedy's hired thug had killed Shelby that day, none of this would have happened.

Victor would have chosen another woman to carry his child. Haldyn. Haldyn would have been the mother of his child. She would have been better than Shelby. *She* would have been perfect.

It would have been perfect.

He wouldn't have ended up here, like this at all.

Shelby had ruined everything.

With a bellow, he lunged at her one more time.

121

IT WOULDN'T BE LONG. SHELBY COULDN'T FIGHT MUCH longer. The drug was taking her. His hands were around her neck, cutting off her air. She wondered if Logan had felt like this that day.

When he had been holding Lacy Deane so tight, after he had already shot Lacy.

Everyone said he'd shot Lacy by accident, though. Said the Sopalmitraln had made him go crazy at the end. Shelby didn't know.

She…no one had given her information about what had actually happened. All she had was what Allen had told her so long ago.

Allen, Izzie. All the family she had.

Logan. Jake.

The only two men she had ever truly fallen in love with.

She wished she could have helped Logan. Wished she could see Jake one more time before the drug took hold. Just long enough to tell him how she felt.

She wanted to tell that man she loved him at least once.

Jake was coming for her. It had to be the TSP fighting

Victor's guards. It wasn't the men who took her—that wouldn't make sense. It had to be the good ones, like Jake and Dom and Mike and the big Viking guy who teased Powell that day. She couldn't remember the man's name now. But he would be there, with Jake.

She had faith in *them*. They would be with Jake.

The sirens were so loud. Cutting into her head.

She knew who it was—it was Jake, and his best friends. The same guys who'd been with him in her driveway that day.

His brothers-in-arms, who he'd said always had his back.

They were coming...*for her.*

She couldn't fight back anymore.

Not now.

She could barely hold her head up. Keep her eyes open. The world was swimming around her.

Someone shouted again. Nearby.

She thought she heard the word TSP. And to stop. To not move.

But it didn't matter.

Shelby wasn't going to just lie there and wait for rescue, with Victor over her. She couldn't. She couldn't just hide from life any longer. Nor could she wait for rescue.

It was time she rescued herself.

No matter what the cost.

Shelby looked at Victor and knew exactly what she had to do.

She pulled herself up, with the stone balustrade. And looked at the pool below. Looked back at the man who had caused this.

Her eyes met blue. He had blue eyes, too. Just like his son had all those years ago. She would never forget those blue eyes. Father or son.

"No! You are not getting away from me now. You will pay for what you've destroyed. And that fish shit will watch his hopes and dreams die with you. Just like mine did the day Kyle died."

Izzie had said something to her once. At Mel's... *"Karma's a bitch*, Vickie...K-K-Kyle got what he deserved. He...he...he... reaped what he sowed. And got exactly what he had c-c-coming. Dying naked on the floor. I know that, you know. My brother told me what happened to him that day. He will *never* hurt another woman ever again. And soon...neither will you."

Jake would make sure of that.

Shelby knew that with one hundred percent certainty. Victor Scott wouldn't hurt anyone again.

Jake would stop him.

Victor lunged at her. Shelby had just enough energy to lift her left hand to fend him off. She clenched the rail in her right. The balustrade was all that was holding her up now.

122

HE WAS TOO LATE.

Jake would never be able to get to her on time. No matter if he sprouted wings and flew. It just wasn't humanly possible.

She screamed. A sound so terrifying it almost froze him where he clung to the damned fence. She yelled. A man yelled.

Shelby fought with Scott, too damned close to the rail. She was too close to the rail. He wanted to yell at her to get back. That she was too close to the edge.

But he couldn't.

Shelby lurched.

Toward Scott.

Victor Scott went over the rail with a cold, terrifying scream.

Shelby tried to catch herself on the rail, but she couldn't. She just hung there for half a second.

Her name was a scream wrenched from his own lips as he watched. As his hands clenched on the fence he was only halfway up.

Time slowed down.

Almost froze.

As he watched the woman who meant everything to him fall.

Jake screamed her name, climbed the chain-link fence as fast as he possibly could. Straight into the barbed wire. It caught on his shirt; he yanked his vest free and tossed it over the barbs. He threw his body over the wires, ignoring the razors destroying his arms.

Jake kept going, despite the damage to his arms, until he landed on the rain-slicked hill behind the fence. The bullet hole in his damned arm caused more of a problem than the barbed wire had.

His damned arms would heal. Jake kept moving.

He scrambled to his feet, vaguely aware of Gunnar doing the same twenty feet away.

Dom waved him on as he ran by the other man, where he secured one of Scott's bodyguards. The other guard wasn't going anywhere ever again, lifeless in the damned rain. "Go! Get to her! Kessler's still alive. Passed out from blood loss."

Jake ran. It took him too damned long to get to her.

And dived. Straight into the water. Still too far from Shelby. The pool was too damned big.

Her hair floated out behind her. The dress billowed next to her hips. It filled with water quickly. Pulled her down.

Shelby wasn't moving at all.

He was a strong swimmer. He'd grown up next to the Italian sea, after all. He just kept swimming. Until he could get to her.

He got to her faster than seemed humanly possible. He flipped her onto her back. "Come on, baby, open your eyes. Breathe. Fight for me. Hell, fight with me! Just open those eyes!"

His feet tangled in the dress. It almost pulled them both under. He tightened his arm around her waist and tried to propel them both to the edge of the pool thirty feet away. What kind of asshole built half their damned pool *under* a balcony?

But if they pool hadn't been there, she'd be on the concrete instead.

He kept swimming.

"Keep going!" someone yelled near him. "I won't let either of you go down!"

Gunnar. Gunnar was right there. Just as Jake went under, almost lost his hold on her, on the damned dress that was as slick as ice and caught on his arm.

Gunnar's hands pulled him back to the surface. He yanked Shelby from Jake's arms. Pulled her another six feet. Getting her head above the water again.

Then Jake had her again. They kept passing her back and forth.

Gunnar climbed out of the pool first. Reached for her.

Jake lifted her as best he could, but the damned dress made it difficult.

Then more hands were there.

Dom.

Dom helped Gunnar steady her. Jake lifted her from the water, while his two friends pulled her the rest of the way.

There was blood welling on her temple. He could see it welling even in the rain.

And she had been under water far too long. Jake pulled himself out of the pool and fell to her side. Rolled her gently to her back. Laid one hand on her chest.

"She's not breathing!"

123

JAKE KEPT HIS HAND WRAPPED AROUND HERS, keeping his ass out the paramedics' way. Shelby hadn't regained consciousness. He kept his eyes trained on her face, prayers he hadn't said in a long, long time moved his lips, but no words came out.

He would never forget watching her fall.

It would haunt him every moment of his nightmares.

Victor Scott hadn't survived the fall. He'd landed on the cement next to the marble statue of his son. Missed the pool by three feet.

His body had sprawled at the eight-foot monstrosity's feet, neck breaking on impact, a crumbled stone hand six inches from Scott's head.

He would never stand before a judge and face punishment for everything he had done. Wouldn't give the answers the TSP needed.

That had been cheated from them all.

Nor would they get all the answers out of him about *who* exactly had hurt Charlotte, Madison, and Zoey.

Those bastards were still out there.

Shelby *never* should have been in a position where she had to fight for her life like that. Never for a moment.

If he hadn't been such a piss-poor protector, she never would have been.

"I'm sorry, baby. So sorry." He whispered it next to her ear. Over and over.

He had let her down. He'd let his own inadequacies push her away. Yes, she'd told him to take a hike. But he knew the truth —it had been to protect her heart from him.

He never should have left her alone.

He should have been there at the damned choir concert, standing proud right next to her. Celebrating her and what she had accomplished, holding a damned video camera to capture every moment. Like the man who truly loved her would have.

She had been in the water far too long. He had been too far away. He should have been able to get her out of the damned water faster than he had.

If Gunnar hadn't followed him in, Jake wouldn't have been able to get her out of the pool in time at all.

Dom had gotten her breathing again. Seconds before the first responders and Daniel had made it to where they were.

Jake hadn't been the one to save her—they all three had. He'd needed *them,* too.

"O2 is too low. Pulse is thready," the female paramedic said. "Prep to intubate."

"We're two minutes out from FCGH," Drew said. Jake had known the paramedic for years. Now all he saw was compassion in the man's eyes. "She'll get good care there."

All Jake could focus on was her face. Her eyes.

They were closed.

She needed to open them again. He still didn't know if her eyes were blue or gray. He wanted the chance to figure it out. He didn't even realize he was begging her to do just that. To open her eyes for him. To just open her eyes again.

Shelby never did.

124

DOM'S ARM BURNED LIKE A SON OF A BITCH, AND HE was having a damned hard time breathing. He'd taken one hard to the chest at the gate, but it had passed through part of the flesh on his arm first.

He didn't say a word about it while Daniel lit into him.

Finally, when his friend and commander's rant was over, Dom said the one thing he knew was true. "I'd do it again in a heartbeat."

"I'm glad you did it, even if you broke a thousand and one protocols and rules," Daniel said, deflating. "When you said you were following a lead, I thought you were going to talk to your informant. I should have realized the three of you were going AWOL. If you hadn't...hell, I just hope you were in time for her. I'll handle anything with IA that comes up from this. Erickson, same for you, too."

Dom checked the other guy quickly.

For once, Gunnar wasn't talking. Now he was just dripping chlorinated pool water and blood all over Daniel's backseat.

With a thousand and one broken memories written on his face.

"She was in the water for less than two minutes, Dan. But...I couldn't see...she may have hit her head on the way in. I couldn't see for sure. That damned statue blocked my line of sight. From at least twenty-five feet up. I don't know how she made it through that. The landing killed Scott instantly. If she hadn't been right over the pool..."

She wouldn't have made it this far.

But the pool may have very well finished what the fall had started.

"She's a fighter," Daniel said. Dom hoped to hell he was right. "She was breathing when she was pulled from the water?"

Dom shook his head. "I resuscitated her. But she never opened her eyes. Breathing, but never opened her eyes."

"Any blood on her that you could see?" Daniel asked quietly.

"Yes. But her damned collarbone was sticking out of her shoulder."

"We need to get there. For Jake," Gunnar said quietly. "Any word on the other three women?"

"Madison is in recovery. There was a disturbance in Madison's room, but I don't know the details yet," Daniel said. Dom's attention sharpened.

"What?"

"We'll know more when we get there." Daniel pulled into the FCGH parking lot, just yards behind the ambulance. "Gunnar, how're the hands?"

"Hamburger. But I'd do it again. Dom? Arm and chest?"

"Same." Hell, he felt like he was going to puke at any moment, but he wasn't about to say that.

Not until they got inside. Saw Shelby for themselves.

Made sure Jake was going to make it through this, too. "Zoey and Charlotte?"

"Still holding on. Heard Zoey is out of surgery, though. Not sure of the prognosis."

"Charlotte?"

Daniel shook his head. "I haven't heard anything on her yet. This is her second surgery. Zoey's third."

Dom just nodded.

Four women injured. What were the odds they'd all four survive? Or survive without serious, life-long injuries?

All because a sociopath had built his life on greed and power.

And it wasn't over yet.

There were still tentacles of the damned evil octopus out there. Threatening them all.

Victor Scott's bodyguard Kessler had vehemently denied that Scott had ordered the hit on Zoey and Charlotte and Madison before he'd clammed up and demanded an attorney when they'd been strapping him down to the gurney.

He'd said the kidnapping of Shelby was a way to screw with Scott's plans.

But Shelby had been found in Scott's possession.

She had gotten there somehow.

Dom was going to find those answers.

125

HE TRIED TO STAY WITH HER. JAKE RAN, JUST A YARD behind the gurney. Behind her. She hadn't opened her eyes. Why in the hell hadn't she opened her eyes?

Shelby had too much damned fluid in her lungs. He knew it. Hell, he'd grown up by the sea. He'd seen drowning victims too many times before. And her damned collarbone had been sticking out through the skin.

Panic was threatening to destroy him. He stayed right with her, next to the gurney.

Someone yelled out. Called his name. Wrapped their hands around his and yanked him from Shelby. Her name was wrenched from his lips.

He fought. Of course, he fought. To stay with her.

"You have to let Jeoff help her!" Gray eyes met Jake's. Eyes so damned familiar he almost yelled. "Come on, Jake, we need you to tell us what happened to her. Right now. Tell me what happened to my sister so we can help her!"

Sister.

Izzie's brother was right there, physically holding him away from Shelby. Izzie's father, too, on the other side. Jake balled up his fist instinctively, ready to lash out at the men keeping him from Shelby. It would hurt, but he didn't give a shit.

Jake met gray eyes with his own. Saw his own fear reflected back at him. Allen loved her, too.

"She fell off the bastard's damned balcony when he was trying to strangle her, Allen. Went over the railing almost three stories up. Hit the edge of the pool. We...were on the wrong side of the fence from her. We couldn't get to her fast enough. I tried. But I couldn't go any faster. I tried. Then we had to get her out of the fucking water. She fell in the deep end. She was going under. The damned dress... I tried to get to her. I did."

His ex-brother-in-law was already gone, following the gurney. Following Shelby.

The woman he loved was in the hands of the man who had abandoned the niece Jake adored when Izzie had needed him most.

Allen was right behind them.

Jake started to follow.

A hard arm was there to stop him. "No, *you* don't. Allen's going in because he's calling in a favor. Hell, your hands are torn to shreds and what the hell happened to your arm? I can't let you be a contamination risk to her, Jake. You're not going in with her."

He looked into Rafe Holden-Deane's dark eyes. Same eyes as Shelby's best friend. "We had to fight our way in to get her. Took a few rounds, I think."

Rafe took a look at the men coming up behind Jake. "I can tell. What the hell did you fight, lions? Dr. Macomber, take Detective Acardi into trauma A. Dr. Kaur, take Detective Erickson into trauma C. Amy, you can help Dr. Deane with Jake, trauma F."

Someone swore behind him. Jake turned.

Jake looked around. Jarrod was there—he'd been out on the

scene at the auditorium, guarding the forensics crew. When had he gotten there? Why?

There was Haldyn, and her pal Rory. Bailey Addy, too. Shelby's attorney was there, pacing erratically, terror on her pretty face. She…made him almost dizzy to watch.

Her fear was almost tangible.

Charlie Fields was slumped in a chair, looking like he hadn't moved in hours. Hell, maybe he hadn't.

The task force was all there now. There were TSP everywhere, still. Waiting on word on the sheriff and Charlotte.

The halls were lined with TSP everywhere he saw. In support of the fallen? Or was it something more sinister now?

Hell, some of the damned cops around them could have been on Scott's payroll.

That could be a damned lot of men.

Even this hospital her brother helped run might not be fully safe for her. Someone could get to her here, too. Could get to Powell, Charlotte, Madison, Haldyn, and Zoey, too.

None of them were really safe.

Not if what Scott's man had said had been true.

Someone had ordered that hit tonight. Kessler had been vehement that it wasn't *Scott*. But someone else.

Jake was going to make them pay for every *second* Shelby and her friends had been afraid.

As soon as Shelby was ok.

Jake pulled himself together. She needed him to keep himself together. He still had to protect her now. He would do a damned better job of it than he had before.

"Gunnar needs seen before I do," Jake said firmly, pulling in a deep breath and really looking around now. Snapping himself back to what he could do. What he had to do. "He…climbed a barbed wire fence barehanded. Tore himself up some."

"Hell, so did you. And you were shot first," Gunnar said, a

look in his eyes Jake would never forget. "I can wait. You first, so you can take care of your girl when she needs you most."

Jake looked at the other man, who was holding a blood-soaked towel to his arm. Gunnar had dived right into the pool almost the same time as Jake. If Gunnar hadn't helped, Jake couldn't have gotten her out by himself.

He would never forget that. "Thanks, Gunnar. I'll owe you one for life for tonight. For her. You and Dom both. I couldn't have gotten to her without you."

"It's what brothers are for. Better believe you will. Get your damned arm taken care of. Then get your ass out here and wait for word on our girl. Go."

Jake went.

He couldn't just sit there in the damned waiting room, or he'd go crazy. Claw his way through the very walls to get to her. Jake would never stop fighting to get to her.

He didn't think he ever could.

126

SOMEONE GAVE HIM EXTRA CLOTHES. JAKE DIDN'T know where they came from. He just started stripping down.

"Jake?" a soft voice asked.

He turned. There was his Annie, with her big blue eyes, sweet smile and Turner Barratt's baby growing inside her. Seeing her, this woman he had had a small hand in getting to adulthood, had him almost losing what was left of his composure. If he was going to lose it, it would be with Annie or Izzie. His family. "Ann...any word on Shelby yet?"

"Not yet. She's getting the best care here. You know that."

"Is she? With Stockton? Why not Rafe or Nikkie Jean?" Her brother was with her. Watching over her like he'd always done. Allen would be just as obsessive over her care as he would be Izzie's. Jake knew that.

It was probably the best he was going to get.

Izzie was on her way with Mel Barratt. And a dozen guards to protect her.

"Because they can't. They aren't taking patients now. Because of Zoey. They just can't. Look at me. Shelby is getting good care here. Stockton is an ass of a father, but he's one of the best trauma physicians around. I have to say that."

"Why wouldn't she wake up? She was only in the water for two minutes at the most. That was it."

"We don't know what happened to her while she was missing, Jake. They could have done anything to her." Her voice broke and her gorgeous blue eyes filled. "Drowning doesn't take even that long sometimes. And...didn't they say she was drugged at the auditorium?"

He nodded. "Chloroform. The bastards used chloroform."

"She might still be under the effects of that now. Stay here, Jake. Don't move. I'm going to go check on her while you finish changing clothes."

And just like that Annie was gone.

Jake never had been good at taking orders.

He followed, shirtless and bloody.

Only to be stopped by Nikkie Jean's brother-in-law. "Where are you going?"

"Where is Annie going? Where do you have Shelby?"

"She's in good hands, Jake. But you're bleeding all over my ER. You can't help her if you pass out." Rafe had one hand in front of Jake.

Hell, he was big enough to be able to stop Jake. If he tried hard enough. Which he probably would. The guy could be damned fierce.

"I got to get to her. I promised her I'd never leave her alone again. Shelby...she hates being alone. She's scared when she's alone. I don't want her to be afraid, Rafe. Let me be with her."

The bigger man stepped right into his space. Got in his face. Two inches of height and sixty pounds separated them, but it didn't matter. "She's not alone, Jake. Allen is with her. You got to her. You got her out of the water and got her to *me*. Let my people do what we do best now. Do you think I don't know what you are feeling right now? Because let me tell you: I for damned sure do. Izzie is going to be here at any minute. Izzie will need you to be the strong man you always have been for her. No matter what. So will Allen. Your family. Hers. So pull it together and let my people do our jobs. Or I'll have Daniel come in here and cuff your ass to the exam table. I'll leave you until we're finished with Shelby, and that may take hours. Take a breath. We need to see what's going on with your injuries. Then we'll handle the lacerations to your hands. What did you do to them?"

"Barbed wire. About six strands of it. I was able to cover half of it with my vest until I got over, but we didn't have time to waste. And didn't have any damned gloves. Not...not once she fell into the water. I just kept climbing. I got over the fence and hit the water. Got her head above water as fast as I could."

"Good. How long was she submerged?"

"A minute. Maybe two at most. Between getting to her and being able to get her head above water and keep it there. We pulled her out. She wasn't breathing. Dom got her breathing again. But she never opened her eyes."

"Shelby is young, healthy, and physically fit. Strong. You promise to cooperate, and I'll check on her now."

That was a deal he could make.

127

Jake was dressed in the borrowed clothes and pacing the exam bay when Rafe returned. Another nurse had shown up to take Annie's place, then Annie had returned.

Jake turned to them. To Rafe, a guy he'd always respected to tell it to him straight.

"She's been intubated and is on a vent for now. Pulse and O2 stats are better. She's injured her shoulder and will require surgery to repair the damage in a few hours once we get her a little more stable. And we are evaluating damage to her spine, Jake. We are running tox screens to see if the bastards who took her drugged her, on top of the chloroform earlier. That will tell us more. But she's holding her own. If Izzie and Allen allow it, I will let you see her for two minutes. Once we get the tox screens back, we'll know the next step in the plan. We're going to do everything we can. For now, she's stabilizing. Holding her own."

Annie stayed with him until he got that two minutes. He had a feeling they thought Annie could keep him in line, if it came to it.

Once he saw Shelby, nothing else mattered.

Jake wrapped one hand around Shelby's, ignoring the bandage across his palm. Ignoring the medical staff around her. The tube down her throat.

Ignoring her own brother, watching every move he made like a hawk.

Jake leaned down. "I'm sorry, baby. I should have been there with you. And I should have found you sooner. I am so damned sorry it took so long for me to get to you. And...to understand. To admit to myself that my place *is* next to you. Forever."

He should have been there.

He would never forgive himself for letting this happen to her. He told her that. Promised her he would make it up to her. If she would just wake up and yell at him again. He knew she liked yelling at him. He promised she could yell at him forever, if she wanted. If she would just wake up.

She never moved.

"Jake, we need to get that X-ray of your arm now," Annie said quietly from behind him. He suspected she'd heard every word. As had Shelby's brother. "Come on."

He wanted to resist. Allen insisted.

"Go. I'm staying with my sister now. I'll be the one to see she's taken care of from now on."

Jake got the message. Allen didn't want him anywhere near her now. Not that he blamed him. Jake had failed her in the worst way possible. "I'll be around if she needs me."

"Noted," Allen said. The fury was on the other man's face. Directed at Jake. "And so will I."

Jake just nodded.

And turned to leave her again.

He was so damned sick of leaving her.

But it was the best thing he could do for her now. But this time, Jake would be back. He wasn't running away from her again.

128

In all the years he had worked with Jake MacNamara, Dom had never seen him break down like this. Not even once.

He'd never seen tears in the man's eyes either, and that was exactly what he saw now. Jake wasn't even that aware of what was going on around him as the hours wore on.

Dom would bet good money on that.

When Izzie ordered her uncle to cooperate when they wheeled him away for an X-ray, Jake just did it. Just quietly went along. Dom suspected Jake was afraid Izzie's husband would kick him out of the hospital if he said or did one thing wrong right now.

It was a real possibility.

Allen hadn't left his sister's side.

That was probably both a knife to Jake that he couldn't be there with her, and a comfort. Someone who loved her was right there with her at all times.

That mattered.

He just wished the physician in charge of Shelby's care was

any doctor in the world besides Izzie's father, though. That probably stung Jake more than a little.

Dom got his own injury treated, not letting on to anyone how serious it was. The bullet had entered just beneath his vest, and exited through fat tissue to lodge in the inside of his vest. He'd be in a sling for a good six weeks, but he'd survive.

Jake just needed stitches and antibiotics. For the hands and the bullet wound beneath his right collarbone that had exited without doing much damage. It had missed anything important.

Gunnar had taken the most significant injury. He'd sliced a hell of a good chunk out of his left hand and arm. They were flying in a specialist in the morning to repair the muscle.

It was Shelby that worried them all.

Rushed tox results revealed what they'd suspected.

Victor Scott had drugged her. Bailey Addy had taken her crew to Scott's place. Two hours ago, she'd called Daniel specifically.

Sopalmitraln, the drug that had been pulled by Rafe Holden-Deane off of trials at this very hospital when suspicious deaths had been reported, had been found at Scott's place.

That drug had driven Logan Lanning mad enough to try to kill the pretty blonde doctor who'd stitched up Dom's shoulder tonight.

All the Sopalmitraln had been pulled and destroyed.

Victor Scott shouldn't have even had the drug to use on Shelby.

Dom was going to find out how he had gotten it.

Bailey had found residue on the bed in a guest room in Scott's house. On the second floor.

Where Shelby's shoes had been found.

Rory had tested it. Sent the results to Haldyn's phone. Haldyn was taking the watch for forensics at the hospital now. Haldyn had told Dom herself—they were running rapid DNA tests when possible now. The lab had everything it needed. Results could come in as little as two hours.

Shelby's DNA had been on the pillow, mixed with the residue.

Her supposition—Shelby had spit out at least half the dosage. There had been two almost intact tablets on the pillow. It had saved the woman's life, that one simple move. Haldyn had made it clear that if she hadn't spit it out, the Sopalmitraln and chloroform together might very well have killed her.

Especially in that high of dosage.

Just that one choice.

He could just imagine what Shelby had been thinking, knowing her only option to save herself from a monster was to risk serious injury or death going over that railing.

Dom just stayed where he was and hoped for miracles. His father stopped by to check on him.

Cherise was in with Madison now.

Max slept on a damned bench in the waiting room right there where Dom could see him.

Finally, the surgeon who had taken Charlotte's case stepped into the waiting room. Virat Patel, Dom knew him well enough. Trusted him.

Patel headed straight to Charlie's side.

Charlie's and the seven cousins and grandmother who had arrived from Wyoming. Seven young, beautiful women who had just sat in the waiting room together and…waited.

Except for the eldest, an FBI agent out of St. Louis. Charlotte's cousin had chased an attacker out of Madison's room with one well-placed roundhouse kick when she'd slipped out of the waiting room into the hallway to call her father and update him.

Dom owed her a damned medal for what she'd done when she'd seen the bastard in Madison's room.

That cousin had Charlotte's eyes. Hard to miss.

Dr. Patel showed exhaustion, but he smiled at the room's occupants. "Charlotte came through the second surgery very well. Odds are cautiously optimistic, at this point. We'll know more in the morning. But for now, she's more than holding her own. And I don't at this time see any reason that should change."

Dom exhaled slowly.

They just needed word on Zoey and Shelby now.

129

"HOW LONG HAVE YOU BEEN IN LOVE WITH MY sister?"

Jake jerked away from the railing. He'd thought he had found a moment to be alone in the damned hallway outside the surgical ward, above the main lobby entrance. Allen stood behind him. Watching him. "The moment I met her at W4HAV. Or the day I carried her over here, bleeding in my arms. The first time I kissed her. The first time she yelled at me. First time she smiled at me. The first time she kicked me for being an ass. The moment I saw her fall tonight. Take your pick. Hell, I think I may have been born loving her."

"Does she know how you feel?"

"I ran like a damned coward. Even though she was the one to tell me to go. I had run from her long before that." Because he had been afraid of what she made him feel.

"Why?" Allen asked.

"Just go ahead and slug me, Jacobson. We both know I'd deserve it."

"You look like someone already has. And I'm not going to hit a man while he's down."

"I'm the last guy who should have touched her. We both know that."

"Why? What's so bad about you that you can't love her?"

That was the last thing he had expected. He stared at Shelby's brother for a moment. "Isn't it obvious? I'm not the kind of man she needs. Everyone has said that to me at one time or another. Hell, her friends, *my* friends. Probably everyone who saw us together. Everyone in the damned waiting room. Me, in my work boots and the cheap T-shirts Iz buys me when she thinks about it. And your sister? The whole idea...I'm not...just not good enough. And I never could be."

"No. You couldn't. As her brother, I don't think any man could be. But...you don't think I'm good enough for your niece, either. That hasn't stopped us."

"You should hate me. I...everything I've done to her. Why the hell don't you hate me?" Jake's bandaged hands clenched.

"I don't think anyone could hate you as much as you hate yourself right now. And just stop it." Allen braced his hands on the rail and looked down.

They were two, two and a half stories up from the front lobby below.

Jake wasn't lost to that. They were just as far up as she had been. He stared at the floor, imagining what Shelby's thoughts would have been as she knew...

"I used to stand right here with Logan and talk, you know. Just talk, catch up. About our days, women. Anything really. You don't think I am good enough for Izzie. And I know the truth—I'll probably never be good enough for her. I think about that fact every day. I have things in my past I regret, Jake. Hell, we all do. When my sister was being attacked five years ago, I was out trying to score with a woman I don't even remember. I didn't even know her last name and was half lit at the time. It's why Shel couldn't get ahold of me and had to call Logan instead. Talk about regrets? I have them in spades. Let's get Rafe in here, or

Turner, or let's get Chance Marshall in here. That would be a story to hear, wouldn't it? We all have regrets. And ways we don't measure up. I don't think I will ever measure up to some ideal man who *could* love Izzie exactly as she deserves to be loved. Be perfect for her in every single way. But I know one thing."

He went silent for a moment.

Jake stood next to him. They were equally as tall, just about the same size in every way. The borrowed polo Jake wore had *Chief of Trauma Surgery* embroidered over the chest.

Worlds existed between them. Jake knew it. Allen had to, too.

"What? What do you know?"

"There is no man on earth who will ever love Izzie more than I do. Could. And I'm working hard to ensure that I remember that each and every day. And all I want for my sister is for the man she chooses to love her as much as I love my wife. Whether he wears work boots or six-hundred-dollar loafers. Something to keep in mind. Shelby isn't stupid, Jake. Nor is she as naive as you think. She saw something in you that mattered to her. Something that had some pretty damned thick walls coming down between you. Fast. Remember that. I wanted to let you know that she's doing well. Stats are rising, getting closer to where they should be. Pass it on to my wife, will you? I'm going back in with her now."

Allen just left Jake exactly where he was.

130

WHEN SHE OPENED HER EYES AGAIN, THERE WAS A blurry shadow looming over her. Shelby cried out, panic filling her.

A warm hand covered hers. "Shelby, you're safe. You're at the hospital."

Her eyes focused a bit better. She forced herself to calm. To look.

Into dark brown eyes and a handsome face.

Zoey's eyes in a masculine face.

She recognized the voice, but not the man. Not exactly. Shelby's eyes slid to the left a little. Searching. No dragon tattoo. That meant...Allen's boss—not Nikkie Jean's husband. This was Zoey's older brother, Rafe. She blinked. She was safe here. "You're Rafe? Not Caine."

"Yes. Good girl."

"J-J-Jake?" She wanted to know where he was, but the thought of talking exhausted her.

"He's ok. I'll get him for you."

"Please...I want Jake. I know he's coming for me."

"He got to you, and he's never left."

"He...he...he came for me."

Truer words had never been spoken. She couldn't remember all the details of what had happened. Her head was cloudy, probably from pain medications. She knew she was in the hospital. She could see that for herself.

But she couldn't remember how she had gotten there.

She just remembered falling.

Victor Scott. Men who had taken her.

Men who had shot...

She bit back the hot panic. A warm hand wrapped around hers.

"Baby? I'm here."

She knew that tone. Knew those brown eyes, too. Some of her fear lessened. "Knew you would come..."

It was the last she spoke for a long time.

WHEN SHE OPENED HER EYES AGAIN, JAKE WAS GONE. There were two other beds in the room with her. Shelby couldn't move a whole lot, the entire left side of her body hurt, and her arm was in a cast. From above her elbow and all the way down over her fingers. She wiggled her fingers, just to see if she could. It hurt, but she could do it.

"I wouldn't move too much," a voice said from next to the bed. Shelby turned as much as she was able. Brown eyes met hers.

Izzie's. Not Jake's. "Where...where...where is he?"

"Walking around downstairs. He's been going crazy since they brought you in." Izzie leaned forward. She held a straw to Shelby's lips. "Driving everyone in the entire hospital crazy, actually. From Wanda all the way to Vincent. Rafe threatened to have Vincent toss him out if he didn't behave."

"Wh-wh-what's he want?" She wanted to see him. So bad it

hurt. But Shelby wasn't about to get her hopes up. She had to look away from his niece. Holding her head in that position hurt.

Her gaze landed on the two other beds in the room.

Charlotte slept six feet away, tubes going all around her. So pale. *Alive.*

Charlotte was alive. Thank God.

There was another woman on the other side. From the hair…Tears hit her eyes at what she saw. What it meant. "Charl…Zoey…"

That was when it came back, when she remembered. She remembered Madison screaming for help… "Wh-wh-where's Madison?"

Terror for Madison had her heart racing.

Soft hands wrapped around her free one.

"She's ok. It's ok. She's ok. She was discharged this morning. Her mother took her back to Mel's place, with Lacy Deane watching over her. She'll be ok. She was hurt the least of you four." Izzie fussed over her. The familiar sight had Shelby's breath leveling out. "Zoey and Charlotte were hurt a little worse, but they are doing ok. It'll take them some time to recover. Now…on to you…I could get a doctor in to tell you? I know one who has been just about driving *me* crazy."

Shelby tried to nod. "I would like that."

Then Allen was there, his hand covering hers. He leaned down, kissed her forehead. The tears doubled. "It's all going to be ok, now."

It wouldn't. Everything had changed for her, for them. Shelby knew it wouldn't just go away.

Not the trauma.

Trauma didn't just *go away.*

She would never forget the men who had come in and almost killed the people she loved. Would never forget Victor Scott.

Tears slid down her cheeks. She would never forget.

All she remembered was knowing one thing—Jake would come for her.

And he had.

She needed to see him. Ask some questions. Find a way to get through this.

She needed Jake, not her brother.

But Shelby didn't know how to ask.

Or if he would even come to her now.

"Where's Jake?"

There was a look in her brother's gray eyes she couldn't interpret. He just stared at her a long moment. "You just rest. I'll go get him for you."

Shelby closed her eyes as she nodded. She thought that was a good idea.

She wanted Jake. If just for a little while.

131

ALLEN FOUND HIM IN THE CAFETERIA. JAKE HAD somehow found his way there half a dozen times in the two days she'd been sedated. He couldn't just sit there in the room, watching her sleep. Watching the nurses coming in and out of 403—same damned room Izzie had been in—just waiting for her to wake.

They'd moved all three women into that room because it was the easiest to *defend* if needed. No one was lost to the fact that the men who'd done this were still out there.

He, Izzie and Allen, Charlie, and a never-ending stream of Zoey Daviess's family were in and out. No one had said much.

Not until today, when they had wheeled Madison into room 403 from the room next door before her discharge.

She had broken down and wept in front of them.

Jake had held her himself until the tears had stopped.

Dom's girl had just clung to him, hurting so damned bad. Jake had felt useless. She'd felt like brittle glass in his hands.

It was going to take a while for all of them to get back to where they were before. If they ever did.

He was terrified of what this was going to do to Shelby.

If he would be able to help her now.

He saw the same nightmares in the eyes of the man across from him.

Charlie had been in and out for three days, never staying at his daughter's side for more than fifteen minutes at a time. Jake got the feeling the other man didn't know what he was supposed to do.

His son had died from a heart condition several years ago. This had to be bringing back some nasty memories. But when Charlie was in there with her, he just sat next to her and stared. Covered Charlotte's ridiculously small hand with his own much larger one.

They hadn't talked.

Other than one time. When Charlie had looked at him and said one thing. "A father is supposed to protect his daughter, Jake. I've failed in that. I don't know how to fix it."

Jake would never forget the torture in the man's blue eyes in that moment.

Jake had stayed with Shelby when her brother wasn't in there. Allen had a couch in his office. The two of them had been taking turns staying at her side the entire time.

Allen hadn't made a move to have him kicked out.

Jake wouldn't have blamed Allen if he had.

Jake had let this happen. He should have been able to stop it. He should have *been there* to stop it. Jake would never forgive himself for that. Ever.

Now he just had to find a way to make it up to her.

"She's awake. Asking for you."

Jake's eyes met Allen's. "What in the hell am I supposed to say to her?"

"How about being honest with her, for once?" Allen asked. He hadn't said another word about how Jake felt about his sister. But the words would never be erased. "Life is too damned short to be stupid about how you feel. I learned that the hard way. Now I tell Izzie every single day. You should try the open honesty thing sometime."

The guy had been snipping at him ever since. Jake figured he owed Allen, considering the things he'd said to the other man after he'd stolen Izzie away.

Hell, Jake knew the truth.

He was scared out of his wits.

But...she wanted him. He was going to get his ass up there.

Jake had to run people out of the room—namely Izzie and Nikkie Jean. Annie was the nurse on duty today. He let her fuss with the computer screen near the bed where they'd entered every bit of data about Shelby for the last three days, then he looked at this girl he'd watched over for years.

Then looked away. Annie looked a bit like Shelby—dark hair, though Annie's was a few shades lighter, and big blue eyes. Though Shelby's were more gray at times, filled with the storms.

It hurt to look at Annie, to see the expression on her face.

She had compassion in those big blue eyes of hers. Understanding.

He wanted Annie to stay right where she was so he didn't have to face the woman in the first bed alone.

Jake checked—Charlotte and Zoey were still out. They probably would be for several more days to come. It had been close, for both of them.

They still didn't know the full extent of the damage to Zoey.

Charlotte would make a full recovery, but it might take a while. Her injuries had been compounded by loss of blood.

It was Shelby who concerned him the most.

She'd hit the water feet first. They had gotten so damned lucky she'd been over the water instead of Victor Scott. She'd been close to the edge, landed in the water, but ricocheted right to the concrete.

Hitting her head, snapping her collarbone, and landing on

her left arm hard enough to break both lower bones before sliding the rest of the way into the water. A concussion, broken bones—they would heal.

Allen had reassured him multiple times that she would heal. She would wake up. She had been out for almost three days, but that had been from the sedatives she'd been given. And from the two surgeries she'd had to endure to fix her arm and her collarbone.

She'd have to have another in a few weeks to fix the rest of the damage to her arm, after the swelling went down.

He'd stayed at the hospital that entire time. Allen had taken pity on him and let him shower in the surgical department. Izzie and Annie and Nikkie Jean had been directing him to the cafeteria when it was time to eat, and Izzie had brought him clean clothes every day. She'd done the same for her husband. He did what he was told. He wasn't going to risk pissing off the people who let him in with Shelby.

Nikkie Jean would probably take pity on him if he did, but he wasn't taking chances.

Jake was going to do whatever it took to be able to stay with Shelby as long as he possibly could. He wasn't leaving her— until the moment Shelby told him to.

Dom and Daniel and Jarrod had been in and out, updating Jake about the next steps of the case. And checking on them— and Gunnar. Gunnar had been discharged from the hospital yesterday.

Gunnar had never left.

Jake didn't know where he had slept, but he suspected Jillian Deane—Rafe's wife—had taken pity on Gunnar and found him a spare bed somewhere.

People were pulling together.

Jake liked that. But he could only stall for so long.

Storm-gray eyes opened. Stared right at him. "Jake."

He just stared.

"It...it...it...wasn't your fault, you know." Shelby shifted a little.

His heart seized and he stepped into the room. To her side. "*Non muoverti, stai fermo!* Stay still. You'll hurt yourself, *bambina*."

"I...I...I can't stay in this bed forever. I'll go...ins...nuts."

"Yeah, you really don't sit still all that great." Jake settled into the chair between her bed and Charlotte's. The light was on next to Shelby, but the rest of the room was dark. "How are you feeling? Are you in any pain?"

Of course, she was. She'd fallen twenty-five feet after physically defending herself from a madman.

"I'm good. Pr-pr-probably going to be doped up for a while." The eyes were clouded with pain. Shooting straight through him. "But...I-I-I am alive. They are, too."

"Yeah. And you'll all make complete recoveries." He hoped. No one knew about the sheriff, or if they did, they weren't talking. At least not to him. But he wasn't about to tell her that. "Then you'll get out of here and go home."

Where he would put her behind stone walls and armed guards and keep her *safe*.

"You look t-t-terrible. Haven't shaved. And your hands... ban...ban...bandages? Why? Tell me."

"Had to climb the fence to get to you. Got a few stitches. Me and Gunnar both. But we're ok."

He wanted to say so much more to her. But hell, what would the words even be?

I'm sorry I left you alone when you needed me most.

That really didn't cut it. "I'm sorry, baby girl. So damned sorry I can't see straight."

"Don't be stupid. You didn't do it. They did. I...knew...you were coming for me. And you did. That's what matters. I knew you would come for me. I just knew. Trusted you would. And you did."

"Always. Every second of every day."

"You found me." She blinked up at him again. "The real me. Did...did...did you know that?"

"What are you saying, baby? You are the most real woman I know." Jake straightened the blanket over her. Tucked it carefully at her side. *Now* he understood why Izzie had a tendency to fuss with things when she felt out of control.

He hadn't felt more out of control since the day his sister died and he was faced with the fact that he had a teenage kid to take care of all by himself.

"No...no...no... I am not saying this right." Her hand tightened on his.

Jake leaned closer.

Someone had washed and brushed her hair, washed her face. Dressed her in a clean hospital gown and thick warm socks. He hated seeing her like this; it was too much like seeing Izzie in the same room not long enough ago.

Jake had been useless.

He had no right to be with her. No right at all.

"I'm the one who has something to say. I never should have left you alone that night at Barratt's. I should have argued with you right then and there. Fought for you. Even if I was fighting *with* you. I just got scared. Used the excuse that I was keeping you safe by doing my job. I was terrified."

"Of what?" Her eyes were the color of the rain now when she looked at him. That pure, perfect gray.

"Of what you make me feel. Of the way my heart only beats like this because of you."

"Of...of...of change. It was change that scared me, too." They both went silent. The only thing he could hear besides the beating of his heart was the machines monitoring Charlotte and Zoey's stats. Shelby's. She blinked at him, still drowsy. "Because...your whole world revolves around TSP. The TSP calls, and you just...go. With no thought of who is behind. With just a little bit of room for Izzie. You don't have room for some… some… someone like me. I'm not…enough…for you. Not forever."

There it was again. The insecurity that he had just not understood at first. But now… "You are *everything* to me, Shelby. Not the TSP, not Iz. *You*. And that was what had me running like a coward. Because what can I give *you*? What do I bring to the table in this relationship? All I have is me—a cop with a bad attitude, and a cat with an even worse attitude. I'm nobody. And I can't give *you* what you need. Not like one of those damned Barratts can. They're better for you than me. Far better. Yet I can't stay away."

"I need *you*. And…and…and…I need *me*." Frustration slipped through. Jake leaned closer.

"I'm not following you, baby." She shot him a look of total irritation that had him smiling for the first time in days. It was how she'd looked at him for ninety-nine percent of their relationship. "You're going to have to elaborate."

"Char…says you can be as dense as a cave…rock."

"I love it when you insult me." He lowered the rail between them. He just wanted to get as close to her as he could.

"It's simple." Her hand rose. To his surprise, she grabbed his FCU T-shirt and yanked him closer. "Listen up…"

"Yes, ma'am."

"I…when I'm w-w-with you, I don't have to worry. I can be-be-be *me*. I can yell at you, you know. The…last…guy…I yelled at was Logan. Because…I don't have to worry about hurting you by not living up to your expectations. I can be *me*. Worry about my *own* expectations, no one else's. I haven't felt that way about someone in a long, long time. More than that…you make me not be afraid. I feel free. So even if you go away forever, I will remember that. And I won't find those two things anywhere else. Only you. And…*that* is what I need. Forever. I found me, by being with you. I love you, Giacomo. A-a-always will. Just deal with it."

Jake just stared at her. The woman meant it.

She wanted *him*.

As screwed up as he was, this beautiful, wonderful maddening woman just wanted him.

"I'm not going anywhere. The reason you found you with me is because without *you,* there will never be *me.* I think we're two parts of the same whole now. And I'm not ever going to leave you again. Ever. I'm going to keep my word." He didn't know where the words were coming from, but they were there. Right in the midst of his soul.

"I think I can h-h-handle that. Handle you."

"I'm certain that you can." He leaned over, carefully pressed his lips to hers. His hand covered her stomach. Jake just needed to see her. Touch her. Storm-gray eyes stared up at him.

They were gray, he realized, with a blue ring around the center. Both gray and blue together. Perfect, just as they were. "I'm not going anywhere."

He told her that, and how much he loved her and that he was going to grab Earl and the two of them were going to move right in with her. That she was never shaking him loose. That to get rid of him, she'd have to call every guy in Major Crimes to haul him off.

That he would never leave her to face any of the wolves of the world alone, that he wouldn't mind the two of them talking about kids someday. But it would have to be soon. He was already close to forty, after all, and he believed in big families.

He just talked to her until she slept again, her breathing steady and even.

EPILOGUE

HE HAD JUST STOOD AND STRAIGHTENED THE blankets over her again after Nikkie Jean had left. People were in and out all the time, it seemed. Shelby just slept on.

Nikkie Jean had stopped by after her latest surgery to check on the room's occupants. And Jake. She'd made no bones about that.

She let out a quiet whoop when he told her he'd figured out how to get his head out of his ass. And that he wasn't ever leaving Shelby's side again.

Apparently, Nikkie Jean had been the one to bet he'd figure that out sooner rather than later. She'd had two hundred dollars riding on him figuring it out by September first. Izzie had bet Christmas. Annie, Halloween. Allen had put a thousand on...never.

Well. Guess Annie and Izzie didn't know him as well as they thought.

He leaned down and kissed Shelby's forehead, just because he had the right to do that now. Jake told her he loved her again. He pressed his cheek to her hair for just a moment.

"While all this lovey-dovey stuff is hugely entertaining...

the...first... thing... I see... when I come back from the dead... should... not... be... Jake MacNamara's... ass... in too-tight jeans. I can't decide if that ass means I'm in heaven or hell."

At the broken feminine voice, Jake jerked around.

To see pain-filled, confused green eyes in a far-too-pale face staring at him from the second bed.

"Well, look who is finally back among us," Jake said. He didn't feel the least bit embarrassed by being overheard. He would shout it from the rooftops, shout exactly how he felt about Shelby for the entire city to hear. "Welcome back."

"Did you get him?" Charlotte turned her head slightly to the right. Looked at the occupant of the third bed. Looked back at Shelby. There was panic in her eyes now. "Where's Mads? Is she dead? Did they kill her? Tell me, Jake."

"She's going to be fine. I swear." Jake was already shaking his head. He stepped over to Charlotte's bed, squeezed her hand and fussed with the blanket over her. "She's going to be fine. Already home with her family, arguing with Dom over resting."

"Then you got the guy?"

"We got a few. Which one are you talking about?" They'd identified Scott as the one responsible for the case Jake had been investigating for three years. Found detailed files in the man's safe. They'd identified Callahan, and had two more names from Shelby's file to track down.

They were going to have the shooters soon.

Dom and Daniel were handling that personally.

It was just a matter of time.

Jake straightened the blanket over his own woman next, and grabbed the call button. He turned back to Charlotte and helped her take a drink.

"The man who shot Madison. I know who he is. Mostly." Charlotte blinked at him. "I want to know if you got him."

"Tell me his name. And I'll have Daniel go get him right now."

"I can't remember his name. But I remember his eyes. I'll never forget his eyes as he shot Mads in the back." Charlotte looked at him as she drifted a bit. "Find him, Jake...because he said he was coming back. He was coming back for *her*. Just her."

"Who her, Char?" Jake asked, quietly. Hell, she looked like a kid lying there. Pale, battered, and looking like her father just along the jawline. His fists bunched.

He wanted to find the guys who had done this to all of them and tear them apart. He hadn't forgotten that two of the shooters—and the driver—were still out there.

As soon as Shelby was safe behind guarded walls—he was never taking chances with her again—he was going to help Dom and Daniel find them. Join the rest of his team and do just that.

He'd just go home to Shelby every night now after.

"*Madison*. He said...he's coming back...for her...Just with her. Said she...wouldn't get away from him again...He's the one who shot her...to teach her a lesson. I heard him say it as he stood over us. I don't think he meant to kill her. Just hurt her. I...will never forget the madness in his eyes when he stared at her. And pulled...the trigger. He's going to come back for her."

Jake did his best to comfort Charlie's daughter while she cried, just like he had her best friend before. Jake grabbed his phone. Dialed Dom's number as fast as he could.

This wasn't over.

This...this was just beginning.

He could officially close his investigation into Victor Scott and the Henedys now. He'd found his answers. It was over.

But Major Crimes wasn't finished. Not by a long shot.

Victor Scott was the end of one criminal enterprise. But Jake wasn't stupid.

There was another one out there. An even bigger one. One that had been building its web around Finley Creek for decades.

And its tentacles had slithered right into the TSP.

He wasn't going to forget that anytime soon.

None of them would.

He disconnected with Dom, then got ahold of Charlotte's father. He wanted another armed detective in the room with them at all times. Just in case.

In the meantime, Major Crimes was going hunting.

For the enemies within.

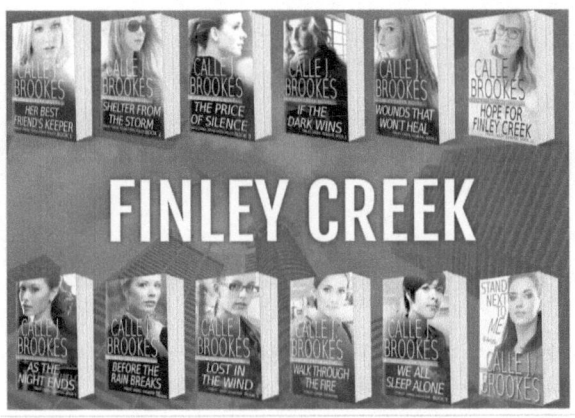

Powell, Haldyn, Madison and Charlotte get their "Happily Ever Afters" with those cavemen of Major Crimes in the next Finley Creek series—

Finley Creek TSP: Enemies Within.

Keep an eye out for more information in 2022.

FOR BONUS SCENES FROM SHELBY AND JAKE

Calle has several scenes that were removed from *Stand Next to Me* available at her blog: www.callejbrookesreads.com.

Calle updates the blog on a regular basis with free reads, excerpts from upcoming books, deleted and bonus scenes, and on-going serial stories.

The next serial will begin in 2022, as soon as Calle decides whether it's a PAVAD story, Masterson, or Finley Creek.

Follow the **blog** for the most up-to-date news about Calle's books and bonus freebies, or sign up for Calle's **newsletter** to be notified about new releases when they go live. (Calle only emails a newsletter with new release information).

To follow the blog visit:

To sign up for the newsletter visit:

ZOEY'S STORY...

Zoey gets her story in Small-Town Sheriff book 2, still untitled, in 2022.

Zoey's "hero" is her co-sheriff, Murdoch Lake. Murdoch was first introduced in Small-Town Sheriff book 1, *Holding the Truth*. If you haven't read it yet, it follows PAVAD: FBI book *HIDING* and is an intense story of healing and overcoming. *Holding the Truth* features Bailey and Clay Addy, seen in *Stand Next to Me*. *HIDING* is the story of Murdoch's brother Cam.

HIDING & Holding the Truth are currently available at most major ebook retailers.

SMALL-TOWN SHERIFFS BOOK 2

WATCH THE BLOG FOR MORE INFORMATION ABOUT WHEN ZOEY AND MURDOCH WILL BE READY FOR RELEASE!

ALSO BY CALLE J. BROOKES

ROMANTIC SUSPENSE

PAVAD: FBI ROMANTIC SUSPENSE

Beginning (Prequel 1)

Waiting (Prequel 2)

Watching

Wanting

Second Chances

Hunting

Running

Redeeming

Revealing

Stalking

Ghosting

Burning

Gathering

Falling

Hiding

Seeking

FINLEY CREEK SERIES

TRILOGY ONE (TEXAS STATE POLICE)

Her Best Friend's Keeper

Shelter from the Storm

The Price of Silence

TRILOGY TWO (FINLEY CREEK GENERAL)

If the Dark Wins

Wounds That Won't Heal

Hope for Finley Creek (bonus novella)

As the Night Ends

TRILOGY THREE (FINLEY CREEK DISASTER)

Before the Rain Breaks (novella prequel)

Lost in the Wind

Walk Through the Fire

We All Sleep Alone

FINLEY CREEK STANDALONES

Stand Next to Me

MASTERSON COUNTY NOVELLA SERIES

Seeking the Sheriff

Discovering the Doctor

Ruining the Rancher

Denying the Devil

Facing the Fire

Trusting that Tyler

Meaning in Masterson (2022)

SMALL-TOWN SHERIFFS

Holding the Truth

SUSPENSE/THRILLER

PAVAD: FBI CASE FILES

PAVAD: FBI Case Files #0001

"Knocked Out"

PAVAD: FBI Case Files #0002

"Knocked Down"

PAVAD: FBI Case Files #0003

"Knocked Around"

PAVAD: FBI Case Files #0004

"White Out"

PAVAD: FBI Case Files #0005

"Buried Secrets"

Calle has several free reads available at

www.CalleJBrookesReads.com

For my grandfather, the best man I have ever known.

You will be missed.

Oct. 2015

For my grandmother, who gave me the courage to try. Without you and
your love of romance, I never would have made it this far.

Feb. 2016

For my papaw, whose children loved him deeply, and will always
miss him.

Oct. 2017

Calle J. Brookes enjoys crafting paranormal romance and romantic
suspense. She reads almost every genre except horror. She spends most

of her time juggling family life and writing while reminding herself that she can't spend all of her time in the worlds found within books. CJ loves to be contacted by her readers via email and at **www.CalleJBrookes.com**. When not at home writing stories of adventure and wrangling with two border collies and a beagle puppy, CJ is off in her RV somewhere exploring the beautiful world we live in, along with her husband of she can't remember how many years and their child.